ENCHANTED EVENING

"We've had a wonderful night," Greg said as they reached her door, "and I want to kiss you."

"I thought you might have changed your mind on the walk back," Kit answered, placing her hands on his shoulders. It seemed almost impossible to believe that this tall, magical man who, several hours earlier, had been only a name to her, was now on the verge of being so much more. "The past few hours have been a surprise for both of us."

The enchantment that had spun itself around them intensified, and for a moment, they just looked at each other, not quite believing this was real. Kit lost herself in the blazing passion that glowed in the depths of Greg's eyes. He traced a finger along the soft line of her cheek and she sighed, moving closer to his lean, muscled chest.

This was what she'd been waiting for, Kit thought as his lips touched hers in tender possession. The man who would make all the others not count, the man who was her present and her future as much as she was his. . . .

Memento

ELEANORA BROWNLEIGH

ZEBRA BOOKS
KENSINGTON PUBLISHING CORP.

For Nancy Evans

Three people may keep a secret,
if two of them are dead.
                    —Benjamin Franklin

Prologue

"My goodness, do people actually *pay money* to watch these things?"

"Not people, Vanessa, *men.*"

"And ghastly excuses for them they must be, too!"

"What I can't get over is that actors do these things and not laugh themselves sick in front of the camera."

"What I can't get over is that we've been sitting here for over two hours watching these things. What one does in the name of business."

"I wonder if I should have the drawing room fumigated?"

"Just be glad that Sin knows how to run a projector and we didn't have to have some stranger here along with us."

"Oh, that awful lingerie—and those black stockings! Are there still women who wear those things?"

"Not anyone *we* know!"

The reel running on the projector came to a clattering end, the jerky images on the screen faded abruptly, and Sinclair Poole leapt up from his seat to turn off the machinery. That task accomplished, and the drawing room returned to its usual lit condition, the six men and women looked at each

7

other in a combination of amusement mingling with disbelief and distaste, wondering how such entertainment could be shown in such elegant surroundings.

Some six weeks earlier, Sinclair, a man long noted for his business savvy and ability to make the best of all possible deals, added to his extensive business holdings by acquiring Hooper Studios. Hooper Studios was a small film factory dedicated to turning out dreadful little one-reel comedies that were really the cover for the blue films that were so dear to the heart of the otherwise respectable Pasadena gentleman who was the studio's founder and sole owner. The owner, Mr. Martindale, had recently died of a heart attack, and his widow, horrified that her husband had been both involved in that awful movie business and had interests she knew nothing about, contacted Sinclair and offered to let him have Hooper Studios—and the real estate on which everything rested.

"How much did you say you paid Mrs. Martindale for her late husband's studio, dear?" Caroline asked with a slightly wifely edge to her voice that suggested her husband might be in danger of joining the late, somewhat unlamented Mr. Martindale if the price were too outlandish.

"Fifty thousand dollars, double what she was asking," Sinclair said, looking very handsome and quite unperturbed for having paid such a sum of money for something that was so questionable in both profit and taste. "Unfortunately, Mrs. Martindale is the sort of woman who'll complain that I cheated her, even though she was the one who made the first offer."

"I didn't think you had much of a taste for either low comedy or alleged pornography," Rupert Randall remarked, and at his witticism, greeted with laughter by everyone else, a clouded look formed in Sinclair's amber-colored eyes.

For a moment he let his glance wander over the large drawing room where the long French doors were firmly closed against the damp night wind and the sound of the Pacific Ocean's waves crashing against the beach could be ever so faintly heard. The years Caro had spent in China as a young woman, combined with their mutual love of Orientalia, made for a sophisticated yet pleasant decor that could take even the clumsy projector and screen which were threatening to mar the perfect pile of the yellow, cream, and gold Peking carpet. He found the pale-lemon-colored walls and cream-colored ceiling soothing, loved the eight-panel lacquer screen that had been divided in half and placed on either side of the fireplace, and was vastly comfortable on one of the deep-pillowed sofas covered in a rich cream-silk damask. But none of the beauty that was his home could rub away the edge of excitement he felt. Even after all of these years of running a multitude of business ventures, each one more successful than the last, there was no mistaking the feeling: he was on to something with this most recent purchase. But there were also so many avenues open to him that he knew he had to be careful. He had thought this weekend would be a help—the people they loved best around them to view all the motion pictures Hooper was responsible for producing and reach some sort of conclusion—but so far his plan was taking on the proportions of a bad joke. Last night, and then again tonight, they had watched the movies—first the comedies and then the blue films—and so far it would have been a more productive evening if they'd rolled back the rug, put on the Victrola, and danced.

"If I were truly interested in pornography," Sinclair said finally, "I could come up with far better story ideas than a lot of ladies in boring lingerie falling off chairs. Obviously, Mr. Martindale's imagination was severely limited. On the other hand—," he looked at the wine coolers holding empty bottles of champagne, their half-filled glasses, and the violet-colored tin boxes that two hours before had been filled with Louis Sherry chocolates. "—did we inhale all of this candy?

9

Damn, I lost my train of thought!"

"I can see why Mr. Martindale kept his identity a secret, but was there really ever a Hooper?" Mallory Randall inquired, her Poiret dinner dress of beige charmeuse with matching lace and embroidered in multicolored glass beads and gold metallic braid swishing luxuriously as she crossed her long legs.

"It was the name of his driver."

"Let's hope he was remembered in his employer's will," Caro said. Her Tappe dinner dress of pale yellow crepe, chiffon trimmed with matching satin and ecru net blended perfectly with the room's decor, and ever the thoughtful hostess, she passed around a fresh tin of chocolate creams. "I'm glad we kept this weekend's gathering down to the six of us. Comedy is strictly a matter of personal choice, but the entertainment we've just seen had better stay between us."

"I'm just glad that Elston is in San Francisco for that conference," Vanessa Worth Harper, Caro's British-born stepmother remarked as she selected a chocolate. In her early fifties, she was still a stunning woman with rich, dark auburn hair and an elegant figure accentuated by her Jeanne Hallee dinner gown of golden brown satin and gold lace. Three years earlier, after ten years of being a widow, she married Elston Harper, a man as much noted for being the father of the popular interior decorator Thea Harper de Renille as he was for being a highly regarded naturalist-explorer. The marriage was an event which thoroughly delighted both women who were endlessly trying to figure out their new relationship to each other. "He's a very liberal and understanding man, but this might unnerve him a bit. Either that or give him the laugh of the year!"

"This is a night one either keeps secret or dines out on for a year!" Gregory West said, and at his definitive comment, the first thing he'd said since remarking on what one did in the name of business, five pairs of eyes turned to him. For the whole evening he'd sat slightly apart from them, occupying a

10

velvet-covered wing chair, sipping champagne and eating chocolates. He was Sinclair's business partner and best friend, and the resemblance between the two men was marked enough for strangers to think that they had some sort of blood relationship. "Am I supposed to make some trenchant comment that reflects on my bachelorhood vis-à-vis these peculiar movies?"

"Only if you think it's absolutely necessary," Sin retorted, sounding like an older brother addressing a somewhat troublesome sibling. "As it is, I just about caught what you said. Do you have an applicable comment, Greg?"

"Only that the projector and screen aren't good for the carpet." His eyes flashed with secret amusement. "You're not still letting them make those movies, are you?"

"Hooper Studios isn't filming anything now; I haven't fired anyone, and I'm still paying full salaries."

"I think *The Pie Man* series has potential," Mallory interjected. "The comedy's a little too broad, but the photography's excellent."

"A constructive comment at last!"

As it turned out, they all had something to say, some input, and Sinclair took this as seriously as a discussion involving millions of dollars. They all had different opinions, but they all concurred on one point.

"So it's don't sell—at least not right now."

"You didn't buy it out of charity," Caro pointed out.

"Or because you like Mrs. Martindale," added Mallory.

"And you can't tell me that you didn't know what you were buying," Rupert said.

"I don't seem to be able to put anything past all of you." Despite his intention to remain serious, Sinclair began to smile. "What do you think, Vanessa?"

"That you know exactly what you want to do," Vanessa replied in her best stepmother-in-law voice. "Of course you may not have reached full realization of it yet and should, therefore, proceed very carefully!"

11

Sinclair laughed, agreed, and turned to Gregory. "Are you going to miss your last chance to get your comments in?"

"You know what I think about moving pictures: they've gotten better than they were; certainly better than some of the second-rate touring companies who feel it's their duty to play Los Angeles," Greg said passionately. He didn't want to sound like a closed-minded snob who couldn't accept change or innovation. It was the shoddy, the second-rate that he loathed, and he wanted to make Sinclair see that. "Look at the films we saw tonight. Can you imagine what they'd be like if they could *talk?* And those so-called comedies weren't any better. If that's all this supposedly new industry can produce, it's better they don't have a voice!"

"Is that really how you feel?" Sinclair asked, an idea forming. It was almost evil, what he was thinking, but sometimes the only way to get results was with the proverbial monkey wrench in the machinery.

Greg looked squarely at Sinclair, and for that moment it was if no one else was in the room. "Yes."

"I'm very glad you feel like that, that you have these strong opinions, likes and dislikes," Sinclair returned evenly. "Don't lose sight of them because they'll be an invaluable source of reference to you."

"A source of reference?" Greg questioned. A warning signal flashed through him, and he had the feeling not of being trapped but rather of having walked into a corner all by himself. "Do you have some special plan in mind?"

"You might say that." Sinclair looked pleased with himself. "I wasn't sure at first, but as soon as you gave us your views, I was. Since I'm going to hang on to this property for the time being, I want to have someone there full time to supervise things. That's you, Greg. Until further notice, you're in charge of Hooper Studios!"

After that announcement, the party began to break up.

Greg quickly covered his expression of astonishment and anger with a smile and a jest, but everyone else in the room knew it was a sham. Out of politeness they wanted to leave him alone until he had adjusted to the new assignment he had been handed. Servants were summoned to remove the movie equipment and to remove the remains of their refreshments, and the guests began to drift out of the room.

"Sin, can you spare a moment?" Mallory asked as they stepped into the large entry hall, all black and white marble, perfect to this Mediterranean-style villa overlooking the ocean. "I may have some good news for you."

"I can use that right now. I should have told Greg this in private, or have at least sounded less gleeful about what I wanted him to do."

"I'm glad to see that you don't need me to tell you about your mistakes."

"No, Caro is going to be more than happy to do that in a few minutes. What's your news?"

"Do you remember the shop next to mine on Spring Street—the one you hold the lease on?"

"Don't remind me, it's the eyesore of the block. If someone doesn't rent it soon, the Merchants' Association is going to come after me. Have you decided to expand?"

"No, I have more than enough space. When you're dealing in antiques, customers always think that the more exclusive and restrained the shop is, the better the merchandise. I may have someone who is interested in it. What would you say to a very, very high quality women's specialty shop?"

"Since I've never paid Caro's bills, personally it wouldn't matter one bit; but from a business standpoint it sounds splendid. Who wants to take it?"

Mallory focused on the rock crystal chandelier for a moment before looking back at Sin. "It's Katharine Allen, and she doesn't know she wants this shop yet."

Sin looked nonplussed. "Excuse me?"

"I usually don't do things like this; but, a while back Kit

wrote me that she's been thinking about opening her own shop, but she doesn't want to do it in New York. I've just written her saying that Los Angeles has a lot to offer—in particular a ready-made clientele with lots of money who'd do anything for a shop offering Paris clothes."

Sin began to laugh. "Well, you can write Kit again and tell her that as far as I'm concerned, the lease is hers."

"I've already done that. Oh, don't look like that. Kit is coming along with Rupert and me when we go to Europe in April, and if she wants to turn it into a buying trip, she has to decide now."

"That sounds logical. In fact, Caro and I are thinking about a quick trip over. May I tell her about this?"

"Please do, I'm sure she'd love to be one of the first to know."

"Even before Kit makes up her mind?"

"Oh, she'll want to come out here—the challenge is too good to resist. One thing though . . ."

"I'm almost afraid to ask."

"I finished my letter just before dinner, and I just happened to tell her what we were doing here this weekend. After all," she went on a little defensively, "you have to admit that it's very unusual to spend a Sunday night watching blue movies. I know you want to keep this quiet, and Kit is very discreet."

"Of course she is, but even if she tells a few people it won't hurt." Sin said as they began to walk toward the stairs. "With all those respectable people back East thinking that all of us in California have to be crazy, it never hurts to keep up the franchise!"

Greg couldn't sleep. It was more than two hours since Sin had dropped his bombshell, and he was still moving restlessly around his room, trying to read, write, or rest. Shock had been replaced by anger—one of the rare times

14

when he was truly furious with Sin—but now that was fading into a sharp annoyance tinged with black humor.

With a sigh of resignation, he got out of the large four-poster bed draped in heavy beige silk, and put his Sulka robe of heavy figured silk on over his pajamas. He was going to run a motion picture studio—what a joke! he thought, as he left his room.

The house was quiet with everyone either asleep or otherwise engaged and not thinking about him at all, but he would have loathed it if any of his friends had offered him words of comfort on his new position. Sin hadn't made him his first vice-president and right-hand man because he turned to others when the going got too tough.

I hate January, he thought, going down the wide staircase. Nothing good ever happens in this month, and everything bad that happened in my life takes place in the first four weeks of every new year.

Forcing himself not to think about what had been going on in his life on this date fourteen years earlier, he went into the kitchen. There were times that Greg, at thirty-five, felt very much older than he was, thanks to the events that had ended forever the last years of his carefree and privileged young manhood; but right now he decided to act quite young and raid the refrigerator. When everything else failed, milk and cookies had the odd knack of helping.

The refrigerator, one of those used by the best hotels, like the rest of the kitchen, was thoroughly up-to-date, and a perusal of its vast and well-stocked interior provided him with fresh, ice-cold milk, while the cookie jar that was the size of a prize-winning pumpkin yielded up the prize of large and chewy oatmeal cookies baked that afternoon.

All of this could be worse, Greg told himself as he went into the servants hall next door where there was a selection of reading matter. I'm not sure how, but this joke could end up being on Sin. I can take it easy all day, sign a few letters, read a few reports, and leave all the hard work back in my

15

office for someone else to slave over.

For a moment he thought about his corner office in the Broadway office building where Sinclair Poole Enterprises occupied two floors; the quarters at Hooper Studios were rumored to be less than passable. Still, it might be worth taking it just to have a few months of ease while appearing to be doing an important job.

But far too much had happened in Gregory West's life—some of it hard and brutal and almost unbelievable—for him to ever take anything at face value. Still there was something in him that hadn't lost the ability to trust and be pleasantly surprised, and he supposed that that was what had saved him.

And as he sat at the kitchen table, eating oatmeal cookies and drinking milk with a boyish enthusiasm, and reading *Vanity Fair,* he didn't bother to wonder if his new assignment—one he was sure would last a short time until Sin decided to sell the studio—had just set wheel after wheel into a series of motions that would leave nothing in its path unchanged.

Part One

The Travellers

. . . there are such opportunities for careers in America now that it makes one restless. With the money we have in back of us and the energy we have stored up in us one hardly knows where to begin.

—Elsie de Wolfe

Chapter 1

Sailing day, Katharine Allen decided, had to be the most romantic words in the English language after I love you. Those two words had an excitement implicit in them, a promise that could and did transcend all but the worst set of pre-travel nerves, and could even make one forget all about silly little problems. Unfortunately, there was no particular expression or words of comfort to the non-weary traveller on the day she returned home. The only reaction was more than likely to be relief at having gotten through the long and boring process of docking, followed by the endless time spent on the pier while the Customs inspector made his way through trunk, after standing dress trunk, after shoe trunk, and ending with becoming part of the massive traffic jam that always occurred on the West Side the day a great liner either arrived or departed.

"And so the estimable Miss Allen arrives back home, not really all that much worse for the wear—provided nobody looks too closely!" Kit murmured wryly, checking her reflection in the mirror that hung above the antique architect's table that filled the entry foyer of the apartment she shared with her mother and stepfather in The Mayfair at 471 Park Avenue. Alone for the moment since Howard, the butler, was seeing that the crew of burly expressmen did no damage to her extensive collection of Louis Vuitton luggage, and Martha—who was Mrs. Howard—was putting the finishing touches on her lunch, Kit made a face at herself in the mirror. Sometimes acting silly was the only way to keep her life in its proper perspective.

She took off her Georgette hat of beige Milan straw with a wide band of cream-colored moire around the band with as much care as she had put in on some four hours earlier in the perfumed privacy of her *cabine de grande luxe* on board the *France*, left her spotless beige kid gloves and gold-chain-handled purse beside it on the table, and left the entry foyer, her heels clicking against the highly polished parquet floors.

I'm not really home unless I look over every inch, she thought mistily, recalling the ritual established when she was six and had just returned with her parents from her first summer in Europe; that of walking through each and every room to make sure everything was just as it had been left. It's twenty-one years and just about as many trips later—not to mention a few changes of residence—and I still do things the same way. Only the next time I come back from Europe, home will be in Los Angeles.

Despite the warmth of the mid-July day, a chill ran through Kit. When she had sailed for Europe on an equally glorious day in April, just three months earlier, there had been no way of knowing that the assassination of Archduke Francis Ferdinand, the heir to Franz Joseph, Emperor of Austria, along with his morganatic wife, Sophie, by a Serbian nationalist in the city of Sarajevo on June 28th, might well be the final act to push German aggression over the edge.

The sight of the living room was soothing. Although Kit hadn't inherited the artistic ability that made Constance Allen such a popular artist, their sense of style was nearly identical, and they had worked together decorating this duplex apartment. In this room the walls had been painted a soft blue-gray with a white ceiling and trim, and the eighteenth-century Chinese carpet was pale celadon and cream with light touches of soft rose. Feeling more relaxed, she sat down on one of the sofas, her Bergdorf Goodman dress of cream-colored Canton crepe with a chemisette of fine mull with a small collar and delicate hand embroidery and trimmed in Roman ribbon contrasting pleasantly against the rose-colored background of the modern chintz upholstery.

She put her long legs up on the low red lacquer table in front of the sofa and let her glance wander over the tables with their displays of silver-framed photographs, their cache of silver and porcelain boxes, and bibelots collected on their travels. I wonder if seeing my home again is so important to me because I don't have one very special man yet? she thought.

By some unbidden impulse, her glance travelled from the cool, elegant landscape paintings to the lacquer-work grand piano. Talk about subconscious impulses, she thought.

"If this weren't so annoying, I could have a good laugh!"

"Excuse me, Miss Katharine, did you say something?" Martha asked, appearing in the doorway. "I was just coming in to ask you where you wanted your lunch served, and I heard—"

"You heard me talking to myself out loud. I was thinking about Sebastian Creighton, and it all just fell into place."

"Then you're going to marry him," Martha said hopefully, coming into the living room.

"God forbid."

"But I don't understand," the older woman said, her face clearly showing her disappointment that she would not be able to bake a gala wedding cake. "Why Mr. Creighton followed you to London. That would be enough to sweep most women off their feet!"

"You may not believe this, Martha, but what I told all the reporters who came on at Quarantine was the truth. He came to London because the musical director of his show was changing the score without permission. That I happened to be there at the same time was just an added benefit."

"Oh, I see. But everyone here is saying that you're both almost engaged."

"There's an area between *almost* and *engaged* that the Twentieth Century and The California Limited both can get through," Kit said significantly, and began to laugh, but her merriment was tinged with regret. How many more men was she going to meet only to have her high expectations dashed again? But was there a plan in this? she wondered. Yes, she wanted to fall in love and get married, but right now she had another, equally important plan to carry out.

"So you're still going to Los Angeles and open that fancy dress shop," Martha stated. "I can't see why that city has so much allure. Why, there's nothing there except a lot of people making movies, looking for oil, and raising orange groves."

"Yes, and they tend to have a great deal of money and wives, daughters, and lady-friends who want to spend those dollars on the best clothes available. You can look on me as providing a public service, Martha. Someone is going to have to open an exclusive women's shop selling the best clothes, and it might as well be me!"

"Of course, Miss Katharine. But if you were getting married—"

"Oh, I'll get married. The only thing is that with me it will be later instead of sooner. There's nothing wrong with that."

"But you'll be lonely."

"Living with the Randalls, not to mention having the Pooles and their social set, I'll have more invitations than I know what to do with, just like I have here in New York," she said reassuringly as she stood up. "Now what's for lunch? I'll have it upstairs, and you can do something gala for dinner in the dining room."

Kit discussed both meals with a slightly mollified Martha. Even though the Howards had been Vincent Lyman's servants before he married Constance Allen, they regarded

22

her with the same feelings of pride and protection that they would have bestowed if they had known her if she had been a presence in their life for more than the past four years. But although she regarded the couple in the highest of light there was nothing they could say to her that would influence her to change her mind at this point. Her real decision had been made six months ago, and everything she did now was simply building on that foundation.

Culinary matters settled, Kit continued on her inspection tour. The dining room had to be visited, as did the library and her mother's studio before she was ready to go upstairs to the second floor of the duplex that occupied half of the sixth and seventh floors of The Mayfair. Six bedrooms opened off the large, square hallway. The two smallest were the rarely used guest rooms, while the remaining four were divided between the master suite and Kit's own quarters.

Her bedroom was all pink and cream with superb French furniture. The bathroom was rich with marble, and the vast closets in the bedroom and dressing room were waiting to be refilled with the spring and summer clothes she'd taken to Europe. But it was the room she'd turned into her office that demanded her attention now.

"I've made this room too pleasant, that's my problem," Kit murmured, eyeing the room where the walls were painted a rosy-red with a rich cream-color for the ceiling and trim. The sofa, easy-chair and hassock were covered in a black-background chintz splashed with pink and red carnations, and a large breakfront held the records of all the projects she'd undertaken in the past seven-and-a-half years.

I haven't done too badly, considering I started out as a twenty-year-old with a couple of half-baked ideas and a not-too-dim talent for telling women how to dress. But I've always done it in such a second-hand way, she thought. Now I'm going to leave this safe corner of mine and test out all my theories in the most direct way possible.

At the fifty-four-inch writing table placed under one

window, Kit ignored the stack of mail waiting for her and removed a letter from her Tiffany-designed letter rack of bronze doré, decorated with Chinese symbols. The cancellation mark on the pale blue envelope read the morning of January 19, 1914, just six months before, and as Kit slipped the monogrammed pale blue sheets out of the envelope, she wondered how many times she'd read and reread the contents since it had appeared on her breakfast tray.

My own women's specialty shop, Kit thought, looking at the straight up-and-down penmanship and the bold blue-black ink. It'll be livelier than Thurn's, have more variety than Lucile's, and all the fun of shopping at Tappe's, but without all the pretensions.

The idea had occurred to her almost a year ago, but she had not acted on it beyond making a few notes and expanding on a handful of ideas. But this idea wasn't a passing fancy, and the urge to do something else, something different other than simply giving advice to New York's specialty shops and buying exclusive items for them on her annual trip to Europe, had taken hold in a very definite way. During the busy holiday season, whenever Kit could spare the time from her busy schedule, she sat down at her writing table and began to make a plan. How she wanted the shop to look, the merchandise she wanted to offer, and the clientele she wanted to attract were all finally translated onto paper. There wasn't an area Kit left unexamined, including drawing up a preliminary budget, dredging up all that she could remember from her last economics class at Barnard. When it was all finished, she made an extra copy of her prospectus and sent it to Mallory Randall in Los Angeles.

Mallory Kirk and Katharine Allen had known each other all through Brearley and Barnard, their friendship cemented on shared interests, as well as their tall heights. Mallory was an interior decorator, working for Thea Harper, a job she continued after her marriage to Rupert Randall in 1910. They spent half of the year in Los Angeles now, where

24

Mallory opened an exclusive shop where she sold antiques and gave decorating advice.

As far as Kit was concerned, Mallory was the perfect person to turn to for advice. But her friend's response had been thoroughly unexpected. Mallory had been complimentary about her budget and enthusiastic about her idea—and had made a direct suggestion:

. . . what you have to do (Mallory had advised, and Kit now reread) is come to Los Angeles. We need an exclusive shop offering fine clothes; New York doesn't. It's as simple as that. Besides, if it doesn't work out, you can go home without too many people knowing exactly what it was you were doing. And, if you're a rousing success—which I'm sure you will be—and decide you want to go back to New York, you can hire a competent manager to run things, come back here for a few months every year, and spend the rest of your time buying the merchandise and working on other projects.

Best of all, the shop next to mine is vacant. A men's tailor and haberdasher was supposed to open, but something went wrong. The workrooms are already set up, as are the fitting rooms, and it's a fifty-foot frontage, and two floors. Sinclair's company holds the lease, and, if you're interested, he'll transfer the papers to your name with none of the stupidity you'd have to take from a New York real estate agent or banker about having some man co-sign.

I know you must be astonished at my suggestion and apprehensive about making such a move. Please don't be. Los Angeles is growing all the time and is very receptive to new businesses. And the weather is fantastic. You'll live with Rupert and me, of course. Our house is huge, you'll have your own suite, and can come and go as you please.

Please think about this.

Rupert and I are going up to San Francisco next week (another highlight of Los Angeles is that you can get on a train after breakfast, have lunch on board, and arrive in San Francisco in time for a midnight supper at the St. Francis or the Fairmont), but we're spending this weekend at Caro and Sin's house in Montecito.

We're just about ready to go down for dinner, and then the evening's entertainment calls for watching blue movies! Sin has just purchased something called Hooper Studios, and these strange little movies are their secret specialty. Sin isn't quite sure what he should do with his latest investment (except stop making those movies!), but tonight should give him a better idea. . . .

"I wonder how that night turned out," Kit said out loud. She laughed and put the letter back in the envelope. "Mallory saw a lot of questionable movies, and I ended up with a signed lease and a Paris buying trip!" She looked at the framed Poiret fashion prints decorating the walls and decided that when she went to Los Angeles in September, she'd take them with her for her new office. "I always knew I did the right thing by walking out of Barnard, and I wonder what the Dean would say if she could see me today!"

College, which was a stimulating and enlightening experience for so many young women in the first part of the twentieth century, was to Kit a gradual disillusionment. She loved her freshman and sophomore years, but her junior year was an unending series of gradual annoyances so that by the start of her senior year all she wanted was to make it through the term and get out of school.

Barnard at that time was going through a conservative period where the administration, aware they couldn't control their girls to the same extent as their New England counterparts, nonetheless decided to take a stand and show that they were indeed standing in *loco parentis,* even when many of the students in question returned to their own homes every evening. The rule that young women students were not allowed to speak to the young men students on the adjoining Columbia University campus when they met on the paths was strictly enforced. Questions were asked as to what parties they were going to and whom they were seeing, and there were lectures about the importance of their college experience and how intense study came before even the most simple and innocent of pleasures. Of all the girls in the graduating class of 1907, Katharine Allen was the least likely to win approval from the college's conservative guiding force. Her late father had been an influential stockbroker with decidedly iconoclastic views, while her mother, to the administration's way of thinking, actually bordered on the dreaded category known as "bohemian," and on every weekday morning when Kit—who was too naturally striking to be ignored—pulled up to Barnard's gates at Broadway and 116th Street in her shiny red Buick roadster and swung across the campus toward her first morning class, there was never a lack of disapproving interest in her progress.

Even if all the little lectures and warnings had come during her first two years at Barnard, when college was still an exciting experience, Kit doubted if anything would have been different. Like her parents, she simply didn't have it in her to be either careful or accommodating when it came to rules designed to stifle. By the middle of October 1906, she was restless and bored, and delighted in annoying the disapproving faculty who wanted her to do as they said. It was, therefore, inevitable that one morning the sound of her Buick's brakes would grate once too often on the sensitive nerves of the powers-that-be, and on a bright, crisp morning she was summarily brought to a meeting comprised of the President, the Dean of Students, and two of the college's

27

most respected advisors.

Why they actually think I can't decide a single thing for myself! was the only reaction Kit could summon up as the lecture droned on and on.

Her classwork was without flaw and showed great potential, they told her, but why did she refuse to participate in any additional activities? She could sing in the chorus and play field hockey and do some properly supervised charity work. It wasn't too late for her to make some significant changes in her life, but if she didn't they were very much afraid that . . .

It was an old song played once too often. Continually interfering advice—pleas to let them play do-gooder for her when she already knew that their suggestions were wrong. Kit was not a joiner in the conventional sense of the word. All she wanted to do was attend her classes, do the work connected with them, and in her free time do the things that interested *her*. Whether she was buying the latest imports at Thurn's, seeing a new exhibition at the Metropolitan Museum of Art, taking in a matinee, browsing in Brentano's, or working on a project at the Henry Street Settlement, Kit didn't want anyone looking over her shoulder. Always before she had politely evaded and eluded these encounters, but today was different. She just didn't care any more.

"No, *you're* not afraid," she corrected when they were finally finished, "you want *me* to be afraid—afraid that I'm going to be expelled unless I do exactly what you say." Kit's voice was clear and definite, something the others definitely hadn't expected, and she pressed her advantage. "I can't sing a single note, I'm already a volunteer at the Henry Street Settlement, and it's a fact that ice hockey ruins the ankles and legs. Why can't my being a good student be enough? Oh, never mind," she went on, standing up. "I quit. I loved my first two years here, nothing can ever change that, but at the end of my junior year I should have recognized that the charm was gone and not come back for my senior year. I thought I could mark time until graduation in May, but I see I'm wrong," she finished, placing her text books on the nearest table and placing the library passes that allowed her entrance to the stacks in the Barnard and Columbia libraries on top of the books. "Thank you for the wonderful education. I know I'm going to put it to good use, but right now it's time for me to leave."

Five minutes later she was behind the wheel of her roadster, steering it down Broadway toward a candy shop that offered a pay telephone station. Once there, she deposited her nickel in the slot, gave the operator her mother's number, explained the situation to her, and a half-hour after that, walked into Constance Allen's West Fifty-seventh Street studio.

Her mother was finishing the last in a series of paintings that would be used to illustrate Mrs. Humphrey Ward's latest novel to be serialized in *Harper's Bazaar*, and as Kit walked in, Constance put down her brushes and held out her arms to her daughter.

"How are you, darling?"

"I hate to say it, but I feel so free," Kit said as they hugged each other. "Are you upset with me because I told them off?"

"Those people may have a string of advanced degrees, but they have no business poking their noses into a student's home life unless there's something obviously wrong. You were at the point where you had to make a decision and you did it. Are you going to have second thoughts?" Constance questioned knowingly.

"Not a single one. If I'd listened to my instincts and not registered last month, I could have avoided this mess. I kept telling myself that at least Barnard is better than Mount Holyoke, or Smith, or Vassar, or Radcliffe, or Bryn Mawr, and it's certainly better than Wellesley where they don't allow boys at the parties, and the girls have to dance with each other . . ."

"But—" Constance encouraged as they sat down on the

chintz-covered sofa, one of the homey touches in the room with its broad windows, easels, stacks of canvases, and cabinets holding her painter's supplies. Mother and daughter bore a strong resemblance to each other, but Constance's dark, acorn-colored hair had a striking streak of silver sweeping back from her left temple, and her eyes were a deep shade of blue while Kit's were a clear, unobstructed shade of hazel.

". . . I would have liked to graduate, to win my degree. You graduated from Vassar, and I wanted you to be proud of me."

"It doesn't take a sheepskin to make me proud of you, and you know that. And as for graduating from Vassar—it never did me any particular good. You get where you are by your own talents, not a piece of paper!"

"Somehow I get the feeling that you've just given that same speech to someone else," Kit said wryly. "Did they call you?"

"Yes, and I've never heard such righteous indignation. Where do supposedly intelligent people get hold of such claptrap? I told them just what I told you, and they called me a bohemian," Constance said. Kit whooped with laughter.

"How trite! What did you say?"

"That if they think I'm a bohemian, I'll be glad to disabuse them of that notion by showing them my latest bill from Thurn's!"

A few minutes later, after Constance had cleaned off her brushes and Kit rang up their apartment and told the cook they were ready for lunch to be sent over, mother and daughter faced each other.

"There should be a bottle of champagne in the ice box. Take it out, darling, and we'll have a special treat. But first were going to have to discuss what you're going to do now."

"You mean I can't sit home all day and sip champagne and eat chocolates?"

"Not likely. Besides, you'd be bored in a week."

"Well, since I can't draw a straight line, that lets out following in your footsteps as an illustrator," she said, admiring Constance's morning output.

"But you do love to read."

"Oh, you have that look, Mummy. Is there something up your sleeve to get me gainful employment?"

"Possibly. The fiction editor at *Harper's Bazaar* told me that they receive dozens of manuscripts every day. You could probably help them out, and when we go to Europe in the spring, they might want you to report back on parties and things like that."

"I'd like that—if your editor would be interested in taking me on," Kit said carefully. She could not quite believe she and her mother were having this conversation. A few hours earlier she'd been a college girl with a day of classes ahead of her, and now she was discussing her first position. *"Bazaar* has good fiction, but their fashion coverage could be better." She put the bottle of Lanson champagne into the ice bucket. "May I change the subject? When you mentioned Europe, it reminded me that our lease at the Osborne is up in August. We've lived there since Daddy died four years ago, and there are newer places being built every day. We should think about moving."

"That's been on my mind also. What's your idea, darling?"

"If we go to Europe in May, and come back in October, the new Plaza will be open and we could take a suite there. Something simple overlooking the park," she added, trying to keep her expression serious.

"As long as it's simple," Constance agreed, and smiled. Like her daughter, she was entranced by the new Plaza Hotel, currently rising like a French chateau that couldn't stop growing at Fifth Avenue and Fifty-ninth Street. She was pleased that she and Kit thought so much alike, and now that Kit was free of the restrictive policies of college, there wasn't a doubt in her mind that her daughter wasn't going to do something grand. "Hardenbergh isn't my favorite architect, but the Plaza looks more than promising. Let's talk about it while we have lunch. We can also get a head start on our summer itinerary."

"That's just the thing to get me over this morning," Kit said brightly as she and Constance moved around the cheerful, sunny studio as they set the table for lunch. "And maybe this will be the summer we either ride the Orient Express or finally get to visit Russia!"

That had been on Tuesday, and on the following Monday, Kit began work at *Harper's Bazaar*, where she spent the next six months reading through the avalanche of unsolicited short stories that the magazine received. She was paid a dollar for every story she read and evaluation she wrote, and whenever she had any free time—which was considerable since Kit was a fast and accurate reader and usually finished a week's worth of work by Wednesday—she visited the fashion editor's office, asking questions and offering opinions based on her own taste and sense of style. Unfortunately, the end of 1906 and the beginning of 1907 were not auspicious years for either *Harper's Bazaar* or its great rival, *Vogue*. Obviously, they were not, and never would be, mass-market magazines aimed toward the great population of American women. Their readers, both magazines proudly pointed out, were from the highest strata of society, with the best level of income; yet, inevitably, they had to change—only the direction this change would take was not yet apparent.

Within fifteen years, the society girl working for a fashion magazine would be an accepted fact of life, but when Kit appeared no one was quite sure how to treat her, and her comments and inquiries were taken with a large grain of salt. Those who make up the vanguard of a new movement are seldom understood or treated well, but for her part, in those brisk fall days of 1906, and through the winter months of

1907, Kit was quite happy just to have a place where she could wear her simple day dresses from Paquin and Poiret, and where no one voiced objections to her carefully made-up face. When it came time for her to leave for Europe in May 1907, the glow was still there, and she hardly noticed that the fashion editor was somewhat less than enthusiastic when she offered to provide her with reports of all the latest comings and goings in England and on the Continent.

The Allen women returned to New York in early October on board the new *Lusitania,* and went directly to the Plaza Hotel, opened just the week before, where a large suite was waiting for them on the fourth floor, with a view of Central Park.

A few days after that, Kit was back at *Harper's Bazaar,* arriving laden down with cunning accessories, a few of the newest hats, and information on the latest fashions and gossip that the regular London and Paris correspondents had missed.

It wasn't until years later that Kit came to realize she had been ahead of her time in the way she saw things and what she did. She stayed at the magazine through December, cheerfully reading manuscripts as well as writing extensive articles for both the November and December issues on what to find in the stores for the best Christmas presents.

She could write, but her forte seemed to be finding out what everyone else seemed to miss. She knew who had the latest hats from Paris first, where the prettiest evening shoes were, and who gave the best facials. Esoteric material to be sure, but it had to be a base for something, she decided. After all, she didn't expect to spend the next twenty years reading manuscripts.

Kit knew she didn't have to work; she could live very nicely from day to day on her trust fund. But her mother had always painted and sold her works, and the idea that she could do nothing and wait until she found the man she wanted to marry was absurd. In early 1908, she heard that the new House of Tappe was looking for a "walking advertisement," a young woman who would wear the House's creations exclusively, be in the salon whenever important clients were expected, and mention where her clothes came from at every party she went to.

Herman Patrick Tappe, late of Sidney, Ohio, had been urged to accept this young matron or that popular debutante, but he hired Kit almost on sight. He didn't want a bored young wife who would look upon wearing his clothes as a possible steppingstone to her first affair, or a nineteen-year-old girl who was too excited at her first taste of freedom to take the expensive clothes she'd wear seriously or be able to impress a new client.

"I expect I'll end up doing your wedding dress, dear," he said as he showed Kit around the salon, pleased that she also wanted to see the workrooms and meet the seamstresses and fitters. "But please try to keep that lucky fellow at bay for the next two years. That's all you'll stay, you're too energetic for what is really a static position—you want more than just a lot of pretty clothes to wear."

Kit ended up staying with Tappe for three years, and when she left in 1911, the salon was as famous for its incredibly pretty confections—both those that were imported and those he designed—as it was for the Fifty-seventh Street salon with two gardens on the luxuriously decorated premises, and an air of total elegance which appealed immensely to the wealthy clientele. Tappe wasn't an easy man to work for, but then few truly creative people are, and if Kit's streak of sensibility was sometimes sorely tested by her employer's antics and attitudes—particularly on the occasion when, displeased with how a trousseau turned out, he refused to let the bride have it—all she had to do was look at how he adapted the best of the Paris collections for New York, and the thrilling dresses, suits, and hats that came out of his workrooms.

Even now, Kit continued to select a good many of her

34

clothes from the couturier. She insisted on paying for them, declining Tappe's offer of a generous discount, and she also declined to go to work for another house in the same capacity. There was only one House of Tappe, and no other specialty shop or import house was going to be the same. She would however, for a fee, give them any advice they requested, as well as bring them back from Europe the latest and most exclusive accessories she could find. It wasn't owning her own shop, she reasoned, but the right moment was coming. . . .

And now it had not only arrived, but the first concrete steps in achieving her goal had already been taken and there was no going back. Or was there?

I suppose if I go into a complete panic and can't get on the train, I could sell my entire stock to a New York shop, Kit thought. No, make that five or six shops, which means with an investment like that, I'm going to Los Angeles even if I have to be pushed kicking and screaming aboard both the Twentieth Century and The California Limited!

Laughing away her anxieties, Kit began the pleasant task of sorting through the mail that was waiting for her. Letters, bills, magazines, charity appeals, and the square, heavy envelopes that clearly announced that they contained invitations were all slit open with her letter opener. The letters from her mother, postmarked Caracas, would be read first; she would handle the others in declining order of interest.

She assumed that if her mother hadn't met and married Vincent Lyman in 1910, they'd still be living at the Plaza. Their experiment in hotel living, begun in fun had turned into a way of life. By the time Constance had met the widowed, handsome, engineering consultant, they were living in a large, sixth-floor suite with two bedrooms, a sitting room, and a dining room, all decorated with their

35

own furniture.

Even though she was now at an age where it really didn't matter any more, and she had an independent social life that kept her quite busy, Kit was fond of her stepfather. A leader in his field, his expertise was in demand by any number of engineering firms with both national and international projects, and that meant the Lymans spent a good part of every year travelling from project to project, and Kit had the vast Park Avenue apartment mostly to herself.

Constance and Vincent had still been in New York on the day she sailed, as had Packard, her stepfather's son from his first marriage who was a highly regarded member of the Boston Exchange, and his wife Daphne. It had been the Randalls' idea—since so many of the same people were coming to see them off—to hold both bon voyage parties in their *cabine de grand luxe,* the most expensive and elegant of the *France*'s suites. The crowd had been overflowing, but there had been more than enough Pol Roger champagne and caviar for everyone, and Sebastian had entertained them all by playing out his repertory on the suite's white Savead piano.

At the thought of Sebastian, Kit stood up and returned to her bedroom, almost as if he were there and she wanted to put physical space between them. She took off her dress, draped it over the chaise longue, stepped out of her shoes and took off her jewelry before going into the bathroom to wash her face. If only it were as easy to wash away knowing Sebastian as it is to wash off my makeup, she thought, creaming the kohl and mascara off her eyes and reaching for the oatmeal soap.

They had met eight months earlier in The Mayfair's elevator on the day Sebastian moved into the building. He was one of Broadway's newest darlings, a songwriter-composer with two musical comedies playing to standing room only every night, and he had lost no time in approaching Kit.

36

If there was an ideal time to start a romance it was in New York during the holiday season, Kit reflected as she put on a simple dress of pink handkerchief linen. Everything seemed to glitter and glow, and it was impossible to have a bad time. The only problem was that that time of year had the knack of making things look better than they really were, and that not only included the merchandise in the shops and the gifts exchanged but also certain people as well.

Sebastian was certainly far more interesting and intelligent than her current crop of beaux. He came from an old diplomatic family and had been raised by an uncle who held a high post in the State Department, but all he ever told her about those years was that, when he was eighteen and had refused to remain in Munich in order to perfect his already apparent musical talent, he had been simultaneously enrolled in Princeton and disinherited.

That had been her first warning, and Kit was a woman who listened to her instincts. It wouldn't hurt to wait, to take her time, to be careful, she told herself over and over, resisting Sebastian's very potent appeal.

Finally, in London, at the end of May, she had the confirmation that this man was not the one for her.

Comeuppance, the show he'd written the words and music for, was playing to sellout crowds at the Drury Lane Theatre. Unfortunately, the musical director had his own ideas as to how the score should be played, and Sebastian Creighton arrived in London straight off the brand-new *Aquitania* to let him know whose music it was.

He had every right to do that, Kit thought, it was the way he went about it that was so distasteful.

She had arrived at the Drury Lane after a morning spent at Lucile's on Hanover Square, ready to collect Sebastian for a promised lunch at Claridges, and walked in on his verbal assault of the musical director. Not a word of obscenity came out of his mouth, and he certainly didn't shout, but the tone of his voice was low and harsh and it not only carried so that she could hear every word, it went on far too long. Unable to bear hearing another word, Kit returned to the outer lobby where Sebastian joined her a few minutes later, acting as if nothing out of the ordinary had happened. She knew he hadn't seen her, but she had the feeling that even if he had it wouldn't have changed anything except that he would have had an audience for which to show off his verbal skill.

Still she continued to see him, to dine and dance with him, and accept his flowers and compliments. Sebastian, she realized, wasn't a man to reason with. The men in London—and to a lesser extent in Paris—seemed to take a step away from her; none of them wanted to interfere with the arrival of a beau from New York, and she wasn't about to let on to anyone—not even her closest friends—that Sebastian wasn't the catch he appeared to be.

Fortunately, there was the matter of buying stock for her shop, and that certainly occupied enough of her time which, had she simply been a tourist, would have been occupied by Sebastian. And for the sort of shop she was going to have, there was no such thing as too much merchandise. Lucile, Poiret, Paquin, Worth, Redfern, Cheruit, Callot Soeurs, Jeanne Hallee, Lanvin Jenny, Martial et Armand, the names of the best of Paris's couture houses floated through her mind. Even now, weeks later, in her own room, thousands of miles from the City of Light, she could close her eyes and see the elaborately furnished salons and smell the air filled with the scent of perfume, fabric, and furniture polish. And she might still be there now if politics hadn't suddenly moved to the forefront of all other events.

It was the beginning of July and they were in Paris. Sebastian had gone back to New York, as had Sinclair and Caroline, who had come over in May, their first trip to Europe in three years, and while Rupert fulfilled appointments with leading Parisian financiers, Mallory made the rounds of the antique shops, and Kit immersed herself in all the details of buying haute couture clothes and accessories.

38

Both women usually returned to their vast, antique-filled suite at the Crillon for tea, but Rupert rarely did, and when he walked in one afternoon they regarded him with surprise and the sudden feeling that something was not as it should be.

At first, all he did was kiss both women and hold Justine, his and Mallory's two-and-a-half year old daughter, but once he had a cup of tea and a selection of pastries in front of him, he dealt with the problem directly.

England and France and Germany were going to war, he told them. It was going to happen soon, quite possibly by the end of the month, and unless they wanted to run the risk of being caught on what might become a battlefield, it was time to go home.

They had had reservations for the *Aquitania*'s early August sailing, but by lunch the next day, that had been moved up to the middle of July and changed to the *France*, the Compagnie Generale Transatlantique, unlike Cunard able to meet their requirements for space.

It had been a mad rush to complete all their tasks in time for the sailing, but they had made it, and if this morning's stories in the *Times* were accurate, it had obviously been the right decision to make. "Now if only all the purchases I made make it to Los Angeles," Kit thought as she returned to her office to continue sorting through her mail until her lunch tray came up.

Even with most people still out of town for the summer there were still several invitations, mostly to theatre parties and dinners in restaurants. Alix and Henry Thorpe's party at the very popular Le Voisin pleased her most of all. She knew the Thorpes didn't care for Sebastian, and she wondered if they had invited him to be her partner or had found another man to fill in.

No, they'll stay with Sebastian, Kit thought. They know I'm going to Los Angeles, and they wouldn't want me to think that they're trying to match-make me out of my move.

Funny, Alix and Henry really didn't like either of the men I was engaged to.

Kit stretched out on the chintz-covered sofa and while she watched the curtains flutter at the slight July breeze, she thought about the two men she'd been engaged to.

Harrison Minot had been first—the first man she said she would marry and her first lover—and Kit still thought of him with affection and high regard. He was wealthy, good looking, witty, and highly principled, and she had said yes the first time he asked. But as the engagement went on, the high romantic feelings began to wear off as Harrison grew more and more protective of her. He wasn't the jealous sort, but he did worry about her. At first it was touching, but it rapidly turned to something quite different, and Kit felt as if he were wrapping her in a cocoon of concern. It wasn't unusual for a man to think that he was one woman's sole protector, and since Harrison was involved in the cut-throat world of high finance he wanted to be sure she was kept far away from anything ugly. But it takes two to agree to make that sort of relationship between a man and a woman work, and Kit's spirit was too independent, and her own sense of pride too strong, to be anything but what she was. With quiet regret, she gave the ring back to him, and almost immediately afterward felt an almost indecent sense of relief.

That had been in 1909, and two years later she was engaged again, this time to Palmer Metcalf, whom she'd known for years. Kit had friends who collected diamond engagement rings the way other people collected stamps, saying yes and then giving back the rings four, five, six months later without so much as a twinge of guilt; but, she wasn't like that and she had sincerely wanted this engagement to work, to last, to turn into a long and successful marriage. Palmer cared deeply about her, and he didn't smother her or think that her knowing about his real estate holdings was something too distasteful for her to know about; yet, it still wasn't right.

She was sure that they could be reasonably happy together, and *reasonably* was the key word. The one thing she didn't want was an old-shoe kind of marriage, one where the couple was so much alike that they could be taken for brother and sister. Her mother and father hadn't been like that, and now neither were her mother and Vincent. She had to feel more than just warmth and affection and respect for the man she would marry, and she was willing to wait until she found the romance she knew was out there.

"Oh, yes, romance is certainly out there," she muttered aloud, tucking another pillow under her head, "but I want something that goes much deeper and lasts and can be built on."

She had thought Sebastian would be that man, and now it was increasingly apparent that he wasn't; yet, she hadn't lost the certainty that one day she would meet the man for her. She didn't worry about not getting married. Among her set it was almost impossible not to marry unless one didn't like men, and usually not even that was an impediment to walking down the aisle. With less and less frowning going on over broken engagements, it was inevitable that the social stigma of divorce would be the next convention to fail, but she didn't want one of *those*.

So I'll wait, she told herself, and it's not as if I don't have anything else to do. Next stop for me—Los Angeles!

Chapter 2

"Alix and I are thinking of moving."

Henry Thorpe's unexpected comment to the small group of men and women who were gathered in the Randalls' living room at One Lexington Avenue as the vanguard of that evening's dinner party caused as much stir as if he'd suddenly announced that he were going back to England to join the army in the war against Germany that had begun the month before. Whenever their friends thought of Henry and Alix, it was always in terms of the Dakota on Central Park West and Seventy-second Street, where they'd lived since their marriage, first in the ten-room apartment Alix had had while she was unmarried, and then in the twenty-room apartment on the sixth-floor complete with ballroom.

"But you two have lived there forever," Rupert remarked as he signalled Dovedale, their very correct and proper butler, to begin serving his justly famous martinis.

"Twelve years—and a bit more in Alix's case—is not forever," Henry replied.

"It would just be so hard to think of you both living anywhere else," Mallory pointed out, looking very striking in a new Poiret dinner dress of dark gold silk with a lampshade tunic edged in maribou, a deep V neck, and a high waist. "There doesn't seem to be another apartment worthy of the Thorpe family."

"Well, we're going to try," Alix said as she admired the Odilon Redon painting of a lush bouquet of flowers that hung over the Steinway concert grand piano. Rupert and Mallory's living room was twenty-eight feet long and sixteen feet wide, and for a long minute, oblivious to her friends' interest, she studied the room's proportions with great interest. "The Dakota is thirty years old, and we'd like to try something more modern," she went on, collecting a frosty long-stemmed glass and sitting down on the richly pillowed ivory-silk damask sofa, her Poiret gown of ivory satin embroidered in crystal bugle beads catching the soft light of the lamps. "Besides, we'd like to see Central Park from the other side."

"I remember when you moved up from the fourth floor." Charles leaned against one of the bookcases and chuckled. "You pressed Rupert and me into service as auxiliary moving men, and when the day was over I knew that I had potential as a day laborer!"

"So speaks one of New York's best literary agents. My back still hurts when I think about it, and the regular movers probably thought we were a couple of rich boys getting exactly what we deserved!"

"In your case, Rupert, I'd say they were probably right," Thea teased, thrillingly turned out in a Lucile gown of Nile-green changeable satin with a tight, lace-frilled bodice. "I know that since Alix and I want to keep our friendship intact I won't be her decorator, but I'm still intrigued with your announcement."

"So am I," Kit put in. So far, Sebastian, who had promised to meet her there, had yet to show up, and she was getting more annoyed by the minute. She wouldn't put it past him to call and say he couldn't come. He'll be sorry if he does, she thought. "But where is it, and when are you moving?"

"When it's built, it'll be 820 Fifth Avenue. The Fred T. Ley

Company, who'll be the builders, contacted us last week. They promised we can work with the architect and have the apartment we want," Alix explained.

"But there's nothing there now but a hole in the ground! It'll be at least a year until the apartment house is built."

"Poor Kit, you sound so disappointed," Alix teased. "But I promise that if all of this works out, Henry and I won't have our house-warming until you can visit us from Los Angeles."

"You know the builders intend to use you and Henry as a draw to attract other renters," Thea pointed out in a slightly critical voice. "Does that bother you?"

"Of course not. I'd rather we had the chance to design our own apartment than have to adapt ourselves to what's on the market. But right now, let's keep this between us," Alix concluded as the Pooles arrived. "Caro is one of my oldest friends, but real estate is a tricky business, and some things are better off not being mentioned for a while."

Kit was so furious with Sebastian that she wasn't even sure how many people were making up Mallory and Rupert's dinner party. For a songwriter, she decided grimly as the waitresses hired for the evening removed their plates of smoked salmon with cucumber sauce, he had the timing of a superbly trained actor, and, all things considered, now, more than an hour since cocktails, she would have vastly preferred that he hadn't shown up at all. He had come in at the last possible moment, just as they had all given up on him and were about to go in to dinner, and with his most charming smile he'd explained to Mallory that although his delayed arrival was inexcusable, something very important had come up. His facile charm had such a great reach that almost instantly his dereliction was forgiven. He was showing off his personality to such an extent that he actually seemed to be overshadowing the women in their couture dresses, expensive jewelry, and rich perfumes—quite a coup for a man

45

whose masculinity couldn't be doubted.

He could do anything short of cold-blooded murder, and they'd think he was wonderful, Kit thought resentfully, watching Sebastian across the wide expanse of the elaborately set table as he alternately entertained Christy Browne on his left and Diana Bernstein on his right. Doesn't anyone see what I see, or has he pulled the wool over everyone's eyes?

"You look as if you're about to turn the same shade of red as our hosts' prized Matisse," First Lieutenant Oliver Beale said in a quiet, friendly voice. As Kit glanced from the striking modern painting hung over the sideboard and then back to the handsome face of Admiral Dalton's favorite aide, she felt her anger begin to fade.

"Have I really been that transparent?"

"Not at all," he assured her. "And I only noticed because I'm admiring your gown and thought it'd be awful if you got yourself out of sorts over Mr. Creighton and ruined the effect you're creating. Did you get your dress in Paris?"

"I spent three months in Europe, a great deal of that time in Paris's haute couture houses, and tonight I'm wearing something from right here in New York," Kit explained. Her complicated evening ensemble came from Henri Bendel's, and was a creation where a foundation of white charmeuse, veiled in shadow, embroidered mull, edged in antique Valenciennes, and draped to Van Dyke points over the skirt; the surplice, draped embroidered mull bodice was arranged so that the decolletage was square-cut in front, cut to a V in the back, and sashed at the waist in pale pink taffeta. She had decided to wear this tonight as her own personal fashion statement. A clear declaration that she didn't believe that only Paris—or in the case of Lucile, London—could create beautiful clothes. "I find that whenever I come home from Europe, I like to surround myself with American things for a while."

"Well, I have no complaints whatsoever," Oliver said, and

46

then leaned closer to her. "And to make you feel even better, I'll tell you that as we were going in to dinner Lucey told me that she thinks a certain gentleman here tonight is a real low-life."

So I'm not in this alone, Kit thought with relief just as the entree arrived. It was tenderloin of veal en crote draped in a truffle sauce and accompanied by saffron rice, all expertly prepared by Mrs. Dovedale, and when their champagne glasses were refilled with Pol Roger 1909, the individual conversations that had gone on during the first course were abandoned in favor of everyone taking part in one discussion.

They were an eclectic group, and their conversations touched on a wide variety of subjects. They played back the political conventions of two summers before when the Republicans, meeting in Chicago, had been even more stupid than usual in denying the nomination to Theodore Roosevelt in favor of the incumbent, William Howard Taft; and the Democrats, convening in Baltimore, had passed over that old bore, William Jennings Bryan, and on the forty-sixth ballot, found the strength in their hearts to nominate Woodrow Wilson, and lead them, for the first time since Grover Cleveland's non-consecutive terms, away from yet another Republican administration.

"If it had been Roosevelt versus Bryan, or possibly even Roosevelt against Wilson, I think T.R. would be back in the White House again," Charles remarked. On Election Day 1912, he had suffered a grave crisis of conscience before marking his ballot for Wilson.

"True, but if he hadn't made that idiot remark back in 1904 about not seeking another term, he could have won again in 1908, saved himself the effort and energy of that third party Bull Moose nonsense, and spared us a lot of problems at the voting booth," Sinclair added. Like Charles, he owed the former President a great personal debt, but he too had voted for the former Governor of New Jersey.

They touched on Ellen Wilson's death from Bright's Disease on August 6th, and then moved on to the even more disturbing and distressing events of the war in Europe. Those of their group who had been on the Continent had made it safely back to New York by the end of July, and the scores of Americans of every economic condition who were even now, the second week of September, still stranded by the hostilities, were an interesting topic of conversation. The Comtesse Solange de Renille, Charles's mother, was the story closest to them, even though it was a tale in reverse.

In July, Charles and Thea, along with their three children and Solange, had driven from Boston to the White Mountains of New Hampshire. One of the authors he represented had loaned them his rather luxuriously outfitted cabin, and they spent their days taking long walks and fishing in the lake, and their evenings reading in front of the fire. No one from the nearest village had thought to come up the mountain trail to tell them the latest news, and it wasn't until they came in for supplemental supplies and the newspapers on the morning of August 8th, that they learned that England and France were at war with Germany. That was Saturday morning, and by Sunday night they were in Boston, but by then it was too late. Cables were waiting for them at the Copley Plaza, messages from Guy and Andre, imploring their mother to stay with Charles in the States.

Stricken, Solange had complied and given up on her insistence to take the next ship back to France, no matter how dangerous, grateful only that her two older sons were too old for front-line service, that her French grandsons were too young, and that Charles was an American citizen. For the time being she was staying with Charles and Thea on East Sixty-sixth Street, but had announced that if they were still fighting the Boche in November, she would find her own apartment.

"I take it Solange is still refusing all invitations," Esme Phipps, Mallory's god-mother observed. "I thought she might come tonight since we're all old friends."

"Thea and I thought so too, but now, to Maman, even twenty-four is a large social event," Charles explained. "She'll accept luncheon invitations, and of course attend any parties Thea and I give, but she said it isn't right for her to lead a frivolous life when everyone in France is suffering."

By the time the salad of Bibb lettuce with endive accompanied by perfectly ripe brie was eaten, they had all agreed that the war in Europe was going to be long and awful, but there was no doubt at all that in the end they'd win over the Kaiser. Far better to have to fight the Kaiser's army again and again than have to live under German rule.

As they waited for dessert, it was only natural that their conversation move on to a lighter topic. Kit tried not to grind her teeth at the thought that someone at the table might ask to hear all the details of her buying trip. She was very proud of how she'd conducted business and of the purchases she'd made, but having to discuss them following the details of the latest war news seemed to her to be the height of bad taste. Across the table she caught Christy's concerned glance, and with instant comprehension she realized that they were both concerned where the conversation might go. Christy's father and stepmother, Morgan and Angela Browne, ran Browne's of San Antonio, a splendid and stylish women's specialty shop, and at almost nineteen and about to begin her sophomore year at Barnard along with her two closest friends, Diana Bernstein and Lucey Sawyer, she knew quite a bit about fashion and good taste. Her Callot Soeurs dance dress of embroidered net over pale pink silk with a V neck and a pink silk dress proved that she knew both how to dress for the right occasion and highlight both her height and her good looks, but with Admiral Bruce Dalton, the new Naval Chief of North Atlantic Operations, for her stepgrandfather, she knew what was going on and what might happen. Just as the waitresses arrived with the lemon sorbet, Christy leaned slightly forward and looked past Sebastian to Diana.

With an almost imperceptible nod of her golden-blond head, the daughter of the man who was the art dealer to King Albert of the Belgians, brushed a fold of her Callot Soeurs dress of white satin with a lightly beaded overdress of shrimp pink tulle. "It's so hard not to want to talk about our friends in Europe now," she said, voicing what they were all thinking, "I don't think we're going to see London, or Paris, or any of the other places we love for a long time. The Atlantic is going to be a very dangerous barrier; and yet, life there seems to be going on as normally as possible."

"People have to do something to keep going, to look past their present troubles," Alix added. She had seen the look that passed between Nela's stepdaughter and Claire's daughter; both of them had superb potential, she decided. "The theater is as popular as ever. And since England has a nice film industry going, this may even help it expand. It may even help ours. God knows, it could use it."

"Oh, I don't know," Rupert said with a sidelong look at Sinclair. "D.W. Griffith is filming something all over Los Angeles. No one seems to know exactly what it is, but the *on dit* says it has something to do with the Civil War."

"France gives us Sarah Bernhardt in *Queen Elizabeth,* and our film makers provide us with *Bronco Billy's Adventures,"* Lucey observed, referring to the first feature-length film shown in America, and a two-reel, extremely popular Western. The image of her mother, Elinor Tierney Sawyer, once San Francisco's youngest and most elegant madam, and since the earthquake and fire of 1906, a very wealthy businesswoman with a wide variety of holdings, Lucey sometimes caused otherwise wealthy and respected middle-aged men to turn and stare at her in the street. "Besides, they don't talk, and there's no color," she continued, tossing her bobbed, dark red hair.

"In some cases, it's better they don't say a word," Mallory pointed out, recalling the motion pictures they'd seen last January.

"I own a motion picture studio," Sinclair said almost abruptly. "Hooper Studios."

"Oh, I know *that.*" Lucey's disdainful voice sent a wave of laughter across the table, laughter that Sinclair joined in, and something in the girl's voice told those at the party who knew the details that she too knew what sort of movies came out of Hooper. "My mother would call that a wild card investment."

"She's right." Sinclair waited until the petit fours and the cafe filtre was served. That same feeling that had enveloped him that January night was on him again. Throw it out and see what happens, he decided. "I own this thing, I have my associate running things over there, and he's going stir-crazy, and neither of us have the faintest idea of what we should do."

"Then why did you buy it?" Alix inquired.

"For investment purposes. Los Angeles is something of a boom town, and sections of the city that were worthless a few years ago have buildings on them now. And the climate is fantastic," Sinclair explained, and then told them about Mrs. Martindale. "I'm rather a good joke in the business community right now."

"But that's no reason to sell," Henry quipped to more laughter.

"This is a little like having a very expensive automobile stuck in the mud," said Sinclair, who owned only Rolls-Royces.

As the conversation surged around the table, Kit sat back in her chair, quite happy to only listen in to what the others had to say. There was more champagne, and additional plates of pink-, white-, and chocolate-iced petit fours, and reflecting that Mallory and Rupert certainly knew how to treat their guests, she amused herself with the fresh supply of food and drink. Even the most dedicated of play-goers among them seemed to have a definite—if secret—interest in

51

the "flickers."

There was a great deal of discussion about the new Strand Theater on Broadway that had opened in April. It boldly advertised itself as America's first motion picture palace, and was replete with crystal chandeliers, heavy marble, thick rugs underfoot, plenty of gilt work, and an eye-catching array of original paintings, and a thirty-piece orchestra to accompany the select films they showed. It was blatantly designed to attract the better sort of audience who avoided the nickelodeons and small, unpretentious neighborhood theaters that were generally thought of as a nice place for the servants to go on their evening off.

"Well, I *suppose* that makes them respectable. . . ."

"That may still be debatable, but I remember reading in the *Wall Street Journal* that Biograph made 151 films in 1909. . . ."

"And that's the same year that the *New York Times* reviewed a movie. . . ."

"Of course, it was *Pippa Passes*—quite charming. . . ."

"Has it really been fourteen years since *A Trip To The Moon* . . . ?"

"Remember, Georges Méliès is a magician. . . ."

"That's what it takes to make those things. . . ."

"Not to mention a touch of larceny. I have a theory that the movie companies that come West prefer Los Angeles over San Francisco because Mexico is a lot closer in case the process server comes to call!"

At Rupert's trenchant comment, Kit almost choked on the sip of champagne she was in the process of swallowing. She knew she'd had far too much champagne, and the best solution would be for her to opt out of this free-for-all entirely. Except that she had an idea. The movies couldn't talk, they had no color, while the few that offered hand-colored plates were painfully false and obvious, and to the sophisticates used to the stage offerings of New York and London, the stories were frequently naive and sentimental.

52

But in a way it was no different than when she'd worked at Tappe's or bought fanciful accessories for the other stores. Things were very rarely all good or all bad. She thought about her weeks in Paris where she'd had to look at the collections through new eyes: before she had simply rejected a garment she didn't like, she had to look beyond her own personal, somewhat rarified, highly developed taste. A dress could be ruined by too much embroidery, a suit or coat by garish buttons, and Tappe had taught her that the selection of material was crucial to the dress no matter how simple or elaborate the design. If it was like that with clothes, why couldn't the same standards be applied to the fledgling motion picture industry?

No one here is really helping Sinclair, she thought, listening to the conversation swirling around the table. All they're interested in is showing off how much they know, or giving their personal opinions. He's looking for a special idea, and mine is as good as anyone else's.

"Sinclair," she said in a crystal-toned voice, and waited for him to turn his attention to her. "I have an idea for you. Why don't you have Hooper Studios make a quality movie, the sort they'd show at the Strand Theater?"

Instantly, silence fell over the table, and with a start Kit noticed that more than a few of her friends suddenly had a "why didn't I think of that" expression on their faces.

"Why did you say that?" Sinclair demanded, not letting himself think beyond this moment, honestly afraid that unless he kept himself totally neutral he'd either accept or reject her idea on the basis of grasping at straws. "I assume that Mallory and Rupert have told you that Hooper's something of a dive."

"Not to mention that some of the movies made there are in questionable taste." Kit smiled and felt a spurt of triumph course through her. "But why should making a movie be any different than making a dress? The little dressmaker or milliner who has taste and style can always dream of becoming a great couturiere—look how far Henri Bendel and Hattie Carnegie have come. If you have the facilities and the resources, all you have to do is improve the product."

"Sinclair, you know there's a reason why you haven't fired anyone from the studio staff," Caroline pointed out. "You've even let me make a few changes there."

"It wouldn't have done me any good to say no," he said, and drained his champagne glass. "The idea of Hooper Studios being able to make a quality movie is the old cliché of making a silk purse out of a sow's ear. But I wonder if it could be done?"

Kit blinked in amazement. Was it all this simple? "Sinclair, are you going to do something with my suggestion?"

"Didn't you mean what you said?"

"Every word!"

"You may have a good idea there, Kit. It's the best idea I've heard all night. I knew I was on the edge of something with this purchase a few months ago, and I certainly didn't want to make a hasty decision straight off," he told her in an expansive voice. "But now I'm willing to take everything into consideration."

"Are the Howards always so generous to you and your escorts?" Sebastian asked as they entered the drawing room to find the lights glowing softly and a tray of drinks set out on the table in front of the sofa.

"No, they're only hoping that if we become serious, I won't go to Los Angeles," Kit responded as they sat down. "Remy Martin?"

"Please." Sebastian swirled the rich liquid around in the balloon-shaped glass. "Are you serious about opening that store? I don't see you as a lady shopkeeper."

"I'm very serious, and while we're on this topic, I could say that I don't see you as a writer of songs for Broadway musicals," Kit replied as she leaned back against the cushions and looked obliquely at the handsome man beside her. How little he understood what she wanted to do, but then she suspected that he cared for little that went on beyond his own sphere of interest. In the short time she'd known Sebastian, she knew that if it didn't affect him, he didn't care. "Since you're doing just what you want, you really haven't any right to question my decisions."

"Just think of it as some gentlemanly concern." With great care he returned the glass to the tray. "Now, shall we see what we can do about making the Howards happy?"

For a split second, Kit considered fighting him off. But the champagne had a delightful effect on her, and right now, at shortly after one in the morning, the idea of indulging in a little affection wasn't a bad idea at all. Part of this past evening was still more than a little unreal to her, and Sebastian was so very, very real.

She twined her arms around his neck and let him draw her closer and closer until she could feel the hard, flat studs of his evening shirt pressing into her skin. He knew all the right things to do, all the things she liked, but almost instantly she became aware that something was off. He was good, much too good, and that bothered Kit more than she was willing to admit, but as his arms encircled her, she had the over-whelming feeling that this was all plotted out beforehand.

Part of Kit didn't care, and there was the delightful urge to push aside all her doubts and enjoy this time with Sebastian. She would even temporarily forget about his too-witty remarks that could border on verbal cruelty, his barely veiled eroticism fueled by his awareness of himself, and the fact that with his money, looks, and talent he could have and do anything. True, he wrote songs about love, paid all the proper compliments, and did all the right things, but she knew he didn't believe, didn't care, and that she couldn't take.

With great difficulty she stopped kissing him and pulled

away, her heart pounding at the confrontation she knew was coming.

"What is it, Kit?" Sebastian asked, his face a complex study of emotions in the soft light. "Do you require an engagement ring before we go any further? I can always send over to Cartier for one first thing in the morning, if that'll make it easier for you."

If I had any doubts left, this had just taken care of all of them, Kit thought, and felt her last vestige of regret fade away. Slowly, she rose to her feet and looked coolly at Sebastian.

"Isn't it time you went home?"

"What about making the Howards happy?" he asked, making no move to stand.

"If you don't leave, I'll see to it that the Howards are very *un*happy." Kit's voice was quiet, even a little cheerful, but she left no doubt as to the seriousness of her intentions. "Howard used to be something of an amateur boxer in his youth—he can probably still pack quite a punch—and Mrs. Howard would be more than happy to apply her rolling pin to you. She thinks you're too good looking for your own good."

"You little tease."

"Look again, Sebastian. I'm not little, and I'm not a tease. And if I wanted to go to bed with you, I'd do it and not worry about an engagement ring afterwards."

"You're still angry about my being late to Rupert and Mallory's," Sebastian said as he stood up. There was a look of cold amusement on his face that Kit didn't care for, but he merely came over to her and kissed her cheek in a rather dry, unemotional fashion. "That was unforgivable of me, and I'm sorry."

"And I accept your apology," she replied, wanting to keep this as civilized as possible.

"When are you leaving for California?" he asked as they left the drawing room. He wasn't so much being a gentleman as being wise enough to know when something was over and done with.

"I'm not sure. It depends on when the others are ready, but it won't be more than another ten days," she said, and felt a slight rush of anticipation.

"Will I see you again?"

"Of course you will, silly. But I'd rather you didn't come to Grand Central to see me off on the Twentieth Century. It might give the wrong impression that if my shop fails I'll be running back to New York and you."

"And you won't?"

It wasn't so much of a question as it was a challenge. He just won't give up on an opportunity to gratify his ego, Kit thought, and as she began to laugh she decided to tell Sebastian *exactly* what she thought was wrong with him.

"No," she said a minute later. "Oh, I think you're wildly exciting, but the only problem is *you* think so also. Not that you're unredeemable."

"And I only have to fall in love to be cured." A speculative smile curved at his mouth.

Kit's smile matched his. "Yes, I think that'll do it. What you need, Sebastian, is a woman to make you quite unhappy. But she'll have to be around you almost all the time. Absence won't do it with you. I can go to Los Angeles and come back again and you won't feel any different about me. But for a woman you'll see every day, who won't leave you alone—well, we'll see who's right."

"I'm not the sort who falls in love," he warned her as they reached the entry foyer and Kit opened the door for him.

"Poor Sebastian, you'll find out," Kit promised, and kissed his cheek. "One day soon you're going to find out that being cynical takes an awful lot of work and is not very rewarding—and that it's a lot more fun to be in love."

"Did I really tell Sinclair that he should have a quality

57

movie made?" Kit asked herself several hours later as she surveyed her elegantly set breakfast tray. The large, red strawberries were swimming in cream, the croissants were golden-brown and still hot from the oven, pats of butter rested in a small dish of cracked ice, and the café au lait was hot and fragrant. The tray set with fine china, the sunlight pouring in through the half-open windows, and the pillows piled up behind her were all ways to ease the way from her party-filled night to a busy day that would end with yet another social evening, and it made the latest war news a little bit easier to read.

Trust the Germans to see to it that the war wasn't going to be fought on their precious Fatherland, she thought, filled with disgust as she read the latest reports about the ongoing invasions of France and Belgium in the *Times* and the *World*. All of the pain and suffering going on, and I'm opening a dress shop.

Pondering the absurdities of a world where men were fighting and dying, and yet the commonplace still went on as undisturbed as possible, Kit put the newspapers aside in favor of sorting through her mail. It was the usual mélange of letters and magazines and bills, and when she was finished sorting it all out, her thoughts turned back to last night's dinner party. They had gone from the dining room to the living room where all attempts at serious conversation had been abandoned in favor of putting on the Victrola and dancing.

It's not all the champagne I drank last night that's bothering me, or all the dancing I did, Kit thought. I know what it is, but am I going to be brave enough to follow up on it? If I had enough nerve to bring up the subject last night, I should be brave enough to find out how my idea holds up in the cold light of morning.

Kit smoothed down her nightgown of sheer white batiste with white floral embroidery and medallions of ecru lace, and reached for the telephone on the bedside table. She gave the operator the Ritz-Carlton's number, and a minute later the hotel's switchboard was ringing the Pooles' suite.

"How are you after last night?" she asked Caro.

"Never felt better," Caro returned, and laughed. "I wish I could say the same for Sin, though. He's been wandering around bleary-eyed and can't look at food. Men simply don't have the stamina for social events."

"Maybe I should give you the name of the Japanese masseur Sebastian uses. He has Saito come by every morning, and swears by him."

"I think Sin is a bit too far gone for even a Japanese masseur, but I'll keep it in mind. Still, my husband is managing to tend to his business, and that's saying a lot considering his condition. Of course, *my* business is taken care of and I'm ready to go shopping!" Caro offered informatively. She knew why Kit had called, and that she was waiting for the right moment to bring up last night; it was a game and they were both experts at playing. "Weren't the girls a delight last night?"

"Absolutely. Christy told me that they call themselves The Three Swans."

"That's charming, and they're smart enough to avoid living in the dorms."

"Lucky for them. When the colleges decide to crack down on the students, the 'town girls' are the last to be affected—as I know from personal experience."

"Education is wonderful, the only thing you have to watch out for is the educators," Caro quipped from the wise viewpoint of a woman who, at seventeen, had chosen the opportunity to go to China instead of college and knew she'd made the right decision. "Still, we're all a pretty intelligent bunch. Lots of ideas," she paused for a crucial half-second, "yours, for instance."

Kit's heartbeat quickened. "It seemed to be the best suggestion to make."

"Don't be modest, darling, yours was the *only* suggestion.

59

What made you think of it?"

"It's the theory of fashion, of using it to look the best you can. You know that, Caro."

"Yes, and so did most of the people at the party, but you're the one who got something concrete together. Sinclair admires that. By the way, I'm meeting Alix at Lord and Taylor at one—a little lunch, a little shopping. Care to join us?"

"Sounds like fun." What did you think, she asked herself, that you were going to hear that your champagne-gilded idea is anything better than a fantasy?

"We're going to spend a little more time in Chicago than we planned. Will you mind?"

"No, I'd like a chance to see the Art Institute properly. Not to mention some of the shops—all in the cause of research, of course."

"Of course," Caro agreed, and laughed. "Sin says Chicago will be the best place for his meeting. He wants to talk to Greg as soon as possible."

"Greg?" Kit tried to place the name.

"Gregory West, Sin's right-hand man. He wants Greg to be in on this all the way, particularly since he's had him watching the studio interests for months and it wouldn't be fair to cut him out of the decision-making process now."

"What is there to decide?" Kit asked with a thrill of anticipation she couldn't suppress.

"What to do about the studio. It can't just sit there almost inactive any longer." Caro sighed. "I wish it were easier to place a long-distance call to California, it would save a lot of difficulties. You really galvanized my husband last night, and now he's looking forward to having Greg meet us in Chicago so we can discuss if it would be feasible to make that quality movie you suggested Hooper Studios produce."

Chapter 3

Gregory West sat at his desk in his office at Hooper Studios engrossed in a three-day-old copy of the *New York Times* that offered a full report of the Battle of Tannenberg, fought the week before. Today, Friday, September 10th, the early editions of all the Los Angeles papers, the rest of the New York papers, the day's first delivery of mail, and the latest issue of *Moving Picture World* all remained unread as he bent his head over the long columns full of details and facts and figures. He scanned the story again and again, half-hoping, half-dreading that he would find a familiar name. For the first time in fourteen years he wanted some concrete news about someone from Russia, the country of his birth that he'd left in secret and in fear for his life one icy night.

Would I be a captain now, or a major? he wondered, folding the *Times* with exaggerated care. Which General would I be serving under, Samsonov of the Second Army who committed suicide in the pine forest because he failed the Czar, or Kliouev of the Twelfth Corps, who entrenched himself with his detachment, held off the Germans with captured guns, and is now a prisoner along with those who survived? Would I be one of the officers who made it back to Russia? Would I be wounded and wandering through a swamp? Or, would I be buried in a forest in East Prussia?

The variations on the life he might be leading now if the events of a single night, a night he could not remember with any sort of clarity, were chillingly endless, and he put the paper aside and stood up, hoping that some sort of movement would ease the thoughts crowding in on him. When he reached the windows and looked out, he actually blinked in surprise. The report of the battle had taken such a strong hold on his imagination that he'd almost expected to see the Tannenberg battlefield spread out in front of him. Instead, all he saw were two workmen carrying a metal foil-covered reflector that they'd taken off a flatbed truck parked at the entrance to the studio.

"We're taking it to the back lot, Mr. West," one of the men called up to him. "They're filming the picnic scene for the latest episode of *The Pie Man.*"

"That's fine, Joe," he replied, "I'm looking forward to the finished result."

Do they have to report every move to me? Gregory thought as he leaned against the window frame and regarded the cloudless blue sky. Another perfect California day, something that even after a dozen years in this part of the state was an endless source of surprise and delight. Considering where he'd been born and bred, the continuing near-perfection of Los Angeles's weather was still something of a near-miracle.

I don't want to be a watchdog, he reflected, but after seven months of having my office here, I still don't have a title. Of course, the real question is, do I want one? Well, I'll find out when I get to Chicago. Sin's finally ready to make a decision, and if he can't wait to get back here to tell me, he has to be pretty definite about what he wants to do. . . .

"It's nice to see that some people can spend their morning looking out the window!"

"Just blame my dereliction on California, Mrs. Rigby," Gregory told his secretary, and gave her a smile guaranteed to melt an iceberg. "One look out the window to see if the city fathers have decided to repave Hollywood Boulevard, and I'm lost."

"That'll be the day they fix *that* street!" Joan Rigby stated with mock tartness. The studio secretary, this direct woman in her early forties had known *exactly* what went on—had gone on—in this studio from the day she was hired by Mr. Martindale three years before. It certainly hadn't been her choice to work in such a place, but what opportunities did a widow with two children to bring up have? She had to pay school fees and the grocery bills somehow. She'd just taken a deep breath, closed her eyes to a lot of things, and done her job. Things had been so much better since Mr. Poole took over, and Mr. West was a dear. But it couldn't go on like this forever, and she was far more worried than she'd ever tell anyone. "Here are the files you wanted," she went on, placing some dusty manila folders on his desk, noting the untouched mail but wisely saying nothing. "Since you're leaving for Chicago tonight, I assume you'll want to send flowers to the Courtlands. Would you like me to contact the florist?"

"Use the florist at the Hotel del Coronado, and tell him just to sign my name to the card. I spoke to Admiral Courtland last night and explained why I couldn't come down to San Diego for the weekend. An arrangement of apricot tea roses and statice will do."

Mrs. Rigby made a note on her pad. "Is there anyone else you want me to call?" she inquired blandly, and Gregory shook his head. She knew, and he knew that she knew, but both of them were responding to a silent code almost as old as time itself, and that the true subject would never be mentioned except in the most oblique way.

Thank God for a discreet secretary, Greg thought, they're as invaluable as the valet who makes sure that one lady never finds out about the other.

Mr. West is such a nice man, Mrs. Rigby thought. Why doesn't he find a nice young woman he can marry and stop all of this business with those married women?

"Are you happy here, Mrs. Rigby?" Greg asked suddenly. "I know you haven't had all that much work since we've closed down production on everything but *The Pie Man*, but at least the premises are in better condition."

"You're a master of the understatement, Mr. West! Why the health department could have closed this place down as a slum. Mrs. Poole and Mrs. Randall have done a splendid job," she said appreciatively as she looked around his spacious office. "Do you think that the special way of arranging the things that Mrs. Poole believes in will do us any good?"

"I'll find out in Chicago. But don't worry, Mrs. Rigby, if Mr. Poole decides to close down the studio, we'll see to it that there's a place for you in our organization."

"Thank you, Mr. West. I appreciate that. I'll call the florist now, and be back with your lunch tray at noon."

Mrs. Rigby left, closing the door quietly behind her, and Greg returned to looking out the window. Here, on Selma Avenue, halfway between Sunset Boulevard and Hollywood Boulevard, the lot that comprised Hooper Studios *was* an eyesore, but he had to admit that the badly tarred expanse of Hollywood Boulevard troubled him far more than the large, three-story ramshackle house that was the main building where all administrative tasks were handled did.

Once the Victorian-style structure had been aired out and scrubbed down and fresh coats of paint applied, he would have quite happily worked with all the left-behind furniture without any trouble, but he'd spent his first three weeks in America working on a road crew in Upper Manhattan, and he could take awful decor far easier than he could the rough roadbed he drove his new Fiat over daily.

That explanation, however, had been totally lost on Caroline Poole and Mallory Randall. Once the house was up to par, when the secretaries, story department people, and salesmen had bright, plant-filled offices to work in—

although there wasn't much work for anyone to do—and the actors' dressing rooms were clean and well-organized, Caro turned her attention to Greg's office.

From her years in China, Caro was a firm believer in *feng shui,* the Chinese art of placement which used the ancient practice of arranging surroundings so they were balanced and aligned in such a way as to bring success. Once the soft white paint was dry on the walls and the Charles Rennie Mackintosh designed carpet of pale tan with an Art Nouveau-looking center grid of black, red, and cobalt blue laid on the floor, she set about to make sure this room would bring forth the life-enhancing energy known as *ch'i.* With the stock of Mallory's shop at her disposal, Caro saw to it that he had an appropriately furnished office. A red wall clock, the charm to keep thieves away, came first, and was followed by a white-glazed porcelain vase with a red ribbon tied around it as a symbol of peace and serenity. In this ancient art, black is a manifestation of water, which in turn draws in money, and although Caro acquiesced to Greg's firm refusal to have a tank with six black fish like the one Sinclair always had in his office, she provided him with a seventy-two-inch-long black lacquer desk and a fancifully modern black lacquer cabinet that she fitted out as a bar. There was a beautiful chesterfield of the deepest, darkest red leather, and several very comfortable chairs—a perfect setting for the business meetings which had yet to take place—as well as a superb mirror in a red and gold lacquer frame.

"Mirrors are necessary to double luck, keep away threats, and bring in positive forces," Greg muttered, echoing Caro's words. He had selected the calligraphy scrolls, but it wasn't until they were framed and hung that Caro had informed him that the characters depicted were all for good luck. "Who knows how much of this will work, but Hooper Studios needs every advantage it can get!"

Greg might be skeptical about the ultimate effect of the art of *feng shui,* but he was quite used to Caroline's cool, jaunty, loving manner as she went about what she called her "social arrangements." If he'd told her not to bother, she would have listened, but a long time ago, Greg had recognized that there was a part of him that liked being quietly fussed over and cared for. For fourteen years, Sinclair had been his surrogate brother, and for twelve years Caroline was probably as good as sisters-in-law got, whether they were real or "adopted." They were the only family he had now. Thanks to the Pooles, he had a home, success, all the pleasures that came with it—and a new name. And since Caro had rarely, if ever, tried to matchmake for him, Greg was perfectly willing to have his new office arranged by her, have Mallory decorate his apartment suite at the Alexandria, and even let Sinclair place him in charge of this white elephant. It was all a matter of trade-offs. . . .

"I'm sorry to disturb you, Mr. West, but this won't wait another minute."

"Doesn't anyone knock around here!" Greg shouted, his very Russian mood of contemplation shattered. He glared, outraged, as Archie MacNeil, the cameraman for *The Pie Man,* strode into the office, waving a letter in his hand.

"It's not as if you're holding a board meeting!" the older man snapped back, his faint Scottish accent becoming more prominent. "I'm one of the few people around here who doesn't earn his paycheck by eating, reading and playing poker. I work, Mr. West—or I'm trying to. My letter of resignation," he finished, laying the paper on the desk.

"Resignation?" Greg forgot all about his interrupted reverie. Archie MacNeil was practially a pioneer in the art of being a cameraman, having gone to work for Thomas Edison at the American Mutoscope and Biograph Company in New York in the early 1890s. He had been there for the first major developments, watching as William Dickson supervised the development of the Kinetoscope, the device that made movies visible on a peepshow basis, and had seen the changes that transformed films from something suitable

66

only for penny arcades to full-length features. The tall, quiet, transplanted Scotsman had come West in 1907 for health reasons, and had worked for Colonel William Selig's movie company as they completed their version of *The Count Of Monte Cristo.*

As far as Greg knew, Archie had never so much as set foot inside the Black Maria where the blue movies were made, and instead confined his talent to comedies that, no matter how silly in plot, were nonetheless beautifully photographed, and even a little innovative. Greg also knew that Archie MacNeil was on a par with Billy Bitzer, D.W. Griffith's own wizard cameraman. Hooper Studios might well shortly cease to exist, but no decision had been made, and he wasn't about to let this man walk. "Isn't this something we can talk about?" he asked as he went to his desk, forcing himself to handle this matter calmly.

"Not with that idiot Coster," Archie said, referring to the studio accountant. "I'm a Scot, and can hold onto a penny, but I look like a wild spender next to that man. I need a new lens, a two-inch f.3.5 Zeiss Tessar, and I went to Coster for approval." Archie's face tightened with disgust. "I told him why we need it, how it will improve the quality of the picture, and that little weasel said it wasn't possible, that I would have to make do with what I have since he couldn't justify such an expense to you or Mr. Poole."

"Sit down, Archie, please. I know Mr. Coster is very tight-fisted, but he feels very strongly about his responsibility to report all expenditures to Mr. Poole."

Archie's look had no pity. "You really believe that, don't you?"

A thin thread of anger ran through Greg at Archie's almost insolent voice, but he also recognized that he thought he had nothing left to lose. "This is a business, Archie."

"And I don't understand that?"

"No, I'm not saying that, but Mr. Poole may want to sell the studio."

"He won't, not if he has half the brains he's reputed to have." Archie leaned forward and shoved the letter closer to Greg. "And I'm willing to stake my job on it. If I'm wrong, I'm out anyway, and if I'm right, you'll have to rehire me in the end. There still aren't too many of us who know what to do with a camera."

Greg glanced at the letter of resignation. "Why is Coster's signature on this? He has nothing to do with hiring and firing."

"I wrote the letter and told Coster that when I went in to see you I wanted his name on it. I want a record of why I had to leave, and who caused it. I want you and Mr. Poole to know that I walked out of here over a camera lens. True, it's an expensive one, but it's only a lens."

"I don't know what's going to happen here," Greg said finally, "but I know you're not leaving here like this." He ripped the letter of resignation in half and scribbled a note on one half. "Take this back to Mr. Coster and tell him to order that lens, and after you've done that, stop by Mrs. Rigby's desk and tell her to type out a letter stating that if Hooper Studios is closed down, that lens becomes your personal property."

With a slow smile spreading across his face, Archie rose to his feet and held out his right hand. "Thank you, Mr. West, and I promise you won't regret this. You don't have an easy job here, but you do know the right thing to do."

When Archie left, Greg sank back in his chair. All of this fuss over a camera lens, he thought, and had to smile. Archie's a perfectionist and Coster's a skinflint with an eye on the bottom line. He's probably having a fit right now, thought I'd be the consummate businessman. If he knew I were Russian, he'd realize that when the final choice has to be made, I'll always come down on the side of the artist, of the one who decides to stake it all on one throw.

His mail was still unanswered, the newspapers—except for the *New York Times*—unread, and he ignored them, choosing instead to close his eyes and remember. Gregory West, the successful Los Angeles businessman, was remembering Gregori Vestovich, Sinclair Poole's erstwhile valet and secretary, and most of all he was remembering Alexander Gregori Dimitri Vestovanova, whose privileged, wealthy, and carefree world had changed because of what had happened on one icy St. Petersburg night. . . .

In St. Petersburg on the banks of the Neva, Peter the Great's city begun in 1703 and built on swamps, the capital of the Russian Empire since 1712, the season was winter. The climate was raw, damp and unsettled, January's temperatures averaged around fifteen degrees, and the drinking water wasn't entirely safe, as at any time during the year. But in those six long, icy months the imperial city came alive. In the daylight hours, the city streets filled with troikas, vehicles drawn by three horses used only in the cold weather, and colorfully dressed vendors competed with each other to sell a variety of goods and foods. Museum-goers forgot about the icy winds outside while they viewed the art collection of the Hermitage. Gentlemen lunched at Dominique's where a billiard room was an added attraction to the excellent food, while further along the Nevski, ladies lunched in the comfort of the Cafe Central. There was the shooting club at Kraskoye Selo, ice skating at the Ice Palace of the Aquarium, and the Cinsielli Circus performed nightly in its theatre on the Fontanka, but most exciting of all—except for the private parties and grand balls—were the theaters. The Little Theatre, which was leased by the Literary and Artistic Society, put on plays by modern Russian dramatists; the Imperial Michael Theatre was the home for French drama and comedy; and the Imperial Alexander Theatre offered Russian drama and comedy; but the magnet that drew both native and visitor alike was the Imperial Marie Theatre—the Maryinsky. Both opera and ballet were performed in the two-thousand seat theater, but it was the ballet that was to some almost a mystical experience. From the end of August to the beginning of May, nearly every performance was sold out, and always in the most fashionable first tier boxes were wealthy, aristocratic men of all ages who came to admire the ballet girls, almost all of whom were beautiful, talented, and, with the right inducements, available to a gentleman with the right qualifications.

Natalia Voykovich was one of those ballerinas, and if she hadn't yet been cast in the principal roles that her closest rival, Anna Pavlova, was achieving, her solo parts were greeted with great enthusiasm by the gentlemen of the audience. Her dressing room was filled with the most expensive of flowers and chocolates, and the dark blue velvet jewelers' cases contained gem-studded trinkets—and from his family's box in the first tier, Alexander Gregori Vestovanova decided that he was going to have her.

There was nothing in the least humble about Alexander. He certainly didn't have to be. With his family wealth, position and power behind him, there was nothing he couldn't do or have, and at twenty-one these privileges had given him a shell of invincibility. Everything he wanted he got, and to his way of thinking there was no reason why Natalia should elude him.

He had first noticed her in *Swan Lake* in August 1899, shortly after he completed his military training and was commissioned a lieutenant in the cavalry. Had he been a graduate of West Point, Sandhurst, or St. Cyr, even though he was from one of his country's finest families, he would have spent the first few years of his commission in some far-flung spot until the military powers felt he'd paid his dues and reassigned him to a spot more fitting his station in life. But this was Russia, what applied elsewhere had no meaning here, and he was assigned to the Barracks of the Horse Guards in St. Petersburg, where his duties were undemanding enough so that most nights he slept in his own bed in his room at the Vestovanova Palace on the south bank of the Moika Canal. It gave him plenty of time to write letters to Natalia, to send her chocolates and search through the fine shops along the Nevski and on Alexandrinskaya Square for presents that would enchant her, to attend every performance she danced in, and then, as the winter season approached, to even meet with her. But now, in the first week of the new century, he knew he would be reassigned after Lent to Moscow, to the Cavalry Barracks on Khamovnivheski Place. In principle, Alexander had no objections to a Moscow posting, and in July he would be reassigned again, to Tsarkoye Selo, the Czar's village of 80,000, where numerous villas and parks and two imperial palaces made a picture-perfect setting; but before he left for these assignments he was determined to make Natalia his.

Among his friends he had always been the ringleader. Even from their earliest nursery days when they'd played together in their correct sailor suits under the watchful eye of their proper English nannies, he had been the one who planned, executed, and led—and usually got away with—all their pranks. With those accomplishments in mind, he met with his closest friends—all as enamoured of Natalia as he was—to plan a champagne supper at midnight. Konstantin Ignatov's brother had an apartment on the Vlasyuk near the Moika Canal that they could borrow for the night's festivities, and once the location was set, everything else fell into place.

"But they say Natalia is under the protection of Grand Duke Vladimir," Sandor Dolgoruky, the most cautious of their number pointed out. "This may not be the safest thing we've ever done."

"If she were, would she have accepted our invitation?" Alexander retorted as they sat in a corner table at Old Donon, the after-theater restaurant much frequented by the demi-monde. "Of course, which one of us she selects is the lady's choice," he continued graciously.

"And you have no doubt as to whom that will be," Georgi Brioukow finished with a sly wink.

Alexander laughed and ordered more champagne for them. The evening was perfectly planned, and when the time came Natalia would choose him. How could she not? Everything would go his way; it always had and always would. . . .

"Mr. West . . . oh, Mr. West, I'm so sorry, but the messenger from the Santa Fe office just arrived, and I thought you'd want your ticket right away. . . ." Mrs. Rigby's usually crisp voice became uncertain as she saw the faraway, almost glazed look in Greg's eyes—a look she had never seen before, and one which startled her. "It's just that you're always such an organized man. . . ."

"I apologize, Mrs. Rigby," Greg said quickly, shaking off the claw-like grasp of the past that was threatening to overpower him with old memories. He motioned for the woman to come the rest of the way into his office. "You must think I've turned into some sort of ogre."

"No, Mr. West, no. It's just that I've never seen you so distracted. You look as if you were a million miles away."

"Not quite that far." Greg's smile was bittersweet as he put his train ticket on top of the reports he was taking with him to Chicago. "I seem to have a lot on my mind today."

"Well, unless there's a fire, I won't disturb you until it's time for lunch," she assured him, backing away toward the door, instinctively aware that the best thing to do was not to linger. Clearly, Mr. West was in a *very* odd sort of mood.

Alone again, Greg spent the next twenty minutes opening and reading his mail, busying himself with familiar tasks until his earlier thoughts once again intruded and he found his work was meaningless.

So Mrs. Rigby thinks I'm so organized, he thought, tossing several letters into his leather letter box. I probably am and always have been, but it's a long way from the plottings of a juvenile cavalry officer looking after his own pleasures to an executive planning a course of action for a failing venture. I don't have enough to do here, that's my problem. The sooner Sin sells Hooper Studios, the better off I'll be.

Greg decided that it was the inactivity here that was slowly driving him to distraction. The last thing he needed was a quiet atmosphere conducive to raising memories he'd much rather leave buried. He longed for his offices at Poole Enterprises. He very rarely thought about the past there. True, he was never free from the events of that January—it was always a free-floating awareness that something in his life had once gone very, very wrong—but it was never as strong as it was today. But the truth remained the same. He could dredge out every memory and still run into the same wall, the same blank spots, the same unending frustration because he couldn't remember what had happened the night Natalia disappeared and his life had been changed forever. . . .

He had never been able to remember what had happened after they arrived at the apartment. He remembered with crystal-like clarity the heated carriage ride from the Maryinsky Theatre; the damp, almost evil feel to the freezing wind; and the utterly delectable feeling of having Natalia beside him, sharing the sable-lined lap robe, her dark eyes dancing with fun as she teased and flirted with him and accepted his compliments about her performance in *Les Saisons*. He remembered the *dvornik*, the yard porter in his *polushubok*, the short fur coat that kept him warm as he sat by the house doors, as he ushered them into the apartment building. In his urgency for the dinner to begin, he neglected to tip the man, and it wasn't until much later when it was too late did he recall that all *dvorniks* were also subordinate police officials.

Even over the space of fourteen years he could still see his friends' faces, conjure up the apartment's rich French mode of decor, and feel how warm it was inside when contrasted with the cold night. The distinctive smell of the gold-tipped cigarettes he smoked, the taste of the caviar, and that first glass of champagne would never leave his memory. It was only with the second glass that the room began to move out of focus and slowly began to spin like a merry-go-round until the blackness overwhelmed him. After that, the darkness lifted only once, and as he came around to find himself stretched out on a sofa that was long enough to accommodate his six-foot-one frame, he watched through a haze as Natalia's limp body was wrapped in an Oriental rug and carried out of the room toward a side door that he knew would lead to a passage to the Moika.

He tried to ask what was happening, but no words came out of his mouth. He tried to stand up, but the last thing he remembered was falling off the sofa, his head striking the sharp corner of a decorative table before he hit the floor. . . .

When he regained consciousness again it was the late morning hours of Monday, January 8th, and he was in his own bed. For one second he had the wild hope that it had all been a nightmare, but when he saw Dr. Butz putting his instruments away a despair almost as all-encompassing as the sickness that was threatening to overwhelm him seeped through his aching body.

"So you're finally awake," the fashionable surgeon said, coming over to check the white bandage around Alexander's head. "That's quite a nasty cut you have. I had to take a few stitches at your hairline, but they'll fade away in time, although the ladies seem to like that sort of thing."

But there was only one lady Alexander was interested in, but when he tried to recall the events of only a few hours before, all he had was a blank spot in his memory. It was if he were back in school where one sweep of the eraser removed all the chalk writing on the blackboard and he was the student too slow to take down the proper notes. But he had never been too slow before, and now he lay in his bed, sicker than he'd ever been in his life from too much champagne and too little food, the blank spots in his memory grew and grew until they resembled a yawning black chasm that he would never be able to close.

His father didn't come to see him until the next day, and one look at Prince Ivan's proud face told his son that there was no mercy from that quarter. The result of eleven-hundred years of aristocracy was stamped on both their faces, but in the past forty-eight hours one horrible incident had forever shattered the close bond between father and son.

"Other young men manage to spend a night with a ballet girl without bringing scandal down on their families," Ivan Vestovanova said directly, staring coldly down at his son. "What did you do to Natalia Voykovich? I would like to hear the story from you before I'm greeted with it at my clubs—and before the Czar himself requests an audience with me for further elucidation."

"I can't remember," Alexander said, fear filling his heart. "All I can remember is arriving at Peter's apartment. Sandor and Konstantin and Georgi were there already—"

"Don't lie to me! And don't drag your friends into your sordid little adventure. The *dvornik* on duty said you were there alone with Natalia. There were no signs in the apartment of any additional parties being present. What happened, Alexander? Did she refuse you, and you had too much to drink and took your anger out on her?"

"Is that how you taught me to behave with women?" Alexander shot back. "Do you think I was so uncontrollably drunk that I murdered Natalia? Why don't you speak to my friends, they'll tell you we were all there together. They'll answer your questions and put an end to this nightmare."

But the nightmare had only just begun, and as the week progressed, a week in which his closest friends and co-conspirators denied that they had been in the apartment with him and had information regarding the disappearance of Natalia, a week where police officers in their somber gray uniforms conducted an investigation at the apartment and then politely presented themselves at the Vestovanova Palace to ask more questions, and a week in which the gossip of what had—or might have—happened made the rounds.

The aristocratic world to which Alexander belonged unquestioningly was now of no protection to him. From the fashionable halls of the English Club, the New Club, and the Imperial Yacht Club, the havens of the high aristocracy and the diplomatic corps, to the New English Club where the English and American residents of St. Petersburg gathered, and even to the confines of the Literary and Artistic Society, the tale of what had happened to Prince Ivan Vestovanova's youngest son was bandied about and bets were taken as to what would happen and how long it would take for the Neva to give up Natalia's body.

Everyone seemed to have some opinion, and the only person cut off from all the controversy was Alexander himself, a virtual prisoner in his room by his father's orders. He stayed in bed, tired, feverish, and confused, waiting to be punished for a misdeed he couldn't remember, and wasn't even sure he'd committed. Something had to have happened, or else why would his closest friends have turned on him, but was it truly murder, and could he be brought to trial when there was no body?

His only visitors in those cold, confused days were his father, cold and unforgiving; his beautiful mother, Princess Dariya, trying to hide her distress at what had happened to her beloved younger son; his baby sister, ten-year-old Vava, who tried to distract him with tales of her life in the nursery; and then there was Boris, who brought him his meals and seemed to be searching him with his eyes as if he were looking for an answer to a question he wouldn't voice. Boris was his father's major domo, and every servant in the household was answerable to this bear of a man who stood at least six-foot-five, but to the Vestovanova children he was as frightening as the stuffed animals in the nursery, and they all adored him.

"You're going to have to leave Russia," Boris announced without preamble as he brought him his dinner eight days after that now infamous Sunday night. "Your father has decided to send you away, and if you're to avoid the fate he has planned for you, we must act immediately."

"Are you saying that my father is going to exile me out of the country?" Alexander asked as he sat down at the table, perfectly set for one with the finest linen, china and crystal, and looked without interest at the variety of dome-shaped silver covers. "Have they found—?"

"Natalia Voykovich's body?" Boris finished, lifting the first cover and serving the soup. "Eat this while it's hot. No, the Neva keeps her secrets well—if there is one to keep. And as to your exile . . . Prince Ivan is sending you to the estate in the Urals, where, after a suitably short time, you will meet with a fatal accident, probably at the hands of the Orenburg Cossacks, since they're good at such things."

At Boris's almost conversationally delivered words, the greatest fear Alexander had ever known coursed through him. His father was going to have him killed. He would be far away from St. Petersburg where such an "accident" would bring only further questioning, and by picking the most remote of the family estates he could avoid too many questions when the deed was done.

He put down his spoon, his soup untouched. "I'm finished then. I'm to be assassinated. Thank you, Boris, at least when my father comes to tell me that he's sending me away from St. Petersburg for a while, I'll know what's coming."

"Do you think I just told you this so you could submit yourself to being murdered?" Boris glowered at him. "Eat your dinner."

"As in 'the condemned eats a hearty meal?'"

"Only if you're willing to accept your fate. If Prince Ivan were to do nothing, you might be brought to trial, and you'd certainly be acquitted, but the damage to the family name will be done. Some young men disgrace their families by transvestism and homosexuality and murder where most definitely is a body," the servant went on, mentioning some of the goings-on that plagued St. Petersburg's best families and titillated its decadent population. "You on the other hand exhibited only the peccadillos associated with any well-raised young man of a superior family, but the incident last week has created a definite strain on the honor of the Vestovanovas."

"I can wait for Sergei to come back from the South of France," Alexander pointed out, referring to his older brother who had been married in December and was on his wedding trip. "He can always talk Papa around."

"You don't have the time to wait for Prince Sergei to return," Basil said. "Prince Ivan has made his plans for you, and they are to be carried out at the end of this week. The stitches come out tomorrow, and after that—"

There was no need for Boris to finish his sentence, but Alexander regarded the family retainer with a slight touch of suspicion. "How do you propose to get me out of St. Petersburg when I'm a prisoner in my own rooms?"

"In this palace, Master Alexander, there are many passages, and when you're in the city the necessary papers can always be obtained—false, but still good enough to fool the authorities—to get you out of the country." Boris paused for a crucial second. "But you must understand if you want me to help you that once you leave this palace, Alexander Gregori Dimitri Vestovanova will cease to exist. You will be who your papers say you are."

Suddenly none of this was quite real to Alexander. But then nothing else since last Sunday night had been real either. "You're talking as if you've arranged things like this before."

Boris looked directly at him, and it was like being stared at by a stranger. "I am dedicated, Master Alexander, to helping those in trouble with the Imperial government, those who have no hope, escape this country and start a new life somewhere else. What I do is a crime, punishable by prison or death, but it is also my duty. My network can save you. I want to save you."

"But why take this risk with me?" Alexander challenged. "I may be the one you can't count on, the one who'll get you caught."

"Every action I undertake is a risk. You're about to be punished for a crime you may not have committed, an action which you did not cruelly plan in advance. It's the only alternative there is for you, and in its way it will be as difficult as the fate your father has in store for you. I know this isn't easy, but I must have your answer now."

My father, whose love I never doubted, is going to have me murdered, Alexander thought, despair closing around him. My whole life is ruined, over, finished by something I can't even remember. . . .

Slowly, he stood up and looked squarely at Boris. "What do I have to do?"

"First, eat your dinner, all of it, you're going to need your strength. The papers are being made right now, and there's no need for you to know anything else until they are ready."

Exiting Russia in 1900 was no easy matter. First there was the matter of a permit of residence, proving that the person leaving St. Petersburg had a legal right to live there in the first place; then there was the difficulty of obtaining a passport, and the even harder-to-obtain exit application with a police stamp. In theory, Alexander knew about all those procedures, but those restrictions had nothing to do with any

79

Vestovanova. When they travelled out of Russia, either on their private train or on the Nord Express, they were not bothered by such annoyances as passport checks and questions from the police, and on Thursday evening, when Boris brought him the necessary papers, he could only stare at them in amazement.

"Will they really work?" he asked as Boris served his dinner.

"They haven't failed yet."

Alexander was still young enough to regard this as a grand adventure. He couldn't conceive that he would be leaving St. Petersburg forever, that he might never see his family again, and despite his recent travail, he was still pure Vestovanova. "Gregori Vestovich?" he inquired, reading the name on the papers. "A servant?"

"A valet," Boris corrected, and gave him the rest of his instructions. "You're going to have to earn your own way, and I decided that you had to have a name as close to your own as possible. Ultimately, our network will see to it that you're sent on to America, but right now you have to prove that you can function as something other than a cavalry officer."

There was a costume ball that night at the Countess Kleinmikhel's, meaning that his mother and father would be gone all night into the early morning hours of Friday. This was his best chance to escape, Boris explained. Prince Ivan and Princess Dariya wouldn't come to his room until Friday afternoon, and with any luck by then he would be well out of reach.

"What will you say when they discover I'm gone?" Alexander asked as he changed into the heavy, well-made and warm, but nondescript clothes Boris brought to him. "I don't want to bring any problems to you, Boris. One of the other servants might have seen you bringing me extra food and these clothes—"

"I've given the others plenty of tasks to occupy their time.

No one is in this wing. Hurry now, the sledge will be here soon, and you'll have just enough time to make the steamer. And don't forget to keep your hat on—that small scar is still pink enough to attract notice."

It had been decided that it was too dangerous for Alexander to attempt to leave St. Petersburg on the train; there were too many stops, too many inspections, too many chances of being noticed, and the Finland Station over the Alexandrowski Bridge was too far away from the Vestovanova Palace, so the journey would have to be made by steamer.

Alexander said his farewells to Boris, and went down the narrow, twisting, rarely used side stairwell alone, the magnitude of the step he was about to take slowly dawning on him. The night was icy, and as he left the palace by the side door that even he'd forgotten about, he remembered Boris's admonishment not to look back. His collar was turned up, his hat pulled low on his face, and the small suitcase in his gloved hand, although obviously having come from a first-class luggage-maker, was now too worn to be used by anyone but a servant. He reached the snow-covered courtyard just as an open sledge, its driver bundled in a greatcoat, fur hat, and many blankets, pulled inside, reining his horses in with an expertise that made Alexander wonder about who this man was and what he did when he wasn't part of Boris's "network."

"Passenger for the Kronstadt Pier?" He questioned sharply.

"Yes, that's me."

"Well, get in, boy, before we both freeze to death. Put your case in back and get in beside me. Warm enough? Good, let's get out of here."

A long time later he would be glad that on that night, as the driver whipped up the horses and the sledge moved away from the Vestovanova Palace, that he was concentrating all his energies on not telling the driver that no one ever called him *boy*. While he was busy holding on to his temper he was too occupied to realize that from the moment he stepped out into the courtyard, Alexander Gregori Dimitri Vestovanova had ceased to exist.

The trip over the Nikolaevski Bridge which spanned the great Neva and led to the Kronstadt Pier where the steamer to Finland berthed at the Nikolayeska Naberezhnaya, was made without incident. From St. Petersburg to Helsingfors and on via Hargo to Stockholm, Gregori repeated to himself as the sledge reached the pier. Without a wasted motion, he retrieved his suitcase and said a quick good-bye to the driver and headed for the gangplank.

The thorough inspection of his papers and luggage went off without a hitch, and as he finally boarded the steamer, Gregori realized that this was *real*. Even if his father should relent, there was no way of his knowing about it save through the workings of the "network." Boris must protect himself at all costs, and, Gregori realized belatedly, so did he. After a period of confusion and pain following that night, his survival instinct had surfaced. He had no doubt that his father meant to have him disposed of, and Boris had been right when he said he was too much of a Vestovanova to go meekly off to his fate. But as a servant? A flash of rebellion burned through him at the idea that in a very short time he might indeed be performing the same tasks that Misha, who had been his own valet, carried out.

But that's only if you make it through this trip, he reminded himself as the steamer approached its berth in the harbor of Helsingfors, which was being referred to more and more by its modern name of Helsinki. The police authorities and customs inspectors came promptly on board, and along with the other passengers, all as nondescriptly dressed as he was, Gregori got in line for the most dangerous part of the long and tedious journey.

Finland, once conquered and colonized by Eric IX in the 12th Century, had been gradually absorbed by Russia in a series of treaties from 1721 to 1809. Created a Grand-Duchy in 1899, it was now an indissoluble part of Imperial Russia with only a limited self-government, a Secretary of State for Finland located in St. Petersburg, and the 22nd Russian Army Corps headquartered in Helsinki. It occurred to Gregori that if he'd already been discovered missing and the authorities notified, he could be captured right here. He hid his fear, kept his answers polite and to the point, and the police inspector stamped his papers with an air born of truly bored officialdom, totally ignoring the simple gold Faberge cuff links that held his cuffs together, as well as the gold Faberge cigarette case secreted in the lining of his coat. Finding those objects could have made the official's career and brought the Okhrana down on Gregori's head, effectively ending his one chance to escape.

For the first time in his twenty-one years, Gregori had faced up to life-threatening danger, and he had won. But what would happen to him now?

The hotel he went to in Brussels, located on the fashionable Avenue Louise, was a new establishment with an Art Nouveau-inspired decor, and the one faint hope that Gregori had been cherishing that the station in life he'd held in St. Petersburg would gain him some special treatment vanished the moment he presented himself to the managing-director.

"I don't know how long we'll be able to keep you here," said Monsieur Boudrin. "People from your city, when they do come to Brussels, prefer the Metropole, but I assume your family has a wide circle of friends, and we'll be as careful as possible."

"I was told you'd have work for me as a valet," Gregori said stiffly, instantly recognizing that from now on no names were to be used. "I've never done this sort of work before. Possibly it would be better if you could just let me rest for a day or two and then I could leave."

"To go where and do what? Forgive my being blunt, Mr. Vestovich, but if you really had doubts about coming to Brussels, you would have gotten on the first liner to America while you were still in Stockholm."

"I'm so tired," Gregori said. "Everything's happened so quickly and I've lost so much control over my own life that I'm not even sure the last few weeks are real. I have papers that say I'm someone I'm not, yet to save my own life I have to become that person."

For one of the few times in his career as a hotelier, Monsieur Boudrin was at a loss for words. He had long ago learned to distance himself from the people he'd helped shelter at the various hotels he'd managed. If he cared too much about the fate of one, he'd care too much about all of them, and then he'd be no help at all. But this young man was different.

But not different enough to deserve special treatment.

"I'm going to take you down to the servants' dining room now," he said at last, forcing himself not to notice the tight look that passed over the younger man's face at the mention of the word *servants*. "You need hot food, and then you can sleep for the rest of the day. You have a lot to learn, and it will all be easier to absorb when you're fully rested and have had a few good meals to take the edge off your discomfort."

Over the next weeks, Gregori discovered that it was more difficult for him to get used to his surroundings than any of the actual work he was learning to do. The entire hotel could fit neatly inside the Vestovanova Palace, and he not only found the difference in size something to adjust to, but the matter of the decor as well. Raised in an atmosphere of signed French furniture, crystal chandeliers, and priceless paintings, the still-new mode of Art Nouveau with its less complicated look left him cold, and it took nearly the whole length of his stay in Brussels to get used to. If he had had to do either manual labor or menial work, his pride at that moment in time wouldn't have withstood the change in his way of life, but being a hotel valet didn't require all that much work. Many of the hotel's guests travelled with their own servants, and often his duties didn't extend beyond unpacking luggage or taking several suits down to the tailor shop in the basement to be steamed. Never before had he had to be concerned about picking up after himself or worrying about so much as a clean shirt, but now he not only had to look after himself but to tend to the clothes of strangers.

He was tough enough to know that he had to earn a living somehow, that although someday he might indeed be successful, he was never going back to the life of privilege, wealth, and pleasure he once lived. But harder than learning how to live with only a minimal amount of money was that to the hotel guests he was a faceless, almost nameless entity, someone to give one's crumpled clothes to, who lived at the mercy of each tip. The only guest who ever took special notice of him was Elliott Bernstein, an American art dealer who sold pictures to Prince Albert of Belgium.

The sitting room of the Bernstein suite was filled with paintings displayed on easels: portraits, still lifes, landscapes, and soft Impressionist oils and watercolors were set up for the clients' perusal, and Gregori, hungry for this sort of beauty, used every excuse possible to visit the suite. That and seeing the glimpse of family life offered by Elliott and Claire Bernstein and their daughter Diana, were the only bright spots through that long, awful winter where one day melted into the next with a gray sameness. Whenever the worst despair closed over him—usually in his small room on the top floor—he'd wonder if he was ever going to get out of this city. Would it have been better to let himself be sent off to the Urals? Could his fate there have been any worse than this endless feeling of belonging nowhere and to no one? The feeling that he'd been pulled out of his own skin hadn't abated. Was this what Boris had saved him for?

"Do you plan to spend the next twenty years learning how to melt into the woodwork and wallpaper?" Elliott asked him on the rainy April morning he and his family prepared to leave. "You obviously weren't born to be a valet."

"No, but it's what I have to do for now," Gregori replied when he'd recovered enough to speak. For the first time in three months he was being spoken to as an equal, with interest and concern, and he strove to keep the shock and surprise out of his voice. "I may be going to America later, but I have a debt to pay here, and I can't leave until it's taken care of," he concluded, adapting his circumstances so that it all sounded plausible. No one would ever believe what had happened to him.

"I understand," Elliott said, knowing very well that some debts had nothing whatsoever to do with money. He handed him a card. "If you come to America, come down to Philadelphia. I may be out of town, but anyone in the family firm will be glad to see you, and we'll try to find a place for you in the organization."

It was an offer Gregori fully intended to take advantage of. For the first time since January, he began to relax. His papers for the next part of his journey—real ones this time—were being readied, and for a while he began to hope that the worst of his experience was over, but less than a month later his world was once again ripped apart.

"Your family has found out that you're in Brussels," Monsieur Boudrin informed him, coming into his room with only a perfunctory knock.

Jerked out of one of the few decent night's sleep he'd known since January, Gregori sat up in his narrow bed, his heart thumping with renewed fear. "Do they know where to find me?"

"No, only that you're in some hotel or other. But after they check the Metropole and the Grand, they'll come here. You have to leave at once. The Red Star Line has a ship sailing from Antwerp this afternoon at four."

"I can be ready in fifteen minutes, but my papers—"

"Are on their way over here. There's nothing but third class available. We'd hoped to send you first, or at least second, but you're young and healthy—Ellis Island won't be a problem for you."

"Wait until I get through it," Gregori muttered, the dark Russian side of his personality coming to the surface before he realized how ungrateful he sounded. "Forgive me, this has been such a surprise that I feel that I'm back where I was in January."

"No, you're finally going to be free of that incident and those who want to punish you for it," the older man told him. "But remember one thing, the papers you'll be given when you leave here are genuine, but since your Russian ones are false, I suggest that if you ever decide you want American citizenship, don't make a move until you acquire an influential connection who can smooth your way."

Like most Russians, regardless of status or background, Gregori had little idea of what he would find in America, except that it was vast enough for a man to vanish in. His reading guides on the matter had been comprised of Baedeker's 1895 *Guide to the United States,* and the 1893 edition of Moses King's *Handbook of New York,* both volumes loaded with endless bits of information, but both of which he'd read with reluctance, not quite ready to admit that studying them would mean he had indeed cut the last ties with the Motherland, and that for better or worse his life now depended on him alone.

Nothing however could prepare him for third-class passage—for sleeping on a hard bunk in a narrow cabin with three other strangers, for almost no amenities, and for food—although hot and plentiful—he considered more suitable for a prison than an ocean liner. And Ellis Island was an equally brutal shock.

What am I doing here? was all he could think on the morning eight days after his hasty departure from Brussels to Antwerp, as he was transferred from the ship to the tender that took him to the vast immigration hall. There he had to suffer the indignity of being hung with an identity tag while he waited his turn to be questioned by immigration officials and examined by a doctor. Three other liners in addition to the one on which Gregori had crossed had arrived that morning, each stopping to discharge its extensive list of third-class and steerage passengers, and combined with those still waiting to be processed, it was a mass of humanity such as he'd never seen.

That long morning he sat on the hard bench, trying to rise above the babble of voices in a tangle of languages that would take an expert in linguistics to identify, trying not to listen to the sound of women crying, trying not to look at the faces filled with anticipation, hope, and fear. He didn't realize it, but even in his undistinguished clothes he still stood out in the crowd—Alexander Vestovanova had taken over from Gregori Vestovich, but the third person who would emerge from those two identities had yet to form.

The only bright spot in the whole processing procedure was Danny Burke, who had come in on the *Campania*. Gregori met the gregarious young Irishman on a line and they passed the rest of the day together, forming a sort of wary friendship. Gregori was still Alexander, a member of an ancient, noble family, too complicated to even think that he could be true friends with someone who, in Russia, would be considered only several steps above a serf; and Danny, with his instinctive native intelligence, instantly understood that any Russian immigrant who sounded like he'd been through Eton and Oxford, had left a life behind him that was best left undisturbed and unquestioned.

"What were you doing in Brussels?" Danny asked, his

curiosity getting the better of him as they waited for the doctor.

"Working as a valet at a new hotel," Gregori replied cautiously. Even if Danny had been his social equal, the betrayal he'd suffered at the hands of his friends, the betrayal that had contributed to his present condition, was still too fresh to risk sharing a confidence again.

"Is it a nice city, Brussels?"

"I wouldn't know, I hardly left the hotel. While they train you, they own you," Gregori explained in a blend of fact and fiction. "First it snowed all the time, and then it rained. The sun came out the day I left."

"Isn't that how it always is? But what about Russia? Did you work on one of those estates or in the city?"

"You don't want to know about Russia," he replied shortly as the line moved forward and they reached the next two available doctors.

He focused on something else during the brief examination. Eyes, teeth, throat, chest; they were checked in such a short time that Gregori began to wonder how they ever decided who was sick or well.

"Get some sun."

"What?" He came out of his self-induced trance with a start. "Did you say something to me?"

"Get some sun," the doctor repeated, trying to hide his astonishment at his patient's superb English. "You're too pale, and since you don't look like sweat-shop material, try and get a job out of doors. Now get out of here—and welcome to America."

"Would you like to come with me?" Danny asked as they boarded the ferry that would take them to New York City. "My uncle will be waiting for me on the ferry dock, and he may have a job for you."

"Out in the sun?" he asked wryly. "The doctor seems to think it'll be good for me."

"What a bunch of incompetents," Danny scoffed. "They can't get used to seeing healthy specimens like us, so they have to say something that makes it sound as if you're two steps from the consumption. You are pale," he went on, "but working for my uncle will take care of that."

John Burke, Danny's uncle, turned out to be a large and genial man who welcomed Gregori with the same warmth as he did his nephew. He was the prosperous owner of a construction company that specialized in the repair of the city's streets, and he was certainly not adverse to starting a young man off on the right foot. "We can always use two more strong backs," he said over dinner at the Burke brownstone in Manhattan's Clinton section in the West Forties. "I can only keep Greg on this project for a few weeks, though—the man he's replacing will be back soon—but it should be enough to give him a start. Now I'm sure my nephew, who has the silver tongue all we Burkes are blessed with, convinced you to come with us, but are we keeping you from some other business?"

"I have an offer to come to Philadelphia," he admitted, and told Johnny about his meeting with Elliott Bernstein. "I thought I might as well look Mr. Bernstein up—out of politeness if nothing else. I have enough money for the train fare, and it isn't a long trip."

"That it's not," Johnny agreed, carving more roast beef and urging a few more slices on his unplanned guest. "It'll give you a chance to see something of America, and when you've had an invitation from a gentleman like Mr. Bernstein, you take advantage of it. Besides, it's nicer to go down there with some extra gold in your pockets. They appreciate things like that in Philadelphia."

"What's the city like?" Gregori asked. He was still dizzy from his first hours in New York, and he was curious to find out if Philadelphia was anything like this vast, pulsing metropolis where good and bad seemed to be crammed together.

"It's very historic, but it's not New York," the older man explained. "In New York, a man can do anything, he can start with nothing and make himself a king, but in Philadelphia—"

Johnny's dismissive attitude toward the city that had been so important to America's early history stayed with Gregori over the next weeks. He didn't doubt that a man could make something special out of his life in New York, but it did seem a bit strange to start out by joining the crew paving upper Broadway near the new homes of Columbia University and Barnard College.

True, swinging a pickax and learning how to spread the mixture that made for a smooth roadbed was hardly suitable employment for a Vestovanova, but Gregori felt that this work was far less trouble than being a valet. Always active, always athletic, the months in Brussels where his only exercise was running up and down the back stairs as he went about his duties, and his only fresh air was what he could get a few minutes a day in the kitchen garden, had taken its toll, and his eight days on ship had reconfirmed how much he missed the freedom to move about as he pleased. Working for John Burke's road crew gave him what the hotel couldn't—a feeling of camaraderie, a sense of sharing, and a source for conversation. In Brussels he'd been a marked man; if those at the hotel didn't know his name and his crime they knew why he was there, and that created a barrier too high for anyone to reach over.

To be sure, he was aware that even in his rough work clothes he stood out from the other men, and knew that among his Irish-American co-workers his British-accented English was the cause of some raised eyebrows before it became the center of some good-natured joking. Most of the men assumed he was born on the wrong side of the blanket, but it didn't matter. The men he worked with and the large, close-knit Burke family both gave him back his sense of belonging and took away his sense of isolation, much the same way the sunny, warm New York weather burned away the ice of Brussels that he thought had permanently invaded his veins.

But when the project was finished he realized that while doing day labor had no shame attached to it, it was certainly not what he wanted to do. He knew that June was no time to attempt a trip to Philadelphia, since all the best families would either be at their country houses or travelling until September, and that meant he needed a job, and that meant valeting at a hotel.

With a supreme self-confidence he presented himself at the Waldorf Astoria on Fifth Avenue at Thirty-fourth Street, and clashed almost immediately with the manager of the most famous hotel in America. George Boldt, himself an immigrant from the German isle of Rugen in the Baltic Sea, was five-foot-six, with a mustache and spade beard that made him look Viennese, and a fittingly autocratic manner. The two men took an instant dislike to each other, and the interview such as it was ended with Mr. Boldt suggesting that since Gregori didn't have much experience he might want to seek employment as a waiter in a smaller hotel, one with less importance, where he could make his mistakes safely. Then he would see about putting him under the direction of Oscar Tschirky, the maitre d'hotel.

Gregori left the Waldorf in a tightly controlled rage, swearing that if he ever made his fortune in America, he'd never spend a penny of it in that hotel. It was a warm, early summer morning, and he walked his frustration off, going straight up Fifth Avenue, past the elegant shops, schools, churches, and the fabulous millionaires' mansions until he came to the Plaza Hotel.

Opened in 1890, the Plaza Hotel was an eight-story building whose 500-foot frontage faced not only on Fifth Avenue but Fifty-eighth and Fifty-ninth Streets as well.

Built of brick and brownstone in the Italian Renaissance style, this favorite of the city's elite caught Gregori's eye, and deciding he had nothing to lose, went in and presented himself to the manager.

He was perfectly willing to earn his way—at least for the time being—as a valet, but the idea of waiting on a table of people, to actually engage in the service of food, was the demeaning act he would not do. He would sooner lay railroad track. With only a slight adjustment in phrasing, he told that to the Plaza's manager, Ben Beinecke, who was as much of a perfectionist as his counterpart on Thirty-fourth Street, but who was possessed of far more understanding, an understanding that encompassed the fact that this fine luxury hotel, rich with marble, bronze, terra cotta, Gobelin tapestries, and Persian rugs, would soon be too small for the swiftly growing city and would have to be replaced by a larger structure. He would have liked to hire Gregori Vestovich, but there were no openings other than that of waiter, which, of course, wouldn't do at all. He might want to check out some of the better men's clubs; he'd be happy to give him a list. . . .

Much to his surprise, he was hired at his first stop on the list, the exclusive Metropolitan Club across Fifth Avenue on Sixtieth Street. The pay they offered was next to nothing, the position wouldn't last past September, but he would get a room and his meals and the tips were his to keep. It occurred to him that if he had come to New York as Alexander Vestovanova, he would have been a welcome guest here, but now he was unpacking luggage and steaming the wrinkles out of suits and once again standing back and blending into the walls. A lonely bitterness filled him, gradually growing until it absorbed the little comfort he'd had with the Burkes. He continued to perform his duties, but his actions were mechanical as his brain endlessly spun out comparisons of his life in St. Petersburg and his new existence in New York. It did no good to tell himself that the money he was accumulating would buy him the right clothes and pay for a room in Philadelphia's best hotel when he went there in September. He was so involved in those thoughts that on one warm summer night he never saw the wet spot on the back stairs until he slipped, his ankle snapping under him in a flash of pain as his body pitched down the stairs.

Less than an hour later he was in a cubicle in Roosevelt Hospital's emergency room, and if he thought being found in a helpless heap on the landing between the second and third floors, having to tell what had happened to him while he waited in pain for the ambulance to arrive was the sum total of the humiliation he would have to suffer, he discovered that belief was totally incorrect when one of the physicians on duty came in to see him.

"I'm Dr. Turner," she announced, pulling the curtains shut. "I understand from the ambulance doctor that you appear to have a broken ankle. I'll just do the preliminary examination, and then we'll wheel you over to our new x-ray machine and see how bad the break is."

Under ordinary circumstances, Gregory would have been delighted to have the opportunity to meet this young woman, only a few years older than himself, who stood beside the examination table looking so tall and cool; but now, wearing only an examining gown, he could only feel a wave of acute embarrassment wash over him.

"I'm sure you're quite competent, but I'd really be more comfortable with a male doctor," he said, wishing he had something to cover himself with—a reaction with a woman that was totally unfamiliar to him. "I've never had a female physician before."

"You'll find it isn't very different, Mr. Vestovich," Alix replied coolly, sticking her hands in the pockets of her spotless white doctor's coat as she read the information sheet the ambulance doctor had filled out. "This won't take long—"

He didn't give up easily, no Vestovanova in this situation would, but like so many situations of the past months, he was defeated in this battle also, and the end result of Alix Turner's careful, considerate examination turned up something more than his broken ankle.

Before he'd been loaded into the ambulance the Metropolitan Club had made it quite clear that they were not in the business of tending to the ills and injuries of temporary employees, and Gregori realized that he was in for a long stay at Roosevelt Hospital, and it seemed that the brief spurt of hope that he'd had a few weeks before was gone.

He hadn't cried since he was a child, but that first night in the semi-private room he'd been taken to once the ether wore off, suffering the twin discomforts of his broken ankle now encased in a plaster of Paris cast and the circumcision he'd had to undergo, he turned his face into the pillow and wept until he was exhausted. When he woke up again, he found his roommate regarding him with obvious sympathy.

Vic Sheehan was recovering from minor surgery, and when his employer, Sinclair Poole, arrived for his daily afternoon visit, he mentioned the younger man in the bed on the other side of the room.

". . . hasn't been in New York very long," Gregori heard Vic whisper. ". . . working at the Metropolitan Club, but they've tossed him out—what else can you expect from that bunch? Poor kid, to break his ankle and lose a slice of his manhood to the surgeon's scalpel. . . . Only time he smiled was about an hour ago when his lady doctor came to pay a call . . . cried himself to sleep last night . . . can't you do something for him, boss . . . ?"

To Gregori's amazement, the impeccably tailored visitor stood up and crossed the room to stand by his bed. "I'm Sinclair Poole, and I understand from my bartender that you're between jobs."

"That's a very interesting way to refer to a man who's not

95

employable at the moment. I'm Gregori Vestovich."

"If you say so," Sin replied. No one who spoke English like that really had a name like Vestovich, he thought with unerring accuracy. The familiar scent of *Jicky* filled his senses, and he looked down to see a lace-edged handkerchief with the monogram A.T. resting on the pillow. "Who gave you this?"

"Dr. Turner. She took care of me when I was brought into the emergency room. When she came to see me this morning she poured some of her perfume on a handkerchief. It's to help me forget some of the hospital smells."

Sinclair's fingers traced the embroidered initials. "What a thoughtful thing to do. And since this seems to be a day for good deeds, would you like to come to work for me?"

"Don't you want to know where I've worked before?"

"Any man who's been dismissed from the Metropolitan Club is good enough for me," Sinclair quipped.

Gregori began to laugh, his discomfort momentarily forgotten, and then he really looked at Sinclair Poole, and a shock of recognition ran through him. This isn't possible, he thought. After all those months of loneliness and confusion to find a bond again, it's simply not possible. . . .

Sinclair spoke first.

"We do look rather alike. Odd, isn't it?"

"These things happen." He strove to sound casual. "Do you have any Russian blood?"

"None that I know of, but my life is worthy of a Tolstoy novel."

"No one has a background free of incident."

"Some of us more than others. Several years ago my father was accused of selling shares in a company that never existed. He was set up by men he thought were his friends. They let him be put on trial and would have let him rot in prison if he hadn't died while the jury was still out. One way or another, I'm going to unmask the men who did this and clear my father's name."

That should have been the moment for him to tell Sinclair his own secret, Gregori realized, but this new employer was fighting an injustice that had been done to his father, not in hiding from a crime he may or may not have committed, and it was not the same thing at all.

"I want to be your valet, and I'll help you in any way I can when it comes to finding the men who ruined your father," he promised.

"Thank you, and I'm going to take you up on that, but first things first. As soon as you're able to leave the hospital, we'll get you a pair of crutches and take you down to Great Jones Street."

"I may not be much of a valet for awhile."

"Then I'll teach you how to read the financial newspapers and how to type. You weren't a valet in Russia, and if you have any brains, you'll want more out of life here. Remember, this is New York, and you can do anything and be anyone you say you are."

And now I'm running a movie studio, Gregory thought, looking at the neat piles of paper on his desk. Did I ever expect things would turn out so well when I was weighed down by my cast? If the wards hadn't been filled, I wouldn't have ended up in Vic's room, and my ability to trust and believe in another person might have withered that night. I had just enough hope left to let myself trust Sinclair. It was like having an older brother again, like having a family. . . .

"Lunch, Mr. West," Mrs. Rigby announced, her voice slicing neatly through his thoughts. She placed the laden tray in front of him and took a few steps back to survey the scene. "You're to eat every bite. You can't tell what train food will be like. You might not get another decent meal until Chicago."

Gregory, who had never had a bad meal on a train, held his peace, promised to do justice to his lunch, and sent Mrs. Rigby off to have her own lunch. The cook working downstairs in the kitchen was a cousin of Mr. Wong, Sin and Caro's devoted chef, and each item of food was a delight, quite a change from earlier in the year when lunch at Hooper Studios meant stale sandwiches and weak coffee. Today, the silver tray set with English ironstone china in the popular pink mist pattern held two well-filled and neatly trimmed ham sandwiches, a large salad featuring a scalloped tomato and a fluted pickle, a generous slice of chocolate cake, and a thermos bottle filled with coffee.

It sometimes amused Greg to realize that in less than ten years he'd be Gregory West for a longer time than he'd been Alexander Vestovanova. And as for Gregori Vestovich— Greg studied half of a ham sandwich with great interest. That disguise had served him well for the time he needed it, from January 1900 to April 1902, when he told the Pooles his complicated story. Sinclair, newly married to Caroline, and finally victorious in his long secret war to clear his father's name, had helped him come up with a new and impenetrable identity—one that would be far more comfortable to live with than the somewhat unwieldy—not to mention illegal—name of Vestovich.

"I may as well stay with Gregori, and just Americanize it to Gregory," he told Sin and Caro. My family never called me Alexander, it was always Sacha, and I'll be better off closing that part of my life permanently. But what does Vestovich break down to?"

With pencil and paper to help, the three of them worked it out, trying any number of variations before coming up with the most sensible approach by dropping the second syllable and trading the V for a W. "Gregory West," he said. And the name fit, belonged on him the way his Brooks Brothers clothes did, and he liked it.

Once in California, where Sinclair knew a Federal judge

he'd once done a favor for, they had seen to making his change of name legal and to arrange for his American citizenship. Then, only twelve years earlier, Los Angeles had been a small and somewhat sleepy city, and Gregory considered his life to have grown and expanded along with the city. He had come here still not quite believing his luck and was quite happy to divide his time between being Sinclair's valet and secretary, living with Sinclair and Caroline in the vast house in Montecito; now he was a full partner in Poole Enterprises, and lived in an apartment suite in the Alexandria Hotel where he had the reputation as one of Los Angeles's most eligible bachelors.

Except for the first few months after he left St. Petersburg, Gregory had never lacked for female companionship, and with a bit of careful planning and some help from his houseman, Moss, the banker's wife in San Francisco, the Rear Admiral's wife in San Diego, the horse breeder's wife in Santa Barbara, and the real estate developer's wife here in Los Angeles, women who all knew each other socially, never knew about each other's special spot in his life. They were all wonderful, delightful women, but—

But I've never forgotten Natalia, he thought. If I could only remember what happened that night, if I only knew what happened after I left Russia, but it's all a puzzle I can never figure out.

It wasn't that Gregory made it a special point to avoid attachment to women who were more available, but his only two encounters with women who were unentangled had both come to incomplete ends, leaving him with the certainty that it was a signal. Despite fourteen years in America, and a manufactured background that he sometimes thought was real, there was still enough Russian in him for him to be superstitious, to believe in signs and portents, and to tread carefully whenever these occurred.

And there was another reason.

In the end, he knew, it all came back to Natalia. Not to

what might have passed between them, that was long ago over and done with, but to the mystery-shrouded night when the life he expected to lead had come crashing down around him.

I'm a man with secrets, he thought, gathering up the papers he would take to Chicago with him. And a man with secrets is best off alone.

Chapter 4

Kit was dividing the few minutes she had left before it was time to join the Randalls and the Pooles at dinner between applying her makeup and making a list of places she wanted to visit while they were in Chicago.

Yesterday, Sunday, September 13th, promptly at two-forty-five in the afternoon, the Twentieth Century, replete with a red carpet running from the gate to the train, had left New York's Grand Central Station, and at nine-forty-five this morning had pulled into the LaSalle Street Station. Kit had ridden the Century many times, and had never known this excellent train to provide anything but the most comfortable of journeys. This time had been no exception, and instead of arriving tired, her adrenaline seemed to be working overtime. Mallory and Caroline's advice that she spend the afternoon resting had seemed ridiculous. Spending an afternoon doing nothing was fine if you were a married woman with a good-looking husband to help you pass the time, but that wasn't Kit and she had to make her own amusements. Staying in her room at the Blackstone Hotel only long enough to tell the maid what to unpack, Kit had taken a taxi to Marshall Field's where she'd had lunch, spent a few hours browsing, and returned to the hotel with a prize purchase—a sixty-five dollar hat comprised of pink velvet rose petals.

"Now that wasn't the smartest thing you've ever done, is it?" Kit asked her reflection in the dressing table mirror, and she wasn't referring to the hat she bought. She finished applying her mascara and reached for her jewelry case. "You were so tired when you came back from Field's that you had to take a nap and ended up missing cocktails. You're lucky that you're not going to have to order from room service."

The telephone on the table beside her bed rang, and Kit left the dressing table bench to answer, guessing quite correct that it was Caroline on the other end checking on her progress.

"How are you feeling?"

"Just fine now, Caro. All I needed was two aspirins and a little sleep. It seems that I heal fast."

"You and Sin's associate, Greg. He came in on the California Limited while you were out, and he had to take a nap also."

"Well, as long as he didn't stop at Field's to buy a pink velvet hat."

"I'll tell him you said that," Caro said, and began to laugh. "We're going down to dinner now."

"I'll be there in ten minutes," Kit promised, and they both hung up. Back at the dressing table, she unlocked the red leather case that held her jewelry and quickly selected a small diamond necklace to complement her Lucile dress. She checked her makeup, adding a little more lipstick, an extra touch of rouge, and a last pat of powder from the selection of Helena Rubinstein and Elizabeth Arden cosmetics on the table in front of her. Finally, a few extra dabs of *L'Heure Bleue* completed her preparations for the evening ahead.

"I hope this associate of Sin's is worth all this dressing up," she muttered, collecting her evening bag. True, she would have dressed the same even if they'd been five for dinner instead of six. The Blackstone, she reflected, closing the door to her elegantly furnished bedroom and crossing the antique-filled sitting room of the suite she was sharing with the Randalls, made one want to look one's best in order to live up to the hotel's superior service and fine decor.

Located on fashionable South Michigan Boulevard, the Blackstone Hotel, which overlooked Lake Michigan, was run by Mr. John Drake to the highest of standards. There was a *feel* to the hotel, everyone agreed, and atmosphere that made it the equal of Boston's Copley Plaza, San Francisco's St. Francis, Washington's Shoreham, and New York's grand triumvirate of the Plaza, the St. Regis, and the Ritz-Carlton. Travellers who had once stayed in Chicago only long enough to pass a morning at the Art Institute, or an afternoon at Marshall Field's before catching a train for the next leg of their journey because of the lack of a true luxury hotel, now stayed long enough to sample some of the city's other attractions.

It was the sort of hotel, Kit decided as she reached the end of the beautiful, wide hall and rang for the elevator, that made every woman feel special.

The mahogany panelled elevator took her noiselessly downstairs, and as she crossed the lobby, Kit reviewed the places she wanted to visit while they spent this week in Chicago. She had to go back to Field's, of course, there was so much to see there; then there was the closest competition, Carson Pirie Scott; and naturally she had to stop in at Blum's on Michigan Avenue, which always had such superb dresses and hats; and Chas. A. Stevens, where a red carpet runner from curb to door and a liveried doorman welcomed customers.

I want to see what the others do to make themselves special, she thought as she reached the doors leading to the restaurant. Like all other patrons, she paused for a moment at the white, damask-covered table that held an arrangement of spun sugar flowers. If you can't sell poorly designed clothes in a pretty setting, the reverse has to be true also. Of course there are women who will buy anything anywhere, but that's not what I plan to offer. Just about ten days to Los Angeles—

The Blackstone's dining room was one of the most beautiful public rooms in Chicago. The rich, perfect, white walls were a superb backdrop for the glittering crystal chandeliers, the small balcony where the musicians were playing soothing music, and the sea of tables, each set with heavy white damask and weighed down by fresh flower arrangements, heavy silver, fine china and glass. For a moment, Kit stood in the doorway, observing and admiring the scene spread out in front of her. How perfect, she thought, and then her gaze found the right table, and all her interest in the dining room's perfect symmetry took second place to another emotion she hadn't expected to be piqued so soon.

How could I ever think that Gregory West was some dreary businessman not worth dressing up for? she asked herself. In a restaurant where every man appeared to be good looking, he stood out, and at their table, where Sinclair and Rupert were undeniably handsome, there was something about this man that not only equalled but also eclipsed them. Even from this distance she could see a special something that went beyond his looks, past his power, and over his wealth.

Of course she was only assuming he had money, and she knew nothing about his character, intelligence, or standards, but from where she stood the learning experience would be interesting. She quietly refused the attentions of the maitre d' who appeared to show her to her table.

"That's perfectly all right, Maurice. I've found my friends," she said softly, deciding that she wanted to make this approach unescorted.

Greg was laughing at one of Sin's more colorful stories when some instinct made him look up, and his darker-than-amber gaze saw Kit making her graceful way toward their table. No one had to tell him who this woman was. Why hadn't Caro told him Katharine Allen looked like this?

He watched her with a quiet intensity he hadn't given another woman in years, and although he made sure the others weren't aware of his scrutiny—his background plus years of working for and learning from Sinclair had made him an expert in the art of looking without others being aware of it—and nothing short of the musicians' balcony collapsing could have diverted his attention. He watched her unhurried progress to their table, taking full advantage to admire how her dance dress of blue net over flesh pink chiffon enhanced the aura she was creating. As she came closer, he saw that the dress was embroidered in diamonds and turquoise, and the small circlet of square-cut diamonds clasped around the base of her throat seemed to throw sparks of blue-white light off her. Another woman, he decided, would put on the same dress and jewels and make up her face in the exact same manner and look cheap and common. But Katharine Allen looked radiant, self-confident, and only slightly exotic, and with a flash of certainty Greg knew that if a man at one of the other tables made a move or even a gesture toward her, he would gladly beat his rival to a pulp.

How atavistic of me, he thought. *How very Russian.* And he stood up.

He was on his feet only a second before Sin and Rupert, but it was enough time for Kit to decide her first impression hadn't been wrong. This was definitely a man she would want to get to know very much better. *He looks as if he's been through it all and that nothing can take him by surprise again. Or can it?*

Somewhere in the back of her mind she summoned up Caro's casually dropped remark that Gregory West wasn't married, but Kit doubted very much that looking the way he did he ever went without a generous amount of feminine attention.

If he has another woman—or women—he'd better get rid

105

of any or all of them, she thought with a swiftness that surprised her. I don't need another gilt-edge encounter, they tarnish very quickly, but even now I'd say this is one very special man, she decided as she reached the table.

"Katharine Allen, Gregory West," Sinclair said at the appropriate moment. In any case, he was not a man given to overlong, effusive introductions, and since he knew that they had both been observing each other, this was most definitely a case of the less said the better.

"I've been hearing a lot about you," Kit said, and held out a hand to him.

"Enchanté, Madame." Gregory had spoken French before he spoke either Russian or English, and now he spoke it in the best restaurants and then only to the staff, but as he and Kit came face-to-face, the words formed naturally on his lips.

"Please, you don't have to speak French to me," Kit replied, touched and amused at the same time. "I'm as American as you are."

To his own amazement, Greg almost said he wasn't quite the American she thought he was, but the sound of a silver tray laden with crystal crashing to the floor instantly cut off all conversations and put him on the other side of this unexpected urge.

"Mrs. Astor's dropped a bracelet," Greg said instead, and his witticism was rewarded by Kit's delighted smile.

"I almost said the same thing," Kit said. How nice his voice sounds, she thought, happily noting that unlike some men—far too many men—he didn't have the strained undertone in his voice that was fair warning to any woman that she was in the company of a complainer. "I hope nothing happens to the poor man who dropped the tray. I'd hate to think that he's going to lose his job over a silly accident."

"I'll have a word with the maitre d'," Greg assured her as she sat down in the chair he held out. He felt himself enveloped by a delicate cloud of *L'Heure Bleue,* and his fingertips brushed lightly over her shoulders. "I'll even speak to Mr. Drake about it—all of these hotels and clubs are insured against breakage."

"I know, but from the way they talk it's as though every broken glass brings them one step closer to bankruptcy." She smiled as Greg took his seat beside her. She had felt his light touch against her skin, a touch that made her momentarily hold her breath. But they were part of a group, and now it was time to postpone their getting better acquainted in favor of being a good guest. "I apologize for being a little late. Have you already ordered?"

"Oh, no," Mallory assured her. "We're all a little late tonight. But right now I think we should all have a glass of champagne while we order." Tonight her dance dress was also from Lucile's, a fragile creation of layers of pale green silk gauze with a silver lame waistband and sash faced in emerald green. Her soft brown hair was swept back into an elaborate French roll and secured with diamond- and emerald-studded hairpins, while a rope of pearls and emeralds rested around her slender throat. "The dance music starts in an hour, and we should be between courses by then."

"It's amazing how hungry one can get from a train trip," Caro said as she leaned back in her chair, her elaborate Henri Bendel gown of pink faille embroidered in silver thread and a scalloped hem trimmed in kolinsky fur drawing its own share of attention. She briefly touched the pink topaz and diamond necklace resting on the flawless skin of her throat. "When we get back to Los Angeles, we're going to have a welcome home dinner and Mr. Wong will make all his Chinese specialties."

While the others discussed their favorite dishes, Kit and Greg stole brief looks at each other over the large ornate menus that their waiter handed around. Neither were particularly innocent in the fine art of dinner party flirtation,

107

but they were both aware that some deep chord had been struck between them and that they were at a crucial point where they could either ignore that first touch of electricity between them or play along with it and see what would happen.

I've been so careful for so long, Greg thought, scanning the extensive menu but not really seeing anything. I never really expected this moment to come, to be like this. Can I take the chance and live out what might be so dangerous?

I wonder if he knows how his eyes change when he's thinking hard about something? Kit speculated as she pretended to be involved in making her menu selections. But if he's being pensive about our meeting, it may not be good. There's nothing worse than a woman chasing after a man who isn't interested. I've never had to do that and I won't start now, but how I'd love to touch the line of his jaw, trace those cheekbones, and see if his thick eyelashes are as soft as they look.

To save time and trouble they all decided to order the same thing, and it took a few minutes of lively discussion to order a complete meal. When their patient, indulgent waiter departed for the kitchen, Greg turned to Kit.

"I haven't been doing much of anything lately at Hooper Studios, but Sin told me that you've come up with a remedy for that."

"Oh, don't blame me if your business partner decided that it was time to put an end to your executive idyll," Kit told him delightedly. "All I did was make a simple suggestion."

"Do you know what it takes to make a quality movie?"

"No, but then neither do most people, including some who earn their living behind the camera."

"Not unless you're David Wark Griffith," Greg admitted as their waiter placed cups of clear consommé in front of them.

"Speaking of D.W.G., what's the latest on him and that epic of his?" Sinclair questioned. He knew and didn't at all like the esteemed director of so many of Biograph Studios best movies, who had recently taken Billy Bitzer, the innovative cameraman, and left to make his own films. "Is he still filming his apologia to the Confederate cause?"

"The word I'm getting is that not only is he periodically running out of money, but there's no script and no shooting schedule and it's all as secret as possible."

"Are you hinting that Griffith is carrying the whole story around in his head?" Mallory asked, and Greg nodded. "It sounds just like him."

"In New York, the word is that his budget is somewhere around eighty-five thousand," Rupert said as the consommé was replaced with a vol-au-vent of fish. "If you do decide to go ahead and make a ten or twelve-reel movie, there'll be no problem with financing, no picking over expenses," he continued, well able to make that promise in his position as the head of the California operations of the Seligman financial firm.

Greg shrugged. "That's very nice to know, but don't look at me. I'm not the one who owns Hooper. Is this what you want to do, Sin?"

"I think this takes more than a simple yes or no," Sinclair said, not quite ready to make a final decision in the matter. "The matter is still open for discussion."

"Of course it is," Greg said as the musicians changed tunes and the opening notes of "Alexander's Ragtime Band" filled the room. "But right now, if no one minds—and even if they do—there's something much better to do with our time."

"And I think what Greg is trying to say," Kit put in as they smiled at each other, "is that we're going to dance."

"Do you remember Sousa's 'Jewel of the Ocean Waltz'?" Caro asked, looking at her husband through her lashes.

"That was what the orchestra at the Linden Trees Golf Club was playing the first time we danced together," Sinclair said, recalling the icy December night, the fact he was a very uninvited guest, and Caro, dressed as a Manchu princess, standing on the terrace. "Did you think that I would ever forget that night?"

"When you want to discuss business in depth at a dinner party, I have to wonder," she chided gently while Rupert and Mallory hid their smiles.

"Is this because you think there may be the elusive scent of romance in the air?" he questioned, and smiled.

"One never knows, but what I really want to do is dance."

"Why didn't you say so in the first place?"

"Do you think this is what we'll have to look forward to when we've been married twelve years?" Mallory inquired of Rupert, managing to keep a straight face.

"Only if we're not very lucky," he responded with a significant look. He stood up and held out a hand to Mallory. "I love a good discussion, but if there's one thing I hate more than false sentiment it's philosophy. As far as I'm concerned, this discussion is closed and it is definitely time to dance!"

"Would you think I was pushing things too fast if I told you that I'm glad the dancing started when it did? I love our friends, but I thought I'd never get the chance to be alone with you."

"I was thinking the very same thing," Kit said as they executed a superb fox-trot around the dance floor. "And as for pushing things . . . sometimes events make their own pace."

"And are we that event?"

"If we weren't, I don't think we'd be dancing right now."

"I was only teasing," he assured her as his arm tightened just a bit more around her. "And no more flip remarks. You were quite a surprise."

"So were you." They were dancing close enough for Kit to identify that he wore Guerlain's expensive men's scent,

110

Mouchoir de Monsieur. It suited him, she decided. "And I also think that you're a man who likes to know exactly what he's doing at all times."

"That's entirely possible, but I don't want you to think that I'm one of those men who has to analyze every situation until it's drained dry," Greg said as he skillfully spun them around.

"Do you promise on your honor that you're not a staid businessman?"

"Do I look like one?" he challenged, and smiled.

"No, you look like a runaway prince from Ruritania."

For a brief moment, the catchy Irving Berlin tune became an indistinct blur. Katharine Allen didn't know, couldn't know, he thought, and yet, in her sincere effort to pay him a compliment, had touched close enough to the truth to stun him.

"That was a compliment."

"Ruritania doesn't exist."

"And *The Prisoner of Zenda* was never my favorite book, but still—" Kit smiled and waited for him to respond.

"Thank you."

"Some men wouldn't like being compared to a hero in a romance."

"There's nothing wrong with a good novel that has a happy ending—and I learned a long time ago to accept all compliments offered."

"For a moment, I wasn't too sure."

"I was thinking about something else—a silly tangent."

"You're forgiven—and you dance divinely."

"Well in that case—" A silent signal of agreement passed between them, and they accordingly increased the pace of their steps until they were almost spinning around the dance floor. At that moment nothing mattered except each other, and the world and its manifold and unending complications could be temporarily forgotten.

*   *   *

When they all returned to the table again, the entree of roast guinea hen glazed with Madeira, stuffed with Malaga grapes and served with mushrooms that had been stuffed with pâté de foie gras was waiting for them, and all pretension at serious conversation was dispensed with while waiters hovered, served, and poured. Between courses, they went back to the dance floor, to tango, and to two-step, and to change partners. There was a hearts of celery salad, and finally there was dessert.

"Did we really order this?" Sin asked as the waiter placed the silver server in front of him. Resting on it was a wickedly rich nun's cake molded with eclair sides, filled with ice cream bonbons and decorated with whipped cream. "Do we think we're children?"

"Is there something wrong, sir?" the waiter inquired politely. "Shall I bring something simpler?"

"Of course not. Serve our dessert, please," Sin instructed amid the laughter of his wife and friends.

"This is the perfect way to finish off our meal," Caro observed as they savored every scrumptious bite of ice cream and cake.

"In any case, we can dance this dinner off," Mallory said. "A few more turns around the floor ought to take care of everything."

"That's one way to survive this dinner," Greg agreed. "But I have another one in mind. Shall we take a walk?" he asked Kit.

"A nice late evening stroll along some of Chicago's better streets?"

"That was the general idea."

"It's certainly a nice evening for it," Kit agreed, and as she took the heavy linen napkin from her lap and put it beside her plate, she admitted to herself that she'd be ready and willing to go for a walk with Gregory West if there was six inches of snow on the ground.

*   *   *

"Do you remember the first movie you saw?" Kit asked as they came through the Blackstone's revolving door and into the warm Chicago night a few minutes later. Unwilling to be separated from Greg for even a few minutes, she had sent a maid upstairs to her room for a wrap, and as soon as her Cheruit evening coat of beige-pink Chinese silk cut like a duster and rich with silk embroidery, was brought down to her they said good-night to their friends and left the restaurant. "Did you have some great flash of recognition that this was a new enterprise?"

"Hardly." Greg tucked her right arm through his left one. "I couldn't believe I was actually paying good money to see such nonsense. I thought it was all a fly-by-night operation," he confessed, and they laughed.

"Was this in New York at the Eden Musee, or was it Koster and Bial's Music Hall?" she asked, referring to the first places in New York to exhibit motion pictures beginning in the late 1890s.

"Neither. When I first came to New York in 1900, I didn't know there were such things as galloping tintypes."

"Hmm," Kit said not very convinced. "What you're trying to say is that you were too busy paying stage door visits with a bouquet of flowers in one hand and a trinket from Tiffany's in the other!"

"Back then I was hardly aware the Broadway theater existed!"

"Somehow you don't strike me as the innocent sort."

"What about my being the nose-to-the-grindstone type?"

"If you were, we wouldn't be taking this lovely walk now," Kit returned in a silky voice. "You would have been so thrilled to discuss business that you wouldn't have done more than register my presence in your peripheral vision."

Greg gave her a sidelong glance. "If I did that, being drawn and quartered would be too good for me. But when I was twenty-one, working for Sinclair was the most important thing. But I've always kept my horizons open."

"I can't tell you how glad I am to hear that."

They walked along the long, elegant expanse of Michigan Avenue, past a variety of expensive shops, all shuttered for the night, and sedate restaurants. They passed other well-dressed people, and even at this late hour there was a good amount of traffic in the form of taximeter cabs, limousines, and private automobiles. For a few minutes they strolled together in a quiet, very compatible silence, and both felt a sense of trust from the other—the foundation that they would need to make their instant attraction to each other more than a superficial thing.

"Do you know where we're headed?" Kit asked at last. She was quite prepared to go anywhere with Greg, but she wasn't going to tell him that—not yet.

"I haven't the faintest idea," Greg admitted cheerfully. "Shall we go to the Art Institute tomorrow?"

"Yes, but in the meantime, why don't you tell me more about the first movie you saw? We got rather off the track of that topic."

"Funnily enough, I saw my first movie in Los Angeles, not too far from where you're going to have your store. It was in a place called Talley's on Spring Street. About a year after we went out to California, Sin decided it would be a good idea to set up a small office in Los Angeles—a place to conduct business whenever he and Caro came up from Montecito—and he took a suite in the Bradbury Building on South Broadway. I was taking a nice lunchtime walk and found not only Talley's but the biggest crowd I'd seen since leaving New York."

"And with a New Yorker's curiosity you had to see what was going on."

"That's just about it. Inside there was a row of kinetoscopes where people paid five cents a round to watch Jim Corbett and his opponent fight a championship bout."

Kit stopped walking. "You faker! I ought to hit you with my evening bag. You didn't see a movie, you saw a version of a peep show!"

114

"Watch how you say things like that, this is one of Chicago's better neighborhoods," Greg advised, his own laughter barely under control. "Besides, if it's on film and it moves, it can be considered a movie. And since fair is fair, what was the first movie you saw?"

"Georges Méliès *Cinderella*. It was the basis for a young people's party at the French Embassy in Washington. We were shown the motion picture and then we were served ice cream and cake. Someone had the bright idea that this was a much more refined entertainment than providing dancing for a group of fifteen, sixteen, and seventeen year olds," Kit informed him. Obviously someone forgot that when you show a movie you have to put the lights out!"

Greg laughed. "Your first visit to the movies certainly wins out over mine. Suddenly I feel as if I did see a peep show. Shall we walk back to the Blackstone?"

"It's a nice night, and I'm not tired."

"Neither am I," Greg said as they turned around and began to retrace their steps. "But I'd like very much to kiss you and not attract too much attention."

Kit regarded him through her lashes, her heart beating in a new pattern. "Oh," she said, not quite ready to give too much away, "why didn't you say so in the first place?"

Kit and Greg walked down the wide hallway to the string of suites their party was occupying. Here on the sixth floor, as in the rest of the Blackstone, things were settling down for the night. Downstairs, the luxurious lobby was almost deserted, the restaurant was dark, and just about the only person to notice them as they came through the revolving door was the night clerk who regarded their passage from the entrance to the elevators as the only spot of glamour he'd have in the hours ahead.

"Do you mind our being an object of interest?" Greg inquired as they reached her door. "The elevator operator's

115

smile was almost paternal."

Kit leaned back against the wall. "I think we gave up that particular privilege the minute we first saw each other."

"We've had quite a night," Greg said, slowly unfastening the ornamental closure that held her evening coat together and then spreading both sides apart so he could admire her lavish dress again. "And I want to kiss you."

"I thought you might have changed your mind on the walk back," Kit answered, placing her hands on his shoulders. It seemed almost impossible to believe that this tall, supple, man who, several hours earlier had been only a name to her, was now on the verge of being so much more. "The past couple of hours have been a surprise for both of us."

"It's not only that," Greg said, and knew with a sort of utter finality that this was the woman he could not tell the story he, Sin, and Caro had so carefully constructed a dozen years ago in order to protect him. "I want you to know that when I first went to work for Sinclair, it was as his valet."

Kit absorbed his words and deliberately lowered her lashes. "Does that have some sort of effect on kissing that I don't know about? Still, it's nice to know that you're a handy man with a hot iron. When my shop opens, I may have to press you into service—"

Her inadvertent pun was awful, but it broke the tension between them, and Kit swayed forward into Greg's arms, their first close contact instantly stilling their laughter. The enchantment that had spun itself around them intensified, and for a moment they just looked at each other, not quite believing that this was real.

"I don't care if you dug ditches," Kit said breathlessly, her legs turning to jelly.

"Actually I helped pave a section of upper Broadway," he said, and kissed her.

This was what she'd been waiting for, Kit thought as his lips touched hers. The man who would make all the others not count, the man who was her present and her future as

116

much as she was his. And then she didn't think at all because it was all pleasure and there was nothing to disturb them. Greg's arms tightened skillfully, and in response she wrapped her arms around his shoulders. It was as though their bodies were melting together, and that where they were was of no importance.

Nonetheless, the reality was that they were standing in a hotel hallway, subject to discovery at any moment, and slowly that fact seeped into Kit's new world—a world in which only two people and a rainbow of their own making existed. She wanted to stay forever like this with Greg, sharing kisses that encompassed a range from tenderness to passion, to hold him close, to share secrets with him, but every dream has an end.

"Someone is going to come by," she whispered, and reluctantly they released each other. Right now, Kit knew, she could unlock the door and lead Greg across the sitting room she shared with Rupert and Mallory to her bedroom. But was this what she wanted at this particular moment—to make love with a man she'd met only a few hours before, no matter how strong the currents between them, no matter how great the promise that they were meant for each other? If this were real for them, it would wait.

"I hate to say good-night," she told him, putting her fingers to his lips to wipe away the traces of her lipstick. "You know I'm not the coy type, but there are things we can't rush."

"And you're very truthful," Greg said, slowly reaching out to push a loose pin back into her hair. "You don't think I'm only looking for an interlude?"

"No, but things happen." She met his darker-than-amber gaze. "We really don't know anything about each other, and we both need time to sort things out. And I must sound like an old-maid schoolteacher," she added.

"Never that." Greg smiled. "It's just that I never thought of Chicago as a place for lovers—and I mean that in the broadest sense of the word. We do have to get to know each other, and you might not like everything I have to tell you," he went on, his smile fading.

Kit took the key out of her evening purse. "You have to realize that if I'm willing to take a chance on going to Los Angeles, I can listen to anything you have to tell me," she said, noting with some apprehension the look that had come into his eyes. What could he have to tell her that was so awful? "Now, why don't you kiss me again so we can say good-night, and then tomorrow we can see if we like each other as much in the cold light of day."

In her bedroom the night maid had opened the bed, laid out her nightgown, and turned on the bedside lamps—all of which made a very comforting sight for Kit when she finally said her last good-night to Greg. She knew that Greg was right down the hall from her, and with all the connecting doors, they could have spent the night together without fear of discovery. But as she locked the door behind her, Kit found herself oddly grateful for her privacy, and she sincerely hoped that Greg wouldn't decide that this was the perfect time to play out a hotel version of the British country house weekend nighttime visit.

He's too much of a gentleman to do that, Kit thought as she kicked off her satin evening shoes and unfastened her diamond necklace, leaving it a glittering strand among her perfume bottles. But by now he must think I'm not all that bright. Why did I say we'd have to see how we like each other by daylight? That's right up there with all those other bright sayings like sweet dreams. I'm too old to be that dumb.

Kit undressed carefully, laying her elaborate dress across one chair and her lacy Lucile lingerie on the other before slipping her pale pink crepe de chine nightgown over her head. In the marble-rich bathroom she used cold cream and oatmeal soap to remove her carefully applied maquillage, and then came back to the dressing table to take the pins out of her shoulder-length hair; each gesture a familiar pattern that kept her from thinking about the man she just might have fallen in love with.

She curled up on the bed, and as a stalling tactic began to look through the books stacked on her bedside table. Did she want to read *Toya, The Unlike,* or the new British bestseller, *Pantomime,* or was tonight the time to reread her favorite mystery, *The Trevor Case?* No, she thought, the only thing she wanted to do was think about Gregory West.

It's happened, the way I always believed it would, but I also have to be careful, she told herself. Suppose it *is* just a momentary attraction, some odd spark struck between us because we're both in a strange city. If we'd met in Los Angeles or New York, this might not have happened.

But it wouldn't have been any different if they'd met in the Plaza Hotel, or the Alexandria Hotel, or on an ocean liner, or in Central Park. The location didn't matter, it was something far more mysterious and wonderful, she thought. It's us, and the rest of it doesn't matter.

Kit stretched out against the cool sheets and switched off the lamp. It would have been so easy for them to spend the night here together, she decided, rubbing her cheek into the pillow. We could be here together right now, but instead we're both alone in our rooms—proving what? That we're willing to wait, to observe proprieties and not offend our friends who wouldn't mind if we did go to bed, and probably think we did anyway.

Kit's mouth curved in a wry smile. She very much doubted that once they reached their bedrooms neither Mallory and Rupert nor Caroline and Sinclair were thinking about her and Greg.

I could go to him, Kit thought, and knew she wouldn't. The first move in that area had to come from Greg. Instinctively she suspected that he had a woman—or women—back in Los Angeles, and she really didn't want to embark on a passionate relationship with him until he was free from those entanglements. And if by some chance he didn't want to free himself entirely, it would be far better to let everything come to an end right here in Chicago.

With a deep sigh, Kit rolled over on her stomach and tucked a pillow under her chin. It was useless to deny that it would have been exciting to have made love with Greg tonight, to have taken her chances, but her sense of caution was too strong, as was her belief in doing things the right way.

All dreams of impetuous romance aside, Kit knew that she couldn't begin an intimate relationship with a man who was still basically a cipher to her. True, they had found each other on a very special level, but the most basic questions were still unanswered.

I can't sleep with a man I know so little about, she thought. I don't know where he went to school or what his middle name is or how he takes his coffee. I have no idea about any of his likes or dislikes or how he'll wear in the long run. If there's one thing I don't need it's another man with a set of eccentricities that a saint wouldn't be able to live with. Tomorrow we'll start all over again, and one of the things I'll have to find out is whether or not he really likes ice cream. . . .

Greg put *The Lone Wolf* back on the night table, no longer feeling the sense of identification with the title of Louis Joseph Vance's newest whodunit. Tonight his whole safe little existence had been turned so completely upside down that the Okhrana might as well have walked into the restaurant tonight instead of the woman he didn't even know he'd been waiting all his life to meet.

For far too long Greg had buried his strong romantic streak under the guise of staying solo for the sake of his secret. Sinclair and Caroline and their children had filled his need for a family, and the women he attracted with no difficulty more than fulfilled his intimate needs.

As much as he had left St. Petersburg behind, as far as he had come from his environment, he was still enough of a product of his social world not to worry much over the fact that all of the women he was currently involved with were married. He was not a lady-killer, seducing a woman away from her husband. They happened because extra-marital flings always happened between well-to-do men and women, and whatever qualms he felt about being found out centered on the effect it would have on his standing in the business community. He'd already ascertained what the effect of such gossip would be on his social standing—it would only increase his popularity as Los Angeles's most eligible bachelor.

Sally is the only one who might be difficult, Greg thought as he considered Admiral Courtland's wife. A younger woman married to an older man, an officer on active sea duty, might want to hold tight to her amusements. She might even want to make trouble—just for the fun of it.

He folded his arms behind his head and smiled. That Kit should never feel that his loyalty to her was divided became very important to him. Not that there would be any conflict where she was concerned. For a moment he considered the idea of going to her room now, not to force the situation, but simply to see what could develop naturally between a man and a woman, but when he thought further about the ramifications of such an action he decided the wisest course was to wait.

He wondered if the Blackstone's florist carried Mystery of India tulips. Kit deserved the most exotic and beautiful flowers he could find to send her. He wanted to give her exquisite jewelry and expensive bibelots for the sheer joy of seeing her face while she unwrapped the package. His rich generosity, stifled far too long by women whose marital status made gift giving a cautious experience, was suddenly

121

blossoming. What Kit would ultimately mean to him, if she were indeed the great love of his life, still had to be resolved, but now, in the dark privacy of his room, with his papers and files piled on the writing table, his clothes folded over various chairs, and the small icon he never travelled without resting on the night table, he knew he was happier than he'd been in years. Happy in a very special way.

Greg had long since lapsed from the orthodoxy he'd been raised in, but he would never travel without the small icon he'd left Russia with, and which he always kept beside his bed. He flinched recalling the difficulty the placement of the religious object had caused him a few years ago, but then dismissed the memory as having nothing to do with him and Kit.

He couldn't remember the last time he'd wanted to devote himself to a woman the way he did with Kit. He wanted to spend time with her, talk to her, share all the things he thought he'd never be able to share with a woman. He could talk business with her and not worry that she either wouldn't understand him or else would repeat what she'd learned to a business rival; they could talk about anything together.

When Greg opened his eyes again it was two hours later and the glittering events of that night seemed very far away. His heart-lifting euphoria was gone, replaced by a certainty he couldn't evade. He had reacted this way to a woman only once before, and she had had this effect on his emotions. It wasn't exactly the same of course, every situation was different, but it was close enough for his heart to begin to thump in a very uncomfortable way. He had felt this way about Natalia.

"Of course I like ice cream," Greg said with some surprise as they sat at their table in the proper dining room of the

Congress Hotel, waiting for their second serving of the hotel's justly famous pale chocolate ice cream. "Was there something in the way I ate my dessert last night that made you think I was one of those suspect people who are happy with a small scoop of vanilla?"

"Well, there was always the possibility that you might have eaten our dessert last night just to be polite," Kit teased, relieved at his response.

"Or possibly because I was so smitten with you, I wouldn't have noticed if dinner had been sawdust and library paste."

"I'm glad you said that first," she said, just as their waiter arrived.

Greg waited while the waiter placed long-stemmed silver dishes filled with ice cream in front of them, left a silver tray holding an assortment of petit fours between them, and refilled their coffee cups. He had started this morning full of resolutions about how to act toward Kit. *Best off alone.* He repeated the old warning again, just for further reinforcement. Katharine Allen was nothing like he'd expected and everything he'd almost forgotten he wanted, but when it came to letting down his defenses with her—well, that was just about as safe as taking a stroll across a battlefield in France. Whatever had happened that night in St. Petersburg still had the power to affect him. Suppose his worst fears were true and he had hurt Natalia; what would prevent him from doing the same to Kit? The wisest course would be for him to try and act as if their attraction of the night before hadn't happened—and he forgot his intentions the moment he saw her coming toward him in the Blackstone's lobby. Her Doeuillet suit of strawberry-pink taffeta fitted her precisely, the hemline was at least an inch shorter than anything Chicago was used to, and when combined with her Georgette hat of black lacquered straw wreathed in black tulle, it was all Greg could do from proposing right there and then taking her to Spauldings or Peacock's and buy her a diamond ring the size of a postage stamp.

Or possibly that was the whole idea behind that outfit.

"Your ice cream is melting," Kit offered informatively, her voice full of laughter.

Greg picked up his spoon. "Do you know that everyone in the restaurant is looking at you? All the men are wondering what I ever did to get so lucky, and the women are wondering where you got that suit and hat." Not that they could look like you, he added silently.

"If people weren't looking at my clothes, I'm going to Los Angeles for the wrong reason." Kit put a spoonful of ice cream in her mouth, savoring the sweetness while she considered how to handle things with Greg. Unlike some women she didn't have the instincts of a district attorney when it came to questioning men. Another woman, she thought, would have had her man relating the exact details of his life by now, but she was too much the respecter of personal privacy to ask the "right" questions. Greg would either tell her all about himself or he wouldn't, and she wasn't about to force the subject. "Do you think I'll like Los Angeles?"

"No one likes Los Angeles," Greg replied, and Kit felt her heart sink. "We complain about it, revel in it because of the weather, make new lives there, and occasionally even grow to love it. But *like*—"

His careless shrug was so European that she forgot her attack of second thoughts. He's not American—at least not born here, she thought with sudden clarity. Last night I thought he might be Sin's illegitimate half-brother, but now I see that their resemblance is just the luck of the draw. But what in his past can be so awful that he's willing to perpetrate such a myth?

"Do you wish you'd chanced New York?" Greg asked unexpectedly.

"It wouldn't have worked." With difficulty, Kit pushed aside her silent questions. "At best I would have been a curiosity, a society girl with a shop," she said, and told him

124

about *Harper's Bazaar*. "I couldn't go through that again."

"And the worst?"

"You're a businessman, Greg. You know the worst. I would have failed. I still might do that in Los Angeles," she allowed, "but at least I'd have a better chance of success. New York is too difficult a place to start, and real estate is the least of it."

In the tangled, complicated world of men and women, Kit knew she might be making a fatal mistake. Her ideal response to Greg, she knew, should have been "if I hadn't decided to come to Los Angeles, I wouldn't have met you," but her innate honesty forbade her from making such a coy, self-evident statement. And if Gregory West thought she was opening a shop to play games or inflate her vanity, she'd better find out now and save herself a lot of problems.

"Do you know Edwin Goodman, who owns Bergdorf Goodman in New York?" she asked.

"I know of him. Mainly through Caro and Mallory . . . and from a few other ladies who always shop there whenever they're in New York," he added, feeling more embarrassed than he thought he could at his string of too-easy conquests.

"Well, very shortly we'll all be shopping at 616 Fifth Avenue instead of 32 West 32nd Street," Kit informed him. "The building is almost finished, but if I had to go through the machinations that he has, I'd be finished. Six-sixteen was originally the site of an old brownstone—a real eyesore— and was owned by Columbia University but leased to the Butterfield family. First Mr. Goodman had to buy the lease, then the building, then have it torn down before he could have construction begin on a six-story building for his new store."

"That's very complicated, but not really that unusual when it concerns a prime location."

"I know that, but I wouldn't want to have to go all through that and still have to rent part of the building for an assured cash income the way Mr. Goodman is going to have to do.

His financing is so complicated. What kind of treatment would *I* get at a bank?"

"You have a definite point. Did you go to Mr. Goodman for advice?"

"He seemed to be the right person to consult with. Except for the three years I worked for Tappe, which meant all the clothes I wore came from his workrooms, my mother and I have been customers at Bergdorf Goodman's for years. When I left Tappe's, I went to Europe for the summer and came back with a trunkful of pretty accessories. I persuaded Mr. Goodman to take a dozen evening bags on consignment. He did it as a favor, and they sold out in four days. When I went to Paris a few months ago, he was good enough to give me a letter of introduction to his commissionaire, Rosambert Freres."

As they ate dessert, Kit explained how the term "Paris original" is actually a misnomer since the garment a customer or buyer purchases is a copy of the original garment one sees at the couture house. Unlike some men, Greg didn't view fashion as some frivolous nonsense he was condemned to pay the bills for, and, fortunately, he was not among the minority of men who would be interested in her conversation because he wished he were wearing the clothes. To him, art—and by extension, fashion—was the counterpoint to the dull, dry world of business, and he listened, fascinated, as she told him how she had visited each salon as many as three times.

"The first time was to see the collection, the return visit to see any model that I wasn't sure of, and the third time to actually place the order."

"And what happens after that?"

"That's where the commissionaire comes in. Every garment that I or any other buyer orders comes with a *reference*. That's a complete list of every item needed to make the dress or suit or whatever—even hats come with *references;* once in a while they'll be really generous and

126

attach a fabric swatch. In any case, it's the commissionaire's job to purchase from the best shops the materials, buttons, and trims in the amounts the buyer specifies so a perfect reproduction of the garment can be made."

"I'm stunned by all of the work that goes into something that looks so easy," Greg said, and Kit was pleased at the admiration she saw on his face. "But how do you know how much material to order?"

"I don't. No buyer does. That's when fashion starts to resemble the roulette table at Monte Carlo." Kit laughed merrily, drawing even more appreciative looks from nearby tables. "I have to calculate how many 'repeats' a garment is going to have. It'll all be a lot simpler the more popular the *confections* become."

"What are they?"

"The first French high-quality, ready-to-wear dresses."

"They sound enchanting."

"And look the same way. Unfortunately Frenchwomen aren't geared to walking into a store and buying a dress straight off the hanger with only a few alterations."

"And American women are?"

"We have very varied lives, and our clothes have to meet different needs," she said, suddenly perplexed as to why he would need clarification on such a thing. Unless he weren't originally an American, and his old teaching, no matter how submerged, would still work on a certain level.

They finished their dessert in silence. Kit didn't mind the quiet moments between them, and this discussion had gone as far as it could go before turning so businesslike that the real meaning behind their spending the day together would be lost.

"Have you given some thought to where you'd like to spend the rest of the afternoon?" Greg asked. They had spent the morning wandering through the Art Institute, but had by no means seen all of its vast collection. "Do you want to go back to the museum?"

"Not really. Today it felt as huge as the Hermitage."

A dull roar sounded in his ears. "How do you know about the Hermitage?" he asked as casually as possible. This couldn't be happening.

"I've been there. It's the most vast place you've ever seen."

"We have to discuss it some time." He motioned to the waiter that he was ready for the bill. "I should have known that even when it comes to travelling, you wouldn't go anywhere ordinary," he said, deciding to take it easy and let his shock fade gradually away.

"Well, as long as you don't expect me to bat my eyelashes at you and murmur something about our not meeting unless I made the decision I did," Kit returned, sensing something more from the man seated across the table from her. It was as subtle as the movement of an excellent elevator car up and down the shaft, but something had changed—was changing—and she was at a loss to identify it. "There's a very exclusive women's shop called Caroline's over on Erie Place, and I want to see how they show off their new imports. If you don't want to come, I'll more than understand."

"Don't even think that." The faintly distracted look in his eyes faded. "When we get to Los Angeles, you'll have to take a full tour of Hooper Studios, so it's only fair that right now I go with you to the area where you're the expert."

"All intellectual discussions aside," Sinclair said when the waiter had removed the plates holding only the remains of the cheese souffle and they were waiting for the wild duck glazed with black currant jelly, served on a bed of wild rice, "can I expect Hooper Studios to have the skill it takes to produce a twelve-reel movie?"

"We'll need an outside director, a good one, and some fresh actors, but with Archie MacNeil for the cameraman the answer is yes," Greg replied. He had thought this out days ago, but now the topic of conversation hardly interested him, and he'd be much happier out on the dance floor with Kit in his arms, the accordion pleated tunic of her ice-blue charmeuse dance dress swinging out as he whirled her around. "I hate to see Archie limiting his talents to *The Pie Man,* but assuming we make this movie, what will you do with it when it's completed, and what effect do you think it will have?"

"A buyer, possibly."

"Drake Sloane is interested in it, as is. That's for the property alone. Drake knows less about movie studios than we do."

"Drake Sloane is a Los Angeles real estate developer," Mallory explained for Kit's benefit. She also knew all about Nancy Sloane and Greg, but that wasn't for her to tell. She leaned back in her chair, showing off her Bergdorf Goodman gown of ivory lace over old blue taffeta to its best advantage. "If he's interested in a certain area, it means that area is going to develop and expand—whether or not it wants to. Of course that's no reason to sell to him."

"I think I liked Hollywood Boulevard and Selma Avenue better when it was a lemon grove." Caro looked chicly amused in Jeanne Hallee's dance dress of silver gray net embroidered with crystals and rhinestones over blue chiffon. "But if Drake's interested, he can't be the only one. Are you holding back on us, Greg?"

"I never could fool you, Caro," he said, and gave her a winning smile. "We're close enough to the Famous Players Studios for Jesse Lasky to be interested, and Carl Laemmle is looking to expand IMF—he's calling it Universal Studios now."

"He makes movies—all westerns and comedies—on a scale that's almost wholesale, and sells them to the overseas market where they're starved for American movies," Rupert observed. "Now that's either the sign of a man out for a fast

129

buck or in for the long haul and looking to expand."

"That would depend on how much money he's offering," Sin said, and turned to Greg. "How much?"

"Double what you paid Mrs. Martindale, and that's negotiable, upwards."

The six friends smiled at each other while waiters hovered, serving the entree and pouring the wine.

"If you sell now you make your money back with a definite profit," Caro said, taking the opportunity to have the first word. "But I think right now the question has just become what are you losing?"

"A white elephant," her husband replied. "Less than twenty years ago, a four-minute film was a great accomplishment, and the results twenty years from now will be equally thrilling, but right now is a shifting, unfocused period where anything can happen. I'm not interested in finding myself standing on quicksand."

"But you won't sell for simply a profit on the real estate and the buildings on it," Caro insisted. "It stands contrary to everything you believe in. It makes you nothing more than a *speculator.*"

"You pronounce speculator the way you do Republican." Sin smiled slowly, trying not to display too much humor at once. "And either label isn't much of a compliment."

"So we're back to Kit's suggestion," Mallory said persuasively.

"I go to some very interesting dinner parties," Kit said to Greg. "But when I made my suggestion I never imagined I'd end up complicating your business life." Or that I might be in your personal life, she thought.

"I can't remember the last time complications made me so happy," he said, his heart speaking, ignoring the warning signals sent out by his mind.

"And what are you planning to do about it?"

"Something different, something very different," he

130

promised as if they were alone at the table, and Kit wasn't sure if he was referring to making a movie or making love to her.

Something different, as so often turns out, is easy enough to say but rather difficult when it comes to translating the concept into reality.

After the hot apricot souffle with hot apricot sauce, followed by several turns around the dance floor, they all returned to the Pooles' suite for café filtre and Remy Martin—and a discussion of what story would make the best movie.

There were the classics, of course. A few years earlier, there had been a version of Wilkie Collins's *The Moonstone,* and Vitagraph had made a film of Tennyson's *Becket.* Both of those movies had been severely truncated as had other one- and two-reelers made in the past five years of dramas drawn from Dickens and Walter Scott and, most unbelievable of all, Shakespeare.

"Making a silent movie from one of Shakespeare's plays is like doing a book about the great paintings of the world and not reproducing a single picture," Sinclair said cuttingly, effectively putting an end to the discussion about their favorite play, *A Midsummer Night's Dream.*

"Besides, if you did that, George Kelly would probably kill you," Greg added, referring to Sin's erstwhile bodyguard, now a private detective, who was a tireless walking reference guide to the Bard of Avon.

"There are more popular books," Rupert said.

"The Amateur Gentleman," Kit, Mallory, and Caro said almost at once. Published in 1913, Jeffrey Farnol's novel told the story of a man of modest birth who inherits a fortune and becomes a leader in Regency society.

It was an excellent idea, and they all had other recent

131

books they loved, but the idea of buying the rights to film a story by a living novelist was still too new to try.

"What about a contest for writers," Greg suggested, surprised to hear his own voice. His first instinct would have been to either negotiate with Carl Laemmle or accept Drake Sloane's offer. But now, instead of looking to end his involvement at Hooper Studios, he was actively seeking ways to extend it. "Everyone wants to write, and you can never tell what will come in."

"And if everyone wants to be published," Kit put in, recalling her days reading short stories at *Harper's Bazaar,* "imagine what the reaction would be for the opportunity to have a story made into a motion picture."

"How do you plan to attract writers, one of whom will hopefully write a good enough story that can be translated into a motion picture?" Mallory asked. "What's the first step?"

"Since I was the one who made the original suggestion, I'd like to make one more," Kit said. "Why not take an ad in a few newspapers?"

"The best newspapers," Caro added.

"About a dozen of them around the country should do the job," Mallory put in.

"What about financial remuneration? No one writes for their health," Rupert pointed out.

"Wait, let's get this all down on paper." Sinclair never liked a meeting unless everyone contributed, this was working out splendidly. He went over to an elaborately inlaid writing table, withdrew several sheets of hotel stationery, and then sat down on the sofa again. He uncapped his gold fountain pen. "How does this sound: a Los Angeles film studio is interested in acquiring. . . ."

A half-hour later, after much discussion, they had their ad:

A LOS ANGELES FILM STUDIO IS INTERESTED

IN ACQUIRING A FICTIONAL STORY SUIT-
ABLE FOR FILMING.... STORY MUST NOT
HAVE APPEARED IN ANY PUBLISHED FORM.
... AUTHOR SELECTED WILL RECEIVE $250.
... SEND ALL SUBMISSIONS BEFORE OCTO-
BER 1 IN CARE OF STORY DEPARTMENT,
HOOPER STUDIOS, HOLLYWOOD BOULE-
VARD AND SELMA AVENUE, LOS ANGELES,
CALIFORNIA.

"This sounds just about right," Sinclair remarked. "Now
for the newspapers. Do you all think twelve will do it?"

They finally selected fourteen papers around the country
as suitable for the ad. The *New York Times*, the *New York
World*, the *Hartford Times*, the *Boston Herald*, the *Philadelphia Bulletin*, and the *Washington Post* would cover the
East; the *Atlanta Constitution*, the *Chattanooga Times*, and
Louisville's *Courier-Journal* would reach the South; while
the *Chicago Tribune* and the *Cleveland Plain Dealer* would
do for the Midwest. The *San Antonio Light* and the *Dallas
Morning News* would reach the Far West, and, finally, the
San Francisco Examiner, would take care of the rest of the
country.

"Aren't you forgetting Los Angeles's newspapers?" Greg
asked as they toasted the completion of this part of their plan
with snifters of Remy Martin.

"No, I'm just exercising some caution. The response to
this ad is going to be tremendous," Sinclair replied. "Once
this ad attracts writers' attention, you're not going to be able
to find your office for the mail, and the last thing you're
going to want is to come in one morning and find an author
sitting outside Hooper's gates with his masterpiece under his
arm!"

Chapter 5

With an exclamation of total annoyance at her inability to concentrate on her work, Kit threw her fountain pen down on the table in front of her and leaned back against the soft, dark blue, plush upholstery in her drawing room and watched the New Mexico landscape as the California Limited continued on its way to Los Angeles. Train travel, as she well knew, was not quite the equal of travelling by ocean liner. It was not quite as clean or as quiet, and there certainly wasn't the same amount of space, but like being on board ship there was the sense of being someplace special, as well as having more than enough time to think.

Looking back on it, their departure from Chicago's Dearborn Street Station at five past eight on Friday evening had looked like a private party in motion, but this train was a worthy place to carry out a house party. The California Limited was the pride and joy of the Atchison, Topeka, and Santa Fe Railway, and in the nearly 2300 miles the crack train covered between Chicago and Los Angeles, its passengers would be provided with all the best that American train travel could provide. It was a known fact that where trans-Continental travel was concerned, a hog or a cow could cross the United States without having to change trains, but humans couldn't. To make up for this difficulty the California Limited—which boasted electric lights throughout, all private compartments, drawing-room Pullman cars, a dining car, a club car, and an observation car—was a worthy continuation for those who'd started their trip on the Twentieth Century, and would make the rest of their journey feeling superbly taken care of.

Sinclair and Caroline had frequently made this journey in a private railroad car either borrowed from friends or rented from the line for the three-day, two-night trip, but this time the Pooles, who liked to spread out, had taken over nearly an entire sleeping car. Their three children, eleven-year-old Laura, nine-year-old Garrison, and seven-year-old Amanda, as well as Rupert and Mallory's little girl, and the attendant nannies, all had compartments, as did all the accompanying servants, while the adults occupied the four drawing rooms, and one compartment was set aside to hold meetings in.

Kit wondered how anyone could concentrate on a business meeting when the changes in scenery over the distances covered were so fascinating. She watched with great interest as small towns with names like Isleta, Sandia, and Rio Puerco, where this train didn't stop, flashed by. On Friday night they'd been in Chicago, by the time she'd gone into the dining car on Saturday morning, Kansas City was fading rapidly into the distance, and by the time they'd all said good-night to each other, the train was through Colorado and on its way to New Mexico. And today, Monday, September 21st, with Arizona's border only a short distance away, they were getting closer and closer to California.

But am I getting closer to Greg? she thought. So far the only thing apparent about being involved with him was that it was very much like playing the children's game of taking one step forward and two steps back. Every time they were together, even in the most crowded spot, a special magic was around them, but instead of wanting to let himself enjoy their attraction, it was almost as if Greg were deciding whether or not he wanted to pull away from it—and from her. At times she felt as if an invisible wall had come up between them—a wall through which they could see each other clearly and talk without obstruction, but which still served to keep them apart in some vital way.

Her work unattended, her books unread, her needlepoint ignored, Kit stretched her long legs out under the table and propped them up on the facing sofa, Gregory West consuming her thoughts.

She was well aware that there were any number of reasons why Greg suddenly seemed so indecisive. He might like being a bachelor (Los Angeles's most eligible bachelor if everything Caro had intimated was true) too much to settle down (oh, couldn't she come up with a better expression than *that?*) with one woman, or he might be seriously involved with another woman and didn't know how to—or if he even wanted to—end it, or he could be one of those fatally flawed men who were incapable of being attracted to a woman unless she already belonged to another man, or he might resent the fact that it was her idea that would keep Hooper Studios going until that twelve-reel movie was made. Or, he might have something in his past that he didn't want her to know about.

Stop romanticizing this situation, Kit warned herself. He has some awful secret and he doesn't want to drag you into it—what a lot of bunk. This may be the one man who is turning out not to be all that interested in you. He may just be trying to find the best way to ease gracefully out of your life—

"Would you mind some company?"

Kit's silent deductions ended abruptly as she turned away from the window and found Greg standing just outside the open doorway. She had deliberately left the door open in the hope he would pass by, but his actually having done it took a bit of adjusting.

"Of course," she said, quickly hiding her surprise under a

137

layer of graciousness. But she made no move to assume a more decorous position, and she looked at him through her lashes as his glance travelled appreciatively over her handmade calfskin shoes, her neatly crossed ankles, and several inches of legs in flesh-colored silk stockings before the hem of her white crepe dress embroidered with deep Chinese-blue figures took over. Is this what they mean about being grateful for small compliments? she asked herself. "Aren't you busy being buried under reports?"

"I managed to claw my way out from under," he said, and with an almost seamless grace sat down beside her. He was close enough so that Kit could feel her heartbeat quicken at this near-contact with him, but not so close as to suggest to anyone passing that he was expecting to establish any intimacies.

It would be so easy for him to put an arm around me, she thought, lowering her legs from the sofa and crossing them in a swish of silk and crepe. But he's not going to, he's just going to sit there and look at me with those beautiful eyes until I can't stand it another minute. I'll either have to kiss him or cry, and that won't solve anything.

"Can you stand a question that has something to do with business?"

The merry, flirtatious look in his eyes faded somewhat, and Kit felt a sharp pang of regret. Had she just put her foot in it? In any case, there was no backing out now.

"Are you . . . upset because I'm the one who first came up with the idea to make a movie?" she said, choosing her words carefully but still determined to get at least one mystery solved. "I know something is wrong—"

"Whatever gave you that idea?" Greg asked, truly startled by her question. "When Sin told me what you'd said at that dinner party, I thought he and I had to be the world's greatest idiots. There we were with the studio on our hands and couldn't come up with a workable idea. I have nothing but admiration for you."

"I thought you might resent me for meddling in your business."

"Movie-making is hardly *my* business. I was thrown into this headfirst," he said, and told her his side of that January night in Montecito. "Sin's favorite party trick is to throw open a discussion and see what happens. *That* tactic either turns people dumb or makes them come up with fantastic ideas."

"Well, that's one question answered," Kit murmured, and wished she hadn't opened her mouth.

"Excuse me," Greg said with exquisite politeness, "but did you make a list?"

"A mental one. Oh, don't look at me like that! I've been engaged twice, and I'm also old enough to know when a man is having second thoughts. Last Monday, we had something very special happen to us, but over the last few days, particularly since we got on the train, you seem to be very uncertain about me, and I knew there could only be a few reasons behind your actions."

Greg looked at her nonplussed, and cursed himself for being a fool. Had he really thought that Kit wouldn't notice the conflict he felt whenever he was near her. He was only being cautious, but he also realized that if he had indeed followed his heart, they'd be engaged by now—engaged and lovers. But he didn't need the intellect of a scholar, or the romantic soul of a poet to know that Kit was a woman who had long since passed the point where she thought that a man who had mysteries he couldn't reveal was exciting. If he didn't meet her halfway, he knew, he might lose her altogether.

"It's not you," he assured her at last, his honest fear that she might reject him winning out over the caution that played such a great role in his private life. "This has to do with me. I never expected to meet you, even though I've been waiting for you for a very long time. Please be patient."

"I don't think I have a choice," Kit replied, certain that

139

now, for the time being, this was the closest he was going to get to a declaration of love.

Before either could say another word or make a move toward each other, the train's whistle sounded, and Louis, one of their porters, appeared in the doorway. "It's just noon, Mr. West and Miss Allen. Will you both be going into the dining car?"

"No, we'll be having lunch right here," Greg responded instantly in a manner Kit found very pleasing. "A nice, quiet meal for two. Can you fix us up, Louis?" he asked the smiling, middle-aged, black man he knew from so many other trips.

They ordered honeydew melon, grilled sole with French beans, and strawberry Melba for dessert. "And a pitcher of ice-cold daiquiris," Kit added, and Greg began to chuckle.

"Are you planning on getting me drunk?" he asked when they were alone again.

"Really, Mr. West, just what kind of girl do you think I am?" She batted her eyelashes at him in an outrageous parody of theatrical flirtation. "Now stop sitting there like the lazy businessman we both know you are and help me clear this table!"

Laughing together they moved her belongings to the other sofa. "Goldberg and O'Connor," he said, looking at her invoices. "Are you going to sell shoes?"

"Not on an extensive basis. I wasn't going to at all, but then I realized that a woman may come in to buy a special dress and may not be wearing the right shoes, or have them in her closet at home, so I went over to the Republic Building and placed an order for a basic opera pump in white satin, black satin, gold and silver, and black patent leather."

"It sounds like a good idea—and I have another one. If by some chance we get a filmable story, would you like to provide the clothes for the principal women performers? Would you like that?"

"Like—?" They were both standing, and without stopping

140

to think, she slung her arms around his neck. "I'd *love* to do it. Or did you just think this up to get a hug and a kiss?" she asked, her eyes turning green with laughter.

"Both," he said, and pulled her closer.

One arm closed around her shoulders and the other around her waist, and then they both forgot that this was—despite the fact that their party had nearly all of the Pullman—not a private car, and that the door was open and they were visible to all passers-by. The same feeling that had enveloped them the first time they kissed in the hallway of the Blackstone, and they held each other close.

I love you, Kit thought, but she couldn't say the words out loud. Doing that now might cause more problems than pleasures, and that declaration, if it were ever made, had to come from Greg. Right now she had to be content to rest against him, to feel that his heart was beating as hard as hers, and know that he kissed better than any other man she'd ever known.

"I seem to have a propensity for kissing you in semi-public places," Greg whispered an endless time later. "Do you mind?"

"Not if the only alternative is your not kissing me at all," Kit said, nuzzling against his shoulder. "I don't want you to ever feel that I'm prying information out of you," she went on, pulling back so that she could look at him. "I can't make you tell me things you don't want to, but if we're truly going to mean something special to each other, we can't build on entirely closed doors. We've found each other, and it's just too easy to let it all slip away."

In the drawing room next door, Mallory and Caro were enjoying their lunch with even more delight since Louis, on delivering their trays, had informed them that Greg and Kit were also lunching together in the privacy of her drawing room.

141

"For a few days there, I thought he was getting cold feet," Mallory said as she put the linen napkin over the lap of her summer frock of lavender and white gingham-check handkerchief linen. "Kit wouldn't say too much either way, but if Greg were going to decide he made some sort of mistake, I don't think she'd let him off without a good explanation."

Caro sampled her chicken salad. "And possibly with a good whack on the head as well. Greg has had it much too easy since he came to Los Angeles."

"So do most men. Seriously though, do you think any of the women Greg's been amusing himself with will make trouble for Kit?"

Caro gave the matter some thought as she leaned back against the plush-covered sofa, looking very cool in her summer dress of green and white striped muslin. "Barbara Lucas won't, she's terribly nice, and I don't imagine Nancy Sloane will make waves. Fortunately with Sally Courtland in San Diego and Peggy Crockett in San Francisco, there won't be too many problems—they are the silliest little snobs, though."

"I can imagine Peggy saying something about Greg taking up with a shopgirl."

"She really shouldn't talk. When her great-grandmother came to San Francisco, she was a girl at quite a different sort of shop."

For a few minutes they chatted about other things before Mallory decided to voice the doubts that had floated around in her mind since the first time she'd met Gregory West. "Caro, all of this business about Greg having come to New York from that little college in Western Pennsylvania isn't true, is it?" she asked cautiously. "In fact, I don't think any of that story has much basis."

Caro's smile was knowing. "It's all a lot of chop suey. But I can't tell you the truth."

"You don't have to. All I wanted to know was that my

instincts were right. But eventually Greg is going to have to tell Kit. I have an idea she's already guessed something is out of kilter—being in love makes you very finely attuned to each other."

"Yes, but it's not going to be easy."

"For either of them." Mallory raised her glass, the daiquiri inside swaying slightly from the motion of the train. "Shall we drink to them? I have a feeling they're both going to need all the luck they can get."

"'All hail, the richest beauties on the earth,'" Sin said as he raised his champagne glass to Caro, Kit, and Mallory in an expansive toast as they all sat in the dining car several hours later. "There are three very lucky gentlemen at this table tonight to have such perfect dinner companions."

Caro touched her glass to her husband's. "How can I help but stay in love with a man who's willing to quote *Love's Labour's Lost* in public?"

"We have a long night ahead of us," Mallory explained to Kit. "When we go over the state line into California, we have a champagne party."

"I'm not known as being against either champagne or parties," Kit said happily as attentive waiters replaced their fruit cups with plates of grilled trout that had been brought on the train in Colorado. "And I have absolutely no complaints about the company."

"Particularly with the right person sitting next to you," Greg added in a low voice only she could catch.

"And then, after we finish a bottle of Moet, when we're finally in the Pacific Time Zone, we all move our watches back one hour," Rupert said, adding a last bit of information.

"So this is what goes on during the last lap of the train trip to sunny California! I've heard that everyone who matters gets off the train in Pasadena because it's too dreary in Los

Angeles," Kit said with great interest.

"That's a lot of pretentious claptrap," Caro said. "We *always* get off the train at Union Station in Los Angeles. Of course, that may make us as affected as the people who won't."

The fish was followed by a roast saddle of lamb with red currant jelly, parsley potatoes, and baby peas and carrots, then by salad and cheese, and finally by apple tart and coffee; the excellent food tasting even better thanks to their free-ranging conversation.

This is the best dining car I've ever been in, and with a roomful of very nice-looking people, we're the best table, Kit thought. Or does everything and everyone look better because I'm in love?

They were the last people out of the dining car and were on their way back to the Pullman when they passed the conductor.

"We'll be pulling into Williams soon, Mr. Poole, if you and any of your party want to get off for a few minutes."

"Shall we see what the train station in Williams, Arizona, is like?" Kit asked Greg.

"It's very dull," he assured her as they let the others go ahead of them. "But if you really want to—"

"I could use a little fresh air, and I like the idea of knowing that the next time I get off the train we'll be in Los Angeles."

For a minute, Greg considered dissuading Kit from her idea. For the ten minutes or so it would take for the crew and engine changes, they would be able to get away from the travelling village atmosphere of the train. But so much could happen in that short time. All his so-called mastery of the situation, the promise that he'd made to himself not to let Kit all the way into his life so easily, might disappear very quickly. Suppose his secret revolted her, and she thought of him as a murderer? He couldn't lie about his past to her and he couldn't tell her the truth, but as for right now—

"I'd like some fresh air also," he said at last, "but you'd better get a wrap first. This may be Arizona, but it's colder at night than you might expect."

It was quite a bit cooler than the unsuspecting train passenger would have expected Arizona to be, and several of the men and women who'd stepped down to the platform hastily went back on board the California Limited at the first taste of cold, but Kit, wrapped in a Poiret evening coat of mauve silk velvet embroidered in silver thread and lined in gray squirrel, and Greg, in a Burberry raincoat over his dinner clothes, were more than comfortable as they walked up and down the wooden platform.

"It seems as if you've collected a few friends here in Williams," Kit said after a few of the cowboys who liked to watch the trains come in greeted him by name.

"I always get off the train during the stop, and I've gotten to know a few of the regulars."

"I like that," she said, "and I'd like it even better to know that I'm the first woman you've ever walked up and down this platform with. Caro and Mallory don't count," she added quickly, catching the look on his face.

"You really want to ask something else, don't you?"

"I don't really want to be one of your crowd, particularly if the rest of them are married!"

They stopped in front of the baggage car, and Greg pulled Kit around to face him. "How much more do you know about me? Has Caro been dropping hints?"

His voice was more amazed than threatening, and Kit faced him without trepidation. "No one has to tell me a thing. If you lived in New York, you'd be busy working your way through the chorus girls of the Ziegfeld Follies, but since there isn't anything like that in Los Angeles, you prefer the London solution—safely married ladies," she told him, and waited for his reaction, perfectly aware that she just might have ruined everything.

He didn't want to feel pleased at her powers of deduction, he didn't want to smile at the proof positive that she cared enough about him to raise a topic another woman wouldn't, and he certainly didn't want to laugh at his so-called sophisticated involvements that took more and gave less than he'd ever dare to admit, but all three emotional reactions took hold of him before he could push them back.

"What's so funny?" Kit demanded, her own amusement beginning to bubble.

"I am," Greg gasped. "You, though, are wonderful, and I love you!"

Those were not the words he should have said, and it certainly wasn't the proper place to make such a declaration, but none of it mattered, and suddenly he felt as young and carefree as he had fifteen years ago.

"Say that again," Kit said, a million tiny sparklers going off inside her.

"I love you," he repeated, and then they were laughing and hugging each other while the train crew and onlookers and a few fellow passengers cheered them on.

Never, Kit thought as they were clasped in each other's arms, her heart filled with joy, delight, and surprise, no matter what happened, would she ever forget that the first time Greg told her he loved her was while they were standing on a wooden platform at ten-twenty on a Sunday night in Williams, Arizona.

Promptly at eleven-thirty at night, Mountain Time, the California Limited crossed the state line into California at Seligman, and in Sin and Caro's drawing room there was the ceremonial toast over champagne and the setting back of their watches one hour so that they would be adhering to

Pacific Time. New York was now three time zones and three-thousand miles away, but with Greg beside her, looking at her adoringly, his eyes full of love, Kit found the thought of the place she would always think of as home only caused a short pang.

But now, at nearly noon, as the train left the California desert behind, she sat in the sunny observation car, arrayed in a Tappe suit of beige linen with a wide plaid ribbon belt, waiting for Greg to join her. Back in their sleeping car, it was a bedlam of adults, children, and servants all involved in the last-minute packing, and Kit, who was already completely ready for the train's arrival in Los Angeles at two-forty, escaped to the observation car to enjoy the side vistas along with the man she loved who was coming down the aisle with a young boy.

"We have some company, darling," Greg announced as he and nine-year-old Garrison Stanford Poole sat down in the large leather armchairs on either side of her. "Garrison here is getting a little train crazy."

"Aren't we all," Kit agreed as a waiter brought them glasses of ginger ale, and several older people seated nearby looked indulgently at them.

"Excuse me for intruding," a dowager seated across the aisle said in stately tones, "but is this fine young man your nephew?"

"This is my Uncle Greg and my Aunt Kit," Garrison said quickly with a brightness that was a younger version of his father's, "and they're not married . . . yet. But last night in Williams, he told her he loved her right out on the platform!"

"Oh, so *you're* that young man," the elegant older woman said in a clear voice that carried up and down the length of the observation car, and to his ultimate embarrassment, Greg began to blush.

"There, you can't try and back out on me now," Kit whispered, feeling as though an attack of the giggles were

147

coming on. "Treat me right or everyone here will think you're a bounder."

"They'd probably form a gang and toss me off the back platform into the Los Angeles Basin," he whispered back, and then they dissolved into laughter.

"You all seem to be having a good time," Sinclair remarked, joining them. "I've come to collect Garrison, and we'll all meet in the dining car at half-past twelve for lunch. Come on, son," he went on in an affectionate voice, "you and Laura are joining us for lunch, and next Monday you'll be back in school."

"The Hollywood School For Girls," Garrison pointed out glumly.

"With only six boys among all those girls, Gar feels a little surrounded," Sin explained.

"In about ten years you'll come to appreciate your vast, early fortune," Greg pointed out.

"As of last night he's speaking from fond memory," Kit added, and Sin laughed quietly.

"See you both in the dining car as soon as the glasses stop shaking."

"What did he mean by that?"

"You'll see in a minute," Greg said. "We're in the Cajoh Pass now, watch our glasses carefully."

As he spoke, the ginger-ale filled glasses on the table in front of them began to tremble and then to shake as the California Limited made the bumpy trip over the summit and into San Bernardino. Gradually the train began its descent into the Los Angeles Basin, and as the track grew smoother the rich vista outside the windows became greener as they approached the first of the orange groves.

"I'm here, really here," Kit said, reaching for Greg's hand. "Breakfast in the desert, lunch in an orange grove, and Los Angeles before tea. All this—and you."

"This is California. And every time I make this trip I think of something Tennyson wrote in *The Lotus-Eaters:* 'In the

148

afternoon they came into a land in which it seemed always afternoon. All around the coast the languid air did swoon, breathing like one that hath a weary dream,'" Greg quoted, his face transfixed. "Somehow those few lines seems more applicable to California than any other piece of poetry I've ever read."

Part Two

The Lotus Eaters

Glamour is what makes a man ask for
your telephone number. But it is
also what makes a woman ask for the
name of your dressmaker.

—Lily Dache

To a woman, the consciousness of
being well-dressed gives a sense
of tranquility which religion
fails to bestow.

—Helen Olcott Bell

This isn't a city, this is a
goddamn conspiracy. It isn't
interested in anything except
selling vacant lots and cures
for consumption.

—irate Hearst editor upon
leaving Los Angeles

Chapter 6

"No, Mr. Garrity, I don't want any of these pinks," Kit said, indicating with a wave of her hand the paint chip samples that Mike Garrity, the building contractor, had brought with him to their first meeting in the store on Wednesday morning. Hopefully, in a short time, this neglected spot would become Katharine's, but the ground rules came first. "The color on the walls of the dressing rooms have to be something much more subtle and delicate. Let me show you—"

She quickly opened the gold filigree clasp of her Mark Cross purse and took out her gold compact and then ripped a page of her Faberge jade-covered notepad, the narrow gold edges set with rubies. With Mr. Garrity watching her as though he were the sorcerer's apprentice, she opened her compact and let some of the finely colored Elizabeth Arden face powder sift down onto the paper. *"This* color, Mr. Garrity. Do you think your painting crew can blend a matching shade for me?" she asked with well-mannered directness. "This is just the right mixture of pale pink and pale beige so that the dressing rooms will look attractive and feminine but won't take anything away from the clothes."

The contractor looked at the face powder with great interest. "When we were in London a few years ago, Mrs.

Garrity ordered some things from Lucile's, and she told me that the fitting rooms there were done in gray."

"A very dull gray," Kit added. "Lady Duff-Gordon won't let anything distract from her clothes. Her theory is a sound one, but it won't work here."

"Well, we'll see what can be done. It would be a help if I had more powder though."

"I'll bring a box with me tomorrow morning," Kit promised. "Now, for the rest of the shop—"

The rest of the shop, including the back rooms Kit intended to use for offices, were to be painted in ivory lacquer, as were the bannisters of the staircase leading up to the second floor where the fitting rooms and stockrooms were located. "I want to see sample chips of marble before I give you the go-ahead to install anything in the bathrooms," she said as they went back downstairs.

"I understand perfectly," Mr. Garrity said, making several more pages of notes in his notebook. "There's still the matter of the last alcove on the selling floor."

"I know. Mrs. Randall and I are going to pick out fabric to mount on the walls. I'll have a decision on that by tomorrow morning. There's so much to do here!"

"I think that's what frightened Mr. Mason off from opening his haberdashery shop. Now watch that pretty dress of yours, Miss Allen. It's a mess around here."

Kit let her glance travel over the dun-colored walls, the sorry, broken pieces of furniture, the balls of dust on the floor, and the large windows that looked as if they hadn't been washed in six months, but she really didn't see any of it. Her mind's eye was already attuned to what it was going to look like.

It's all mine, she thought triumphantly. And it's going to be beautiful.

"I'm personally going to see to it that your shop is going to be a masterpiece, Miss Allen," Mr. Garrity promised. "But I will miss not having a haberdasher's. My daughter's getting married in November," he explained, "and Mr. Mason promised me a suit of morning clothes for the wedding. Well, I can always find another tailor, but possibly you could help Mary Alice out."

Here it comes, Kit thought, biting back a smile. The first bribe. Let's see how well I handle this.

"I'm not selling bridal ensembles, Mr. Garrity," she said, making her voice sound as regretful as possible.

"Oh, no, Mary Alice has her dress already, from I. Magnin in San Francisco, but she needs a lot more things for her trousseau. Now if you could help her and my wife out with a few nice things when you open, I can guarantee this shop will be in ready-to-open condition before you know it!"

So that's how it's going to be, Kit thought, amused. There's a price to everything, but at least this one is easier to take. Look considering, just like this is a great and important decision. Now smile. . . .

"I can't give clothes away, Mr. Garrity, as a businessman you know that's a bad practice." Kit sounded thoroughly charming, completely versed in business, and quite ready to put a deal together. "But what I can do is offer Mary Alice fifty percent off her bill under the agreement that whenever anyone asks, she tells them where she got her clothes. Do you think she'd agree to that?"

"She'd better," Mr. Garrity replied, surprised that he wasn't going to have to bargain a bit more. "But there's my wife, and the bridesmaids."

"As long as they all come in together, I'll be very happy to take fifty percent off their bills as well—for that one time only." Kit walked over to the rickety oak desk that Mr. Garrity used on all his jobs, and took her memo pad out again. With nothing in the shop safe enough or clean enough to sit down on, she used the wall as her desk, and with her gold pencil wrote out her agreement with Mr. Garrity and signed it. "Here," she said, and held the page out to him. "And please tell your wife and daughter that they'll both be

155

invited to my opening day party so they can not only admire the clothes but your handiwork as well."

Michael Garrity chuckled as he took the note. "I'm going to charge you a pretty penny for all the work you want done, you'll pay my bill promptly because you're not only smart about business, but a lady as well, and then you'll earn it all back through Rosemarie and Mary Alice."

Kit matched his smile. "That's business, Mr. Garrity."

"So it is. Now, I want to take a few more measurements, and I'll be back in the morning with my crew, ready to start work."

"Fine, and I'll be next door in Mrs. Randall's shop if you have any questions."

Collecting her purse, Kit walked toward the back of the shop and then off to the right where the doorway that she and Mallory had discussed had been neatly cut, her Lucile dress of green and black gingham-checked silk trimmed with a wide collar of hemstitched organdy and a black patent-leather belt rustling softly. The interior of Mallory Randall, Antiques, was the complete antithesis of what her own premises currently looked like, and for a minute Kit stayed where she was, breathing in the very pleasant combination of fresh flowers, furniture polish, and expensive perfume.

Mallory's shop, opened in April 1911, was run as an adjunct to Thea Harper de Renille's decorating firm in New York, although neither woman went out of her way to advertise the fact. Those who were cognizant of the connection between the two showrooms knew that decorating advice was available for a fee, but Mallory preferred to work on a ten-to-four basis, selling both original antiques and reproductions, as well as a variety of chintzes, and the occasional rug. Life on her half-yearly basis in Los Angeles could be very nice, she told Kit, provided she didn't clutter it up with too many clients suffering major fits of indecision when faced with redecorating their houses.

Kit banished the last of her cobwebs by admiring

Mallory's way of transforming her shop from what could just have easily been yet another antique dealer's jumbled display into an extremely elegant showroom. Everything was arranged in a variety of settings, a series of vignettes that the best of Paris's antiquaries would be proud to claim. An assortment of discreetly placed cabinets and vitrines showed off their porcelain treasures of small cache pots and oriental bowls and vases in the patterns of famille rose, famille verte, and tobacco rose; there was a carefully chosen selection of sofas and chairs, covered in either pale silks or pretty chintzes, and a wide variety of tables and chests from several periods held either small ornaments, bouquets of flowers, or tasteful-looking lamps.

"And every single thing is for sale," Grazia D'Ettiene said, getting up from behind her inlaid satinwood writing desk as soon as she saw Kit. Tall and very slender, her hair was the color of burnished taffy, and she was wearing a Paquin beige-and-cream-checked summer dress trimmed in ribbon. "This summer I actually sold a flower arrangement."

"You're joking," Kit said as they walked toward the center of the shop whose proportions were exactly the same as they were next door.

"Not at all. I was just about to close for the day when a woman dashed in. She told me she was giving a dinner party and the florist had lost her order, so I let her choose."

"Why do I get the feeling that that could only happen in Los Angeles?" Kit asked whimsically.

"I see you're picking up fast on life out here." They paused in front of a Louis XV two-drawer walnut commode with a serpentine front and panelled sides, and Grazia made a great show of rearranging a pair of French silver candlesticks. "I just heard about you and Greg. Congratulations, he's really swell, and I think you're just what he needs."

"How nice of you to say that," Kit returned, feeling pleased and mystified and a little curious. "Of course we haven't settled anything between us. With my shop and his

157

movie studio we're both a bit preoccupied at the moment. Were you and Greg—?" She paused delicately.

"Oh, *no*. There was nothing like that, absolutely nothing. When I came out here two years ago to live with Sin and Caro, I was still very lost after my parents' death. The *Titanic* was such a public thing—really, I felt sometimes as if I were walking around with a sign on my back. At any rate, Greg was very kind to me, and Caro tried very subtly to promote something there."

"But it didn't take?"

Grazia giggled like a schoolgirl. "I don't think Greg was even aware of anything happening. And I didn't want it. He is wonderful looking, but there's too much difference in our ages, and our names— Can you imagine us as a couple?"

"Grazia and Gregory." Kit had to smile. "I always think that couples with alliterative names sound a little strange, but the two of you together would have sounded like characters out of a very sophisticated children's book!"

"We wouldn't have added anything to the history of great romantic couples," Grazia agreed. "Look, Kit, did Mallory mention that I'd be very happy to help you out?"

"She said that you're always saying there isn't enough to do. I can promise you plenty—you've seen the mess next door—but I don't want you to feel that you're being asked to pick up after me."

"With all those gorgeous things you're going to sell, plus what Mallory has, never! And the door between the two shops is going to be terrific."

"Mallory and I are counting on a lot of cross traffic. Was it a mess when they cut through the wall?"

"Not too, Mr. Garrity's people are very careful."

"I'm glad to hear that. Is Mallory very busy right now?"

"Go right on back, she and Julie ought to be done with the inventory list they were making."

Located in the back of the shop, Mallory's office was incredibly tasteful and largely noted for its lack of clutter and urge to show off, something quite rare in antique dealers, most of whom loved to work amid the results of their buying expeditions. Everything was done in the faintest possible shade of gray-green: walls, carpet, and upholstery. The surface of the large kneehole desk had a writing surface covered in pale-green leather sprigged with tiny gold roses, and across the room the small niche formed by the two very useful closets was filled with a sofa covered in a pale-gray chintz with a loose design of butter-yellow primroses and gray-green leaves.

"There you are," Mallory said, looking elegant in a Lucile dress of beige embroidered linen with a black satin belt, as she and her salesgirl-secretary, Julie Harrison, looked up from the sample books they were conferring over. "From the look on your face, I take it your first conference with Mr. Garrity went well."

"It went *very* well," Kit agreed, putting her purse down on a tulipwood writing table holding a large crystal vase filled with white and yellow peonies and surrounded by a selection of auction house catalogs. "Of course in order to get the job done quickly and right I had to promise to supplement his daughter's trousseau at half-price."

Mallory laughed. "Oh, what are a few dresses? I had to redecorate his dining room and give general advice on the rest of his house."

"What a great racket, and Greg told me Michael Garrity's an honest businessman."

"He is—no cost cutting, no drunk or disorderly workmen, and all the best materials, only you don't get a nice big house on West Adams Boulevard plus a nice parcel of land in Beverly Hills by not doing a little graft."

"I like him though." Kit came over to the desk. "How pretty," she said, admiring the fabric samples spread out over the surface. "But most of these are English and French, aren't they? How are deliveries?"

"So far so good. Of course I'm ordering in larger

quantities just to be safe, and warning all clients that there might be a delay in arrival. Julie, show Kit what I picked out for her."

Julie, a pretty strawberry-blonde in her early twenties, wearing a simple Lanvin dress of rose linen with collar and elbow cuffs of white organdy, put aside the lists she and Mallory had been working on and pulled out two samples for Kit to see. "Look, here's a glazed white chintz with pink peonies and a cream-colored linen with pink carnations," she said brightly. "There's plenty of ready stock on both. Mallory, if there's nothing else for the moment, I'll go back out to the selling floor."

"That's fine, but don't you want to tell Kit about your cousin first?"

The girl blushed slightly. "My cousin, Delia Stewart, is visiting us from Cedar Rapids, and I know she'd love to go to work for you instead of having to go back home," Julie explained.

"Does she like clothes?"

"Oh, yes. Delia gets everything in Chicago or New York. We also look a little alike, if that'll be of help to you. Del's met a young intern who's doing his training on my father's staff. Daddy brought him around for me, but since I definitely *don't* want to marry a doctor, I'd like to keep my cousin around!"

"I can see where Cedar Rapids isn't any easy commute from Los Angeles," Kit said, and smiled. "Tell Delia that in the interest of romance, I'll interview her next week."

Julie left, and Kit and Mallory surveyed the variety of chintzes, fabrics, and papers; many of them featuring the renewed interest in roses. There were samples featuring exaggerated cabbage roses, neat moss roses, beautifully drawn roses reminiscent of the Queen Anne period, and rose bouquets after the style of the late eighteenth century. In addition there were graceful violets and lilacs, as well as delicate camellias and primroses, every single one of them fit for a garden.

"They're all lovely," Kit said sincerely, "but I'll stay with the glazed chintz sample Julie showed me. I want to keep the fuss to a minimum, and I prefer peonies over roses."

"So do I, but there seems to be some sort of rose revival on. Now that people aren't cluttering up their homes with horsehair, Belter, plush, and poor-taste knicknacks, everyone wants to see what these prints *really* look like. Besides," Mallory went on smoothly, "Greg might want to do a little redecorating, and I decided it was only right to let you have first look at all my new things."

"Aren't *you* his decorator?" Kit replied blandly, deliberately misinterpreting her statement. She knew that Greg lived in bachelor splendor in a suite at the Alexandria, and was very curious about how it looked. "He may be perfectly happy with his rooms, and most men don't like to change unless something drastic makes them do it."

"Does falling in love fit the category?"

"Greg only said he loved me, he didn't ask me to be his wife." Kit didn't like the reality of her statement, but a day and a half after her arrival in Los Angeles was too soon to start looking for trouble. "I'm having lunch at the Alexandria with Jessica Gilbert, who writes the women's page for the *Los Angeles Statesman-Democrat*," Kit went on, deciding to change the subject. "Hopefully, she'll want to write up my shop."

"Let's just hope she's not the jealous type—none of us really know."

"How catty you sound, Mal." Kit couldn't resist a smile. "Who is Jessica Gilbert married to?"

"No one."

Some of Kit's certainty that she knew all about at least one facet of Greg's private life seeped away. "That's not in line with what I've been hearing."

"Oh, I never said that anything serious went on between them in private, but for a while there they did seem to be

161

seeing a lot of each other, then it sort of tapered off."

"I couldn't fall in love with a nice, uncomplicated man, could I? It would certainly make things a lot simpler. Not to mention boring," she added, answering her own question, and both women began to laugh.

"Do you know how many so-called suitable men I could have married in the four years Rupert and I didn't see each other? It was all completely useless. I knew he was the only man I'd ever love, and I had to wait until things were right for us again." Mallory leaned back in her chair. "Do you have time now to come upstairs to my storeroom and see the furniture I've put aside for your shop?"

Kit consulted the velvet-banded Cartier watch around her right wrist. "No, when Jessica called me last night I agreed to meet her exactly at noon, and it's a quarter of now. Then I have an appointment in the Bradbury Building with Benson Paper Boxes to order dress boxes and hat boxes, but I should be back here about three. Is that all right with you?"

"Fine. Oh, Kit, one thing—"

"Yes?" Kit stood up and went over to one of the closets to retrieve her Talbot hat of hard beige straw with a firm brim and black and green silk wrapped around the high crown.

"You know it's my and Rupert's fourth anniversary tomorrow night," Mallory began, and the rest was patently self-evident.

"Oh, the first peril of being an indefinite house guest! No wonder you're so eager for Greg to ask the significant question." Kit laughed, and looked into the mirror attached to the back of the door to adjust her hat. "It's all right, you have nothing to worry about," she went on. "Greg and I are driving out to Pasadena tomorrow night for dinner and dancing at the Huntington Hotel, and with your celebration in mind, we'll be sure to get back to Los Angeles very, very late!"

The Los Angeles that Kit had arrived in on Monday

afternoon, September 21st, 1914—*La Reina de Los Angeles,* formally founded by military order on August 26th, 1781— was a city of undeniable contrasts that so far showed no signs whatsoever of slowing down. Settled in a series of mass migrations, this metropolis that had long since passed the one-million population mark, was literally civilizations over civilizations: the Indians, the Spanish settlers up from Mexico with their vast land grants that had produced the haciendas that older Angelians could still recall, and the men and women who had come from the East Coast and the Middle West to farm, or to ranch, or to just do something different from what they'd do back home. Pundits liked to speculate that the warm climate released some sort of vast creative energy surge. New arrivals liked to compare the metropolis with its growing multitudes of sections and neighborhoods, to a great new cocktail full of varied ingredients waiting to be shaken up by an expert bartender. No one knew whether all the tastes would blend—whether it would be a place where traditions would not only melt together but be able to form new traditions of its own.

But on this warm and sunny September noon as Kit walked the short distance along Spring Street to the Alexandria Hotel, it was agreed that Los Angeles had continued to grow despite various panics or depressions because the climate made things easier. It was already a headquarters for shipping, manufacturing, and railroads, but they were only the spokes of a very complicated wheel that go into making a major city. Los Angeles still needed a hub, a center, one industry that would gather others, and all that summer and early fall, as the allied nations of Europe battled against Germany and Austria, the rumors, the whispers, the feeling in the air of this city where so many people seemed to be striving for so many different things, was that the cohesive force it was seeking just might be the movies.

*   *   *

The Alexandria Hotel was the gathering place for Los Angeles's elite, and the lunch hour was quickly reaching its early pitch when Kit came through the revolving door and into the lobby and walked into the Palm Court. As usual when she was trying to create an impression, she looked straight ahead, and today she had the satisfaction of literally halting the self-absorbed conversations of several businessmen who would later admit to themselves that they were very glad they'd taken this day to forsake the club-like atmosphere of the hotel's elite Indian Grill Room, as well as attracting the considering eyes of several of the women lunchers as she allowed the maitre d' to show her to Jessica Gilbert's table.

"I think our fathers knew each other," Jessica remarked easily in her somewhat throaty voice. She had been watching Kit's calculated progress with amusement and approval, having created the exact same stir only fifteen minutes before. Except for Kit, Jessica was the best-dressed, best-looking woman in the restaurant. Her dark ash-brown hair was swept up under a Reboux hat of cream-colored Milan straw, banded in blue moire, and Kit immediately identified her dress as Poiret's cream-colored silk linen with a collar and belt of pale blue satin. Instinctively she knew that her onetime rival was studying her with equal interest. "Mine was Harold Gilbert, president of Gilbert Brothers Mercantile Bank—and a greedy bunch they are."

"I'm glad you said that first. Daddy always said that your father knew more than the rest of his family put together," Kit replied as she sat down. "I know we went to different schools and saw each other only occasionally at very large parties, but you did drop out of sight after your father died and your uncles took over the bank."

"Oh, I've been here in California all the time," Jessica said breezily. "I took my jewelry and emptied my bank account and came out to stay with my godmother, Vera Wallach, in Pasadena. By luck I drifted into writing newspaper features.

But enough of me. I'm fascinated by what you're going to do, Kit. It sounds *so* elegant."

"You wouldn't think so if you saw the mess the shop is in, but I like to think that it's going to be worth it. That women who go up to San Francisco to buy clothes are going to come to me. If you don't mind my asking, did you get your dress at Poiret's or at an import house?"

"At Poiret's this summer. *Early* this summer," she added, and they exchanged bittersweet smiles at the meaning behind her words. "We probably missed each other there as well."

"I wouldn't be surprised. But if we had met you might have told me too much about one of Los Angeles's most successful citizens." Kit looked up at the Palm Court's decorative stained glass ceiling. "Shall we order lunch?"

Sure that Jessica had caught the meaning behind her words, she signalled their waiter, who presented their menus with a flourish, making suggestions and informing them of the specials of the day. Both women ordered jellied turtle soup, to be followed by zucchini stuffed with lobster and garnished with artichoke hearts, raw mushrooms, and green mayonnaise, and decided to end their lunch with trifle.

"When you phoned last night, you mentioned you might be interested in a series of stories on my shop," Kit said. "Can I take that to mean that you want to start writing about it now straight through to opening day? I have to attract customers," she explained, "make them *want* to come in and buy something, even if it's only a hat or a pair of gloves and a bottle of perfume."

"But you are an exclusive shop," Jessica insisted, her sea-green eyes turning dark.

"Only in terms that the merchandise is the finest I can offer. And there won't be any charge accounts." She and Jessica exchanged knowing smiles; there was no need to say anything else—they were rich, they paid their bills on time, but were all too aware that many of their number did not.

165

"There's nothing like a little self-protection."

"Yes, self-protection generally works well in most situations."

There was a message there that Kit didn't miss, but as much as she wanted to discuss Greg, he had to wait until business was out of the way.

"I have an appointment with Timothy Benson so I can order boxes. Would you like to come along and give your readers an exclusive look at how things are going to be?" she asked just as the waiter arrived with their soup. "Tomorrow morning you could come by with a photographer for a few pictures. If nothing else, I'd like a record of Mr. Garrity's progress."

"I think that could be arranged." Jessica put down her spoon. "You're no more a society girl with a bright idea than I am. Where did you work before?"

"You mean where do my ideas come from? From one Herman Patrick Tappe."

"And they say people from Ohio have no imagination. He taught you well."

"Thank you."

"Are you going to hire Grazia D'Ettiene to help manage your shop? Mallory sells the best antiques, and does very well, but there isn't enough going on there to really keep her busy."

"From what I've seen of her, Grazia should be splendid handling both shops, and to make access for everyone concerned easier, Mallory had a door cut through our connecting wall. She has two reproduction Venetian blackamoors, one points left and the other points right, and we'll each take one. Touches like that seem to go over big in Los Angeles."

"You've caught on quickly. Wait until you see the Bradbury Building. Sinclair had his original Los Angeles office there, and I don't know how he could leave it for that monster-sized building further along Broadway where he has two floors now," Jessica offered. "Oh, I know he needed the space, but the Bradbury—"

"It must really be outstanding." Kit loved interesting and unusual architecture. "It can't be a very new building though."

"No, it's 1893, and for this city that's getting on in years. It's only five stories high, and the brick front isn't very interesting, and neither is the arch you enter under. Everything is inside. It's built on the open court style with two open cage elevators and two staircases. Everywhere you look there's wrought-iron railings and grilles, the floor space becomes wider with each floor, and the ceiling is a complete skylight raised on a clerestory. Stand under it and you feel like you're in the Hagia Sophia in Istanbul!"

"I've been in the Hagia Sophia. If the Bradbury Building is even a quarter as powerful, it will be a remarkable place."

"You've certainly done your share of exotic travelling. How did you get to Istanbul?"

"On the Orient Express!" Kit said, and they both began to laugh. "I always say that whenever anyone asks me why I wasn't in Mallory's wedding party. My mother remarried in May 1910, and she and my stepfather left immediately for a long honeymoon in Europe. I was in New York, supervising the details of decorating our new Park Avenue apartment, and in July they cabled me that they had decided to ride the Orient Express and wanted me to come along. I caught the *Mauretania*'s last July sailing. Mallory came back from Europe on the ship's reverse crossing, and got engaged to Rupert shortly after that. When they were married in September, I was wandering through Istanbul's bazaars instead of being a bridesmaid."

For a few minutes both women talked about places they'd been and places they still wanted to go. Kit and Jessica had the same longing to see India and the Orient, as well as South America, and gradually their topics became more specific. There was still a lot to discuss when it came to fashion, but they also discussed books and the latest Broadway offerings, in particular the newly opened musical, *The Girl From Utah,* whose Jerome Kern score—in particular the song "They Didn't Believe Me"—was sweeping the country.

In time it was inevitable that their conversation would turn to the discussion of men.

Instinctively she knew that Greg was going to be a topic of conversation between them. Did she still care about him, still want him, regret whatever had happened to end whatever romance they had before it ever really began? Kit thought.

I wonder how much I should say to her? Jessica speculated silently. I'm sure she already knows that Gregory West is one in a million, but there's also something about him that's kept carefully hidden. Right now, Kit's gotten further with him than I ever did. Maybe she'll be the one to unlock what he doesn't want anyone else to know.

"Are you glad you came out to Los Angeles?" Kit asked at last, deciding that this was the best way to begin.

"Oh, yes. The weather for one thing. Frank Rundstadt had just purchased the *Los Angeles Statesman-Democrat* when I came to town, so everyone he hired had to be willing to pitch in and do extra jobs in addition to their regular assignments. Believe me, it's a lot easier to follow a police story in January in Southern California than in New York."

"Do you get lonely out here though? Or do you live in Pasadena with your aunt?"

"On and off. I keep a room here for when I'm working late—or playing. Mallory decorated it for me, and you'd be surprised how convenient it is." Jessica looked around and then lowered her voice. "You can use the room for your cover, if you like. I'll give you a key, and then if anyone asks you can say you're visiting or waiting for me."

"There are arrangements like that in New York. We just tell the doorman we're going to see someone, have the elevator man leave us on one floor, and then use the service stairs to go up or down to the right apartment," she said, and

168

they laughed about the machinations they went through in order to spend time alone with men they cared about. "I was wondering how things like this were worked out in Los Angeles. There's plenty of open spaces, but a genuine lack of large apartment buildings."

"Oh, we can get quite inventive out here," Jessica offered. "It may have something to do with the movie business, and speaking of which—"

Kit laughed. "You still can't quite picture Greg overseeing Hooper Studios much less supervising the making of a twelve-reel motion picture!"

"Something like that. He does have a deeply artistic side, and he isn't ashamed of it or doesn't try to hide it the way some men do. Of course that may have to do with his working for Sinclair while he was importing antiques from the Orient. You can't work in that sort of atmosphere and not absorb some of it."

"I agree, but there's more to it. Greg's instincts are very finely bred."

"I always thought so, too," Jessica said, and both women looked at each other.

They both knew that while gentlemen did not discuss ladies behind their backs—or at least bring their names into the conversation—ladies had no such compunctions. It was nothing to them to discuss in great detail the men in their lives. It was all part of female friendships.

Except that Katharine Allen and Jessica Gilbert weren't friends. At least not yet. And telling each other about the man the former loved and the latter had once been interested in was not the way to start building one.

"If I were another sort of woman," Jessica said slowly, pausing while the waiter brought their salads, "I'd pretend that I still had more than a passing interest in Greg. All I will say is that we were always out of time with each other. Pacing between a man and a woman is like J.M. Barrie's description of charm: when you have it, you don't need

169

anything else; and if you lack it, nothing else helps."

Kit appreciated Jessica's words more than she could say, but she still regretted the conversation they couldn't have. She didn't want to discuss any of her deeper feelings with either Mallory, who might think she was acting too silly for a grown woman, or Caroline, who probably knew more about Greg than any of them but would say nothing.

"Thank you for saying that," Kit said finally. "I'm not going to tell you anything that sounds intimate—mainly because nothing like that has happened yet—but I do have to know if you agree with me about something."

"That sounds reasonable."

"One night in Chicago, Greg took me to the College Inn. It's very romantic there, with the soft light on the dance floor and those little lamps on the tables that you turn up when you want to signal a waiter. We weren't taking *anything* very seriously, and at one point I asked him if he always dreamed about being a successful businessman when he was growing up."

"And for a second he seemed to close off."

"Yes. I thought it might have been something I did."

"I doubt that very much," Jessica said with not a little touch of envy. "I wouldn't be surprised if at one time or another every woman Greg knew—except for Sally Courtland who isn't concerned about anything except the reflection she sees in her mirror—hasn't wondered what she did wrong in asking about his boyhood."

"I know, but in one way it isn't very unusual. Lots of men," she said, her memory touching on Sebastian, "have had terrible childhoods and don't want to relive them for any reason."

Jessica agreed, and their conversation went on, but even as it moved on to the far safer topics of shoes and cosmetics and whether or not Guerlain's *L'Heure Bleue* was the most romantic of all perfumes available, Kit continued to think about Greg. She thought about funny little things: how

170

precisely his hair was barbered, almost as if he followed a military style, only a little longer; how his eyes crinkled at the corners whenever he smiled or laughed; that he not only had the nerve it took to kiss her for the first time in a hallway at the Blackstone, but to tell her that he loved her while they were standing on the station platform in Williams, Arizona, and didn't care who heard.

It was all very pleasant to think about, but one fact, as solid and uncompromising as concrete and steel, was certain and unavoidable: what, she wondered, could have happened to Greg when he was younger that made him not only try to blot out his early years but also be so cautious about loving her now?

Chapter 7

Although only seven miles separate the city halls of *La Reina de Los Angeles* and the Crown of the Valley, the driver behind the wheel of his car may have difficulty telling exactly where Los Angeles and Pasadena end and begin, but upon reaching one or the other, the difference is almost audible.

If Los Angeles was nouveau riche trying to put a good face on its uncohesive and clashing architecture and continuing sprawl, Pasadena represented the establishment almost beyond the definition of the word; it was above common necessities, a calm oasis of Craftsman and Spanish Colonial Revival houses. Going there was like visiting a dowager aunt who kicked up her heels once a year, which, in Pasadena's case was every January 1st, for the annual New Year's Day events of the Tournament of Roses, and the Pasadena Rose Bowl in the Arroyo Seco, a stellar event in the world of college football.

Residents of Los Angeles cheerfully admit that they enjoy having a bit of fun at the expense of poor Pasadena with its fine gardens and staid citizenry, but since Los Angeles in 1914 was not a city that offered a wide variety of respectable entertainment at night, livelier members of the leading social sets had to find a place to go on those evenings when the idea of dining and dancing once again at the Alexandria or Levy's Cafe paled. Since Los Angeles wasn't a theatre town, and the Hollywood Hotel was a temperance stronghold, and the Van Nuys Hotel was too old hat for words, they had to go somewhere to drink champagne and tango and two-step the hours away, and had subsequently adopted Pasadena's Huntington Hotel as a very pleasant place to spend—in a manner of speaking—a night on the town.

Opened in 1907 as The Wentworth, it had been designed as a posh resort hotel that would attract well-heeled visitors from the East Coast looking to forget about the icy insults of winter in a spot of sunshine and flowers. Unfortunately, it wasn't much of a success until railroad magnate Henry E. Huntington added it to his vast real estate holdings in 1911, and brought in his architects to bring the newly renamed hotel up to the level he expected to find in a grand hostelry. The six-story building and central observation tower had the dun-colored plaster walls and red-tile roofs that southern Californians now took almost for granted, but the massive walls were so rich with growing ivy that the vines were becoming an attraction in themselves. It also had an impressive central entrance court that Greg turned his new Fiat closed body town car into with a proud crunch of gravel shortly after seven on Thursday evening.

"They're always very nice to me considering that I own only one automobile at a time," Greg observed wryly as the doorman greeted them and then turned the car over to an attendant. "That's not quite the way things are done here."

"I've already picked up on that," Kit replied as they entered the hotel. "Sin and Caro have five Rolls-Royces, and Rupert and Mallory have three Cadillacs. Is there some unwritten state law about not being allowed to own only one motor car or place of residence? From what I've been able to put together over the past few days, all your friends not only have homes in Los Angeles but beach houses in Santa Monica or Hermosa, or ranches in the valley. Are you really going to tell me that you live modestly in the Alexandria and have only one car?"

"The Fiat is it as far as transportation goes, but I do have a small place in the Santa Ynez Mountains," Greg said as they walked arm-in-arm into the Huntington's glittering lobby. "I'll tell you about it another time, right now I just want to concentrate on us and celebrate the end of my being just another extra man in a dinner jacket."

"Oh, you were never that," Kit replied softly. How she'd missed Greg over the past few days when they'd both been too engulfed by business to spend any time together. Even several telephone calls a day couldn't make up for not seeing each other. Tonight, however, was for them. They would have a private and romantic evening together, a chance to be alone that might very well lead to something more. "And as far as I'm concerned, you're the best looking man here!"

"All your compliments are very cheerfully accepted," Greg said with a pleased look, "but right now most of the people in this lobby are probably wondering who that is accompanying that glamorous New Yorker, Katharine Allen! Jessica did quite a story on you for this morning's women's page."

"I have you to thank for that, but we can discuss it later," she said as they paused in front of the area separating the men's and women's cloakrooms. "I'll see you in five minutes."

"Not a minute more. I still haven't seen what you're wearing to dazzle everyone with."

In the women's cloakroom, Kit handed the attendant her Poiret evening coat of black satin embroidered in gold leaves, and then paused in front of one of the dressing tables to check her hair, makeup, and dress. When Greg had arrived at the Randalls' house, she had been all ready to leave, eager to be out of the house before Mallory and Rupert came downstairs; tonight was their wedding anniversary and there was no reason for them to be either host

175

and hostess or interested and encouraging friends because she hadn't gotten ready quickly enough. Of course, Greg had thought it was funny that she had been practically standing on the doorstep, and teasingly asked if Rupert was coming after him with a shotgun, but he had agreed that they shouldn't linger, either to enjoy one of Dovedale's excellent martinis or for him to admire her dress.

She had already drawn several covetous female glances in the powder room, and now, as Greg saw her in the Callot Soeurs dance dress that was layers of gold tulle and lace on a foundation of gold cloth, she knew she'd made the right choice.

"This isn't too much for Pasadena, then?"

"No, but it may be too much for my heart. Don't you believe in not creating envy in the customer for the owner of the shop?"

"Certainly not, then I wouldn't be able to wear any of my own clothes. Besides, the clients I want to attract won't want to find the owner in sackcloth and ashes," Kit said as they approached the restaurant, the heels of her gold evening shoes clicking on the marble floor. "Incidentally, how do you know about that particular dress shop trick? You give yourself away, Mr. West," she said lightly, her recent conversation with Jessica running through her mind.

"I told you I wasn't only a businessman interested solely in the bottom line."

"Lots of men like to watch the women in their lives buy clothes, but not too many know the secret little details." Kit didn't like the direction her questions were leading them. So Greg knew that in some couture houses, when a very wealthy client was due, only the plainest mannequins were used to show the clothes in order that the woman would feel that there was no competition. So what?

So he's giving me his past in such broken little bits that he isn't even aware of it, she thought as the maitre d' greeted them with the sort of smile reserved for only the most

176

welcome of patrons. There was the usual exchange of greetings before they were shown to the quiet, secluded table Greg insisted on instead of the more prominent one the maitre d' thought they would want. For the next twenty minutes there was no chance for Kit to further explore her thoughts as both their waiter and the wine steward arrived. Unlike some men she knew, Kit was delighted to find that Greg didn't feel that ordering wine was some mysterious process reserved for men, and together they decided on a bottle of Henriot 1908.

"A fine year from an excellent house," the sommelier complimented them. "So many Americans pass Henriot over, but it is the champagne of choice for the royal houses of Holland and Russia."

Ordering their food took a bit longer, and with the waiter making a few tactful suggestions the decision was made for clear consomme, crabmeat Newburg, breast of guinea hen on wild rice, green salad, and glacé Manchu.

"Alone at last," Kit said. "I don't know why anyone worries about chaperones, the waiters and the rest see to it that a couple never have too much time to themselves."

"You don't know the meaning of the word chaperone." He was so close to her that it almost hurt not to touch her. "Not that I care."

"Somehow I didn't think you would. In any case, it's much too late for both of us."

"You mean you don't want a man who'll protect you and worry about your reputation?" he asked in mock concern.

"That's what my first fiancé did—all the time—and that's why he became my former fiancé. Funny," she went on, "he couldn't understand why I didn't appreciate all his efforts."

"Should I take that as a warning?" he inquired lightly. He'd known all along that Kit was the sort of woman who didn't want a man's protective hand—no matter how well-intentioned—guiding her through the shoals and pitfalls of life. And since he never had the opportunity to find out if he were the sort of man who would consider it his sworn duty to keep the woman he loved from anything distressing, that was a fantasy that was best left on some back shelf.

Kit looked at him through her lashes. "You'd better—that is, if you meant what you said in Williams."

"I meant every word, and then some," Greg said, and his hand closed over hers. "I want to kiss you, but this is Pasadena, and being chased out of the Huntington by an outraged mob of guests wouldn't be a proper end to tonight."

"Pasadena doesn't strike me as the sort of community that rides people out of town on a rail for kissing," she parried, weaving her fingers through his. He was right in a way though, she had to admit. Their table, while secluded, was far from private, and there were certain rules that polite people had to obey in public. "However, they *might* be moved to arrest us as a warning, and somehow I don't think Rupert would be very happy about coming down to the city hall to bail us out."

"This is the second time that the thought of incurring Rupert's wrath has stopped me from a certain course of action."

"And when was the first time?" Kit inquired, her heartbeats quickening. She knew what he was going to say, but she hadn't expected to hear it from him quite so soon.

"The night we met. I almost decided to unlock a few doors and come to see you," he said, his voice low. "The only thing that stopped me was that I didn't know which room was yours. I knew that if I opened the wrong door Rupert would probably take some very definite action against me."

"He probably would," Kit agreed. The orchestra was playing a Strauss waltz, small candles and tiny bouquets of roses decorated each table making everything and everyone look better, but she didn't need a romantic-looking atmosphere to increase her feelings for Greg. It would be just as wonderful if we were together in a roadhouse, she

178

thought. "But I can tell you how happy I am that we're thinking the same way about that night."

"I suspected as much, that's why I've been so inaccessible since we arrived in Los Angeles," Greg explained, going from sexy to serious. "I didn't want to see you again, to make more memories between us, until I tied off a part of my old life. If cross-country telephone calls weren't so difficult to place, I'd have taken care of all of it before we left Chicago."

Kit understood instantly. "And has it all been successfully concluded? I'm not only going to learn all their names eventually, but there's a good chance they'll be customers of mine, and we'll all end up socializing together." She gave him an oblique look. "Or did you pick the sort of woman who'll call me a shopgirl?"

He thought about Sally Courtland; her reaction on the phone had been as bad as he prepared himself for. "Not all of them. Barbara and Nan are very happy for us and want to meet us. Peggy lives in San Francisco, but she'll probably be a client if not actually friendly—she's just a bit difficult to get to know."

"Three out of four?" Kit began to feel very lighthearted. "Not too bad. Grazia and Jessica were very complimentary about you."

"Then I'm a very fortunate man," Greg replied as the waiter and wine steward arrived, and as the attentive men served and poured, he realized how fortunate he truly was, not only in how he'd survived the dangerous circumstances he'd found himself in, but also in the women he'd known as well. The black speck in his life that was that night with Natalia, and, which, at any given time, grew larger or smaller, now receded to near nothingness. "And I'm luckiest of all to have found you."

"It took us long enough. We might even have saved each other a lot of entanglements."

"But then we would have been at the mercy of our friends' matchmaking efforts."

Kit gave a mock shudder. "Don't remind me! We could have met on our own though."

"How?"

"Caro mentioned that you have a particular fondness for the Plaza," Kit told him, enjoying her moment as a lady of mystery. "I lived there with my mother for a few years. Think of all the times we must have missed each other when you were in New York on business. You could have gotten on an elevator a few minutes after I got off; we could have been seated at opposite ends of the Rose Room, or the Champagne Porch; or been at opposite ends of the taxi line."

"The possibilities boggle the mind." From that first moment when he'd seen her in the Blackstone's restaurant, Greg had been deeply aware that he and Kit operated on some deeply instinctive level with each other. He knew he could trust her completely, but she could still surprise him. "When did you live at the Plaza?"

"From almost the day it opened to June 1910, nearly three years. If my mother hadn't remarried, we wouldn't have moved to The Mayfair on Park Avenue, and eventually we would have stumbled over each other in the lobby."

"Do you know that you're an unqualified romantic—with some very modern overtones."

"So are you, my darling Gregory, and you're also very traditional when it comes to certain types of behavior. Only a true gentleman would end his previous entanglements before—before—," Kit stopped, not at a loss for words, but because anything she might say to complete her sentence would sound too leading, and she never wanted Greg to say or feel that she had tricked him. "I can't tell you what that means to me—not in public, at least."

"I never thought I was making an empty gesture, and I wouldn't have minded stumbling over you in the Plaza's lobby."

"My mother would have found that very interesting."

"Do I have to worry about doing any explaining now?"

"No, my mother and stepfather are in Venezuela. I'm glad the Panama Canal finally opened last month. It'll make getting from South America to California easier. Of course," she went on teasingly, "if you really do break my heart, I can always get in touch with my stepbrother in Boston. Pack's very fond of me."

"How fond?"

The light, easy tone of his voice was gone, and Kit looked at him in amazement. "What do you mean by that? You almost sound as if Pack and I . . ."

Greg felt a curtain of embarrassment drop over him. What had gotten into him? he thought. This wasn't St. Petersburg, and although that didn't mean such things didn't go on everywhere, he had no right to take things for granted or to be suspicious.

"I'm sorry," he said at last. "I have an upbringing where such things are very common, and your wording—"

"Means one thing in America and another in Europe," Kit finished, another confirmation made, another piece of the puzzle dropping into place. "You weren't born and brought up in this country."

Greg felt his heart lurch. "How long have you known?"

"Since our lunch at the Congress Hotel. At first I thought you might be Sin's half-brother, but then you made a movement, a shrug, something only a European can carry off," she said, silently adding, only a well-born, well-educated European. "It doesn't matter to me. I don't care where you came from, or what you've done. What matters is what we do with our lives right now."

For a long minute they didn't speak. Around them the restaurant filled up with couples, the orchestra continued to play a variety of tunes, and to cover the sudden silence between them, they finished the consomme and sipped the champagne. The waiter presented the next course and refilled their glasses, and then Greg spoke, their earlier, light-hearted conversation clearly over.

181

"When we first came out to California to live," he told her in a quiet, serious voice, "the three of us came up with a background for me. We decided that if anyone wanted to know, I would say that I was born in western Pennsylvania, in one of those god-awful steel towns, that I was an orphan raised by the local high school principal and his wife who educated me and sent me to a small college nearby. By the time I 'graduated' they had died, and I came to New York and went to work for Sin."

"What a story—I'm lost in admiration at your facility not only to work out a story that really can't be checked out, but to have one that's so oblique that people will think you're Sin's brother."

"There are times I think he is. At any rate, Pennsylvania was Sin's idea. His father had gone to the western part of the state several times in 1878, conducting business with the steel companies, and since I was born in 1879, a logical connection could be made."

For a long minute, Greg and Kit simply looked at each other. There was so much still to be said, still to be revealed, but for the time being this had to be it.

"That's the story we made up and that everyone told everyone else," he went on. "But it isn't the truth, and I knew from the minute I met you that I could never tell it to you except as the lie it is."

"I'm not used to driving in California yet," Kit said several hours later on the drive back to Los Angeles. "How far along are we?"

"Almost halfway," Greg replied, not taking his eyes off the road ahead. "Are you all right?"

"Fine, it's you I'm concerned about."

"I've just had dinner and gone dancing with the woman I love, we have a nice drive home, and I have a movie studio to run. There's nothing to be concerned about."

"Hmm." Kit smiled and studied Greg's beautifully defined profile. "Do you know that it's generally nice to smile while you're dancing the tango?"

"Come to think of it, I must have looked like I was trying hard not to forget the steps," Greg said, and slowly began to smile. "I tend to hold on to moods longer than I should. My little speech must have put more of a damper on our evening than I thought."

"I've had a wonderful evening, and I don't mind your being introspective."

"Is there anything else?" His smile began to deepen.

"Do you think you can find the long way back to West Adams Boulevard?"

"I thought you'd never ask."

With a skillful turn of the steering wheel, the Fiat was off the road, and he pulled it into the shadow of several large willow trees.

"I think right now the longest way back to Los Angeles is attainable by simply not going anywhere for the time being."

"Funny, that's just what I was thinking. But aren't we a bit advanced for this? Pulling off the road to make a little time is more for college students."

"I was never a college student," Greg pointed out. He turned off the ignition and slid across the soft gray velvet seat until he was close to Kit. "Do you really mind?"

She slid her arms around his neck. "Whatever gave you a silly idea like that?"

"It was just a stray thought." One arm was draped along the back of the seat and the other came to rest on the side of her waist, and his body rested close against hers. Kit couldn't remember ever feeling so expectant with any man, and she raised her face to his, eager for the next step.

Greg kissed her so gently that she felt a new wave of tenderness sweep over her. This was the first time they could exchange affection in total privacy without worrying that anyone was going to discover them. Just a few hours before

183

he had admitted to her that the young life most people had thought he'd led was just so much carefully made-up fiction, and he'd still given her no indication as to what the truth might be, but if he trusted her enough to tell her that much, she could trust him enough to wait for the rest.

"You kiss so perfectly," she whispered, stroking the back of his neck. "I feel so right with you."

"And I feel the same way with you. I wasn't looking to fall in love, and meeting you was like being hit with a railroad tie." Slowly he undid the fastenings of her evening coat. "It feels wonderful."

"So do you." Her arms were around his shoulders and she could feel the quiet strength of his long, fluid muscles as he pressed against her body. How marvelous his hands felt as his fingers travelled lightly down the column of her throat, tracing the low neckline of her gown and the tops of her breasts. "I love you so much. With you, I feel more special, more cherished, more cared about than with anyone else," she told him, moving her hands over his dark, thick, carefully barbered hair.

"Do you really mean that?" In spite of the tenderness in his voice, there was an edge of anxiety in it that Kit had never heard before. "Do you mean that even though I've admitted to you that the background I've told everyone is mine isn't true?"

"If you didn't love me you wouldn't have told me what you did. That's a very big admission." It was hard to make out his face in the darkness, but she had to say this now. "I don't love you for your position, either former or present, or for whatever it is you went through. I love you for being *you.*"

"No one has ever said that to me before," he told her, and in that moment he knew there was no going back for him, no breaking off this relationship, and no using that long ago night in St. Petersburg as a shield against the ultimate involvement. Now he had to go forward no matter what the end results were. "I want you to marry me, Kit."

"Oh, Greg, do you mean that?" Her hands went to cup his face, her heartbeat increasing. Was this proposal too soon? No, it was too unexpected. Was this what living in California was all about—everything in a hurry? "Do you really want me to be the woman you spend the rest of your life with?"

"Yes," he said, drawing her into his arms, holding her close, breathing in the intoxicating nimbus of *L'Heure Bleue*. "You're the first woman I've ever asked to marry me."

"I want to marry you," she said, and her heart filled with love for him. She reached out to trace his face feature by feature with her fingertips. Alone together in the luxury car, the heavy trees making the road seem a long way off, they revelled in their seclusion. They were adults, not grappling twenty-year-olds, but there was the same semi-illicit thrill.

They explored each other through the layers of their expensive clothes. The gentleness of his first kiss was quickly replaced by a far more demanding force, and Kit responded quickly and eagerly to his demands and made a few of her own. The tenderness his first kiss had evoked was rapidly turning into something much more potent as his tongue moved across the roof of her mouth while his hands moved to find the most sensitive areas of her back. She held on to his shoulders, wondering if the next wave of delight was going to be the one to push them over into an endless sea of pleasure. In this new world made up of black velvet and sparkling gems there was only one slim streak of reality. *Do you want the first time for the both of you to be in an automobile?* it asked with the cold glint of steel in the sunlight, and slowly she began to draw away from him.

"We'd better start back to Los Angeles," she said as soon as she could get her breath when the kiss ended. She pressed her lips against Greg's temple as he rested his head against her shoulder. "We both have to go to work tomorrow."

He kissed the side of her neck and laughed quietly. "So the prosaic business world intrudes," he teased.

"Is running a motion picture studio really commonplace?"

185

she countered.

"It is when nothing special is going on. I sit at my desk all day and think of you. But I'd do that no matter how much work there was."

"Compliments, my love, are going to get you everything," Kit said as they parted reluctantly and Greg slid back behind the driver's seat. "But right now we've had our ration for tonight."

"Do you realize that the rooms you have at Mallory's and Rupert's were mine when the house was Sin and Caro's?" Gregory said sometime later when he pulled into the driveway of the twelve-room Tudor-style house in the six-hundred block of West Adams Boulevard.

"What an intriguing thought," Kit said as he switched off the ignition. "But Mallory's redone the rooms, and if I remember correctly you didn't live there very long since you were just marking time until the Alexandria opened."

"That's true, but you know how Mallory is about showing off her handiwork, so I know exactly what your bedroom looks like."

Thanks to the softly diffused light coming from inside the house, Kit could see the laughter on his face, and she slid sideways on the seat to kiss him. "First your rooms, then my rooms, but I think it would be better if the guest suite never became *our* room. There are some places a couple should never go together."

Greg laughed. "Then I can't charm my way upstairs into your boudoir?"

Kit felt amused and serious at the same time. "As much as I'm in the mood to be charmed, it wouldn't be right, and I think you know that already."

"I do, and it's not the sort of thing I like to do in a friend's house, no matter how liberal they are."

For a second, Kit half-expected Greg to ask her to come

back to the Alexandria with him, but instead he got out and came round to open the car door for her. Mallory and Rupert weren't keeping tabs on them, but the same didn't hold true for their servants, and as soon as Greg opened the door on her side the front door opened, and Dovedale could be seen silhouetted in the light coming from the entry foyer.

"Shall we tell him our news?" Kit asked as she stepped from the running board to the driveway, the gravel crunching softly under her shoes, her hands warm in Greg's.

"Let's. That way we not only assure Rupert's esteemed butler that we're still perfectly respectable, but we can get used to telling everyone that we're engaged."

"As long as you've put it that way—"

Laughing, they approached the front door which Dovedale opened all the way for them. "Good evening, Miss Allen, Mr. West. I trust you had a pleasant evening in Pasadena."

"Very, very pleasant, Dovedale," Kit said, proudly tucking an arm through Greg's as they stood together in the large, airy entry hall which the Randalls used as an art gallery to show off their collection of prints and watercolors. "We have some very happy news, and we'd like you to be the first to know."

"Tonight I asked this very beautiful lady to marry me," Greg continued, "and I'm very happy to tell you that she said yes."

"My best wishes to you both." Slowly, Dovedale's serious face became wreathed in a smile. "And I'm sure Mr. and Mrs. Randall are going to be delighted when you tell them your most delightful news."

"We certainly hope so, but that will have to wait for daylight," Kit answered.

"Would you care for some champagne. There's a split of Moet in the refrigerator, and it won't take but a moment."

Kit and Greg exchanged glances. "No, thank you, Dovedale," he said quickly. "We've already had champagne tonight, and I still have to drive back to the Alexandria. We'll just go into the drawing room and say good-night."

"Of course, Mr. West. If you and Miss Allen change your minds about the champagne, just ring for me, I'll be in the dining room. Mr. and Mrs. Randall had quite an anniversary feast tonight."

"We've been warned," Kit whispered as they went into the drawing room.

"I can't say I like knowing that I'm expected to keep to my best behavior, but it's nice to know that even here in Los Angeles, Dovedale is loyal to all the proper traditions. My houseman, Moss, is like that—very discreet, but I always know he's there."

"Remember, you have your reputation as the city's most eligible bachelor to start living down."

"Don't remind me."

"Only this once," she said as they closed the double doors behind them. "I love this room. Was it very different when this house was Sin and Caro's?"

"More Oriental, with one of those spectacular pictorial rugs. But I like it now, it's very modern."

In the large, square room, Mallory had had the wall behind the marble fireplace paved with squares of antique mirrors so that no matter where one stood their reflection was thrown back. The rug was a modern creation, woven in Tiensten; a thick, lush wool pile of varying shades of celadon with touches of black and lemon, making it a perfect background for the cream, brocade-covered furniture, as well as a perfect setting for the paintings hung around the room.

"Only Mallory and Rupert would move to Los Angeles and then purchase a painting showing an early spring view of Central Park," Kit said as they admired the painting by the American Impressionist Willard Metcalf.

"It rather belongs, but that may just be a result of Mallory's skill. But my favorite is Robert William Vonnok's field of poppies, and—oh, the hell with the paintings," he said sharply. "Right now, I don't care about them, I want to kiss you!"

"And the feeling is very mutual," Kit said, and locked her hands behind his neck. She was ever conscious that Dovedale was just at the other side of the entrance hall and that they hadn't locked the doors, but she was even more aware of Greg, and as soon as his long, hard body pressed against her it was time to forget about propriety.

His hands curved around her waist and his lips touched hers in light kisses; once, twice, there was no rush, and the atmosphere around them became warmer and more urgent. She moved closer to him as their kiss deepened and his embrace became more demanding. She felt the room begin to spin around her and Greg was the only solid object left. It was like riding some wonderful carousel, and she never wanted it to end. . . .

"I have to go now, or else I'll take you upstairs," he said thickly, reluctantly, the reality that this was neither the time nor the place dawning unhappily upon him.

"Oh, that sounds so wonderful." Kit rested her cheek against Greg's, both of them flushed with the desire their close contact had raised. Technically, they were free to do as they pleased as long as they remained within the bounds of good taste, but at this moment they had too many entanglements around them to act as they wanted. "I hate to say good-night to you. I want tonight, right now, to go on and get better and better. But we'll have to stop and begin again tomorrow," she finished regretfully.

"I suppose I should thank you for saving our reputations," Greg murmured whimsically, pressing his lips against her temple. "For a man who supposedly can handle any situation, I suddenly feel like an awkward boy."

"No, you're not. You're wonderful." She tightened her hold on him, stroking the back of his neck under the stiff collar of his dress shirt. "You didn't calculate tonight, we just

189

let it all happen between us. That's the way it should be when you're in love, and if you'd planned out every single detail, every move you made, right down to your proposal and each kiss, I'd really doubt if you really loved me."

Upstairs in the master suite, in the four poster bed with posts of heavy glass topped with glass plumes and curtained on four sides with cream voile lined in pale pink chiffon, under the pink satin comforters, and between the pale pink cotton damask sheets, Mallory lifted her head from her husband's shoulder and stopped caressing him.

"Why did you stop?" Rupert inquired in a contented voice. "You were just getting someplace interesting."

"Kit is home," she said as she sat up in bed and tucked the expensive, handmade sheet around her. "I heard Greg's car drive up, and now he's just left."

"That's Greg's loss," Rupert muttered, and pulled Mallory down to him again. "She's on the other side of the house and probably couldn't care less about what we're doing."

Mallory laughed softly as Rupert's arms encircled her. For a moment she buried her face in the warm hollow at the base of his throat, revelling in the satiny feel of his skin. "Of course she doesn't, but Greg *is* something of a mystery man—rather like you."

"Me, a mystery?" Rupert laughed softly. "My life is an open book."

"So you like to think," she shot back, and they grappled across the bed, laughing together as their play turned into something much different.

"And that's enough about other people, even if they are our dear friends," Rupert commanded. "It's our anniversary, and the only thing we have to concentrate on is each other. Four years ago we were at the St. Regis for our wedding night, and it's time to relive that moment."

"What a perfect way to celebrate." Mallory ran a hand

lightly along Rupert's spine, delighting in the feel of his body as his arms closed tighter around her. "You are my husband, I love you with all my heart, and right now I think it's time I show that to you all over again."

Kit adored the guest suite, and she thought that Mallory had ample reason to be proud of her skill as a decorator. The cream-colored walls were set off by grisaille panels which were repeated on the decorative screen, the black and white marble fireplace was echoed in the marble tops of the two-, three-, and four-drawer chests, and the white-painted furniture were excellent reproductions of graceful eighteenth-century pieces. The thick carpet underfoot was of a deep rosy hue, while the fabric covering the comfortable chairs and the lit de repos had peonies splattered on a pure white background, and vases full of rich flowers rested on book-laden tables. The rock crystal-based lamps were already turned on when Kit returned, and now, several minutes after she and Greg had said their last reluctant good-night, she sat down at the writing table, determined to draft a cable to her mother.

"The cable is going to be easy," she said aloud, leaning back in the cane-backed chair, "but what am I going to say in the letter?"

The long cream and pink silk curtains fluttered in the nighttime breeze, and the clean California air that circulated around the chamber and mixed together the scent of the flowers and her Guerlain perfume only resharpened her longing for Greg. If Dovedale hadn't been downstairs when they returned, they might well have been together in her bed right now.

We love each other and we want a life together, she thought. Rupert and Mallory wouldn't have thought we were disgracing their home. Of course, with a little more forethought on both our parts, we could have gone back to the Alexandria, and if we were only a bit more uninhibited we could have made love in the Fiat's back seat.

That's semi-public love, not a very pleasant memory to look back on, she reminded herself. When the moment is right, we'll both know it.

Fortunately, Kit knew, her mother wasn't the sort who cared overly about genealogy, but she would want to know something about the man who was going to be her son-in-law. Still, what could she say?

She wrote out the cable quickly, and then decided that the letter could wait. She was starting to feel tired, and anything she wrote now would look like gibberish in the morning.

I have a busy day tomorrow, Kit thought, standing up and kicking off her evening shoes. I have a shop to get ready for a grand opening, and now I have my wedding to plan. I knew that Greg and I were meant for each other the moment I saw him, but how am I going to tell my mother that I'm going to marry a man who reinvented his life at the turn of the century?

Chapter 8

"What was the first thing that Sin and Caro said when you told them that we're engaged?" Kit wanted to know as Greg drove along the bumpy road off Sunset Boulevard.

"Are you sure you want to hear this?"

"Why, is it that awful?"

"That depends on what you consider awful. Sin said that he was worried I was going to turn into a stupid twit and let you go."

"And Caro?"

Greg began to smile. "She wanted to know why we couldn't get this settled in Chicago, and then asked what I was going to do for a ring."

"For her or me?" she asked archly as the Fiat passed over what seemed to be a small boulder. "What kind of an excuse for a road are we on? Another rock like that and the undercarriage of this expensive car is going to be on the ground."

"The ring, my darling, is for you, as if you didn't know. I phoned Shreve's in San Francisco yesterday morning. It seems they have your ring size on file from a previous visit, so they aren't going to have any problems. Do you want me to surprise you, or shall I ask them to send a salesman down on the next train with a selection of engagement rings?"

"Oh, I want to be surprised. Speaking of which, I wrote a long letter to my mother yesterday. I even sent along some snapshots of you that I took in Chicago and on the train."

"That should reassure your mother that I'm a respectable man with honorable intentions," he said, just managing to get the words out with a straight face.

"Not with that smile you're not! Besides, my mother's an artist. She looks for other qualities."

"I'm glad to hear that—I think."

"You'll like my mother, but I'd better warn you about one thing."

"What's that?" Despite the fact that in a very short time from now, after he told Kit his story, their happy conversation might very well be a fond memory, he couldn't lose his sense of the absurd. But he couldn't put off the inevitable any longer. All day Friday, even while he called the San Francisco jeweler and the development company here in Los Angeles, he knew they were at a turning point. He had told her that the past he told everyone else about was a lie; now he had to tell her the truth.

"She'll probably want to paint you. She has an excellent eye for bone structure."

"Then she must never stop painting you."

"Not since I was sixteen. About then, between mothers and daughters, there's a blurring of illusion and reality, and that's a situation the artist is better off not exploring. That's a lot of artist talk in case you're interested."

Greg's graceful hands tightened on the steering wheel. "I know something about illusion and reality, and it exists beyond mothers and daughters," he said, not taking his eyes off the road, not trusting himself to look at Kit. In a few minutes he'd tell her about his past, but he had to keep control now. "That's what life is, what my life is, what people think is real about me and what I know is the truth."

*   *   *

"Would you care to tell me where we are?" Kit asked five minutes later when Greg turned off the road and pulled the Fiat to a stop at the edge of what looked like a field covered with some unidentifiable vines. "I'm lost whenever I leave downtown, and this looks like a farm."

"We are now standing in the municipality of Beverly Hills," Greg supplied, and managed a slight smile, "and we're north of Sunset Boulevard. I spoke to Burton Green, the area's developer, and he thought we might like to come over and take a look at eight acres he has available. After we decide one way or the other we can go over to the Beverly Hills Hotel for lunch. It's not much to look at—a rather unattractive building covered in ivy—but the food is very good."

Kit looked doubtful, not at the idea of lunch but at where they were standing. She wasn't a snob, but this was not West Adams Boulevard or Chester Place. "I know everyone's talking about Beverly Hills as *the* up-and-coming place, but what *are* those vines we're looking at?"

"It's a lima bean field."

"Is the movie business so bad that you want to become a vegetable farmer?" She paused and took a deep breath to calm her increasing heartbeat. Something was wrong, and her instinct told her she was about to find out what, the only question was would she be better off *not* knowing? "Or, are we here for another reason?"

"This parcel of land *is* for sale, but I did drive us here with an ulterior motive. I have something to tell you, and I wanted to take you someplace where we couldn't be interrupted."

"Then let's get out of the car. It's a beautiful Saturday morning, and I'd rather hear what you have to tell me out in the sunshine," Kit said, and without waiting for Greg, she opened the door and stepped out of the car. It had to be at least eighty, Kit mused, taking off her Poiret auto coat of blue striped linen to reveal a Poiret summer dress of ecru

195

linen with rich blue embroidery. I wonder if after you've lived here awhile the beautiful weather makes you discount trouble. I haven't gotten to that point yet, and I hope I never do.

Kit left the coat on the front seat and then walked toward the front of the car. "Aren't you going to join me?" she asked, leaning against the shiny black fender. "And if you have something to tell me I'd like to hear it straight out."

Almost as if he were using a delaying tactic, Greg took off his suit jacket and rolled up the sleeves of his white shirt before joining her, leaning against the fender so he could see her face under the wide brim of her Panama straw hat. He knew that she wouldn't ever try to hide her reactions or dissimilate her feeling about what he was going to tell her, but he wanted to look directly at her while he spoke.

"I'm not going to insult either of us by saying you're free to break our engagement when you hear my story. We both know that you'll do exactly as you please, and I wouldn't want you to be anything but your independent self." His little preamble was over, but he wasn't sure how to begin. At the beginning, he thought, and just be thankful that Kit isn't the sort who spreads stories. "You were right when you said I wasn't American-born, and that Gregory West isn't my real name."

"Yes." Kit instantly decided that for the time being the less said the better.

"Gregory West is my legal name, though, thanks to a helpful Federal judge here in Los Angeles. My real name, no, that's not right; the name I was born with was Alexander Gregori Dimitri Vestovanova," he said, and waited for her reaction. Would she be able to identify the name?

She did. No one who had been to St. Petersburg, even if they moved only on the fringes of the most elite society, could help but know the name.

"Are you a member of the Vestovanova family with the palace on the Moika Canal?"

196

"Yes." For a second, that one word was all he could manage. The wounds he thought had closed years before were about to break open. "I'm the youngest son of Prince Ivan Vestovanova. I was born in that house on the Moika, and on one frigid night I had to leave there with only a little more than the clothes on my back and a lot of identity papers that said I was someone else."

It was only the barest outline, the slightest hint of what had happened, but it was the absolute truth, Kit had no doubt about that. And she couldn't say a word. Any questions or comments she made now would sound inane, or, worse, curiosity-ridden. The only thing she could do was stay close to him and listen.

"In America, in a family that would be considered the equivalent of mine, a son would have to run away because of his disgust with his parents' wealth and how they lived and spent their vast fortune," Greg said after a long minute spent gathering his varied thoughts together. Now, of all times, he couldn't forget a single detail or leave anything out. Nothing was to be filled in later, and the Russian turn of his nature insisted that if he made the slightest evasion he would lose her. "That's not how it was with me. I don't want you to think for one minute that I left for a high-minded reason. I ran because I was a victim of circumstance—and because I may have murdered someone."

His voice, always so low and rich, held such an uncompromising note that for a long minute Kit could only regard him while a slow wave of surprise welled up in her.

"You've never murdered anyone," she said, and Greg found himself drawing unexpected strength from the certainty in her voice.

"I don't want to think I did. I don't want to think that for one night a very dark side of my personality surfaced and took over. But I have to face the reality that it might have happened."

"Did this . . . incident involve a woman?" Kit asked. Her

heartbeat was still rapid, but some of the awful feeling of dread that had been building in her had receded, not enough for true relief but enough for rational thought. The puzzle was almost in place now, only the corners remained to be filled in. "When a man looks like you, it should be—has to be—cherchez la femme."

"Thank you," he said, and for a moment they held each other close. "When you told me you'd been to Russia, I was in shock, and then when you seemed to glean things about my past using nothing but your instinct, I wanted to keep you at arm's length, not to get as close to you as my heart wanted to be, but I was already in love with you by then."

"I'm glad you're a man who listens to his heart," she said, resting against him. How wonderful he felt to lean against, and how much she loved him. And it was also a measure of his love and trust that he was willing to take this risk and tell her about his past.

"If I'd really listened to my heart, I would have asked you to marry me five minutes after I saw you in that pink taffeta suit."

"Strawberry," she corrected gently, kissing him under an ear and letting her tongue trace the outline.

"That tickles."

"Anything to have your attention," she began in a low voice.

"You're whispering. Are we in danger of being overheard?"

"Haven't you heard that lima beans love to talk?"

"They're the gossipy sort then?"

"Absolutely." She trailed a row of kisses along his hairline. "May I ask you a question?"

"Anything at all."

"Did you have an affair with Anna Pavlova?"

Their few minutes of much-needed silliness was at an end and he slowly pulled away from her, but kept his hands cupped around her shoulders.

"If I had, I probably wouldn't be here with you, and where I would be is something I don't want to think about too often. I was a brand new cavalry officer."

Another theory explained, she thought, but all she said was, "Going into the Maryinsky is like stepping into a magic world. Even if you didn't want to, you couldn't help but be attracted to one of the dancers—it's an almost mandatory reaction for a normal man."

"Don't give me virtues I didn't have when I was twenty-one," Greg said roughly. "Believe me, Kit, when I went to the Maryinsky, it wasn't solely for the dance." Suddenly, with an unexpected smile, he asked, "If it had been Pavlova, you wouldn't have minded?"

"You don't have to look so raffish! And no, I wouldn't have minded, and if you can't guess the reasons why, you're not the man-about-town you say you are."

"I've never claimed that distinction—other people have been more than happy to do that for me."

"Oh, I know that attitude well," she said, and then they both knew they were down to the real details. "Greg . . ."

He told her the whole dark, tangled, twisted tale. He told her about his family, about his friends and the experiences they'd shared together in the heady, opulent atmosphere of St. Petersburg, and, most difficult of all, he told her about Natalia and the night that was like a photograph with the center cut out of it.

At some point during his recitation they walked to the edge of the lima bean field. With their arms around each other they were such a picture of two people in love that if an official of the Rodeo Land and Development Company happened to come out to see how they were doing, he would automatically think that they were deciding on what sort of house to build, and which architect and landscape gardener to hire. He would never believe that their topic of conversation was anything but joyful.

"After Boris said he could get me out of Russia, everything

happened so quickly that I had no reaction. I just did what I was told," he said as they walked slowly back to the car. "I know my survival instinct must have surfaced at some point, or I never would have made it to Brussels let alone New York. But I was so damn confused and numb that I couldn't focus on anything or anyone."

"And you were terribly, miserably lonely. Everything you'd been brought up to believe in, every privilege you had by right of birth was taken away."

"No, it wasn't taken away. I gave it up. I gave it up because I was afraid of my father's wrath, afraid to take the consequences for a murder that if I did commit I certainly didn't mean to do." Abruptly, he sat down on the running board, his face a study in bitter remembrance. "I was only twenty-one, an officer almost without responsibilities, all the money I could spend, and friends as eager for adventurous escapades and beautiful women as I was."

"I'm not interested in passing moral sentence; first, because my own life isn't particularly blameless, and second, because you went from *jeune garcon bien eleve* to *homme du monde* by a very rocky road."

"Why is it that certain phrases always sound better in French?" Greg asked as Kit sat down beside him, and without waiting for an answer he plunged on, "Do you still think I couldn't murder anyone?"

"A human being is always capable of murder, but if you want to know if I think you murdered Natalia, the answer is—and will always be—no."

Greg felt the chambers of his heart fill with love. "And I haven't shocked you?"

"Not at this point in my life."

"But there is still one constant, something that won't change. *I can't remember what happened!*"

"Which can mean that you weren't responsible."

"Which is something I can't be sure of. And I may not be the man you think I am, even now. Maybe I'm only honest because the situation to be dishonest didn't present itself."

"Don't say that—don't you even think such a thing!" Kit exclaimed, jumping to her feet. "Don't you realize that at a certain point you stopped being a victim of bad circumstances and made a clear choice? You chose to be the very best person you could be."

"It was circumstance. I had no choice," Greg insisted as he got to his feet.

"I don't want to hear your Russian superstitions. Any man who looks like you," she went on, grabbing his shoulders, "could have found some rich woman to support you. If your aim in life was to be a lap dog, you wouldn't have worked on a road crew or as a valet, or taken a chance with Sinclair when he was supposed to be the most notorious man in New York."

"I just don't want you to have any romantic illusions about me," he said. "I may not be worth it."

"Oh, yes you are! You're going to have to tell me something more recent than over fourteen years ago."

"There's Jessica."

"She said that you would have to tell me about that."

"Generous of her. No, I mean that."

"She said it wasn't terribly intimate." Kit knew that he wasn't about to tell her details about any of his married ladies since they could not be considered her competition, but Jessica Gilbert *did* fall into that category, and he wouldn't hide anything from her. "Were the two of you in love?"

Greg laughed and shielded his eyes from the sun. "I think we were very taken and delighted with each other, but we weren't in love, and the . . . disagreement we had was the best thing that could have happened."

"I agree with you."

"You're thinking about end results again, aren't you?"

"It helps to get past the bad spots. Did you sleep with Jessica?"

"Almost. It was the night after Wilson's election, and we came back from a victory party full of champagne and playfulness. We were in my suite for a nightcap—something neither of us needed. One thing led to another, and when she saw that I had an icon on my bedside table she asked if I would consider removing it. I said no, and then we said some interesting things to each other, effectively ending what never started. Do you object to an icon?"

"How large is it?" Kit asked, recalling some of the reliquaries she'd seen in St. Petersburg and Moscow. With their frames of precious metals and studded with the finest stones, they had left her with very mixed feelings, but she couldn't very well deny Greg what might be the last link with the life he'd left behind.

"It's a schoolboy's icon."

"I see. But I have to let you know that it isn't what's beside your bed that bothers me, it's who kept you company *in* your bed that matters to me!"

"There are two bedrooms in my suite," he said, and drew her into his arms. "One of them is, for obvious reasons, in need of being totally redecorated, and the other is my private preserve. Can you guess which one the icon is in?"

Chapter 9

On Sunday evening, Caroline and Sinclair gave a Chinese dinner for their friends in their Norman-style twenty-room house in exclusive Chester Place. Located between Twenty-third Street and Adams Boulevard, and surrounded by a beautiful wrought-iron fence, this elegant oasis was home to Los Angeles's most prominent and wealthy citizens, and was owned in its entirety by oilman Edward L. Doheny, who resided in a mansion built in the Spanish Gothic style on grounds landscaped to resemble a Victorian garden.

The Pooles had been in residence in this enclave since early 1911, but they had already purchased several large parcels of land in Bel-Air and Hancock Park as well as the municipality of Beverly Hills in preparation for their next move. They were not the favorites of their more conservative, traditional neighbors. In a city that boasted a large number of weekly Wednesday-night prayer meetings, Caroline and Sinclair were the undisputed leaders of the most eclectic, sophisticated social set. They and their friends had the best and fastest automobiles, the most expensive clothes, and the most handsomely decorated houses where, whether it was a formal dinner or, like tonight, an informal gathering with the men in business suits and the women in silk dresses, it was *the* place to be. With apparently the greatest of ease they appeared to be racy, while in actuality they were able to avoid any of the more spurious overtones that the word and attitude implied. In the large dining room where an eighteenth-century Chippendale table and chairs with the overhead chandelier from Waterford and side tables holding silver candelabras and an assortment of Oriental porcelains provided a formal, elegant tone, the atmosphere was almost theatrical, boarding-house convivial with platters being passed back and forth without a break in the conversation.

Tonight was a welcome-back-to-California party as well as an informal celebration of Kit and Greg's engagement, and they invited their closest friends. Rupert and Mallory, of course; Drake and Nan Sloane, who were willing to tear themselves away from their brand new Bel-Air mansion for the feast of Chinese food; and Barbara and Winston Lucas, up from their horse ranch in Santa Barbara, had motored over from their Hancock Park house (besides, Caro told Sin, she was sure both Nan and Barbara were consumed with curiosity about Kit, and wouldn't miss this chance to see her if they were serving sawdust and library paste). Jessica Gilbert came with her publisher, Frank Rundstadt, and Grazia D'Ettiene was with Frank's associate, Matt Arnold.

The centerpiece was a colorful Chinese export tureen filled with white carnations instead of the usual lush arrangements favored on more formal evenings, champagne had been banished in favor of tall glasses filled with Danish beer, the china was a simple blue and white pattern, and although each place was set with Tiffany's uncomplicated Shell and Thread pattern silverware, all were making good use of the chopsticks which were also supplied.

The winter melon soup was finished and had been perfect preparation for the butterfly shrimps, the fried rice, and the Peking fried rice, while the spring rolls were a very welcomed side dish for the hacked chicken in a spicy sauce, the shrimp in lobster sauce, the sautéed scallops in black bean sauce, the shredded chicken with sesame sauce, and the whole sea bass in brown sauce.

"So it's going to be Beverly Hills for the two of you?" Sinclair asked. "Are you going to build now or wait for the lima bean harvest?"

"Funny," Greg said, putting down his chopsticks. "I think you really want Kit and me to be the pioneers out there, getting all the rough spots out of the way before you and Caro decide to build."

"What else is an associate for?"

"Don't listen to him, just go ahead and start interviewing architects," Caro advised. "Robert Farquhar did this house, and we can recommend him."

"There are a lot of good architects around," Rupert put in. "But you have to know what you want."

"Drake and I have hired Irving Gill from San Diego to do our new beach house at La Jolla. He's so devoted to authenticity that he's going to have Hopi Indians who are skilled in adobe work build the house," Nan Sloane told them. "Do you like the Spanish mode, Kit?"

"It's bad enough there are so many awful-looking Spanish-style houses around, I don't have to compound the problem by living in one," Kit told the tall, pretty, auburn-haired young woman seated across from her who had once amused Greg in his leisure hours. She wasn't about to be jealous at this stage, but she wasn't going to stifle her opinions for the sake of appearing agreeable. "A hacienda is a working ranch, not a style of architecture. Who was responsible for putting up those awful faux-Spanish and Victorian gimcrack buildings?"

"You can stab me with your chopsticks, Kit," Drake Sloane said. Dark, sleek, and handsome as a matinee idol, Nan's husband reminded Kit of Sebastian Creighton, except that the wealthy real estate developer, whose family had come to southern California in 1876 when the Southern Pacific built the first railroad into Los Angeles, had a healthy sense of humor. "It was my family that built those monsters. Just the Spanish ones, though," he added taking two more spring rolls before passing the platter to Grazia. "The hideous architecture began in the late 1880s when the first large group of settlers from the Middle West came out. That's where the badly designed bay windows and overlay of gingerbread comes in."

"Tell Kit why there are so many front porches," Winston Lucas said. He was a tall, rangy man in his early forties with a pleasant face.

"These new arrivals in Los Angeles built their new houses with front porches so they could sit out there and enjoy the twilight," Drake told her in a voice that clearly stated that this was a private "inside" joke. A joke that Kit was already aware of.

"There really aren't any twilights here, it gets dark almost immediately. Didn't those people realize that *before* they built?"

"This is Los Angeles where you don't have to notice anything you don't want to see," Rupert said wickedly.

"Still, that doesn't forgive you for the previous sins of your family," Jessica added, and everyone else around the table began to laugh.

"All right, all right, stop laughing—I'll admit to this blot on the Sloane escutcheon." Drake put a hand over his heart in mock sorrow. "Back about twelve years ago, my father and the band of happy real estate subdividers he was a part of decided to forgo the luxury of an architect and let the contractors build an assortment of Spanish haciendas."

"And it's equally obvious that none of the contractors bothered to find out what hacienda really means," Greg finished. "No wonder the Mexican aristocrats who came up here to get away from the revolutions keep to their own little enclave on West Adams. They're probably plotting revenge right now."

"Now, *that's* a new version of the Mexican Peril," Matt

206

Arnold said, impatiently pushing his wire-rimmed eye-glasses back up his nose. "I'm originally from San Francisco—"

"Don't worry, we won't tell anyone," Greg interrupted with a sly wink, playing out the subtle rivalry the two cities engaged in.

"And I can't quite get used to how people down here get jumpy about the least little thing," Matt went on, unperturbed. "Look at the way all the society folk here won't have anything to do with anyone who's involved with the movies."

"I know, and it almost makes one forget that President Eliot of Harvard once referred to reporters as 'drunks, deadbeats, and bummers,'" Greg said. "And since you live at the Garden Court Apartments which pride itself on being so exclusive, you're probably glad that it's taking the heat off you."

"Touché. But I paid my dues during my reporting days for the *World* in New York by living at 144th off Riverside."

"We've all paid our dues—one way or another," Greg said quickly, not wanting to let this conversation go down *that* path. "Now we can all pick our neighborhoods and pay the rent."

"As long as we're back to the subject of real estate, why don't you and Kit buy some property in Hancock Park?" Barbara Lucas asked, her berry-brown eyes bright with friendship. "We'd love to have you as neighbors."

"Thank you, but you know that in Hancock Park, the residents don't let people build when they won't join the Los Angeles Country Club," Greg reminded her.

"Sin, don't you think this rule you have about your executives not being allowed to join any country clubs is a bit arbitrary?" Winston asked.

"No, I don't. If I can play golf on the Municipal Links, so can anyone who works for me, and since most people building houses today are putting in tennis courts, that sport is also taken care of," Sinclair replied with absolutely no trace of humor. "I remember the clubs my father and I belonged to, and I remember the letters asking us to quietly resign so we wouldn't have to be embarrassed by their expelling us. I have no objection if one of my executives goes as a guest to a party in a private club, I've done it myself. It's being a member and conducting business on the premises I can't stand. It's *wrong*."

Sinclair's voice was so firm, so unyielding, everyone at the table grew serious and it took several minutes for their conversation to get back on track. Their usual slightly provocative exchanges resumed, however, and when the platters were scraped clean for the last time and everyone had eaten every possible mouthful, Caro stood up in a crisp rustle of Cheruit's blue taffeta with white charmeuse and lace.

"Everyone upstairs for tea and almond cakes," she announced, "and anyone who complains about the location doesn't get invited back!"

"Caro means that, too," Greg whispered as he put an arm around Kit's waist. "What do you say to a nice walk in the garden? I'll show you the night-blooming jasmine."

"Is that the outdoor equivalent of showing me your etchings?"

"You'll have to come outside to find that out."

"Then lead the way."

They were in the entrance hall of Caen marble with its large curving staircase before Sin caught up with them.

"In case you missed it, you're not heading in the direction of the stairs."

"No, but this is the way to the garden."

They stopped beside the statue of the Chinese deity Quan Yin which dominated the center of the hall and was lighted from above by a spotlight concealed in the Empire chandelier hanging overhead.

"Apparently giving a newly engaged couple a splendid dinner party isn't enough to keep them around for dessert."

"Come on, Sin, you just enjoy being a host too much to let anyone escape from your reach."

"The only thing worse than having a wife who remembers all my party tricks is having my closest associate remember them as well!"

"That's how it is, Sin. We all know things about each other, some sad, and some funny," Greg said, pulling Kit close to him. "You know a great deal about me, and if you let Kit and me go out to the garden so we can be alone together for a while, I promise I won't tell anyone that Mr. Wong told me back in 1902 that it was a good thing you and Caro were getting married, because her excellent Peking accent was definitely superior to your very execrable Cantonese intonation!"

"We had the hedges trimmed yesterday; don't fool around near the calla lilies, Caro says they're very innocent and sensitive, and in general don't do anything that'll attract the neighbors' attention—they don't care for us very much as it is, and on the whole we'd rather move on our own than be chased out of Chester Place because two guests indulged in some interesting high spirits," Sin said with vast amusement, managing, as usual, to have the last word.

"This was the very first time I was able to refer to my past in fun," Greg said as they walked along the garden path bordered by tall, pyramidal and regal mounds of mixed phlox. "There isn't anything that Sin and Caro don't know about Alexander Vestovanova, but it's almost like having a mad relative hidden in the attic—we never mention it."

"Do you want me to call you Alexander when we're alone like this?" Kit questioned softly. She knew this was a delicate and potentially explosive topic, but she also felt that there was no reason why Greg—at least when they were in private—had to act as if his past hadn't happened.

"I was never Alexander, my family and friends called me

209

Sasha," he said as they walked past bushes of New Marguerite carnations and Marchioness of Lansdowne peonies. "That's a fine name for a boy or a very young man, but I get uncomfortable when I think of it being attached to a grown man."

"You have a very definite point there." In the silvery, diffused light coming from the house, her double tunic Paquin dress of pale green silk turned shimmery. This part of the garden was full of night-blooming plants; small, delicate flowers. Calla lilies and camellias and night-blooming jasmine abounded, making the area a very romantic bower. They sat down on a small stone bench, and her slit skirt showed off her legs to their best advantage. "I don't think I could call you anything but Greg or Gregory. Except for darling, dearest, sweetheart and assorted other endearments," she went on, leaning against him. "Did we really eat so much food?"

"We did, but wait until Mr. Wong makes his famous Peking duck—otherwise well-behaved people turn into a starving horde."

"I can believe that. And I suppose Mr. Wong will have a cousin handy to come and cook for us when we build our own home?"

"I'd be very surprised if he didn't. Are you really adamant about not having a Spanish-style house, or were you just being contrary because of Nan?"

"And wouldn't that just feed your male vanity?" Kit laughed. "But really, I don't want a house reminiscent of old Spain or Mexico, not even a properly authenticated one designed by a major architect. I'd be much happier with a colonial, or even something very beaux-arts, if you want to be very formal."

"We have plenty of time to make a final decision," Greg said as they settled back to enjoy the warm night. "But there's something I'd like to ask you that may seem a little foolish."

"You want to know how I came to visit Russia twice," Kit hazarded.

"Are you a witch?"

"No, it just seemed to be a logical progression. St. Petersburg and Moscow aren't right up there with London and Paris as the cities Americans abroad love to visit."

"You're not the usual tourist. Was it a very strange visit for you?"

"Yes and no. At first I thought I was living in a fantasy, and then there would be something familiar like a flower seller or a confectioner's shop."

"When was your first visit?"

"In 1907. My mother and I had been trying to decide whether to ride the Orient Express or go to Russia, and when Mummy was commissioned by *The Century* to illustrate a new Russian novel they were going to serialize, the decision was made for us."

"St. Petersburg isn't particularly welcoming for two women alone."

"We knew that, but our embassy was very welcoming. The ambassador gave a dinner for us at the Restaurant de Paris, and we had invitations to all the after-theatre dinners at A L'Ours and Danon."

"I trust that was the new Danon near the Pyevtcheski Bridge. I'd hate to think of you and your mother dining among the raffish clientele at Old Danon," he told her humorously.

"Spoken like a man who must have been a very good customer."

"It was where I plotted what turned out to be my downfall."

There was no possible way for Kit to reply to that, but she couldn't resist asking, "Do you ever think about being able to go back?"

"I can't. If I ever show my face in St. Petersburg again, I'd be arrested—or murdered."

"But you can't be sure." Kit pulled away from him. "Isn't it possible that your father changed his mind?"

"You don't know my father."

"Isn't it possible that it was all some sort of awful prank, and Natalia isn't dead? It's not that I want you to go back to a way of life that's alien to you now, I'm only asking because I love you and I don't want you to be any more unhappy or distressed than you've been."

"I know that, and I love you even more for your concern, but I can't make use of your suggestions. I can't even hope that Natalia didn't die that night, either through my fault or by some other means." A strained look appeared on his face. "When the Imperial Ballet made its first American tour in 1910, I went to see them dance in San Francisco. Peggy gave a party for Anna Pavlova, and against my better judgment I went. Pavlova looked at me oddly for a moment, and someone else said something to me in Russian, but gave up when I said I couldn't speak the language."

"You were very brave to go to that party."

"And I thought I had to be the greatest fool. I spent the first half-hour near the door so that I could run the moment I was recognized. That didn't happen, and Peggy was a little annoyed with me."

"I'm sure that you were able to charm her out of her miffed mood," Kit couldn't resist saying, and she reached out to trace a finger around the outline of his rich mouth. "All you needed was a secluded spot and a comfortable sofa, and after a few minutes Peggy probably didn't care that you'd been a bit of a reluctant guest."

"You're jealous, aren't you?" Greg asked, and couldn't help feeling a bit pleased. "You don't have to be now."

"Oh, I know that, and this is just about as sticky as I'm going to get about it," she said, resting against him. "You've told me what you couldn't tell another woman—except Caro—no matter how much you cared about her, and the only thing I'm indignant about is that she had you before I

212

did. Of course, when you soothed her it was probably never on a garden bench or in the back seat of an automobile!"

"But on the other hand, I'm not soothing your ruffled feathers, I'm only asking you questions about St. Petersburg —which so far sounds like a very correct visit made by a mother and daughter."

"Helped out by a simple suite at the Astoria Hotel and nice bouquets of flowers from the American Embassy, the New English Club, and the Literary and Artistic Society, and a few invitations to display on the mantelpiece and use to suitably impress the help," Kit said wryly. "It was the same way in Moscow at the Hotel National."

"Did you go to Moscow's Great Imperial Theatre?"

"Of course. And to a grand dinner at the Hermitage restaurant. The concert garden was in full bloom the night we were there, and we ate in the restaurants of Petrovski Park."

"On your first trip, you could only have gone to the Yar and the Mauritania; the Stryelna is open only in winter."

"We ate there during our second visit three years later— and that was the least of the differences. My mother and Vincent Lyman had just gotten married," she said, and told him how she came to join them in Europe, and their journey on the Orient Express. "We were back in Paris when Vincent was invited to come to St. Petersburg to give a series of lectures at the Engineers' Palace. We were all having such a good time we decided that that sounded like fun."

"And was it?"

"It was different that time—very, very different—and not because it was the beginning of November and not the end of August," she told him carefully.

Greg instantly picked up on the hesitation in her voice. "You can say anything you want to me, I'm as American as you are," he said, echoing the remark she'd made to him when they met. "You can't say anything that will insult me."

They looked at each other for a long minute, and Kit knew

that Greg had left Russia at exactly the right time in his life. Had the incident happened earlier, it might have destroyed him; if it happened when he was older, when his way of life and what he did and thought was set in concrete, he would never have been able to adapt, to change, to become the person he now was.

"On the surface it was just *more*. The hotel suites at the Astoria and the National were larger and more lavish, the flower arrangements bigger, and there were more invitations. When we went to Faberge, the salesmen showed us the best trinkets, and the antique dealers suddenly discovered a 'little something' they had tucked away that would be just perfect for us. In a way, I almost expected that treatment. Vincent's first wife had been a duke's daughter whose grandfather had been a British ambassador to Russia, all of which made my stepfather close to the peerage, and no society is too grand not to accept a proper Bostonian."

"And that was not the way you'd been treated when you and your mother were simply two wealthy women with no man."

He would never say "to protect you," but he knew that to Russia's ever-watchful, always suspicious secret police, three Americans with the best of connections would be of great interest.

"It was that and more. We had guides, servants, and officials hovering around us, bowing and scraping, but there was something about their smiles—," Kit hesitated for a long minute. "I think we were followed, if not all the time then part of it. For the month we were in Russia, I couldn't shake the feeling that someone knew our every move, and just for the fun of it would check through our mail. Greg, tell me I was imagining things."

It was growing cooler in the garden, but the flowers were still as fragrant, and as a cool breeze whispered through the thickly leaved trees, Kit wondered why they weren't taking

214

rich advantage of the voluptuously scented privacy. But I know why, she thought. Our attraction to each other was so immediate that we're still trying to fill in the missing pieces.

"Was I imagining things?" she insisted.

"No, and you and your mother were probably under some sort of surveillance on your first visit as well."

"What!"

"Don't look so shocked. The Okhrana is an accepted fact of life in Russia."

"Do you mean to tell me that you and your family were—?"

"No, not in the way you mean. But we all knew what was done and to whom." Greg was discussing things he hadn't even allowed himself to think about for nearly fifteen years, yet with Kit it was like having a normal conversation. "Artists are always suspect, well-to-do women artists are unexpected, so any interest they paid to you in 1907 was cursory."

"Meaning they didn't know what to make of us then, but three years later we were of more interest. My mother would have a fit if I told her," she said, well aware that she couldn't mention a word of this if she were to keep Greg's secret.

"Did your mother and stepfather have their suspicions?"

"Oh, yes. Vincent always thought our guides were a bit *too* conscientious and friendly, and he thought that his lectures at the Old Michael Palace were almost too well attended. Mummy said that she was never comfortable when she went out to sketch, she always felt someone was hiding behind a tree—and my mother doesn't care if someone looks over her shoulder while she works!"

"I can't wait to meet her," Greg said, kissing the side of her neck. "Shall we walk through the garden? That way, if they send a search party for us we can evade them."

They stood up and Kit put her arms around Greg's neck. "Do you think anyone in the house will believe we've only

215

been talking?" she asked, and began to kiss him.

"No," he replied, laughing quietly as her lashes fluttered against his cheeks in butterfly kisses, "they're probably expecting us to come back with grass stains!"

"Well?"

"Let's surprise our friends—for tonight at least," Greg said huskily, savoring their closeness as he kissed her forehead, her throat, her cheeks, and finally her lips.

"There is nothing better than being kissed by you," Kit said as she pressed her arms around his strong shoulders, "except for the next step."

I can't believe I just said that, Kit thought. I must sound like some passion-starved old maid. But I want to make love, and I want Greg to feel the same way—and he has to make the first move.

It was a foolish bit of etiquette, one of the silly games men and women play with each other. Had they relied on their first instincts, she knew, they would have been lovers that first night in Chicago, but now—

"We seem to have a slight logistical problem, don't we?" Greg said, his amusement obvious. "I think we're caught in our own good intentions."

Kit nodded in agreement, and a certain realization dawned. Could it be that he thought she was—? Could that have been one of his problems with Jessica? Well, he was going to find out sooner or later, and she'd rather tell him right now.

"You're not the first," she said quietly, as conversationally as she could, and waited for his reaction.

"Am I going to be the last?" he said, and his look told her he already knew the answer.

"I wouldn't have it any other way—provided it's mutual."

"I wouldn't have it any other way," he repeated, and there was no further need for words.

"We should go back inside," Greg said reluctantly a short

216

time later, and with equal reluctance, Kit agreed. When it was right for them again, when they felt the same heedless delight that they had in the Blackstone, they'd know it. Certain things had a natural progression.

"When do I get to see Hooper Studios?" she asked as they wandered along the neat brick pathways, arms around each other's waist.

"Tuesday."

"What's wrong with tomorrow?"

"I want to prepare a welcoming committee—it'll give most of the people something to do!"

"I was going to say thank-you."

"For that remark, you're going to have to earn your personally conducted guided tour. It's only one question, but if you don't answer it correctly I'll leave you with my secretary, Mrs. Rigby, who never knocks on my office door before walking in, while I sit at my desk and read the *Wall Street Journal.*"

Kit gave him a sidelong glance. "I'm absolutely terrified. Are you going to ask, or are you still thinking it up?"

"You're not going to be an adoring, eager-to-please fiancée, are you?"

"You wouldn't want me if I were!" Kit laughed. "The question, please!"

"Since you insist. Now, Russia can be forbidding, surprising, opulent, and unexpected, but it can never be called dull, except in one instance."

"And you want to know what it is."

"Take a guess."

"I don't think I'll have to," Kit said, wrapping her arms around Greg's waist and bracing herself against his diaphragm. "The only dull thing in Russia is the train ride between St. Petersburg and Moscow. It's almost eleven hours on a straight route, and the scenery is so boring that you can scream. What do you say to that?" Their heights

217

were so compatible that their faces were delightfully close together. "Do I get my personally guided tour of Hooper Studios?"

"Better than that," he assured her, his arms tightening skillfully. "You've not only earned a tour conducted by me, but at least one more kiss as well before we go back inside and make polite conversation when all we really want to do is be alone together."

Chapter 10

"What the hell are you doing in my office?"

Kit never thought that Greg had a typical Russian personality—one that shifted moods the way one could adjust a Venetian blind. It was obvious he had blue periods, of course, but then so did she and most people she knew, and she suspected that he had a quick temper, but the last thing she expected was for him to change from the laughing, happy man who'd spent the morning showing her around Hooper Studios to the cold-voiced, imperious-sounding man she now heard.

From the moment they'd arrived at Hooper Studios, Kit had felt like visiting royalty. Everyone wanted to meet her, and she wanted to meet everyone and to see everything. Greg was more than happy to accommodate both ends.

In the newly modernized kitchen, Mr. Chu, who was one of Mr. Wong's numerous cousins, wanted to show her what he was preparing for lunch; the wardrobe mistress made a great event of taking her through the dressing rooms so she could see how well-organized they were and how the makeup was the newly developed Supreme Greasepaint, eyeshadows and pencils from the lab of Max Factor, the onetime Polish emigre who had been the chief makeup artist for the Moscow State Theatre before coming to Los Angeles in 1908; and

Wilbur Covington, the former vaudeville comic who played the Pie Man in the continuing two-reel serial that was the tale of an average baker and his comic adventures in running his own bakery, couldn't wait to tell her all about the latest episode. Margery Haskell, the woman who ran the editing room, showed her how the film was run back and forth through the projector while the director watched, signalling with hand-held buzzer whenever the projectionist had to stop so that a piece of paper could be inserted in the machine's uptake reel, so the editor would know where to begin or end a cut; and Archie MacNeil forgot all about being a cautious Scot as he showed off not only his new camera lens but his brand-new, just-delivered Pathe camera, explaining to her how, by and large, acting wasn't important, it was all in the casting and lighting.

Kit was taken in turn to the carpenters' shop and the property shop and the story department before Greg introduced her to his secretary. Mrs. Rigby was thrilled to meet her, and while she was showing off pictures of her children, Greg excused himself, saying he had to make a quick phone call before showing off his office.

"My goodness, but Mr. West certainly sounds annoyed," Mrs. Rigby remarked as they heard Greg's decisive voice. "I certainly hope you get him to watch his temper."

"I certainly hope I won't," Kit replied as she got up from her perch on the edge of the secretary's desk, her Bergdorf Goodman dress of pale beige maletesse with rose silk trimmings rustling expensively. "But I think I'd better see what's going on."

Her curiosity overruling caution, Kit stepped over the threshold. Greg had already described his office in great detail to her, so there was nothing unexpected to distract her from the sight of her fiancé glaring at the black-haired young man seated behind the massive desk, the early edition of the *Los Angeles Times* in his hands.

"Do you see anything on my desk that interests you?"

Greg asked, ice dripping off every word.

"I'm sorry, Mr. West, but I'm one of those people who are a pushover for a stack of newspapers. I was sitting on the chesterfield like any other good but uninvited guest, but the lure of the papers was too much for me. Kit, will you please tell your fiancé that I'm perfectly respectable?"

"Hello, Charlie," Kit said. "I never expected that you'd follow the siren song to Los Angeles. Greg darling, this is Charles Lasky, a friend from New York."

"You're not related to Jesse Lasky and his crew over at Famous Players," Greg stated. Trained by Sinclair, he knew how to carry out the delicate task of sizing up new people. "Although they might want to claim you at various times."

Charlie's laugh was short and not too humorous. *"They* used to deal in musical instruments, if my sources are right. *My* father is the theatrical producer," he went on, not bothering to add that his mother's family was British and titled, and that he himself was an alumnus of Dwight and Harvard. Like any other rich, well-brought-up man, he knew certain things were almost self-evident—that is, if the listener was one who was also tuned to observe such niceties of life. "And I *am* sorry about sitting behind your desk. Please believe me that I wasn't raised to treat other people's property like my own."

He stood up, a tall, well-built man in his mid-twenties, with black hair and sapphire-blue eyes, and came around the desk to stand in front of Greg.

"I want to be the director for the motion picture you're planning," he said directly, and with quite a bit of caution on both their parts, they shook hands.

"I'm glad to see that you really do like to read newspapers," Greg said with a faint touch of amusement. "But before we discuss a lot of mundane details, wouldn't you rather kiss the bride-to-be?"

"You're very cavalier this morning," Kit said, but she was laughing as Charlie kissed her cheek. "How are your parents, and David and Cordelia and the baby?"

"Everyone's in perfect health and they all send their love." He took a step back and regarded them with a smile. "And I'm going to be very happy to report back to New York that your fiancé is up to snuff!"

"I think we've just passed inspection," Kit said to Greg. "But now that the social notices are taken care of, what shall we all do?"

"Since it's too early for lunch, and definitely too early for a drink, why don't we all sit down?"

When they were all on the chesterfield, Greg's eyes narrowed slightly. "Why do you want to direct a motion picture?"

"You make wanting to direct a movie sound like a disease that you pick up in South America," Charlie returned, unperturbed.

"I prefer the stage."

"On behalf of my family, I thank you. But here we all are." He held out both his hands. "Are you going to give me the job?"

Greg looked casual. "Are you in need of work?"

"If I were, you wouldn't hire me."

"I still may not."

Kit leaned back against the expensive leather, took off her Maria Guy hat that combined a beige organdy brim with a black straw crown banded by black faille, and decided to enjoy the conversation. She knew that both men were testing each other, showing off their superb verbal skills in setting up the best deals for themselves. She knew they were going to end up with an agreement, a good working relationship, if not actual friendship, but when were *they* going to realize it?

When they get tired of playing games, she thought.

"Kit probably thinks we're behaving like a pair of idiots," Greg remarked, and once again Kit had confirmation of his high degree of perception. "This is my day to show Kit around Hooper. I want everyone to see how lucky I am, and

222

I want Kit to see that I do more here than just sit at my desk and read the *Times*, the *Examiner*, the *Herald*, the *Express*, and the three-day old New York papers."

"I am impressed with everything here," Kit interjected, "but actually this day is a trade-off—I see the studio and Greg spends a day in my shop."

"I'm envious. Who wouldn't want to spend a day in a shop full of perfume and Paris dresses and populated by beautiful women?"

"Kit, I think you may have just made a new customer," Greg joked.

"Charlie, you are full of wonderful compliments—all of which I expect you to translate into purchases for all the women you know in a couple of weeks when I open."

"That sounds appropriately expensive."

"I think you can break loose a few dollars," Kit responded, biting back her laughter.

"I will if your fiancé hires me."

"Spoken like a man without a trust fund," Greg said dryly. He knew enough about the Lasky family—the theatrical, New York Laskys—to guess quite accurately that Charlie was playing poor-mouth for effect only.

"You know we theatricals never let on that we have more than ten dollars in our pocket."

"Then I'm glad you don't need the money, because Hooper isn't going to pay you very much."

"Ah, down to brass tacks at last!"

"Not really, it's almost time for lunch. Now we can meet for lunch tomorrow at the Good Fellows Grotto and drag it out, or we can get it all settled now."

"Shoot," Charlie responded, and smiled.

"You have to work with Archie MacNeil, the cameraman, the two of you together. I don't want any Broadway pretensions, and Archie's already assured me that he's more than willing to share his secrets with the right director."

"And that's me."

"Now if you all only had a story to turn into a motion picture," Kit couldn't resist adding.

"Trust the woman I love, the woman whose shop will probably earn enough in profit for the first year to remove the United States from the list of debtor nations, to come up with the most salient point," Greg said, and when they stopped laughing he fixed Charlie with a piercing dark-amber gaze. "Before we go downstairs, would you mind telling me how many films you've directed?"

"A couple of years ago I directed a few shorts at Vitagraph."

"I thought so."

"You don't care?"

"You know all about the Broadway stage, and that matters," Greg said as he and Kit stood up. "Besides, I didn't really know what I was getting into when I came here; why should you be any different?"

Lunch was served buffet style in the dining room with everyone helping themselves to cold salmon and lobster salad and assorted sandwiches, fresh vegetable salad, and ending up with rich chocolate ice cream. Plates in hand, they all moved out to the back porch and the lawn where long tables were set up under the trees. It was a combination office party and company picnic, and was as much an occasion to introduce Kit as to help keep morale high. Eventually, their talk turned to the theatre, to who was touring in what: How the *Ziegfeld Follies,* which had opened in June at the New Amsterdam Theatre had gone; why *The Girl From Utah* at the Knickerbocker was worth a second visit, and to discussing the pros and cons of *Under Cover,* currently attracting audiences at the Cort.

"I think I'm going to like working here," Charlie said when the talk about the New York theatre was over. "Plenty of sunshine, warm weather, and good food to eat."

"All the important things in life," Greg concurred. He could remember when he wanted nothing more than warm sunshine to work in and a decent meal to eat. But laying a roadbed had nothing to do with directing a movie. Or did it?

"No, you already have the most important thing," Charlie said directly.

"I think we've just been given a very nice compliment," Kit said, and reached for Greg's hand.

"I agree, and I'm very glad that as crazy and put-it-together-as-we-go-along movie business is, some good things aren't lost."

One by one, the actors, technicians, and office personnel finished eating and began to drift back to work until only Kit, Greg, Charlie, and Archie were left on the porch. They were talking about the Battle of the Marne, about Paris's narrow escape from occupation by the German army, and the sudden importance of the airplane in battle. It was a conversation that could have gone on for the rest of the afternoon, except that Archie stood up and gave Charlie a significant look.

"I have to go over some camera angles I want to try out tomorrow, and I'd appreciate a stage director's advice."

"Sounds good to me," Charles said as he also stood up. "And while we're at it, we can plot out some angles for the movie we're going to make."

"That *has* to be a new one, deciding on a series of camera angles for a nonexistent motion picture," Kit remarked wryly when they were alone.

"And as far as I know, Archie hasn't taken advice from anyone regarding his work since he left Edison in New York."

"I wonder if Charlie realizes that?"

"We all have to be indoctrinated into the world of the flickers, and everyone has to make their own mistakes," Greg said, and they were still laughing when a pleasant-faced man in his forties wearing the uniform of a post office

225

supervisor came out on the porch.

"I'm sorry to disturb you, Mr. West," he said, taking off his cap, "but your secretary said you were out here."

"It's perfectly all right, Mr. Winters." Greg quickly made the proper introductions. "Is there something wrong with our mail delivery?"

"Not exactly, Mr. West. Do you remember how you said the studio might be getting more mail because of the contest?"

"I know, I overexaggerated. If we get five stories a day, it will be a lot. I hope I didn't disrupt things too much at the post office by asking you to put aside special space for us."

"It's disruptive all right, Mr. West," the older man said. He began to smile, and the certainty of what he was going to say rippled through Greg and Kit at the same time. "I drove over here because I wanted to prepare you. The packages you warned us about started pouring into the post office this morning. We're all just amazed that people like to write so much. I'll see to it that the deliveries start first thing tomorrow, but it's only fair to tell you that it doesn't look like it'll be stopping any time soon."

Chapter 11

Was it really the last week in October? Kit thought as she stood on the threshold of her new office. And even more important, was today *finally* opening day for her shop?

Working under the strict eye and explicit instructions of Michael Garrity, his workmen had completed their job in record time and with great care. The stock had arrived and been arranged, the salespeople hired, the furniture set out, and all that remained was to open the doors.

And hope for the best, Kit thought on a surge of nerves, and she began to wander around her office that Mallory had decorated in cool and relaxing colors. For a moment she fussed at the raw silk curtains, making sure that there wasn't a misplaced speck of dust on the cream, blue, and yellow Portuguese needlepoint rug. She restacked the already perfect piles of *Vogue* and *Harper's Bazaar* set out on the gray-marble-topped tables, and moved the handwoven basket that held a half-dozen cymbidium orchids resting on a nest of green moss, eucalyptus and baby's breath that Greg had sent her to the center of a round table covered with an antique linen tablecloth. There wasn't time to sit down in any of the chairs or the loveseat covered in a yellow-rose-splashed chintz or behind her pale yellow desk with grooved legs picked out in blue. But there was enough leeway left to check her reflection in the full-length mirror attached to the inside of the closet door.

Even without ever having been to southern California, Herman Tappe knew what was right for this eccentric city, she decided, surveying the coral silk dress with white dashes, two horizontal tucks on the skirt and a tie sash belt that her former employer had sent her as a present with the instructions that she was to wear it to open her shop. She tucked a pin back into her hair and smiled as she recalled the telephone call she'd made to New York the day after her visit to Hooper Studios. Transcontinental telephone calls were expensive for the caller and difficult for the telephone company to connect and there was no guarantee that either person would be able to talk through the static on the line, but the call to Tappe had sounded as if he were no further away than Pasadena.

"Of course I'm going to do your wedding dress, my dear. Who else is there?" Tappe had replied when she told him about her engagement. "Now, just give me the date and tell me all about that lucky man."

"We don't have an exact date yet. It depends on when Mother and Vincent can leave Venezuela. Let's just say sometime in December for now. And please, Herman, no Victorian ruffles and frills."

"Now, Katharine dear, would I dress you against type? I may be sentimental about the brides I dress, but I'm not a fool. What does your fiancé do?"

"Greg is Sinclair Poole's business partner, and right now he's running a motion picture studio."

"Then I definitely can't do anything that even remotely resembles hearts and flowers. You always seem to know exactly what you're doing, and do it in the most dramatic way possible."

Well, I'm going to find out very soon just how successful I am, Kit reflected, closing the closet door. On her desk, her Faberge two-color gold clock with the circular white enamel

228

face set in a trellis-like frame studded with pearls and diamonds read just after nine-fifteen. At ten, she would unlock the front door for the women invited to come and see the selection of clothes, and later there would be champagne accompanied by small sandwiches and cakes catered by Levy's Cafe. She knew Jessica's articles were going to bring her a full house, but having them actually buy was another matter.

She left her office to make a final inspection of the packing room with its neat stacks of dress and hat boxes, all covered in glazed white paper with "Katharine's" emblazoned across the surface in a modern serif, and piles of pristine, perfect white tissue paper just waiting to enfold dresses, lingerie, and millinery; checked the business office which Grazia would use when dividing her time between her and Mallory's shops, and the room she'd set aside for the saleswomen to relax in. A four-panel decorative screen hid this section of the back room from view, and in front of the screen, just as she and Mallory had discussed, was the reproduction Venetian blackamoor pointing the way to Mallory's, while, on the other side of the open door, was its twin, urging customers in the opposite direction.

Kit patted the blackamoor on the head as she walked past the figure, her handmade pale beige calfskin pumps sinking into the pile of the elegant beige wool rug with stylized designs in navy blue, purple, green, and pink that had been created at Poiret's Martine School of Design, and stopped as she reached the edge of the selling floor.

How could such two dull words as selling floor be a fitting description? Kit wondered, surveying the area in front of her. It's glorious, just what I wanted, and thank you Michael Garrity for doing it all so perfectly!

This was every plan she'd made back in New York come to life. There were no display windows, since the last thing she wanted was either a dress dummy or a wooden head to show off a hat, and the large, flat plate glass windows on either side

229

of the door provided all passers-by with a clear look inside, which was just what she wanted. In her articles, Jessica had chronicled the transformation of this shop from a dingy would-be haberdashery to an exclusive and expensive women's shop with accuracy and devotion to all the unfolding details, telling her readers to watch for lacquered walls downstairs, walls the color of face powder in the dressing rooms, for satinwood-and-glass vitrines and Biedermeier-style cabinetry showcasing accessories and perfumes, but none of it would do any good unless the customers who walked through the door actually made purchases.

Don't get nervous before you have to, she warned herself, and soothed her jumpy feelings by wandering around the delicate bleached oak tables and chairs and framed mirrors where hats would be tried on, and then made sure that the representative selection of hats from Georgette, Chanel, Reboux, Talbot, and Maria Guy were ready and waiting. For added calm she looked lovingly at the vitrines that held the perfumes, beautiful bottles of worldly and expensive scents from Guerlain, Caron, Houbigant, Poiret, and D'Orsay. Sixteen fragrances from five different perfume houses, each in a different bottle and each with its own distinctive packaging, with enough of a scope in their individual blends to please even the most fussy of shoppers. Just looking at them had an almost hypnotic effect, but when she heard someone rapping on the door, her butterflies returned full force.

But only for a moment.

It was too early for customers, deliveries went around the back, the saleswomen weren't due quite yet, and Mallory would come through her own shop. Her mystification as to who was looking for entry lasted only as long as it took to look from the perfume bottles to the door, and then she saw Greg leaning against the glass, his arms full of pale, pale yellow champagne roses and a look of love on his face.

Kit ran lightly across the rug and swiftly unlocked the door.

"Why didn't you tell me you were coming!" she exclaimed as they embraced on the threshold. "This is the best surprise, and I love you!"

"This is the best way to start the day," he responded, and with his free arm around her waist began walking them backwards, the lush flowers still between them. He stopped at the bottom of the stairs, both of them laughing. "And you'll note that I closed the door behind me—I can tell that there are several eager women lurking around Spring Street, waiting for the first excuse to dash inside."

"You think of everything," she said, bending her head for a moment to breathe in the roses rich scent. "Except that you haven't kissed me yet."

"Los Angeles can take just so much attention so early in the morning," he quipped, but his deep-amber eyes grew even darker, and as he pulled Kit even closer to him the roses fell to their feet, the green florist's paper rustling.

Kit put her arms around his shoulders, letting all her concerns about the opening of her shop float away as Greg began to kiss her. Every kiss they shared was a promise of what was still to come between them, she decided as their embrace became closer and their kisses more searching. They tasted each other's mouth and tongue, and for a minute they hovered, lingered on the edge. Desire that was real and right encircled them, but there was reality as well, the reality that reminded them that they were visible from the street and had a public persona to maintain.

"Can you stay here for a while?" Kit asked as they slowly drew apart and she rested her cheek against his.

"Do you think you'll attract more clients with me here?" His voice was teasing, and they began to laugh together.

"Is movie-making really that boring?" Kit asked as she picked up the flowers. "Oh, these are so lovely. Come with me while I put them in water, and then I'll show you everything. Are stories still coming in to the studio?"

"At least forty of them every day," Greg said as they went into her office. "We have two mail deliveries a day, and at least four or five mail bags. It's past the time specified in the ad, but until we find the right story I'll accept everything that comes in."

"Those poor girls in the story department are going to need eyeglasses by the time you're finished," Kit remarked, coming out of the bathroom with a tall crystal vase filled with water.

"Everyone is going to need eyeglasses. We've all been reading stories," he said, admiring her newly framed fashion prints. "On Friday, I finally realized that there are quite a few colleges and universities in the area, and I began phoning the various English departments and asked if they had some students who'd like to make a little extra money by reading stories."

Kit placed the rose-filled vase on her desk. "That's a great idea!"

"I'm glad you agree with me. Compared to some of the reactions I got, we positively love the movies. The head of the English Department at the Normal School on Vermont Avenue reminded me that they're training future teachers, and educators are divided on the merits of motion pictures, and I had to convince the priest over at St. Vincent's that I wasn't trafficking in sin."

"The legacy of Hooper Studios."

"Don't remind me. Naturally, the English professors I spoke to at USC and Occidental saw fit to remind me that their students really weren't in need of extra pocket money."

"It doesn't sound very productive so far," Kit said as they left her office.

"I had to take two aspirin when I was finished. But as doubtful as the professors were, no one actually turned me down. They promised to let their students know, and they must have kept their word because the first contingent of

232

volunteers arrive today," he finished triumphantly.

"That's wonderful, but why didn't you tell me this before?"

"Because of this," Greg responded, gesturing at the selling floor. "I knew that this was the most important thing to you, and for the moment my news could keep."

As he finished speaking, Kit put her arms around his neck. "I read once where Russian and American men were alike because they always behave honorably toward the woman they love," she said, looking into his eyes. "Even with that part of your life over, I'm very glad that certain characteristics and standards are still there."

"You always know the right thing to say to me," he whispered adoringly. "But right now I think you'd better show me around. Those big, shiny windows of yours are making us this morning's favorite sight."

"Then it's definitely time for intermission. I want you to see how things have improved since the last time you were here. No more painters and plasterers to duck."

Raised in splendor that could never be equalled, and, except for those months between leaving St. Petersburg and going to work for Sinclair, never having lived in an atmosphere that was devoid of luxuries, he responded instantly to the beautiful creation Kit had wrought. Nothing missed his attention, not from the masses of pink and white tulips arranged in round crystal vases placed at strategic spots on the selling floor to the elegant use of cabinets and vitrines to display the carefully edited selection of accessories. The only thing he did blink at was the vast variety of hats.

"Do women really buy so many hats?" he inquired, gazing at hats with broad brims, and narrow brims, afternoon turbans, fanciful luncheon hats, hats in a wide variety of straws, felts, as well as satin, lace, and velvet, both plain or trimmed with ribbons, silk, and veiling.

"You've obviously never lived intimately with a woman," Kit rejoined lightly. "Of course while that delights me, it also

233

shows me that your education has a small hole in it as far as women and their clothes are concerned."

"Such as how many hats constitute a well-dressed woman's wardrobe?" He was enjoying this conversation. "I can understand a large quantity of dresses and ball gowns, I can even understand a woman needing a lot of shoes, it's just that hats are a bit much to understand."

Kit picked up a white chip-straw hat with a graceful length of blue chiffon draped over the crown. "This is from Reboux. It's a class model, although it may be a little after the season, even for Los Angeles."

Greg fingered the brim. "But you can almost give me a guarantee that this hat is going to sell?"

"It will—eventually—and possibly on sale. But the point is that this creation is going to be just what one woman wants."

"Hopefully not two. Can you imagine two customers in a dispute over this?" he suggested wickedly. "Two respectable Pasadena clubwomen, possibly."

"Thank you very much, that's just what I want to think about on my first day of business!" Kit put the hat back on the table and tried to glare at Greg, but her laughter overcame her annoyance. "Besides," she went on, "this is not a clubwoman's hat, not unless she's been fooling around in the potting shed, breathing in the mulch."

"I think you may know your hypothetical customers a bit too well."

"That's why I'm not having any charge accounts. But even when it's cash or check only, a woman always needs another hat. It's rather like men and their ties," she finished, casting an amused look at Greg's discreet regimental stripe.

Greg began to smile. "Should I be happy that I won't have to pay your bills?"

"Of course—provided that you remember that even if I didn't have this shop you still wouldn't see a bill of mine much less pay it," she said, and held out her hands to him.

"Come on, I want you to see everything else."

The first alcove was for daytime dresses and suits, and the second for evening clothes, and Greg noted the careful placement of the mirrors and the small sofas for the customers to sit on. The whole atmosphere was one of unquestioned luxe, from the lacquered walls, crystal chandeliers and the scent of Guerlain's *Rue de la Paix* in the air, to the thick carpeting underfoot, to the small silk-covered sofas and chairs, and Greg felt as if he were being allowed a look into some complicated and intensely feminine ritual.

"As you can see, I've kept the touches of *Feng Shui* down to a minimum. I agree that the placement of mirrors is very important, but I didn't think my clients would like to see the tank with the black fish. Fortunately, Caro agreed with me."

"I'm glad you got off this easy with her. When it came to my office, we had a battle worthy of the conflict on the Marne." He looked appreciatively at a Martial et Armand gown of pink mousseline trimmed with pink satin ribbon. "This isn't your entire stock."

"Of course not!" Kit tried to look insulted, but failed. "This is a representative sampling. I don't like shops where all you see when you walk in are silk draperies and velvet chairs and you can't tell what they're selling, but I'm not running Lord and Taylor, either. My customers can get an idea of what is available and what they're looking for, and their *vendeuse* will bring out other selections."

"No wonder women can spend hours shopping. Brooks Brothers and Tripler's have never been like this."

"I certainly hope not. Now, on to the next alcove." She took his hand. "You're the first man to see it all set up."

A man could have only one of two reactions to this room, Greg thought. He could either start looking for the nearest exit, or else not want to leave this very special spot where even more closely guarded feminine secrets were revealed.

As Kit had specified, the walls of the third alcove had been

235

covered in a pale pink watered silk that had been almost too fragile to mount, and it gave the semi-circular area a highly intimate feel, the kind that almost all women understand and respond to because they recognize it as the perfect backdrop in which to view elegant, expensive and exquisitely fragile lingerie.

Somewhere in the United States were women who wore only the most modest of nightgowns and peignoirs and undergarments made of pristine white lawn, cotton, or cambric, trimmed with nothing more than a little eyelet embroidery and pale pink or blue ribbon, but they weren't going to be catered to here. From first glance it was clear that this establishment dealt only in the pretty, the frivolous, the sensuous, and the most subtly romantic of creations. A reproduction of an oversized Queen Anne secretary had all its drawers and panels open to serve as a display piece for camisoles and teddies and other small items, while polished armoires were set up to hold nightgowns and negligees.

As Greg admired the creations of silk, satin, lace, ribbon, charmeuse, and chiffon, Kit began to think about him, about them. The immediacy of their attraction to each other had been so overpowering that they both knew that time was needed for them to have a proper courtship.

Together they had spent the last month exploring Los Angeles and its environs on foot and by automobile and even occasionally taking the Pacific Electric Railroad, the "big red cars," which was the interurban line that pushed out in all directions from the center of the city, making the mountains, the desert, and the seaside all convenient locations. They played tennis on Rupert and Mallory's private court, played golf on the Municipal Golf Links, and took long horseback rides through the Hollywood Hills. Now that things were actually moving again at Hooper Studios, Greg felt he didn't have to be there as often as he had during the time when the studio's immediate fate had been in doubt. There was time every weekday for a long lunch at the Alexandria, or Levy's

236

Cafe, or the Good Fellows Grotto, that popular business-men's lunch spot where Greg never failed to tell her that even the most engrossing business conversation couldn't go on when she walked in wearing one of her Paris dresses and outstanding hats.

The papers had been signed and the deed registered, making the Beverly Hills property theirs, and soon they would begin interviewing architects, but on Sundays they still engaged in the popular Los Angeles weekend pastime of buying real estate. In between Sunday picnic lunches and drives to the Huntington Pier, or the Seal Beach Pier, they frequently stopped at the roadside stands real estate developers set up. The lots they now owned in Hancock Park and Bel-Air were for eventual resale, but it was agreed that they'd probably keep the orange grove in the San Fernando Valley.

She still wanted Greg as much as she had that night in Chicago, and occasionally she did wonder if it would have been better if she had just taken the chance and become his lover. It wasn't that delay was making the idea impossible—they were making as good use of the Fiat as a couple of college kids—but the idea of *when* never stopped circulating in her mind.

He isn't like all the other men you've known, she reminded herself. Greg is real, honest, and considerate, and there are a lot of men out there who might not be so willing to get rid of their other women. On the other hand, the fact that he doesn't have what the British call "side" doesn't change the fact that way down deep he still comes from a family that considers the Romanovs to be arriviste. . . .

"Catch!"

Kit came out of her thoughts just in time to see Greg toss her a small blue-velvet-covered box. There was a schoolboy's grin on his face, and she deftly caught the box, her heart pounding. The box could contain only one thing and for a second she held it in her hands, waiting for Greg to cross the

237

floor so he could stand beside her.

"It was delivered last night," he said, standing behind her and putting his arms around her waist. "I've been trying to decide the best place and time to give it to you. I thought champagne and candlelight was the proper setting for us, but this lovely place is even better." He tenderly kissed the nape of her neck. "Open it."

For every morning since the night they met, except for the three days on the California Limited, Greg had never failed to send her flowers. And not just any flowers, but lush and extravagant blooms like the pink Mystery of India tulip, first grown in 1830, the red-streaked yellow Flaming Parrot tulip brought to Holland from Turkey, as well as full-blown pink, white, and lavender peonies, orchids ordered from Hawaii, fuzzy pink dianthus, bright red calla lilies, baskets of paper-white narcissus, perfumer's roses with incredibly long stems, and exotic tiger lilies. But he never sent her anything else, not chocolates, not perfume, not any of one hundred and one trinkets that a man usually gives his fiancée, and now Kit knew why. Glittering up at her from its bed of white satin was a ten-carat starburst cut natural brown diamond nestled in white diamonds.

"I've never seen a ring like this. Oh, Greg, when I said you should surprise me, I never expected anything so exquisite!" Kit turned in his embrace. "I want you to put it on for me, but first I want you to kiss me. . . ."

Greg's arms tightened skillfully, and Kit felt her knees go weak as they drew closer together. His kisses were enough to make her forget she'd ever kissed another man. They clung together, parted long enough for Greg to slip the ring on the fourth finger of her left hand, and they continued to stand close together, gazing into each other's eyes.

"Is the ring too heavy?"

"A little . . . but I'll get used to it." With her left hand, the exquisite cut of the ring catching the light, she reached up to brush back his hair. "I almost wish we could forget our

238

responsibilities for just a few hours right now."

"Almost?" His voice was softly teasing, but there was an undertone that she caught immediately.

"That's the key word—the dividing line between fantasy and reality."

"I like your thought though."

"When we're together—to celebrate or do anything else— I want us to have a wonderful long stretch of time. I don't want us to be lovers for the first time—or any time after that—with either of us keeping an eye on the clock."

"That's not the way I want to love you either," Greg agreed, his lips pressing small kisses against her hairline. "We'll be alone together—"

Greg's voice stopped, and Kit opened her eyes to find Mallory standing only a few feet away from them. She was wearing a Tappe frock of crimson georgette crepe, topped by a full-brimmed black satin hat faced in crimson silk, and she looked at them as if she came across this sort of thing every day.

"Am I interrupting?"

"Yes!" They spoke together, and Mallory gave them a cool, considering look.

"The champagne is on ice next door, and the waiters will bring the food over about noon." Her gaze flickered over Greg. "Don't you have an office to go to?"

"I know," he said good-naturedly, "there's nothing so unnecessary on the opening day of a very exclusive shop as a man who isn't either paying the bills or buying a present."

"I couldn't agree more." Mallory's eyes were full of amusement. She knew something very special was going on, but she wasn't about to treat it seriously. "Then what are you doing here?"

"You might say I had to make a delivery."

"Just a small trinket," Kit interjected, and held out her left hand. "A little something to seal our affections."

Mallory's own six-carat, emerald-cut diamond engagement ring from Tiffany's was hardly insignificant, but for a moment she could only stare at Kit's ring.

"It's magnificent," she said finally, "and it's you."

"I certainly hope so," she said, slipping her free arms around Greg's waist and exchanging a secret smile with him. "When we talked about my engagement ring, I told Greg to surprise me, and it's obvious he's a gentleman who takes all requests very seriously."

"And I was wondering why the only presents you ever sent Kit were flowers."

"Thank you, Mallory," Kit said wryly, and her friend sighed and gave them a look of great forebearance.

"Well, since it looks like I just put a Carcion and Manfre handmade shoe in my mouth, I think the time has come for me to temporarily return to my own shop. See you soon."

She turned and left them, her perfume, Guerlain's *Vague Souvenir* wafting like a light and fragrant cloud around her. Mallory, like her cousin Alix, didn't know the meaning of leaving a situation in either embarrassment or defeat.

"I hate to say this, but I think it's time for you to leave for the studio. You probably have a stack of work waiting for you, and I have the usual last-minute details to check over."

Together, they walked out to the selling floor, and through the large windows they saw Mallory and Rupert's shiny new seven-passenger Cadillac limousine complete with uniformed driver parked at the curb. Most of the time Mallory drove around in their three-passenger laudaulet coupe, and on nights out she and Rupert had their five-passenger inside drive limousine.

"I'm glad to see Mallory considers the opening of my shop to be a state occasion—that's just about what it takes for them to use that car," Kit said, and as she finished, a 1913 Silver Ghost laudaulet painted a rich shade of burgundy pulled smartly in front of the Cadillac, and a moment later the uniformed driver opened the door for Caro. Resplendent in an elegant Doucet dress of rose-colored silk with a two-tier clinic and a bodice that crossed over and tied in a bow at the high waist, she looked at them from under the brim of her large picture hat, and waved.

They returned her wave, and Caro motioned that she was going into Mallory's shop.

"Now you can be sure you're a state occasion," Greg remarked, pleased, laughter evident in his voice. "We both know that Caro is known about Los Angeles by the yellow Rolls-Royce two-seat phaeton she drives. The driver's uniform gets moth holes from wearing to wearing."

"No, it doesn't!" Kit laughed, but quickly grew serious when she noticed two women waiting nearby. "It looks like they might be customers—or again, they could be loitering."

"You're going to be fine," Greg said, taking her hands in his. "I know you had to be wondering why all I sent you were flowers. I did it because I didn't want anything to detract from this ring."

"I knew that the moment I looked at it."

"This is the first engagement ring I've ever given."

"And it had better be the last."

"I don't think I could go through the waiting for the jeweler to finish again. I was sure you were going to throw my latest floral offering at me and call me a cheapskate."

"You're anything but. But it isn't the cost that matters. You put all your heart and your love into this ring, and I wouldn't care if it came from a box of Cracker Jack."

"I used to think I was best off alone."

"But not any longer?"

"Not since the night we met," he said, and pulled her into his arms. "I'll be back around five, and you can show me the rest of your shop—and your receipts."

For a minute, to the delight of the ladies who were gathering outside, Kit concentrated on brushing some nonexistent lint from the front of Greg's suit jacket, made sure his white carnation was secure in his buttonhole, and straightened his Charvet tie. "Don't be late," she whispered, kissing him lightly. "I'll save a bottle of champagne and we'll celebrate."

"I promise to make only one stop on my way over from Hooper."

"Not a jewelry store, please. I can't take another piece of jewelry today."

"No, I'll only stop at Ralph's." Greg's eyes were alight with fun. "We need something special to go with our champagne, and I think a box of Cracker Jack is just the thing!"

Chapter 12

Gregory West wasn't a sentimental man. Everything in his background, his education, and the dark incident that had so radically altered his life served to remove him from the soupy, syrupy sort of attitudes that affected far too many people. In no particular order he believed in God, the Constitution, Woodrow Wilson, the reform wing of the Democratic Party, and the utter necessity of freedom of the press. If Russia had a free press like the United States, he often reasoned silently, if it had developed a talent like the *New York World*'s most celebrated reporter, Herbert Bayard Swope, the horror of that night might well have been solved. He felt keenly for those who were disenfranchised and denied due process of law, because that had once been his fate, too, and he loathed unfairness of any kind, but popular, pre-conceived, honey-coated notions were not for him.

Sentimentality, he knew, had nothing whatsoever to do with love or being in love. That was affection, caring, laughter, and plans for the future, and a feeling of rightness and belonging that had never been found with another person. It was even a good shouting match, a few tears, and kissing and making up. It was knowing that sensual satisfaction could wait because it was the final step, and in order for everything else to be right it had to come last. And

243

it was the certainty that whenever he heard *Alexander's Ragtime Band* he would think of the Blackstone Hotel and the first dance he and Kit had together. What it wasn't, could never be, should never be, was an experience to be draped in tacky lace, decorated with overblown roses, scented with cheap perfume, and set to the music of weeping violins.

But today, Wednesday, November 4th, ten days after Kit had opened her shop to a rousing success, Greg sat at his desk and wondered if he were the only person in the world who thought like that. He very much doubted it, but so far it seemed to be his fate to have Hooper Studios attracting writers of stories, who, for the most part, didn't have a clear or unstereotyped thought in their heads. Why was it that so many of these stories were disturbingly alike? he wondered, reviewing the carefully typed synopses that the story department prepared for him on a twice daily basis. Did these people all know each other, or were these stories symptomatic of the poor quality of imagination abroad in the land?

Every story that arrived was given a reading, and so far the avalanche of manuscripts were falling into one of three categories. In the first category, and by far the one into which most of the manuscripts were slotted, the story went directly back to the writer with a polite note thanking him for his contribution; in the second category the writer also received his manuscript back, but with a note that his story showed promise and belonged in a magazine, or should be expanded into novel length; and in the third and smallest group the writer didn't get his manuscript back, but received a check for twenty-five dollars and a letter telling him that although his story wasn't the one they were looking for, it was good enough to option for future consideration. This was Greg's idea. Should they find the story that would make the movie they all wanted, it would mean that Hooper was viable to produce other films, and the best move they could make was to have a backlog of stories ready to be translated into scenarios.

But no story rose above the others to say "film me." It wasn't so much that Greg knew what he was looking for, but he definitely knew what he *didn't* want, and it fit in exactly with his views on cloying sentimentality.

He didn't want a war story. Let D.W. Griffith with his awful taste in clothes, his suits a race track tout wouldn't touch, topped off by floppy Panama hats, use his movie as a forum to display his own vicious prejudices; doing that was asking for trouble. And he didn't want a farm or country story. If he saw one more story about how good people were who lived in small towns or down on the farm compared to the evil people who lived in big cities, he'd write to each of those authors and tell them exactly what he thought. Did it ever occur to these people that the prisons were full of men who'd never seen a large city? Stories based on an overt religious theme fell into the same category. A person's religion—or lack of it—was a private matter and not a fit subject to be displayed on a movie screen.

A comedy, however, was different. He would love to see Hooper Studios make a full-length comedy along the lines of *Tillie's Punctured Romance. The Pie Man* was their ongoing success, but to continue it had to remain in its two-reel format.

"And where are all your high standards getting you?" he muttered, checking through yet another list. "Why don't you pick one likely sounding story and get it over with?"

"Did you say something, Mr. West?" Mrs. Rigby asked as she appeared in the open doorway.

"I'm just castigating myself for being too particular about the stories that are coming in," he said, and spied the sheaf of papers she was holding. "I take it those are more synopses?"

"Yes, for all they're worth," she sniffed, setting the thick stack of papers on his desk. "The only good thing about all of this is the college students who've been helping out. They're really very enthusiastic about this."

245

"As opposed to the rest of us."

Mrs. Rigby smiled. "I never knew there were so many untalented people in the world who considered themselves to be writers."

"Just like certain men who think they're able to run a motion picture studio," Greg couldn't resist adding. "But maybe it's the same hope—the one chance to do something different."

"Well, that person who is going to make a big difference to us had better show up soon," Mrs. Rigby said tartly, and then left as suddenly as she arrived.

Greg smiled quizzically, and decided to give Mrs. Rigby a raise. She knew exactly what went on here and never hesitated to let him know how the wind was blowing. For the next hour he checked some reports, reviewed a budget, and signed some letters he'd dictated the afternoon before. For a minute he considered calling up Kit. It was her birthday today, and tonight he'd planned a special dinner for the two of them, and the evening might well end on a very different note. Unfortunately, a quick look at his watch showed that right now she'd be making a decisive survey, walking through the fitting rooms and the selling floor before putting on one of her hats and joining Mallory and Caro for lunch at the best table in the Alexandria or Levy's Cafe, as much to be seen as to eat.

He uncapped his fountain pen, and, as usual, began to make X's next to most of the descriptive paragraphs. Trash, stupidity, vulgar garbage, not too bad, he thought, marking off three X's and finishing off with an O for option, and turned the page.

A young Russian cavalry officer from a noble family becomes the devoted admirer of a ballet dancer. Their infatuation for each other brings them both to the brink of despair, pain and tragedy.

He was so used to rejecting proposals that he almost passed it right by, almost but not quite.

It caught his eye and he reread it twice before it finally registered to his brain.

Not letting himself think, he buzzed for Mrs. Rigby, who immediately appeared in the doorway. "I have a synopsis here that sounds promising," he said as calmly as he could while his heart began the low, sick pounding he hadn't had in years. "It's signed C.D. Do you know who did the reading?"

Mrs. Rigby looked thoughtful. "That might be Cecilia Downes. She's a student at USC, and very popular."

"I'm glad to hear that. Would you ask her to come up here and bring—" he glanced down at the page again, "—bring *Ballet At Midnight* with her."

Less than five minutes later, Cecilia Downes appeared in the doorway, holding a manuscript, a slightly apprehensive look in her bright blue eyes. "I'm Cecilia Downes, Mr. West," she said in a clear voice. "Mrs. Rigby said that this manuscript is very important to you."

He might be in danger of going into shock, but Greg would never forget his manners, and he stood up and showed her into his office, remembering to ask her about college and how she liked reading manuscripts at Hooper Studios before turning to the subject of *Ballet At Midnight*.

"I finished it this morning and typed up the synopsis right away," she told him. "It's really very different. Truthfully, it's the best one I've read."

"I see." He took the thick sheaf of pages. "O.L. Pinchot," he read from the title page. "There's not much to go on, is there?"

"Could this be the story you're looking for?"

"We'll have to see. But if it is, I'll let you know." He smiled at the girl's surprise. "There's a special bonus for the reader who discovers the winning story."

Alone again, he began to read a well-prepared, well-constructed story, an interesting tale, what was in essence not only the story of his youth but also the story of what had happened on an icy night in an elegant St. Petersburg apartment.

This couldn't be happening, he thought, feeling the same fear build inside him that he had known on those January days in 1900 when he knew Natalia was missing and that his father was going to dispose of him. Not now, not after all this time. Who could know all of this?

Almost against himself, Greg found that he was captured by the story. Even if it weren't paralleling his own nightmare experience he would keep turning the pages. The writer was obviously an amateur, but the talent was there—and so was the story.

He finished reading and sat there absorbing the words he'd just read. The first panic was beginning to subside, and he concentrated on viewing this with some sort of detachment.

"Chto delat?" he said, speaking in Russian for only the second time since he'd arrived in the United States. *"Chto delat*—what to do?"

Chapter 13

"Oh, Kit, I love this dress. Do you really think it's for me?"

"Absolutely," Kit told Mary Alice Garrity as the pretty young woman with the soft black hair and brown-gold eyes looked at her reflection. She was wearing a striking Lucile evening dress that began with a foundation of yellow-pink taffeta, was overlaid with a cream lace tunic that flared into a pannier effect on the sides, and finished with a French blue girdle. "It's a very complicated dress, but you have the height and coloring to carry it off. Also, I didn't order any repeats on it, so it's an exclusive here, and since it is difficult for everyone to wear, it may turn out to be one of the few bought from the original collection."

"Then I won't see myself coming and going?"

"That's not too likely." Kit smiled. "What about the other things you've been trying on?"

"I'm definitely taking the Paquin," she said, indicating a frock of pink and white flowered crepon with a black velvet belt and double ruffled hem, "and Lucile's orchid chiffon with the silver trim, but I'm not sure about the Doucet—."

Kit spent a few minutes helping Mary Alice make her numerous selections, turned her over to Delia to complete the extensive sale, and then went into the next dressing room where Mrs. Garrity was admiring a Lucile afternoon dress

249

of dull gold georgette with a large collar of pink ninon de soie and a gold cord belt.

"This is just perfect, Kit," the older woman told her. "In fact, I think I'm going to wear this to Mary Alice's wedding instead of the dress I picked out at I. Magnin's!"

"I couldn't have a nicer compliment, but please don't mention it to Mary Anne Magnin."

"Don't you worry about that. And speaking of weddings, it won't be too long until yours. Have you and Greg set the date yet?"

"We're discussing it now."

"If you don't mind a word of advice, dear, don't delay too long. Gregory West was a very eligible bachelor and when men have had that sort of popularity, no matter how much they say they didn't care about it, they tend to have second thoughts."

There was very little Kit could say to that, except to deftly move the conversation on to another topic, and then move on. It was the middle of the afternoon, and she visited each of the dressing rooms, all decorated alike with an excellent three-way mirror, a fifty-one inch Louis XV reproduction marquise and Louis XV reproduction fautueil, both covered in a cotton floral print. She consulted with her saleswomen to make sure all was running smoothly before going downstairs to the selling floor. She saw that Beatrice de Jonge and her assistant Lila Evans, who had both worked in the millinery department at Robinson's, were waiting on several women who looked as if they were intent on buying extensively, and that Susan Marshall was showing another customer a selection of evening purses. With a smile and a nod toward her employees, Kit went into her office, closed the door, and sat down behind her desk.

Happy birthday, Katharine, she told herself, looking at the small milk-glass vase filled with nerine, muscari and lily-of-the-valley that Greg had sent her. You're twenty-eight today, and everything is wonderful. I like Los Angeles more than I thought I would. I have the shop I planned, and so far it looks like more of a success than I even allowed myself to hope for; and then there's Greg. His whole life is almost unbelievable, but it's all true and he not only made the best of it but made himself into a new person. I love him, and today I want him to know how much.

She studied the jewelry that had come with the flowers. A pair of gold bangle bracelets and a small ruby heart attached to a long, delicate gold chain; both had arrived with the flowers and served to reinforce the decision she'd come to.

But first there was the current crop of paperwork to see to, and she uncapped her fountain pen and lifted out the contents of her letter box. Grazia was turning out to be an excellent manager, but Kit let nothing pass out of the office without her approval. Jessica's series of stories about the shop and its transformation to its current elegant state had drawn all the interest promised. Frank Rundstadt hadn't owned the *Los Angeles Statesman-Democrat* long enough to transform it from the last and the least of the city's papers, but thanks to Jessica, the women's page had a steady and devoted readership, and Kit not only had customers turning up in person, but writing to ask about a particular dress or hat, and she answered each one.

She was signing the last letter when the phone rang. "Katharine Allen," she answered crisply despite her quickened heartbeat.

"This is Moss, Miss Allen. I'm ringing up to let you know that I've just spoken with Mr. West and I gave him the message as you instructed." The soft-spoken, deliberately bland voice of Greg's houseman came through the earpiece, and Kit held her breath, waiting for him to continue. "Mr. West has informed me that he will be home within the next ninety minutes."

"Thank you, Moss," Kit replied. So far, her plan seemed to be working, but there were many parts to this, and she'd better be cautious until everything was in place. "I'll be over

251

in a half-hour."

Hanging up only long enough to break the connection, she had the operator connect her with the Randalls', and got Mrs. Dovedale on the line.

"Everything's almost ready, Miss Katharine," she said cheerfully. "Just a minute or two more in the oven for the last batch, and we'll be ready to leave. Are you sure you don't want a birthday cake?"

"No, thank you. The menu we worked out will be fine. I hope this won't be too much of an interruption on your evening off."

"Not at all. Mr. Dovedale and I are going to see *Tillie's Punctured Romance,* and then have dinner at the Van Nuys Hotel, so it won't be any trouble at all to drop off your order at the Alexandria."

Kit had to smile at the mention of the word "order," and as she and Mrs. Dovedale completed their call she was very glad that four years of working for Mallory and Rupert had immured their cook against the sound of the rules of etiquette between men and women being broken. On the surface, this was going to be a tea party, but still—

The best thing about owning her shop was that there was no need to worry about getting the right clothes together, Kit thought as she stood up and went to her closet. It didn't take long to change from her Lucile suit of beige silk trimmed with beige silk braid and pearl buttons to a Lucile afternoon dress of black georgette satin draped gracefully with bands of white satin and a collar of white embroidered batiste. Once everything was fastened, she headed for the door that led to the stockrooms. From the racks of dresses she quickly selected a Lucile dance dress of striped chiffon over green satin with a sky-blue girdle and a pair of silver evening shoes, and from the shelves of exquisite lingerie packed in tissue paper and delicate boxes, she took a nightgown and negligee of ecru-colored mousseline de soie trimmed with frothy Valenciennes lace.

Unexpectedly, the box slipped out of her hands and landed at her feet with a slight thud. What am I doing? she asked herself as she bent down to pick up the box. This isn't a game, this is real. An hour from now, I'll be with Greg in his suite, but if anything happens, he has to want it first. I never want him to say that I take too much for granted.

That matter was paramount with her, but she was also aware that the time had come to let Greg know that all the rituals of courtship were becoming an impediment to real life. On Sunday night, after they'd returned from a day spent exploring the nearest missions, Kit had decided that it was time she paid a visit to Greg at the Alexandria. He was taking her out for a night of dinner and dancing to celebrate her birthday, but what could possibly be wrong with having tea together first—all carefully planned, of course. Getting Mrs. Dovedale to make some of her famous pastries had been easy, she'd barely finished explaining before the cook happily and eagerly agreed; but approaching Moss had been another matter, and it had taken a bit of carefully worded request to get the correct houseman to agree to call Gregory at Hooper Studios and tell him there was an emergency at home.

Now, the first part of her plan was set, and it remained to her to carry the rest of it out.

Fully aware that if she had use of the lingerie she'd need clothes for tomorrow, she chose an elegant Lucile suit of off-white serge ornamented by a row of jade buttons, collected all the necessary lingerie and accessories, and took everything into the packing room. There she found Millie, the eighteen-year-old girl who did all the packing, carefully placing a small afternoon hat of gold tissue swathed in brown tulle onto a nest of white tissue paper.

"Oh, Miss Allen, let me take all those things! You must have made quite a sale."

"You might say that," Kit agreed, feeling a bit light-headed as they put everything on the linen-draped work table. "So someone bought this hat," she went on, peeking into the box. "I have to admit, Millie, that I had a few doubts about this number when I ordered it at Alphonsine's. Do you know who bought it?"

"A Mrs. Garr who's visiting from San Diego. When I finish here, I'll bring it over to her at the Alexandria."

Kit's butterflies began to fly. Was this the reassurance she was looking for?

"I'm on my way over to the hotel now, so I'll just take it along with everything else," she said as calmly as she could.

"Of course, Miss Allen." Millie reached for several fresh sheets of tissue paper. "I love your dress. There's something so striking about black and white."

"There's a secret to this combination. Don't let anyone tell you that men only like to see women in pastels. They do, but every once in a while you have to put on something very dramatic, and there's no better way to make an impression than in black and white!"

And I'm soon going to find out how effective this dress is, Kit thought a minute later, looking in the mirror as she put on her black satin hat with a wide brim wreathed in white flowers to match the facing.

I may end up with pastry all over my face, she admitted, but I'm going to make every effort and have a good time doing it. Today's my birthday, and I'm interested in only one very special present!

Almost staggering under the stack of boxes, Kit reached the door to Greg's suite on the fifth floor of the Alexandria. Somehow managing to balance the boxes so she had a free hand, she rapped on the wood panel and was instantly rewarded by Moss's prompt response. As apprehensive as she was, all she wanted to do was put her collection of boxes down.

"Good afternoon, Miss Allen. Here, let me take those

254

boxes from you," Moss said pleasantly. He was a tall, spare man in his fifties who, like so many others, had come to Los Angeles for his health. Gregory West wasn't the first bachelor with an active social life that he'd worked for, but this was the first time he'd seen a fiancée arrive like one of the other ladies, each of whose presence he had been at such pains to hide from the other, and since Miss Allen would soon be Mrs. West, certain adjustments were called for. "Mrs. Dovedale is setting things up for your tea."

"Thank you, Moss," she replied, not unaware that the man's voice and attitude had warmed several degrees since their telephone conversation of a short time before. "If you take care of the boxes, I'll see how everything is coming along."

Greg had told her that he'd taken this suite when the Alexandria was still in the blueprint stage, and the architect had been quite willing to make several changes, but he had never elaborated beyond saying that a closet had been turned into a small pantry so that he wasn't dependent on room service for a cup of coffee, and, of course, that Caro— and more recently, Mallory—had taken care of the decorating.

"I guess he really couldn't describe any of this," Kit murmured as she saw Moss disappear into one of the bedrooms. "It really has to be seen."

For a minute she stood by the door, taking in the reserved beauty of the room without seeing any one piece of furniture in particular, but gradually beginning to register it piece by piece.

There was almost no entry area to speak of, but the illusion of a foyer had been created by a glass-fronted bookcase on the left, and on the right was a fifty-inch-wide and thirty-five-inch-high First Empire chest of drawers made of dark mahogany with ormolu fittings and a black marble top. A bronze figure of Kwan Ti, the Chinese god of literature, rested on the center of the surface while a circular

Federal mirror hung on the wall over it. The walls were painted a soft, pale yellow with rich white trim, giving the living room a more spacious feel.

With a soft murmur of appreciation, Kit walked across the Oriental carpet of cream, yellow, and black, the deep pile silencing her footsteps. The entire room seemed perfectly suited to Greg; she could almost see him relaxing in one of the low, well-stuffed armchairs or the comfortable sofa that were covered in an expensive yet quiet chintz of soft gray splashed with yellow flowers; or playing Mozart on the black Steinway concert grand piano; or writing letters at the Chippendale secretary. In fact, the imprint of his personality was so apparent that the sense of missing him that she always had when they were apart was somehow assuaged by being here. She could close her eyes and almost feel him standing beside her, his arms encircling her as his mouth came closer and closer to hers. . . .

The sound of china and cutlery rattling reminded Kit that she wasn't alone in the apartment, and stopping only long enough to leave her hat, purse, and gloves on the nearest surface, she looked behind a painted leather screen with Chinoiserie motifs to find Mrs. Dovedale busy taking plates out of a cabinet.

"There you are, Miss Katharine. I heard Moss let you in a minute ago," she said cheerfully. "He's a little bit stuffy, but his heart's in the right place."

"I'm sure it is," Kit replied, peeking into the bakery boxes on the counter. "Oh, it all looks scrumptious. I know we're going to eat it all down to the last crumb. Is everything all right here?" she questioned, looking around the pantry. "It looks like a scientist's dream for the kitchen of the future."

"As far as I'm concerned, all it shows is how poorly a bachelor is forced to live," Mrs. Dovedale said tartly, opening one cunningly built cabinet after the other to reveal bottles of Dole's pineapple juice, an assortment of Franco-American soups, cartons of Kellogg's corn flakes, puffed wheat, shredded wheat, Quaker oatmeal, an assortment of teas and coffees, a tin of Maillard's breakfast cocoa, and a few boxes of Wilbur's chocolate buds. "There's a cereal cooker and an egg boiler and a percolator, but imagine, soup from a tin. It's not proper for a gentleman to eat like that, or very healthy either. Marriage is the only cure for poor eating habits!"

"Well, I'll take care of that as soon as I can," Kit assured the cook brightly. The kettle began to whistle, and as Mrs. Dovedale occupied herself brewing the tea, Kit took the linen, china, and tray back to the living room and began to set up for tea.

The red and gold lacquer coffee table in front of the sofa was the most logical location, and she placed a cloth of cream-colored tulle edged with a wide border of black lace over its gleaming surface. Next came a black mirror tray with bevelled edges that was almost the size of the coffee table, and on top of that she arranged the large gold luster cups and saucers, gold and black plates, a sugar and creamer made of pink opaline, Tiffany forks and teaspoons, and for the finishing and just slightly scandalous touch, little black napkins. She was admiring her handiwork when Moss returned, and she knew from the look that passed over his features that he didn't approve of how the tea table was set, not at all.

"I've placed your boxes in the second bedroom, Miss Allen," he said in his perfectly modulated voice. "I trust you and Mrs. Dovedale are finding everything to your satisfaction?"

"Yes, thank you, Moss. There's no trouble at all."

"I'm very glad to hear that, Miss Allen. Is there anything else you need?"

"That will be all for right now. If Mr. West needs anything, he'll ring you."

He left, and shortly after that, Kit sent Mrs. Dovedale off to join her husband. "Yes, I'll keep the kettle on the hot plate

257

and put out all the cakes myself. Don't worry, if I can run a shop I can certainly handle a pot of tea. I'm sure you and Mr. Dovedale are anxious for your evening off—I can't thank you enough for all your help. . . ."

Alone, she thought, closing the door behind the cook who had much more romance in her than the restrained Moss. Alone, that is, until Greg gets here. I can't go back now, and waiting for him to walk through the door is going to be the hardest part.

For a moment she looked at the reflection of the tea table in the gilt-framed mirror hanging over the mantel which was graced by a pair of blue cloisonné incense burners flanking a fine Tiffany carriage clock.

Was this all too deliberate, too risque, even for her? she wondered, suddenly seized by a wave of self-doubt. Would Greg be delighted that she loved him so much that she'd do a little extra maneuvering so they could spend some extra time alone together, or would he start thinking of her as one more demanding woman in his life?

But even as questions about how, if at all, she was compromising her high principles, Kit was aware that being alone here offered too much of a temptation to explore to ignore. Simply wandering around the living room, taking her time while she looked at the paintings and books wasn't enough, and she went toward the bedroom doors, selecting the one Moss had carried her boxes through a short time before.

"So this is the infamous second bedroom," she murmured, amused, as she looked around her. "Nothing to find fault with, it's certainly nice enough, but there's something missing. . . ."

The bedroom had been done by Mallory in 1911, shortly after her arrival in Los Angeles, and Kit could see that her friend had used her excellent taste and talent to create an almost monotoned chamber with the walls, ceiling, and carpet done all in pale gray and touched with lilac. The pale gray sateen curtains had bunches of lilacs printed on them, the headboard of the bed had painted lilacs on it, as did the tall screen, and the armchair and loveseat were covered in a flowered chintz.

"It's a fine spot for an afternoon tryst, but it's not my sort of place," she said, going over to the boxes resting on the quilted pale gray sateen bedspread. She discovered that the two roomy closets were empty, but that the dressing table held a full selection of perfume and cosmetics. For a moment she hesitated about the proprietary gesture of putting her clothes away, but reasoned that since they were going to dinner it only made sense to hang up her expensive evening dress.

Her tasks didn't take long, and her next destination was the one she longed to see—Greg's bedroom. She supposed that every woman when first granted access to the inner sanctum of the man she loved felt like this—half intruder and half detective—but was she the only one to feel such a rush of emotion at her first sight of the beautifully furnished room that, five stories above busy Spring Street, was bathed in sunshine and quiet?

Oh, Greg, do you think about me in my room the way I do about you here? she wondered.

She admired the rich Oriental carpet with its center grid of soft sage green and surrounding border of green, dark blue, and taupe that made the highly polished walnut furniture glow with a deep brightness, and for a long minute simply looked at the large fourposter bed draped in soft green silk. It looked like a very comfortable, very masculine resting spot, and Kit couldn't help the feeling of triumph that so far no woman had shared this room with him.

She glanced out of one of the large windows down to the Alexandria's main entrance. No sign of either Greg or his Fiat, and the urge to continue exploring was too strong to ignore.

On one of his bedside tables, both of which were designed

to have bookcase fronts, she saw the icon Greg told her about, and taking a closer look, she recognized it as a rendering of Our Lady of Vladimir, and had probably been painted about a hundred years before in Mystera.

And at one time it had probably reposed in a repousse and gilded riza encrusted with jewels, Kit thought, acutely aware that when he left St. Petersburg disguised as a servant, Greg had had to leave such outward signs of his wealth behind. She could understand Jessica's reaction to the religious object, she might even share it, but knowing Greg's story she'd never say a word about it.

Almost without realizing what she was doing, Kit looked through his closets, at precisely tailored business suits in weights and colors ranging from Palm Beach light to Wall Street pinstripe worsted, all proper and correct depending on the weather and the city he was in; at three sets of dinner clothes and two full-dress suits; the tie racks that held a full selection of ties from Brooks Brothers, Sulka, and Charvet; and two heavy silk dressing gowns. There were the appropriate morning clothes and riding and tennis gear. His hats were few but his shoes were numerous and in perfect condition; she could imagine Moss patiently polishing them to the highest possible gloss. He had a Burberry raincoat, a velvet-collared chesterfield for evening wear, and a heavyweight topcoat obviously reserved for winter trips to points north and east. The multi-drawered chests revealed spotless, flawless stacks of shirts, underwear, pajamas, and socks. The labels were Brooks Brothers, Tripler's, Jaeger, Sulka, Charvet, and Turnbull and Asser; all the markings of a fastidious man who could put on his clothes and then forget about them.

The bathroom revealed the usual shaving things and aspirin tablets and other necessities of life, as well as bathtub-side baskets holding Guerlain's sandalwood and *Mouchoir de Monsieur* soap, and bars of Jockey Club and Knize soaps which he ordered from Caswell-Massey in

New York.

It isn't Greg's secret that kept him from getting married, it's this apartment, Kit thought wryly. It's perfect enough to keep a man a confirmed bachelor!

She returned to the living room, still trying to sort through the feelings that her tour had brought up in her, when the long English Georgian writing table placed against the back of the sofa caught her eye. How could I have missed this? she wondered, looking at the selection of silver-framed photographs arranged on the brown leather surface. The first photograph to catch her attention was of Caro standing between Sin and Greg, her arms around their shoulders.

They all look so young and carefree, she thought, and realized that it must have been taken shortly after their arrival in California.

She was glad to see that the assortment of photographs included a few of the snapshots taken of them in Chicago and on the California Limited. And in the center was the formal photograph that Madam Lallie Charles had taken of her in London in May.

And then she knew why the second bedroom had left her cold, and it had nothing to do with jealousy over the other women who had graced it for a few hours.

It's just a classic hotel room, only with more style, but there's no real feeling there, no soul. Greg's personal imprint is so strong I can feel it everywhere else, but not in the other bedroom, she thought, heading for the pantry.

Working quickly and carefully, she filled the large gold teapot with the scalding hot, deeply fragrant tea, brought it out to the tea tray, and then returned to the pantry to arrange the pastries on the serving plates. Suppose Greg had decided not to come, to stay at Hooper Studios until the close of the workday? She could be in a silly, sticky situation. True, Greg had to come back here to change before dinner, but the last thing she wanted was for him to come in and see her waiting with a cold pot of tea.

She spent a minute trying to figure out how to get out of the apartment without leaving any trace of having been there in the first place, but she gave up on that struggle.

I can't be noble, she decided. I came here because of Greg, and I'll wait for him. No hasty departures leaving a trail of pastry crumbs behind for me!

Kit was aware that she knew Greg well enough to know that he wouldn't turn either cold or hostile because she was surprising him, but exactly what his reaction would be was a mystery to her.

Don't make up a scenario that isn't going to come true, she warned herself as she heard a key turn in the lock and the door open and then slam shut.

"Moss!" It was Greg's voice, clear and quietly authoritative. "Moss, what is this emergency—"

He was out of the small entrance foyer before he finished talking, and as his voice trailed off, they simply looked at each other.

Kit had never seen Greg when he didn't look like a magazine illustration. Even in more informal situations he never looked anything but clean and crisp. But now, for the first time, she saw how he looked at the end of a working day. His long, lean body slumped a little, his hair was rumpled, there were lines of exhaustion etched on his face which was pale under his tan; she now knew that he had to shave twice a day. And she never loved him more than at this moment.

"Hello," he said, not taking his eyes from her.

"Hello," Kit responded, her heartbeat turning erratic.

"I don't suppose I should ask where Moss is, or what the emergency is." Like reading *Ballet At Midnight,* he couldn't quite believe this was happening, but unlike four hours ago, this was a situation to enjoy.

"There's no emergency, it's only my birthday," Kit said, barely keeping a smile under control. She saw the corresponding look in Greg's eyes. "I love the flowers and the jewelry you gave me, but I decided I wanted to give myself a present."

"And that is—?" Greg asked, the smile in his eyes finally reaching his mouth.

"You and me and a French tea party with no one else around." She stood up in a rich swish of satin georgette and walked over to Greg, putting her arms around his shoulders. "I hope you didn't have a lot to eat for lunch."

"I seem to recall something that was probably a chicken sandwich," he said, his hands encircling her waist as her fragrance, Guerlain's *Apres le Ondee,* enveloped him. Now was the time to put aside all the old demons that were stirring. He had the woman he loved, the woman who staunchly believed that he was incapable of committing murder, and all the confusion and conflict launched by the arrival of the last story he ever expected to see was momentarily stemmed. "Have I met your requirement to be properly prepared for a tea party?"

"That sounds just about right." She wanted to run her fingers over Greg's well-defined mouth, she wanted to kiss him and not stop until they reached a point from which they couldn't retreat, but all she allowed herself was to kiss him on the cheek. "Before we eat, do you want to ring Moss? When he left here, I was sure he didn't think very much about fiancées who use a loyal servant to deliver false messages!"

"Then how did you get him to do just that?" Greg asked when he stopped laughing.

"I just said it was my birthday—"

"Which is the truth."

"And that you've been working very hard."

"Also the truth."

"And that I thought that you deserve a very special treat, and that since he was such a loyal servant, he would want you to have some special time to relax." He was too close to resist, she thought, but she had to, at least for a little while longer. "Finally, I told Moss how much we were looking forward to him being our butler when we build our house in

263

Beverly Hills."

"That did it. My darling, you knew exactly how to reach that proper Englishman I employ! In his heart of hearts, he really doesn't approve of how I live. He may have a few qualms about your tactics, but since he knows that you're going to reform me from my wayward bachelor ways, he decided to carry out your request."

"I think he might have had a few second thoughts when Mrs. Dovedale arrived with the pastry boxes and I set the table. What do you think?"

Greg studied the tea table. It was the perfect recreation of a Paris tea, where, unlike London, they don't waste time with tiny cucumber sandwiches and brown bread and butter and hot scones. The magic of the pastry chef rules, and he looked at perfectly formed pains au chocolat, incredibly rich and dark chocolate cake, and golden-brown pastry barquettes where large red strawberries rested on a bed of creamy custard. He took a deep breath, and the scent of vanilla from the glazed apple tart blended irresistibly with the aroma of jasmine tea.

Kit placed her cheek against his, enjoying the unfamiliar sensation of the light scrape of his beard. "Well?"

"I'm overwhelmed," Greg said, and then he proved that any man, no matter how sophisticated or wealthy or accomplished, can turn into a twelve-year-old boy in an ice cream parlor. "And are those Mrs. Dovedale's famous pains au chocolat made with *two* strips of chocolate?"

Chapter 14

An hour later, the teapot was empty, the plates held only buttery crumbs, and Kit and Greg were stretched out together across the sofa. Their shoes were off and Greg had draped his suit jacket and tie over the nearest chair.

"The last time I felt like this," Greg said in a newly contented voice as he lay with his head nestled against Kit's shoulder, "I was twelve, our new pastry chef had just arrived from Paris, and I ate my way through his specialties. For a few years after that, I confused eating pastry with another equally pleasurable activity."

Kit laughed softly. "That's not a bad comparison. And you look so much better now. Just before you came in, I was wondering how you'd react to the tea table," she continued, stroking the back of his neck just below his perfectly barbered hair, and slipping her fingers under his open shirt collar. "It was a few minutes of pure stage fright!"

"And this from a woman who gave up her life in New York to come to Los Angeles and open her own business!"

"Some pioneer, dressed by Tappe, Poiret, and Lucile!"

He nuzzled at the side of her neck. "The very best kind. And all I saw when I walked in the door was you. I didn't focus on the tea table until later." He shifted his head slightly so he could view the remains of the treat Kit had so carefully planned for them. "Do I own all of these plates and cups and that tray?"

"Of course you don't! Your pantry is an architect's delight and a bachelor's nightmare. The forks and teaspoons are yours," she allowed, "but I bought the rest of it in Mallory's shop."

Slowly, he raised his head from her shoulder, her dress rustling as he shifted position to look down at her face. "So now all of this is ours?"

Ours, Kit thought, the magic word. If this was all that happened this afternoon, it was worth it to hear that word.

"All ours," she repeated, her fingertips tracing over his high cheekbones and down his cheeks to touch the slight indentation in his chin. "We'll use it every time we have tea, if you like."

"Black napkins included?"

"They are a bit much."

"Oh, I don't think so. They seem to be in keeping with the spirit of the occasion." His head dipped down for a moment to kiss the base of her throat where her pulse was beating at a steady pace. "I'm crushing your dress," Greg whispered. "Do you mind?"

"Not from you," she said as his mouth moved to the side of her neck. "I can have it steamed, and—," For a moment, Kit hesitated, but there was no reason for subterfuge, "and I have another dress with me."

Greg's eyes were knowing. "Only one?"

Her last bit of apprehension faded. "Two. One for tonight, and one suitable for daytime—and all the accessories to go with them."

"Do you mean to tell me that this tea isn't a replacement for the dinner I was going to buy you tonight?" Greg inquired with mock surprise.

"Why you stingy—!" Kit feigned a swing at his ribs. "I always thought Russians were supposed to be so generous!"

"I'm American now."

266

"Yes, but don't try claiming New England thrift with me."
She felt so relaxed, but their closeness, their ever-increasing
intimacy was never far from her mind. For the past hour she
had kept her love for him on another plane, more concerned
with easing some of the tension he'd walked in with, but now
she was filled with longing for him. She was achingly aware
of his closeness and of all the possibilities they could share,
and no amount of witty exchanges was going to lessen the
heavy air between them. "I know how generous you really
are."

"And you know that flattery is even more effective on a
man than French pastry. It can make me forget all sorts of
things."

"It's nothing you really want to remember." Kit could feel
his limbs pressing against her legs, his hands gently touching
her face, and his dark-amber eyes seemed to look right
through her. "Oh, Greg, I love you."

"I love you," he said, his face transfigured as his arms
closed around her. Was he insane? he thought in the brief
moment when time was suspended between them. Remember what happened earlier, remember the story, the story
that's in your briefcase right now, it could change your life all
over again. The past, always the past, but not now, now is for
the future. "And right now I want to make love to you."

His mouth fastened over hers, and for a moment Kit felt
herself perched on the edge of a new passion, one that would
bind them together forever. The magic that was never very
far away from them spun its web again, and their tongues
met in a passionate exploration.

When the kiss was over, Kit was lost between gasping for
breath and pressing extra kisses on Greg's face. "If we stay
here on the sofa, we'll never be able to look at it with a
straight face again."

Greg's hands moved lovingly over her, igniting new fires in
both of them. "Why is it that I have the feeling you're now
familiar with much more than the contents of my pantry?" he

asked, love and laughter mingling in the rich amber eyes she loved.

His attitude was the key to just how much she could tell him. "You have that certain feeling—among others more appropriate to the moment—because you're a very perceptive man." She kissed him again. "My darling Gregory, I not only know how many suits you have in your closets, but the brand of aspirin tablets you use!"

They were still laughing a minute later when he carried her through the bedroom and set her on her feet beside the bed. They exchanged another lingering kiss before Greg spoke.

"I don't have any secrets left, do I?" he asked with gentle humor.

"Only one," she rejoined, touching his forehead with hers.

"About the other bedroom—," he began, but Kit pulled back and quickly placed a hand over his mouth.

"No, you don't have to explain a thing to me. The minute I walked into that room I knew what was missing. Your body was there but not your personality. Your essence, that's here in this room and in the living room. All that other bedroom shows is how considerate you were of the women who came here in terms of privacy and comfort. It takes nothing away from me—or from us."

Greg took her hand from his lips and began to kiss the soft skin. "Doesn't anything that I do ever shock you? Do you always have to understand me?"

"Oh, Greg, you're the most uncomplicated complicated man I've ever met! And as long as you didn't show me to the other bed—."

Her voice turned into laughter as Greg suddenly swept her up into his arms and deposited her on the bed. "This is the only bed I've ever wanted you in," he said, his body following hers to the seductive comfort of the mattress and pillows. "I've dreamed about it and wished for it since the night we met." His mouth descended to the long swan-like column of her neck. "The hot water faucet on my bathtub is rusted closed by now. . . ."

Together they dissolved into laughter that faded into something quite different as they began to touch and kiss. Kit ran her fingertips over Greg's richly made mouth, a new urgency building inside her. There was no more need to hold back or keep themselves in check because the time or place wasn't right, or postpone the fulfillment they both longed for in order to be sure what they had was real.

They sat up, and Greg undid the long row of tiny, satin-covered buttons that fastened her dress down the back, and as Kit leaned against him he slipped the dress off her, letting it fall on the floor beside the bed.

"I've never sacrificed a dress for a better cause," Kit said as they pulled down the bedspread and the quilted silk puffs to reveal creamy percale sheets. She began to return the favor, unbuttoning his shirt. "Greg, my fingers are shaking. . . ."

"I'm not very steady myself," he whispered thickly as the last button on his shirt was opened and Kit began to remove his cufflinks. "This isn't how we're expected to act, you know."

"I wouldn't have it any other way."

He took the pins out of her hair, removed her pearls, and, as his breathing changed and heartbeat became swifter and heavier, his long-fingered hands tangled in the silk, lace, and ribbons of the princess slip she wore.

Eyes closed, Kit lay back against the pillows as he removed her lacy lingerie, opening her eyes only as he carefully unhooked the bandeau that supported her breasts. She waited expectantly as he gazed adoringly at her. In another minute, he pulled off the rest of his clothes, and free of the awful-looking underwear men had to wear, he stretched out alongside her.

Kit gloried in her first sight of Greg's fully aroused body, and they reached for each other at the same moment, their embrace merging them in their first truly close contact as male and female without the encumbrance of clothes. For an endless moment they held each other very close.

"You are so glorious," she breathed. "Even better than I dreamed about."

"So are you." He caressed her creamy shoulders and moved down to cup her breasts. "Let me love you, Kit."

"Yes . . . yes . . . oh, Greg, just like that—." His hands were moving down her sides, over her hips to her thighs, gently parting them, and their contact became even more intimate.

Instinctively, Kit threw one leg over Greg's hip, and for a moment they stayed together without moving before a skillful twist of his body moved her to her back. He was kissing her: tiny kisses at her hairline, nipping little kisses at her throat, and passionate kisses on her mouth; and in turn she was caressing and exploring every inch of him that she could reach.

She felt his desire throbbing against her, felt the burning heat of his skin, and thought that she would melt from her own mounting desire. It had never been like this before, and when neither of them could stand it another minute, Greg brought them together with one swift thrust, filling Kit to overflowing.

She was in a new world, one made up of white lightning, brilliant colors, and the deep flash of heat that was Greg. It was the most overwhelming act of love that she had ever experienced. Each thrust of his body took them further away from the separate lives they'd lived before this afternoon and closer to a new life from which they could never be sundered from each other again.

She knew that her mind had closed off to everything but the sensations he roused in her; she was full of love for him, revelling in what they were discovering together, and wishing it could go on and on.

But that wasn't the aim of their spiraling passions. He was

slowing his strokes now, and she matched herself to his new rhythm, responding to him over and over again, telling him how much she loved him just as his passion-heavy voice said the same thing. They made the same promise, and as they reached the zenith of their love-making, the shattering crescendo burst over them in colors more than worthy of the most magnificent of firebirds.

"Would you like me to tell you a secret?" Greg asked a long time later, after they'd awoken from the deep, dreamless sleep they'd both fallen into after that first shared climax. Now they lay in the center of the bed in perfect, utter completion.

"I'd love to know any secret you have to tell me," Kit replied in a throaty voice as she trailed a hand down Greg's chest, delighting in its hardness and in the silky hair that grew lightly down its center. "Is it a good one?"

"This time it is." For a brief second his mind flashed to the story inside his briefcase, but with Kit in his arms, every luscious, curving inch tucked alongside him, there was no time to dwell on words written on paper. "Tonight, after dinner, I was going to use all my male charm to woo you into my bed. Naturally, when I walked in and saw you, I realized that you had a few plans of your own!"

She kissed the hollow at the base of his throat. "You make me sound like such a calculating woman! Well, I *did* plan out the birthday tea with the possibility of an ulterior motive," she amended humorously, "but I wasn't going to vamp you into making a move you didn't want to—that would be useless—but an assortment of French pastries have been known to be very effective!"

"Now that you know that a pain au chocolat is all that it takes to make me putty in your hands I'm absolutely at your mercy!" Greg laughed and began to kiss her. "From the first, I felt we were very finely attuned to each other—we wouldn't

271

have fallen in love with each other the way we did if we weren't—and this afternoon proves it."

"There are times when the only thing you can do is trust your instincts," Kit said as she nestled closer. "And I love your philosophy, but let's talk about something more important right now."

Greg smiled. "Such as?"

"How thick your eyelashes are, how perfect your mouth is, and how making love with you is bliss, better than any fantasy."

"I return every compliment," he said, wrapping his arms around her and taking her back into the bed's welcoming softness, gently wedging a leg between hers, his desire surging. "There's one thing we have to give special consideration to though."

Kit ran her hand down his strong back, enjoying the play of his muscles as she reached the base of his spine. "Only one?"

"Yes . . . it's a matter of timing. You decided on this afternoon—."

"And you were planning on tonight. But I think I can safely say that the advance hasn't upset you."

"Never . . . we simply have to perfect our timing. We both have the right ideas, we just have to bring them into closer alignment, and—"

"And we should immediately get to work on it in the best way possible," Kit concluded as he molded them together. She ran her hands up his back to the nape of his neck. "You're so right, darling. Now stop talking and kiss me so we can find out how much in tandem we really are!"

"I hope the elevator operator is going to appreciate your largesse!" Kit teased several hours later when they returned to his suite after dinner and dancing. Greg had worked out the entire menu with the Alexandria's chef in advance, from the chicken and turtle soup accented with sherry to the filet of sole prepared with shrimp in wine sauce and served with asparagus and rice, through the lettuce and hearts of palm salad, and ending with an ice cream bombe and the birthday cake with the correct number of candles. But once the evening was over, there was the logistical problem of the best way to get back to the fifth floor to solve. Coming downstairs had been easy by comparison. Kit had simply walked down the stairs to the lobby, arrayed herself on a sofa and waited for Greg to join her a few minutes later. But at midnight, with their love giving them a new daring, they had abandoned the plan for Kit to get off at Jessica's floor and then use the stairs, and Greg had taken out his billfold and handed the operator a twenty-dollar bill. "It was an absolutely brilliant stroke," she said as Greg went over to the bar set up in a corner of the living room.

"I didn't see why we should carry on like characters in a French farce. Hotel staffs always seem to glean onto things anyway," Greg replied. He kept his voice light and amused, but the moment was fast approaching when he would have to discuss a deeply serious matter with Kit. "Shall we have a cognac?"

"That would be nice."

He poured out two snifters of Remy Martin and carried the glasses over to the sofa. "Tonight would be perfect for a fire. You would look ravishing in that particular light, but in case you haven't realized it, the fireplace is false."

"I thought it looked a little strange." She cupped her hands around the balloon-shaped crystal to warm the rich liquid inside. "But it doesn't matter, and next year at this time we'll have our own home with a real fireplace. It's something to look forward to."

"You're very optimistic."

"Tonight I am—thanks to you," she said, looking at him over the glass. "Are you in a Russian blue mood tonight?"

Greg began to laugh, then stopped, suddenly serious. "Do

I look or act very Russian to you?"

"If I didn't know your background, I'd say that you were either born in Europe or were taken there for your first years," Kit said honestly. "It's just certain mannerisms I've caught. Oh, I forgot to tell you this earlier, but Sally Courtland came in on Monday. She looked at a lot of things, bought a pair of gloves, and then cornered me for a nice little chat." Kit took a sip of her drink, and her engagement ring flashed in the soft light. "She wanted me to know that she didn't mind your defection to me since she has a charming French naval officer paying attention to her, and you're really better off with me since you're *so* American!"

Greg almost choked on his cognac. "You made that up as you went along!"

"I only wish."

"That's not what I ever expected Sally to say about me. Somehow I suspect she was insulting me."

"It's a matter of perception, and Sally sees you as an all-American sort of guy. She has no idea of your past."

"But someone else may."

His words, so quietly and conversationally delivered, were more shocking than if he'd spoken in either anger or fear.

"How—?" Kit could barely get the word past the sudden tightness in her throat. "Did someone say something?"

"No, they wrote it in a story and entered it in our contest," Greg said, feeling oddly calm as he told Kit what had happened, how he had discovered the story, and how he felt when he read it. "I've spent years waiting for this to happen. I always thought that one night I'd be having dinner in a restaurant and a stranger at the other side of the room would stand up and point to me and shout, 'That's Alexander Gregori Dimitri Vestovanova, the murderer of Natalia Voykovich!'"

"Don't say that!"

"I don't want to discuss whether or not it might be true," he said a bit shortly, followed immediately by a sharp pang of regret. "Kit, I didn't mean—"

"I know, darling. After the day you've had you must be exhausted. I'm starting to feel pretty worn out myself. Why don't we discuss this in bed?"

A faint smile tugged at his mouth. "I'm not about to refuse that suggestion."

Kit put down her snifter. "You're being awfully calm and patient about this."

"I'm not calm, just rather numb about this possibility, and as for patient—, whenever I look at you, I start to feel very impatient."

"That's all I need to hear," she said, smiling as they stood up and went into his bedroom.

The maid had already remade the bed, returning it to its pristine condition, and turned on the bedside lamps so that the room was bathed in softly glowing light. His pajamas were neatly folded on the top sheet, and Greg held out the top.

"Shall we share?"

Kit thought very briefly about the expensive nightgown and negligee in the other bedroom—she didn't for one moment think that Greg didn't know she'd brought all her ornaments of allurement with her—but there was no real decision about what she really wanted to put on right now.

"I'll only be a few minutes," she assured him, taking the proffered top. "I know how concerned you are about that story—would it be possible for me to see it?"

"It's in my briefcase," Greg said, looking a little surprised. "I want very much for you to read it and tell me what you think, but I was worried that you'd think I plan to make bringing home business and taking it into our bedroom a regular occurrence."

"We'll make an exception just this once." She gave him a quick kiss. "Be right back."

Kit was consumed with curiosity as to what that story might contain, and she undressed quickly, leaving her shimmering dance dress draped over a slipper chair. She noticed that the maid had been here too, turning down the bed and laying out her nightgown and negligee.

But not tonight, she thought, and headed for the bathroom to wash her face.

"I've just realized that this is the first time you've seen me without my makeup," Kit remarked as she rejoined Greg.

"I have no complaints, and seeing you in my pajama top is enough to make me say, what story." The look in Greg's eyes as they faced each other at opposite sides of the bed became very appreciative as he gazed at Kit. Because of her height, she didn't have the little-girl-lost-look a smaller, slighter woman might have projected; she only had to turn back the cuffs once, and the loosely fitted jacket made of the finest white Pima cotton and edged in gray stopped some inches above her shapely knees. "You look so entrancing—"

"You're pretty enthralling yourself," Kit said. She bit her lower lip. Greg needed her to read that story, and she wanted to be his sounding board. He wasn't calm and accepting about this, she realized, he was in some sort of shock. But something else had also happened today, and they were still at the point where nearly everything else could be put aside. "Greg—."

They met each other in the middle of the bed, and the manuscript stayed where it was on the bedside table. The past was an armreach away, but the present and the future had a much stronger pull on them.

"Are you *really* Nikolai Taranov?" Kit asked with great interest sometime later as they lay back against the pillows reading the manuscript together. "He seems to have a penchant for gold-tipped cigarettes, and I've never seen you smoke."

"But I did—and those very same gold-tipped cigarettes. I

didn't smoke between the time I left St. Petersburg and arrived in New York, and when I did start again it was only a couple of Pall Malls a day," Greg explained quietly. "When Sin had emergency surgery twelve years ago, I made a promise that if he recovered I'd never smoke again. It was a very frightening night, and any offering I could make seemed to be the right thing to do."

"It was a very noble gesture, one made from your heart." She turned a few more pages. "Apparently, your fictional alter ego doesn't have many altruistic thoughts."

"Neither did I then," Greg remarked, and his face tightened. "Read on."

Kit did, and as she turned each page she became more and more enthralled in the tale. She could overlook the choppy construction, the slightly awkward pacing, and the over-blown bits of dialogue. Whoever sent this in could tell a story, could write, and she told Greg that.

"How couldn't I agree. My blood is on every page, but I still couldn't stop reading. There's something there."

"Your younger life?"

"More or less."

"You love being cryptic, don't you? All right, let's start with less. What's wrong here?" she asked as they reached the last page. "It can't be flawless."

"No, it's not. Whoever this O.L. Pinchot is doesn't know the first thing about the Russian cavalry. I never had any of the duties and responsibilities afforded to Nikolai; it sounds as if the writer is familiar with the American army. And the unit he's assigned to doesn't exist. But that could be a well thought out trick to throw me off the track."

"And it could be a coincidence. Greg, look," she said as his expression turned incredulous, *"everyone* knows about ballerinas, particularly ballerinas from the Imperial Ballet and their aristocratic protectors. It's impossible to walk into Brentano's and not find half a dozen romantic novels with just that premise. The writer may have just decided to use a familiar topic and twist the ending."

"It's a possibility," Greg allowed, "but there are just too many similarities with how it was between Natalia and me, even down to the shop where I bought her chocolates. It's all there."

"But it doesn't mean that it was written by someone out to destroy you!" Kit protested, unable to bear the look of pain on his face, but hating the words as they came out of her mouth. Why else would someone write this story except for some sort of monetary gain? "There has to be an answer, one we just haven't come up with. I wish I could think of where I've heard the name Pinchot."

A faint look of hope appeared in Greg's eyes. "Do you know the name?"

"It's usually a Bostonian one—old and good, just the way they like it."

"Unfortunately, it's still no help to me. I can't even tell if *Ballet At Midnight* was written by a man or a woman."

"It was written by a man—and don't look at me like that. A woman can always tell when a particular sort of story is written by a person of the opposite sex. Something is always off because male writers don't listen very carefully to women or observe how they act."

"The hardest thing is going to be telling Sin about this. Still, he wouldn't appreciate me waking him up at one in the morning."

"He'd probably turn you in to the Okhrana himself."

To his own surprise, Greg began to laugh, and with a swift motion he removed the manuscript from the bed and deposited it on the floor before turning off the lamp and taking Kit in his arms.

"I wouldn't doubt that at all, but that's about the only consequence I won't have to worry about."

Kit wrapped her arms around his shoulders. "Then you

278

don't have some vast, complicated plan?"

"No," he said, unbuttoning the pajama jacket she wore. "I was thinking more along the lines of our indulging in an advance class in mutual exchange and observation."

"You can knot your tie without looking in the mirror!" Kit remarked as she came into the bedroom shortly after seven-thirty, fully dressed except for her hat, gloves, and lipstick, to find Greg leaning against the tall chest of drawers, casually flipping the ends of his maroon and gold-strip tie over each other.

"Is this supposed to be something of a parlor trick?"

"Most men I know have to look in the mirror."

"Since I'm not given to waking up with other men, I'll have to take your word for it," Greg said, and gave her a smile that made her heart leap.

This is *not* the time to get nervous, she thought, fussing with the jade buttons on her suit. They'd both been delighted to find that they were early risers, and now they were ready for a long and private breakfast together. For a moment Kit mentally debated the decision that had come to her in the middle of the night when she'd awakened for a few minutes and looked at Greg sleeping as peacefully as a child beside her. Should she bring up the matter now or wait a few minutes until they could face each other over coffee cups?

Now, she thought, and sat down on the edge of the bed.

"I hope you're as deft with the percolator as you are with a tie," she said brightly despite her apprehensive heartbeat.

"A bachelor picks up certain skills along the way. You'll have to drink Kaffee Hag though. Caro thinks I drink too much coffee, and she's foisted off the new caffeine-free coffee on me."

"Oh, it's not that bad. We both have a long day ahead of us, and this is the best way to start it." She took a deep breath. "I was thinking about what we should do later on."

Greg began to move the perfect knot up toward his collar. "Lunch?"

"Actually, I was thinking we should get married."

His hands fell away from his tie. "Are you proposing to me?"

"Of course not." Kit raised her left hand so that he could see the brown diamond glittering on her finger. "You did that. I'm simply setting the date."

"I'm glad I have the chest to lean against," Greg said almost whimsically. "You certainly know how to take me by surprise."

"I'm very serious about this. After breakfast, we can go over to the county clerk's office for the license, and then we can have that nice Judge Foley marry us. It's very simple."

"And like most simple solutions, it's wreathed in endless complications."

How could he be so calm? Kit wondered. It isn't that he doesn't care, it's as if he won't allow himself the luxury of either agreeing with me or hating the whole idea.

"Do you still want to marry me?"

"Yes! There's nothing I want more than to make you my wife."

"And I want you to be my husband," she said, drawing new resolve from the strength of his words. As she rose to her feet, she noticed that something was missing. "Greg, where's the manuscript? You haven't—?"

"*No!* It's back in my briefcase. I want a typist to make a clean copy before I show it to Sin."

"I see. That sounds like a good idea. But to get back to getting married—."

"I may be waiting for a call from a blackmailer," Greg pointed out as he finished dressing.

"And when the cobwebs grow on your phone we can get married?" she asked, coming over to him. For a moment, she enjoyed the pleasurable, possessive task of fussing over him, making sure his tie was straight and lapels free of even the most infinitesimal speck of dust. "I don't want to wait that long, and neither do you."

"All right," Greg said, placing his hands at her waist. "Even if that story didn't exist there would still be complications."

"Name them."

"Think of all the people we'll disappoint if we elope today. Not only your mother and stepfather, but Mallory and Rupert, and Sin and Caro, and all our friends."

"I wouldn't hurt any of those people for the world, but we're entitled to our own decisions. And there is another thing, but I don't want you to be hurt when I tell you," Kit went on, resting her hands on his shoulders as she looked into his eyes.

"There isn't anything you can say that'll upset me—except if you change your mind about marrying me."

"That's what we're discussing, darling. Oh, Greg, everyone expects us to have a big wedding, and I just don't want one. For me, big society weddings were events I went to or was a bridesmaid at, not something I ever really wanted for myself. You matter to me, not a lot of stupid, overblown frills. And most of all, I don't want all your old flings to watch while we get married!"

"Oh, my darling—" In spite of his own conflicts, conflicts strong enough to make another man reel, and which were leaving him not quite sure from which direction the next blow would come, he reacted instantly to the distress on her face and in her voice. He held her in his arms. "I never knew that you felt that way about being a bride."

"It's the idea of being *on display*. I'm too old to play the innocent bride."

"I'd never ask you to do that," he said as they left the bedroom. "I thought you would want all the glory of being a bride."

"The glory is our being married to each other."

281

"What about the reception Sin and Caro are planning for us, and the sukiyaki party Mallory and Rupert want to throw the night before we get married?" Greg inquired.

"They can still give us the parties." Kit sounded unperturbed. "*Everyone* wants to entertain a newly married couple. It's really like some sort of competition. I promise you, we'll be just as popular."

For the next few minutes they concentrated on making breakfast. Boxed cereal was all well and good in its place, but Kit had held back several of the pains au chocolat, and she put them on the breakfast tray.

"*Deja-vu?*" Greg suggested with a somewhat wicked smile as he put the silver tray he was carrying on the coffee table.

"A little, but it's only been about fourteen hours since we sat here the last time."

"Which was also the first time."

"But definitely not the last." Kit poured out the coffee. "How do you take your morning coffee?"

"With warm milk, quite a bit, and one sugar," Greg said, enjoying the cozy intimacy of the moment. "If we were married, would we have breakfast like this every morning?"

There was an undertone of fun to his question, but Kit recognized that it was essentially a serious one. "I'd like to think that we'd have breakfast either here or in bed, but with only one change."

"And that is?"

"Matching china and silver! The contents of your cabinets look like you were the salvage firm for all the odds and ends your friends didn't want."

"There's usually something wrong with a bachelor who has full sets of china and silver," Greg replied, and Kit was reminded that most men always thought that something was effeminate. "And couples who elope don't get wedding presents."

"That's what you think! A week from today, we'll be choking on chafing dishes. There'll be more wedding presents than we know what to do with."

"You have an answer for all my arguments, don't you?"

"The only concrete reason you could give me for not wanting to get married is that you've changed your mind, that you don't love me. Greg, you're not thinking about lying to me for my own good, pushing me away from you because you love me too much to hurt me," Kit finished a little more bitterly than she intended.

"No, I love you too much to let you go unless you wanted to leave first. Underneath it all, down to my very last layer, I'm still Russian enough to hold on to you for as long as you want me. My family may be noble, but I don't have the nobility it takes to be self-sacrificing."

"A fact for which I'm very grateful," Kit said, leaning over their coffee cups to kiss him. "And since I'm not willing to give you up, I would just have to stay around you, make enough of a fuss to ruin both our reputations, and generally make your life miserable!"

"I believe you would," Greg said, and grinned.

"And now that we have *that* settled, shall we set the date?"

He still wasn't ready to give up. "Don't you want to get married just before Christmas? We can have a small and very private ceremony, and a big reception afterwards," he said, aware that what he was suggesting was, in its own way, almost the same flouting of the rules of etiquette that Kit wanted to ignore. But if he could convince Kit—and himself—to wait, the intervening weeks might well provide some solution, some explanation to why this manuscript had suddenly arrived in his life.

"That's six weeks. Weeks of preparations and presents and plans. That's just what I want to avoid for all the reasons I told you about and because *I don't have the time*. I won't sacrifice the time I have to put into my shop for a lot of bridal fuss."

"What about our honeymoon?"

"Did you think you were going to get off easy there?" Kit

flashed him a flirtatious smile as she cut the last pain au chocolat in half. "If we get married today, we can drive up to Montecito tomorrow, and the day after that you can show me your horse ranch. We can spend a few days there, and later in December, when your movie project is under way and the Christmas shopping season is almost over, say around the twenty-first or the twenty-second, we can go up to San Francisco for our honeymoon."

"You have this all planned out." Greg's voice was full of delighted wonderment.

"It never hurts."

"What about your friend Tappe?" he asked, and Kit knew he was reaching the end of his list of excuses. "From what you've told me, it sounds as if he's putting in every stitch in your wedding dress himself."

Kit laughed. "I'll have to place a long-distance call and tell him. Herman will be disappointed, but he's a romantic, and I'm sure he can make a few adjustments so instead of a not-too-bridal-looking wedding dress, I'll have a ballgown with bridal overtones."

"Do you really want us to simply present everyone with that much of a fait accompli?"

"Greg—"

"When a couple runs off and gets married, it's usually for a reason."

"Well, if we didn't want to go to bed with each other, we'd really give the gossips something to chew on. It would also be very hard—no, make that impossible—to spend the next six weeks waiting for our wedding night. And I don't want that night to lose all its specialness for us by our meeting here every chance we get."

"There's nothing that I can say to that because I feel the same way. It's taking every bit of control that I have not to pick you up and carry you back into the bedroom. I want to take off that beautiful suit you're wearing, as well as everything underneath it, get rid of what I have on, and then put you right back in my bed."

"*Our* bed . . . and I agree with you," Kit said, putting her arms around him. "Regina and Ian MacIverson are back from the Orient, and Mallory and Rupert are giving them a dinner tonight to welcome them back to California. It's a very small, very intimate gathering, and it wouldn't be any trouble at all to add Judge and Mrs. Foley to the guest list, and have Mrs. Dovedale make a wedding cake instead of a chocolate roll."

"And Judge Foley can marry us before dinner."

"You were in agreement with me all along!"

"After my initial shock and surprise wore off. Everything you've said is true. You're the fourth person in my life to offer me not only great change and challenge, but a chance to rebuild my life," Greg told her in a quiet voice that was powerful with emotion. "First there was Boris, then John Burke in New York, and finally Sinclair. Each offer, like yours, was made with a full heart and no motive beyond the offer itself. I love you with all my heart, and I'm not enough of a fool to postpone the next step in our lives for another day."

Part Three

The Movie-Makers

*I was led by the grace of God to the
movies. I would like the industry
to be more aware of what they're doing
to influence people.*

—Dorothy Arzner

*We have a little catch phrase in our
family which somehow fits almost everyone
in the movie colony: "Spare no
expense to make everything as
economical as possible."*

—Frances Marion

Chapter 15

Kit stood in front of the full-length mirror in her bedroom, checking her reflection, waiting for the moment when she would pick up the large bouquet of rich gardenias tied with silver gauze and white silk ribbons that Greg had sent her, and walk out of the room and down the stairs to marry the man she loved.

The certainty that in less than an hour she and Greg would be husband and wife sent a long wave of excitement through her. This day had been so crammed with the events that led to this hour, she had had almost no time to think about the ceremony itself. But now it was almost time. She had come to Los Angeles to start a new life, and there was no better way to do that than by getting married. It was the closing link in this new circle.

"You look absolutely beautiful. You make almost as lovely a bride as I did," Mallory said as she entered the bedroom, looking stunning in a Lanvin gown of silver lace over pink chiffon.

"Thank you, I take that as the very highest compliment," Kit said as she turned away from the mirror. "When I bought this dress, I wondered where I'd wear it—it's so understated compared to some of my evening clothes. But then a

289

wedding dress is supposed to be that," she finished as they both admired the Tappe evening gown of rich white satin. The crossover bodice had a low square neck that merged into the high waist, and a small train fell gracefully from the skirt and swirled around her white satin evening pumps. "Is that an early wedding present?" she asked, finally noticing that Mallory was holding an oblong box whose familiar robin's-egg-blue color announced it was from Tiffany's. "Jessica called me this afternoon. One of her sources at the county clerk's office tipped her off that Greg had been in to get a marriage license, and she wanted confirmation. I can't believe how quickly word gets around. Was there a Tiffany trinket around someplace?"

"I think you're too important to Greg for him to give you a present from a cache of gifts he has put aside."

"This is from Greg! Why didn't you tell me right away?"

"Here, and here's the note to go with it. He brought it with him and said you were to open it right away."

"When did Greg get here?"

"About five minutes ago. Rupert has him in the library, regaling him with tales about our wedding."

While Mallory went over to the dressing table and closets, murmuring something about checking to see if Kit had left anything important in her first round of packing, Kit undid the ribbons and opened the glazed pasteboard box with trembling fingers. She pressed the hidden spring that released the lid of the black velvet box, and gasped when she saw what lay on the white satin bed. For a long minute she looked at the double strand of large cream-colored pearls with a snowflake-shaped clasp set with diamonds and cornflower-blue sapphires. Briefly she thought that they were too large to be real, but she knew that any gift of jewelry coming from Greg would not only be real but the finest and most imaginative of its kind. Placing the jewelry box on the closest table, Kit opened the letter.

My darling Katharine—

My mother had pearls just like these, and a long time ago she promised that when I married, she would give them to me for my bride. I can't obtain the originals, but the replica is as exact as possible.

I'm still Russian enough to believe in signs and portents. I contacted Tiffany's the day after I asked you to marry me. They arrived late this morning. When I see you wearing them in a little while, it will not only be for the first time, but at the start of our life together.

With all my love,
Gregory

"Oh, they are exquisite!" Mallory exclaimed. "May I put them on for you?"

"I wouldn't have anyone else help me." Kit quickly folded the note, slipped it back in its pale gray envelope, and put it beside the jewelry box. Together, they lifted the pearls from the white satin, placed the necklace around her neck, and Mallory worked on the intricate clasp. "I can't thank you enough for everything you've done today," she went on, reaching back to touch Mallory's hands.

"It's not over yet. The best part is coming."

"I mean it, Mallie. You've been wonderful. You didn't even blink when I walked into your office this morning and told you that Greg and I wanted to get married tonight."

"It's a good thing I decided to come in early today."

"Yes, and if you had said forget it, I would have run over to the county clerk's office and told Greg we were getting married right then and there."

"I remember that there were quite a few times I wished Rupert and I had eloped."

"Did you really?" Kit asked, carefully crossing to her dressing table to add a few more strategically placed drops of

291

Guerlain's *Rue de la Paix.* "I thought you loved every minute of your engagement and wedding—or, that's what everyone said."

"I loved it only because every day brought Rupert and me closer to getting married. But the endless gifts and parties and decisions were a terrible strain on both of us." Mallory paused for a moment as if remembering an unpleasant result of those days. "Our case was different though, because of the four years we didn't see or speak to each other. Still, I think couples should either have a good long engagement or else get married straight off."

"I told Greg I was too old to play the innocent bride," Kit said, deciding not to mention anything about Greg's old girlfriends. "Of course, getting married here tonight with our closest friends isn't really eloping, it's more what the French call *dans le plus stricte intime.*"

"The French do have a certain way with words," Mallory agreed just as Caroline opened the bedroom door.

"Are Regina and I welcome?"

"Don't even ask that question," Kit said happily, embracing Caroline and then Regina Bolt MacIverson. "Are you upset because we've turned your welcome home dinner into something else?"

"Don't you dare even *think* that!" Regina's Doucet gown of old-gold taffeta and brown chiffon swished expensively as she sat down. "All Ian and I have done since we docked in San Francisco last week is go to parties in our honor where we had to answer endless questions about China and Japan. It'll be nice to have another couple be the center of attention."

"Greg said something to the effect that our getting married like this might hurt our friends who were planning parties for us. He was really just spinning out excuses, using the time to get used to the idea of being a married man, but I want to make sure that no one here feels like that."

"Oh, for goodness sake." Caro, resplendent in Jeanne

Hallee's gown of nude charmeuse studded with brilliants over blue draped chiffon, looked utterly amazed. "I can't speak for every other anxious hostess in Los Angeles, but for my part I'd much rather have you and Greg getting married right now in a blaze of happiness because it's what you want to do, than just go through the social motions six weeks from now because it's what others expect of you."

"And we've all been to enough of *those* functions," Regina added swiftly.

"And you certainly know my views," Mallory put in, and Kit's last bit of concern that she might be inadvertently hurting the people she cared most about vanished.

Before anyone could speak, Patsy, one of Mallory's maids, appeared at the door. "Excuse me, Mrs. Randall, but Judge and Mrs. Foley have just arrived."

"Here we go!" Mallory said excitedly. "Now I know how Alix felt a few minutes before my wedding. She had all the fun of being matron of honor and none of the nerves of being the bride!"

"Thank you so much," Kit murmured wryly. This whole day had gone by in a flash, the minutes and hours pushed along on a surge of having to get everything in order by early evening, and now time seemed to have slowed to a crawl. "I really didn't have to hear that."

"Caro, it's time for you and Regina to go down and play hostess for me," Mallory instructed, in charge again. "Patsy, you and Rosita get our bouquets out of the refrigerator, and while you're there, tell Doverdale to wait exactly fifteen minutes and then put the record on the Victrola."

"Something old, something new, something borrowed, something blue—we're down to that," Mallory continued when they were alone again.

"I bought my lingerie last summer at Lucile's, new is just about everything else, there's the blue garter you wore, and Caro's earrings take care of borrowed," she finished, touching the large, dramatic-looking pearl and diamond earrings that Caroline had loaned her and went so well with her wedding present that she was pleasantly sure that her friend had known all about the pearls. "This is just about it, isn't it?"

"It's all over but the walk down the stairs," Mallory said, recalling herself just over four years ago, swathed in white satin and Duchesse lace, not thinking about anything except seeing Rupert again. "You and Greg are going to be fine."

"I know we are, and before I forget—," Kit quickly switched her engagement ring from her left to her right hand, "our rings are being sized at Shreve's, but Greg told me he found suitable temporary rings for us at an antique shop on Broadway," she said as the young maids, pretty in their evening uniforms of pale blue taffeta, came in with the gardenia bouquets. "They look even more beautiful than when they were delivered." Kit took her flowers. "Shall we go downstairs before Greg decides this is all a terrible mistake?"

"Not if he's smart he won't," Mallory said as they left the room, Patsy and Rosita holding up the short train of Kit's gown. When they reached the upstairs gallery the maids ran quickly down the stairs and signalled to Dovedale, who was waiting beside the Victrola that had been moved to an appropriate spot beneath the staircase, and a moment later the strains of "A Midsummer's Night's Dream" began to play.

"It's finally happening, Kit thought with a thrill of anticipation. Did I push Greg into this? What is Mummy *really* going to say when she gets my cable? Am I doing the right thing?

The three questions raced through her mind as she saw Mallory take the first step down the stairs. Last-second doubts assailed her, but she knew the decision made twelve hours earlier was the right one. Greg was a man of strength and firm resolve; no one, not even her, was going to make him do one thing unless he too wanted it. Her mother was hardly the type of woman devoted only to the idea that her daughter's wedding had to be the social event of the year. And as for being the right thing to do—she had spoken from her heart this morning, and that was never wrong.

Kit counted to five and began to walk down the sweeping staircase.

At the foot of the stairs, she stopped for a moment to smile at the servants who would watch the ceremony from the doorway. This is how I've always wanted to get married, she thought as she walked toward the drawing room, swaying slightly on her high heels. It's small and quiet, and filled with love.

The drawing room was filled with flowers: large vases held great bouquets of white and pink flowers and were placed at strategic spots around the room, while the fireplace was banked with pots of white orchids and gardenias in celadon bowls. Candlelight flickered gently, softly diffusing the light from the silkshaded lamps, and the scent of flowers mingled with the faint aroma of furniture polish and the scent of perfume.

The first person Kit saw was Judge Foley standing in front of the fireplace. Rupert was standing with Caro and Regina and Mrs. Foley by the long sofas, while Mallory stood at the judge's left, and finally, standing next to Sinclair, was Greg, and she thought her heart was going to overflow with love for him.

He looked utterly resplendent in his dinner clothes, she thought, and his face above the perfectly starched wing collar of his dress shirt was only slightly pale. Just a little while longer, she told herself, and then she was handing her flowers to Mallory and turning to Greg. Instinctively, they reached for each other's hands.

The music stopped, and in the moment of quiet that followed the lifting of the needle from the record, no one seemed to be breathing. It was an almost church-like quiet, and the ceremony itself, which could so easily have been something almost furtive and pasted together and slightly shoddy, instead took on the quiet patina of a small and highly cherished occasion.

"Dear friends—," Eric Foley, Federal judge of the California court, still handsome and athletic at fifty, paused for a moment to warmly regard his wife, his friends, and the couple he was about to marry, "there are those people—otherwise good and warmhearted people—who believe that a civil ceremony is not really a proper wedding, that that can only take place in a house of worship because otherwise there is no spirituality. After tonight, however, I am going to be very happy to tell them that their theory is false. That the spirituality that comes from a happy pair does not need a special setting in which to flourish, and the couple, the friends, I am about to marry are proving that right now.

"Gregory West, do you take Katharine Allen . . ."

"If I'd known that getting married was so easy, I think I would have asked Kit to marry me at the first opportunity," Greg said a half-hour later as they all gathered in the dining room. The ceremony had concluded, congratulations exchanged, and the photographer hired for the occasion had taken their pictures. "Every other wedding I've been to seemed to be an exercise in excess."

"I hope you're not counting ours on your blacklist of overdone weddings," Caro said as Dovedale began to fill their glasses with champagne. "Sin and I have always considered our ceremony and reception to have been a model of good taste."

"And it was, but I was the best man there and not a guest," he explained adroitly, quickly pressing Kit's hand in a silent signal that let her know he knew how close he'd come to stumbling into a social gaffe.

"Well, I've always found that the happier we are the more we think our wedding was the simplest and best run," Adair

Foley observed, placing a large damask napkin over the lap of her Callot Soeurs dress of iris-colored chiffon and silver lace. "And how large it actually was had nothing to do with the matter."

"The only thing I remember about my wedding is Caro in the drawing room of that apartment in the Osborne," Sinclair said as he rose to his feet, champagne glass in hand. "And this brings us to the first toast, which I shall endeavor to make as interesting for the groom as possible. Now—"

When she had been faced with seating a party of ten at her English Regency dining room table, one couple being the bride and groom, Mallory had wisely thrown all the rules of etiquette in this matter out the window. She and Rupert were at opposite ends of the table, with Sin at her right and Judge Foley at her left. Her husband divided his considerable wit and charm between Caroline and Mrs. Foley. Kit and Greg were placed together between Sin and Mrs. Foley, and Regina and Ian were across from them.

After that, decorating the dining room with its panels of old paper showing scenes of Venice had been much easier.

The shining Honduran mahogany table was draped in their best damask tablecloth, rich arrangements of white flowers in full bloom and placed in silver bowls filled the center of the table, and while she had left the candles off the table, they were flickering gently in silver holders placed on the sideboards, throwing shadows on the fine Impressionist paintings on the walls.

"I hope, Kit, that you're enjoying the special privilege we both have tonight," Regina teased as the waitresses under Dovedale's watchful supervision served the crepes filled with crabmeat and mushrooms.

"If you mean being able to sit beside my husband for the first and last time at a dinner party, I certainly do," Kit said, picking up a fork. "I know that after tonight all our friends are going to work out their seating plans so that we're at opposite ends of the table."

"It's supposed to make you more appreciative of quiet dinners *a deux,*" Ian said. "Believe me, though, you can get a crick in your neck very quickly from trying to catch a glance at each other from opposite ends of a table that looks like the length of the playing field at the Rose Bowl."

Whether it was the rush of the day or the excitement generated by the past hour, everyone was hungry, and the crepes were replaced by boned jumbo squabs stuffed with wild rice accompanied by creamed spinach, and followed by a hearts of palm salad with a fine, runny Camembert. After each course there were the toasts, each guest rising in turn to raise their champagne glass to the newly married couple, making remarks that were funny and touching and heartfelt without being at all silly or sentimental.

There was a superb orange sorbet, and then there was the wedding cake.

It was a three-tier cake, perfectly frosted and trimmed and ornamented with the same bride and groom figures that had graced Mallory and Rupert's cake some four years before. If Mrs. Dovedale's creation was smaller than the one Mr. Wong would make for them in a few weeks time when Sin and Caro gave them their formal reception, it nonetheless managed to affect everyone at the table.

"It's just perfect for us!" Kit exclaimed, rising to her feet as the cake was wheeled in. "I know Mrs. Dovedale was disappointed in not being able to make a birthday cake for me yesterday, but she certainly outdid herself tonight!"

"Everything's been outdone tonight," Greg said, also rising to his feet. "We have all of you to thank, and thank-you doesn't seem to be nearly adequate."

"Oh, God, now they're getting sentimental!" Sin said with a mock groan.

"Get the photographer and cut the cake before the treacle begins to drip!" Rupert advised, and joined in the good-natured laughter as Kit and Greg took their places behind the cake.

The photographer was summoned from the breakfast room where he had been enjoying exactly the same dinner, and he quickly set up his equipment before posing the Wests in the traditional pose of cutting their cake. Mrs. Dovedale knew they both loathed fruitcake, but pound cake was too plain, and she couldn't bring herself to make the rich, dark chocolate cake they so loved, so a compromise had to be reached.

"Marble cake!" Greg said as he offered a forkful to Kit. "I don't think this is going to start a new style in wedding cakes, but it'll be a tradition that's going to be all ours."

"My darling husband," Kit savored the words as she fed Greg a piece of cake. While he was still in the process of swallowing, she put down her plate and picked up her champagne glass. "It's time for my toast," she went on, raising the tulip-shaped glass. "For Gregory West, who is my love, who is wonderful in every way, who took care of all the details involving our wedding brilliantly, and will be perfect in my eyes if he tells me one thing."

"When you put it like that, you know I'll tell you anything you want to know," Greg responded, adrift on a sea of love.

"Did you remember to tell the Alexandria's manager that when we walk in there tonight we'll be a perfectly dull and respectable married couple?"

"Maybe I should have forgotten to tell the manager that we were getting married tonight after all," Greg said as he swept Kit up in his arms to carry her over the threshold and into his apartment where Moss had left the lights soft and dim. "It would have saved us the reception we received downstairs."

"Oh, you didn't mind that much! Weddings, even unexpected ones, make people want to do something special," Kit said as he set her down in the center of the living room. "At least they didn't throw rice at us."

299

"Probably because it would be too much of a problem to sweep it off the carpets. But none of that seems to be very important right now," he went on, pulling her closer to him, her perfume filling his senses. He removed her Poiret evening wrap, the same one she'd worn that night in Williams, Arizona. "Thank you for wearing this again."

"I thought it would add the proper touch."

"If Sin and Caro hadn't lent us their newest Silver Ghost and Taylor to drive us, I would have pulled us off the road and into some quiet spot for an early start on our wedding night."

Kit laughed and locked her arms around his waist. "I wouldn't have minded very much, but can you imagine the hotel staff that was lined up to welcome us, how they would have reacted to our arriving very late and rumpled?"

Greg's smile was touched with a pirate's glee. "It would have been worth it."

She brushed her mouth against his. "Of course it would."

"Then why are we standing here?"

"My flowers."

"What?"

"My flowers," Kit repeated, picking up the great armful of rich gardenias. "There wasn't anyone to toss it to, and I can't let it wither away. Do you have an extra vase?"

"If I don't, we'll find a reasonable facsimile."

"There's something very intimate and lovely about standing together in a kitchen," Kit murmured a short time later as she filled a vase with cool water. Greg's arms were wrapped around her, and his chin rested on her right shoulder. "We'll have to remember to do it often."

"This is a pantry, and there's no place for us to stand except very close to each other," he said, nibbling gently against the side of her neck. "I never thought I'd spend the first hour of my wedding night anywhere near the kitchen sink!"

Kit laughed and deposited her bouquet in the vase. "I

300

know this isn't quite what's expected of a just-married couple—particularly anyone like us—but every aspect of tonight, from the way our friends acted, to Judge Foley's words, to the rings we exchanged, means so much to me. It's the first affirmation of our love, and I want to treat it with care and respect." She threw him a look over her shoulder. "Could it be that some of your Russian sensibilities have rubbed off on me?"

"You don't have to be Russian to care about all the right things," Greg said quietly, kissing her hair. "Do you think the flowers will be happy for the night now?"

"Not as happy as we're going to be."

It only took a minute to leave the flowers on a side table, and then they were in the bedroom, leaning against the closed door, taking their time as they exchanged kiss after kiss. Holding tight to each other, they were in no overwhelming hurry. They had all the time in the world on this, their first night together as husband and wife.

"We did it," Kit murmured between kisses. She leaned her head back against the wall, her senses starting to spin. "When I woke up this morning, I decided that when I went to bed tonight it would be in this room again and as your wife. Now it's all finally starting to seem real. No headstrong, let's-do-it-our-way business. Just long and slow and just for us."

"We've astounded everyone we know, and now we can lock the world out and please ourselves," Greg agreed, his hands moving down her back, unfastening the tiny, stiff hooks and eyes. "I want to love you for the rest of my life. There's no one else I want to have a future with, and no matter what happens we'll have each other."

He took off her dress that was so complicated in its simplicity, and while he draped it over the nearest chair, Kit took off her shoes. She closed her eyes and let the sensations wash over her as he removed her filmy lingerie, but when she was wearing only her cream charmeuse and ecru lacy teddy, she stopped him from going any further.

"No," she said, opening her eyes. "I think it's time we got a little more equal. And if you feel like I do right now, you can't be very comfortable in those stiff dinner clothes."

Greg's hands reluctantly left her waist. "You already know the answer to that."

"Would you like some help?"

"A cufflink or two would be nice," he said, holding out his arms to her, "but why do I have the distinct impression you're about to do a little admiring?"

"This is also known as equality in marriage." Kit removed the left cufflink, then the right, and placed the mother-of-pearl objects on the nearest table. "And you've been doing the exact same thing from the minute we walked in here!"

Greg laughed and began to remove the pins from her hair. "One last husbandly privilege, and then I'm all yours."

"I think I'm going to bob my hair," she said as the carefully done French roll tumbled down close to her shoulders.

"As long as you don't do it for a few weeks. I've been dreaming about taking your hair down since the night we met," he said, running his fingers through the silky, perfumed strands before taking off his dinner jacket.

"That's a nice start."

"Shall I continue?"

"You're a careful and considerate gentleman, but I'd never say that you were the modest sort."

"You know me too well," he said, pulling at the perfect black silk bow tie, and then the rest of his clothes followed swiftly. "Do I pass inspection?"

"You'd never fail." Kit took a step forward and lovingly ran her left index finger down the center of his chest as his breathing became more uneven and his cool skin warmed and his warm flesh expanded.

Little by little they made their way across the thick carpet toward the bed. His pajamas and her most lavish nightgown were laid out on the nearest chair and they stayed there. Kissing her shoulders, Greg eased down the thin satin straps of her teddy, and he moved lovingly over her curves as the shimmering garment slid down to the floor.

"What do you suppose other people's wedding nights are like?" she asked suddenly as she continued to touch and rub and caress every inch of Greg that she could reach.

"Not like ours," he assured her as his legs pressed closer to hers.

At that unmistakable signal, Kit put her hands against his chest, and together they tumbled onto the bed.

"Oh, this is lovely," Kit breathed as she felt the cool sheet make contact with her sensitized skin. "And so are you."

"Me?" Greg's hands were molding them together so tightly that there was no space between their bodies. "Compared to you, you beautiful creature, I'm very, very boring."

"Never say that," she told him, letting her hands drift down the length of his back. "You're wonderful, and I love you so much."

He returned her words, and when he entered her it was like an explosion of shooting stars. This was the moment that bound them together for all time, erasing the past and pledging them to the future. Their voices whispered words of love, their bodies merged into sensual perfection, and the problems of the present all but disappeared into unimportance.

"I was a fool to think I could wait six weeks for us to get married," Greg said as they lay entwined in the bed. They had made love to each other three times on a rush of passion and longing, and now it was almost dawn in Los Angeles. In a few hours they would leave on the almost one-hundred mile drive to Montecito, but right now they felt as if they had all the time in the world. "And if you have any lingering doubts that you pressed a little too much yesterday on our getting married, I want you to know that I'm very glad that you did."

303

She kissed the hollow at the base of his throat. "It did take all my skills as a negotiator, and I still wasn't sure you'd agree."

"I couldn't have held out for too long. You gave me the surprise of my life yesterday morning, but right now I have to tell you that you were right all along."

"The best way to learn about being married is just to get married. We'll work everything out along the way."

"Is that your philosophy?"

"Yes."

"I think I'm going to like it."

"I knew you would. I've been thinking about what I should do with my bouquet. I'm going to save a few gardenias, of course, and one of the ribbons, but I want the rest of it to go someplace special. Do you have any ideas?"

Greg thought for a moment. "Do you know about Felipe de Neve's place in the history of California?"

"He was the first military governor of Spanish California, and he gave the order for the founding of Los Angeles in 1781. One of my best customers is one of the Native Daughters of California," she explained.

"De Neve was also a young military officer from an aristocratic Spanish family when he arrived here," Greg said quietly. "I think that if I ever write a book, it will be a biography of him."

"I can see where you find a lot of parallels between both your lives," Kit said, nestling closer. "There must have been times when the young governor felt as strange to be here as you did."

"He must have. I have an idea that's why he took the time to indulge in a little city planning. He actually set out the first plan where the streets were to run diagonally, northeast and southwest, so they would get the morning sun."

"It must have been a wonderful plan, and it's too bad that no one is following it today. I think the city's idea of city planning now is to put up a building on a vacant lot and see what happens," Kit remarked, but she began to see where the conversation was leading and she liked the idea. "At any rate, before we leave for Montecito, we'll go over to the monument to de Neve that the Native Daughters of California had erected so I can put my bouquet on it as a symbol of understanding and good luck."

Chapter 16

"Greg, what was Sin's reaction when you told him about that manuscript?" Kit asked as she began to unpack the handmade English Royal Ascot picnic basket.

"Do you mean *Ballet At Midnight?*" he asked with mock ingenuity, dropping down beside her on the steamer blanket to unfold the tablecloth.

"Oh, don't give me that Boy Scout look!" Kit wasn't sure whether to laugh or get upset. She handed him a corkscrew and a bottle of Lanson champagne. "Is there a story I don't know about?"

"I'd rather talk about lunch. Hasn't all this fresh country air made you hungry?"

"I'm famished, but don't try to change the subject."

"Am I?"

"Do you know how infuriating you can be?" Kit asked in amused exasperation. She pulled off her taupe suede Chanel hat, tossed it beside the picnic basket, and kissed Greg. "But since this is the first part of our honeymoon and only the second day we've been married, why don't you do something husbandly like opening our champagne?"

It was just after one on Saturday afternoon, and they were on their way to Greg's horse ranch in the Santa Ynez Valley. They had spent Friday night in Montecito where Elston and

Vanessa had greeted them with joy, and after an early breakfast Kit and Greg started on their long drive into a part of the country some consider to be the most romantic part of California.

It is in this triangle-shaped area formed by the mountains and valley with the rich and sweeping views that sharply reminded one of the days of the land grants that had reached 40,000 acres and of the hundreds of *vaqueros* who worked that land. The five towns of the valley, Los Olivos, Santa Ynez, Ballard, Buellton and Solvang were there for supplies and necessities, but they were not spots to socialize in. Even now, in the twentieth century, this area was devoted to the working ranch almost to the same extent as it had been in the days when the *rancheros* had ruled.

"I'm still lost in all of this splendor," Kit said as they sat under the shade of an oak tree. "Vanessa was right when she said you really can't understand or visualize old California until you've driven from the ocean to the valley and into the mountains."

"Then the bumpy ride didn't bother you?"

"Not too much—not with the view we've had. And even though the road is really more of a wide trail, it's not too noticeable with the car we have."

"I can definitely agree with you on that point," Greg said, looking over at the automobile parked under a nearby tree. It was more than simply another of Sin's Rolls-Royces. This was the 1913 Continental, the famed "Alpine Eagle," that the company had tested on the endurance trip of July 1913 from London to Vienna. "This is one of the few cars that can make the trip with any ease. When they brought in the furniture for my house, it was on a wagon drawn by Belgian draft horses." He pulled the cork out of the bottle and reached for the glasses. "What do we have to eat?"

"Too much, I think," Kit said as she unwrapped the serving dishes and reached for the Lowestoft plates and Reed and Barton silver. A new thought, one she hadn't given much

308

consideration to, surfaced. "Sweetheart," she said carefully, "your house does have a kitchen?"

With the true eye of a trained gourmet, Greg regarded their lunch. He looked at the terrine of chicken and hazelnuts, the salmon en croute, the mushroom quiche, the paper-thin slices of Scotch salmon placed between equally thin rounds of Swedish pumpernickel, the crisp fresh vegetables, the long baguettes of French bread, wedges of brie and camembert, fresh fruit and chocolate torte.

"There's a kitchen," he said after a suitable pause, and he couldn't conceal his smile any longer. "I also have a nice couple who look after everything for me, Brand and Georgiana Kirby. He was a cowboy with one of the Wild West shows that always toured Europe, now he looks after the property and horses, and Georgie's a splendid cook."

"Do they live in your house?" Kit asked, handing him a plate with generous slices of quiche.

"The Kirbys have their own house. In fact, it's the original house on the property. It's been thoroughly renovated, and my house is the new one."

They paused for a minute to toast each other.

"For us, and our new marriage—our first and only marriage," Greg said as he touched the crystal rim of his glass to hers.

"Our first and only marriage to each other and no one else," Kit added. "To having each other—always."

"I think this is going to be our toast to each other from now on," Greg said, leaning over the glasses to kiss her.

"We are doing rather well for ourselves, and I'm looking forward to seeing your horse ranch. You never did tell me how you got the property."

"From Barbara and Winston Lucas. Does that bother you?"

"Of course not! I like them very much. Did they arrange for you to buy the land?"

"About two years ago, I was talking to them about my

interest in buying some land and a few horses, and after a bit of discussion they looped off a hundred acres and sold it to me along with a few thoroughbreds to use as breeding stock. They were there with lots of help and advice. But after a few rough starts the basic running of a horse ranch came back to me. Of course it helped that it was all on such a small scale."

He didn't have to tell her where the large scale operation had been and who it had belonged to.

"It's a wonderful thing to have friends you can share things with. Which brings me back to my question. What did Sin say?"

Greg raised his glass to the sunlight. "I haven't told him yet. Don't look like that. I will. I was going to tell him the first thing on Thursday morning, but another important event intervened."

Kit smiled. "Weddings—particularly unexpected ones—tend to overwhelm nearly everything else."

"After I got the license, I had to talk with Judge Foley, and by the time I got to Sin's office all I told him was that there was going to be a wedding sooner than anyone was expecting. And when I thought about it, what else I had to tell him, it all became very inappropriate. I'll tell him when we get back to Los Angeles."

"I wasn't trying to be a nagging or inquisitive wife. I just thought that the two of you must have discussed it, and you didn't want to bring it up just yet."

"No, I wouldn't hide anything from you." He helped himself to the salmon en croute. "The hell of it is, *Ballet At Midnight* is still the best story."

"Greg, are you aware that a psychoanalyst would have a field day with you?"

"Me?" Greg tried unsuccessfully to look astonished. "I'm just a good businessman trying to be a creative producer."

"You know what I mean!"

"My darling, I know perfectly well that if I told my life story to any qualified, concerned professional, I'd be sent to some quiet rest home while my psychoanalyst braved the

North Atlantic and various battlefields to get to Vienna and speak with Dr. Freud. I'd be worthy of a multi-part article in a medical journal, or even a chapter in a textbook."

"With footnotes."

"I wouldn't have it any other way," Greg assured her as they dissolved into laughter.

They talked about other things, ate the fruit, and devoured the chocolate torte. Even here, over a hundred miles north of Los Angeles, it was warm for November, and the day was made to enjoy the pastoral setting and the feeling of endless space with no one else around.

"Do you think we should be discussing something serious?" Kit asked as she reclined with her back against the tree while Greg lay stretched out with his head in her lap. "We've eaten every bit of food and drunk all the champagne and we should talk about something important but I can't."

"I'm afraid I'm not going to be much of a help. All I want to do is look at you."

"Typical new husband," she said lovingly, bending over to kiss him. "Of course it's so private here that we can take up something quite important that isn't at all serious."

"That sounds like the sort of invitation made for a honeymoon," Greg said as he sat up and put an arm around her waist. "But there's a very nice bed waiting for us about an hour or so from here."

"So there is a bed," she teased, tracing an invisible line around the outline of his mouth. "For a while, I was wondering if there was an indoors for anyone but the horses and the caretakers."

"There's an indoor everything in my house," he promised. "I'd be happy to eat peanut butter sandwiches and drink lemonade with you on a park bench, but as long as I can afford something better, I wouldn't deliberately take you someplace where we couldn't be as comfortable as possible."

It didn't take long to pack up the picnic things, and this

time, with Kit behind the wheel, they began the last part of the drive. She had told Greg that years of driving in New York's traffic had given her all the experience needed to handle the somewhat steep road. "And I've never driven a Rolls before. I'm not going to let you have all the fun of driving."

Handling the Rolls took all her driving ability, but the fun of being behind the wheel of this expensive, perfectly designed vehicle, and of being able to show off her skills with Greg beside her made it all worthwhile.

The road they travelled on had been a cattle trail at one time, but as soon as she turned the car onto the private road that led to Greg's ranch, she forgot all about the sometimes steep and bumpy road.

"Surprised?" Greg asked, his smile spoke for itself.

"I'm glad you didn't tell me too much about your place. Oh, Greg, it's beautiful . . . the perfect honeymoon hideaway."

Resting her arms on the steering wheel, Kit admired the new vista ahead of her. Straight ahead, nestled in a perfect pastoral setting, was a two-story Dutch colonial house. Small but enchanting, it was painted white with bright red shutters and set among white and live oaks. Further on, she could see a simpler, one-story house, a paddock, barns, white-washed fences and the rich green pastures.

Greg was silent while he watched Kit's first reaction. The last thing he'd had in mind when he purchased this land from Barbara and Win was a honeymoon hideaway. He had bought it because the urge to own a piece of land had been too strong to resist. But now he was glad he'd not only put in every improvement but also put in quite a few luxuries as well.

"I have to tell you that I put in a lot of things because it was too much fun not to."

Kit looked at him through her lashes. "Building your own Tsarskoye Selo is fun, isn't it?"

"It does have a certain appeal, and now that I have my own czarina to share it with," he went on softly, sliding along the seat until they were close together, "we can look on it as a laboratory for what we'll do in Beverly Hills." He kissed the side of her neck, and laughed. "We've spent a little too much time lately necking in my car, and I don't think that's good form for a Rolls."

"Are you trying to tell me that you're not going to kiss me properly until we're inside the house?"

"That among other things. No, leave the luggage here. Brand will bring everything in later. He and Georgiana have probably gone up to the Lucases for extra supplies. They'll want everything to be perfect for us."

"It already is," Kit assured him as they walked toward the house. "What made you decide on Dutch Colonial?"

"It fit in best with the rest of the buildings. The Kirbys have a modified chalet, but I wanted a little bit more," he concluded, opened the door, and lifted Kit into his arms. "What do you think?"

"That your carrying the bride over the threshold technique is perfect," she said, kissing him under an ear. "Are you *sure* you haven't been practicing?"

"I'm a neophyte in that particular area, but I plan to get in a lot of practice with you."

He set her down, and she wrapped her arms around his neck. "I have absolutely no complaints."

Kit was a big-city woman; she wasn't even fond of weekends in the country. She always made a joke of it by saying too much green grass and trees made her nervous, but it really was the truth. She had suggested they come to the mountains for a few days because she knew it was the place where they could have almost perfect privacy, but now, much to her own surprise, she found that the jittery feeling that usually afflicted her in the wide open spaces wasn't bothering her.

She concentrated on kissing Greg, eager for the taste and

313

feel of his mouth. Her passion built slowly but steadily as they pressed closer to each other. This was no hotel corridor or Pullman drawing room where they had to worry about discovery. This was home.

"Now this," he said when they finally separated and he could breathe again, "is the best way to start a honeymoon. And we haven't even gotten to the bedroom yet."

"If it looks anything like the downstairs, I think we should see about extending our long weekend. A month or so sounds just about right," she said to Greg's delight as she got her first close look at the light and airy room that managed to look like it belonged in the country without being at all rustic. It was impossible to miss Mallory's distinctive touch in the quietly rich room done in tones of brown, cream, rose, and dark green. The gleaming hardwood floors were partially covered with a fine needlepoint rug; the sofas were upholstered with a brown moire-taffeta and accented by large throw pillows of woven cotton-satin. There were books everywhere: in the shelves of the small lacquered secretary, on the large coffee table in front of the fireplace, and on the tables covered with skirts of glazed chintz.

"How do you ever tear yourself away from here?" Kit asked, leaving her hat on one of the side chairs that was covered in cream and rose velvet. "It's country, but it's also formal. I'm amazed that you don't want to trade in running a movie studio for being a gentleman horse breeder."

"Do you want to know the truth?" Greg asked a little shame-facedly, stepping over the needlepoint footstool to come over to Kit. They sat down close to each other on one of the sofas, pushing aside a handsome fox throw. "This house wasn't finished and decorated until six months ago. Before, whenever I came up here for a weekend, I stayed with Brand and Georgiana. Their house is very nice, but it's not like this."

"Just how many times have you stayed here since Mallory finished decorating?"

"Counting right now?"

"That would be nice." Kit smiled gently, already suspecting the answer.

"Twice. Haven't you noticed that it all looks a little too crisp, a little too unlived in?" With a graceful movement, he stretched them out on the sofa in a soft whisper of fur and moire-taffeta. "I gave Mallory carte blanche to create a country house for me, and when I came here in May, I hadn't been so lonely in years."

"My poor darling," she said as they nestled together on the sofa, their bodies molding intimately against each other. "We both smothered a lot of trepidation to come up here."

He raised his head from her breast. "Didn't you want to come to the country?"

"I *hate* the country! It makes me nervous, and I'm always cold. I suggested we come here because I wanted a few days alone with you with no interruptions. Why didn't you tell me how you felt?"

"Because I wanted to be alone with you also, and this is just about the best place for us. Also, I loved that you trusted me enough not to care too much what you might find here. I could have been camping out."

"This is a wonderful tent," she said, drawing him down to her.

For a few minutes they were too busy to talk, and Kit luxuriated in their growing passion. With fresh air and food and champagne, their feelings were rising quickly.

"Isn't there another room you'd like to show me?" she questioned a little breathlessly.

"It's four bedrooms and two baths—with room for expansion should we need it in time," he finished, intently kissing the side of her neck.

"Are you thinking in terms of a nursery?"

"In time, that's just the sort of adding on I'd like us to do."

She smiled as he began to undo the small buttons on her cream silk blouse and the waistband of her heather tweed skirt. His hands moved slowly up to cup her breasts beneath the silk and lace that confined them, and she caught her breath as his thumbs moved over her nipples until they hardened.

Stirring restlessly under him, she reached out to unbutton his shirt. "Do you think the Kirbys will be back soon?"

"If they do, we'll hear them—their car's something of a jalopy."

"When we're together, I don't listen for cars that backfire. I'm interested in another sort of fireworks."

His laugh was rich. "You're so delectable in this blouse and skirt, but I like you better without it. I should have brought our luggage inside."

She placed her hands on his shoulders. "Don't you have a pair of pajamas in one of the bedrooms?"

"I'll see what I can find—later," he promised, getting up from the sofa and gently pulling Kit along with him.

"Please don't carry me upstairs," she said, stepping out of her skirt and slipping off her blouse. "I'd rather reach our bedroom under my own speed. "Think of it as saving your back for other activities."

"I'm not about to complain that I have such a considerate wife," he said, and held out a hand to her. "Shall we do some exploring?"

Upstairs, the same color scheme of brown, cream, rose, and dark green prevailed. The master bedroom was dominated by a four-poster bed draped in a cream and brown print that had to be French. The same material framed the windows in billowing curtains, and the fitted carpet was a deep, rich shade of rose.

The furniture was inviting and there was a large, modern bathroom, but Kit hardly noticed any of it as she and Greg concentrated on each other, undressing each other, leaving their clothes where they fell. The bed was cool and welcoming and very quickly they were in the center of it, eager and laughing.

"Did you lock the door?" Kit asked as she rose to her knees, pulling Greg along with her. "Isolated country spots have a habit of suddenly getting very crowded."

He closed his eyes as Kit caressed his back and moved down to his buttocks. "All locked," he said thickly, lowering her into the mass of soft pillows, his hands tangling in her hair. "We're alone together, just the way we want."

Their need for each other was too great to hold out for any extended love-making, and they merged together, their limbs entwined. His thrusts were quick and deep, and Kit felt herself caught up in an onrushing tide of passion. His searing hot body was still new enough to her so that she was willing to let him set the pace of their love.

The house was nestled in the mountains, but making love with Greg was like swimming in the Pacific; it was rich and blue and the waves were crashing. Only there was no danger, and the undertow, instead of promising peril, was a force that gave them the ultimate pleasure.

"Now I know why I never liked the country before," Kit murmured a long time later. "You weren't there."

"Funny, I was just going to tell you the same thing." He pulled her even closer to him and adjusted the comforter more snugly over them. "The first night I spent in this bed was the worst that I'd had since—well, since a very long time before. I dreamed that I was in the estate in the Urals, and I knew that when I went out riding in the morning the assassins my father ordered would be waiting for me."

Kit put her hands on his chest, her eyes filling with tears. "How awful for you."

"I'd had any number of bad dreams over the years, but never that one—and I never had it again. But then I haven't been up here since then."

"I thought I'd be roughing it in a rustic cabin, my blood turning to ice; and you had to face coming back to a house you were almost sorry you'd built." Kit laughed shakily, and a tear coursed down one cheek. "It seems that we're a good match in every way."

"I'm not sorry I built this house any more," he said softly, brushing away her tear. "And don't cry for me—please, darling, I can't bear it."

"I won't . . . as long as I can help you so that you never have that dream again."

"I'm going to look forward to coming here on a much more frequent basis."

"Then I think we should start thinking about this house as our home. What would you say to our ordering our own car to drive up here, either an Alpine Eagle or a heavy duty Pierce-Arrow?"

"I'd like that very much, but since this is now our home—or one of them—we should do a little more to establish our territorial rights."

"That sounds like a very good idea." Kit smiled and pressed herself closer to him. "We have a lot to discuss, but right now is really for staking our claim, to prove that even though we sometimes go stumbling around, we do manage to come up with a right answer or two."

Kit had a theory that any person—no matter what their background and provided they were open to new experiences—couldn't help but be changed for the better by travel, particularly travel in Europe. And as far as she was concerned, Brand and Georgiana Kirby, an attractive couple in their late twenties, were absolute proof of this.

It was obvious that while on their often long stays in Europe while Brand had performed as a champion rider and roper with the rodeo, they had taken full advantage of their surroundings, and as they all sat at the circular table in the small dining room, the conversation centered on sightseeing, museum-going, and shopping.

The dining room was small and set aside from the living room by a set of glass doors. The needlepoint rug was a twin to the one in the living room, butler's tables served as sideboards, there was a large oval mirror in a gold-painted frame, and the table—just big enough for four—was set with a forest-green tablecloth, embroidered Madeira linen place-mats, simple Limoges china with a narrow gold band, and Tiffany crystal and silver flatwear. The room's rich and intimate feel was further aided by pleasantly flickering candles, the laughter-punctuated conversation, and a bottle of excellent California burgundy.

Despite the fact that they looked after the grounds and the house, the Kirbys weren't servants, and since Greg had always lived in their house every time he came up here except the last, Kit was not about to insist on any sort of formalities. Besides, she liked them on sight. Brand was from Oklahoma, Georgiana from Texas, and their conversational abilities were the first-rate kind she truly enjoyed.

"Greg, does it bother you that you're the only one of us who hasn't been to Europe lately?" Brand asked as they finished the crab bisque, their conversation centering on London's theatre season which had included such shows as *After The Girl* at the Gaiety, *Kismet* at the Globe, and such actors as Gerald du Maurier in *The Clever Ones,* and Marie Tempest in *The Duke of Killicrankie.*

"Not really. I ran away from Europe fourteen years ago and I've never been in much of a hurry to go back," he replied, but to Kit, his delivery sounded like he was repeating a line from a drawing room comedy, a line everyone could laugh at but no one could take seriously. "And it's not much of a tourist spot at the moment."

"I read in the papers where Cunard is letting the *Lusitania* sail on a regular schedule," Georgiana pointed out.

"That is asking for trouble," Kit observed. "Jessica told me that she's trying to convince Frank to send her to England as a correspondent."

Greg looked amused. "The war'll be over before Frank ever agrees."

"I wouldn't bet on that."

"I read everything she wrote about your shop," Georgiana told Kit. "First I couldn't wait for it to open, and now I can't wait till we get to Los Angeles so I can see it and do a little shopping—and I usually make all my own clothes."

"Georgie can copy just about any dress she sees in *Vogue* or *Harper's Bazaar*," Brand said with a proud look at his wife who was wearing an expert replica of a Paquin dinner dress in pale blue silk with a pagoda tunic.

"I can't say that Kit has that particular skill, but I can brag that my wife is getting some of the wealthiest women in Southern California to part with their money in return for some expensive clothes."

"And each to her own talent," Kit said. "Georgiana, is this recipe one of Mr. Wong's?"

"Almost all of my best recipes are courtesy of Mr. Wong or Mrs. Dovedale. I took some cooking lessons in Paris a few years ago, but those two could show my teachers how to improve their techniques. What's even funnier," she went on, collecting the soup plates, "is that Mallory made *complete* floor plans for me so that when the furniture arrived, I'd know exactly where every piece went."

"That's Mallory. Thea taught her never to install rooms but always to provide a detailed floor plan."

"Brand's mother once wrote to Thea Harper, asking if she'd like to come out to Oklahoma and redecorate the ranch house."

"It was a good offer, but she decided to elope to Mexico with Charles de Renille instead," Brand finished. "Anyway, it's time for me to help my wife. We'll be right back."

"Would you like to know why Charles and Thea *really* went to Mexico in 1904?" Kit whispered when they were alone again.

Greg took a minute to get another bottle of wine from the sideboard. "Are they really married?"

"Of course! But they didn't elope to Mexico," Kit

continued in a low voice. "Thea used to be one of the people Theodore Roosevelt depended on to help him out whenever there was a sticky situation. Ten years ago, when they were starting to dig the Panama Canal, there were a lot of rumors that the Germans were going to cause trouble, and T.R. decided that Thea and Charles should go to Mexico City and listen in on things. The marriage was supposed to be in name only, with a convenient annulment later on. You can use your imagination as to what happened next," she finished, and smiled.

"Sometimes," Greg said in an equally quiet voice, "it helps to know that I'm not the only one with secrets."

The Kirbys returned before Kit could reply, and they turned their attention to helping Brand and Georgiana with the profusion of platters they carried in. There was a rosemary-scented rack of lamb that was a tender pink inside, accompanied by small roast potatoes, string beans with almonds, and small, warm dinner rolls worthy of those in a fine French restaurant.

They talked about New York and Chicago and riding the Twentieth Century and The California Limited and Los Angeles and San Francisco. Eventually, the talk turned to the movies, and Greg explained why Hooper Studios was looking for a movie scenario and how *Ballet At Midnight* had arrived.

"I had a letter from Odette Derrenger the other day," Georgiana said. "You remember, Brand, we shared a compartment with her and Jean-Luc on the train from Paris to Brussels two years ago. They've been in San Francisco since June."

"Are they in some sort of financial trouble?" Brand wanted to know. "We could help them out—."

"No, no. Odette says they're managing right now."

"Were they caught here when the war started?" Kit asked, buttering a piece of roll.

"Jean-Luc is a musician. In fact, he's the new second viola

in the San Francisco Symphony. Here's something that should interest you, Greg—Odette was with the Paris Opera Ballet."

For a second, Greg looked down at his plate. "Was your friend the costume designer or the wardrobe mistress?"

"No, she was a soloist."

Kit thought that she could almost see the wheels of Greg's mind turning. She knew that he believed that some things happened, and then linking events kept on happening and there was nothing one could do about them. Now she too believed certain events followed other events. The leitmotif was still very loosely woven, but the pattern was waiting to be formed.

"Is she dancing in San Francisco?" she heard Greg ask. "I imagine the ballet company there is very enthusiastic about having such a star with them. She must have her choice of roles."

Before Georgiana could reply, Brand put down his fork and gave his employer and friend a searching look. "Greg, do you have any idea of how obvious you're acting?"

"That bad?"

"Worse."

"I'm glad you said it first, Brand," Kit remarked.

"So much for secrecy," Greg said, and began to smile. "If I'm going to make a movie about the ballet, I need a ballerina for the heroine. Georgie, do you think your friend Odette would be interested?"

"That would depend on the money. Odette wants to open her own ballet school."

"And who knows," Greg said mysteriously, raising his wine glass to the light. "I may be the one to help her have her dream. There comes a time when we can all help each other, and since I've been helped at a time of great difficulty in my past, it may be time for me to help someone else," he continued. All too aware that the conversation had reached

322

waters he didn't want to sail on now if ever, he skillfully moved the topic on to another far more neutral subject.

"Are you cold?" Greg asked an hour later as they walked through the garden, the light from the house and from the full moon providing all the illumination they needed. Dinner was over, and now that the wine was drunk, the lamb consumed, and the open-faced glazed apple tart and twice-perked coffee enjoyed, they had decided to take a short walk. "It can get pretty cool up here at night."

Kit pulled the black velvet coat she'd put over her Lanvin dinner dress of cornflower blue taffeta closer around her. "I don't mind. This really feels like the weather I'm used to. All the sunshine and warm weather in Los Angeles can start to be a little odd."

"Don't worry, the rainy season is about to start." Greg unlocked the gate to the latticework arch. "I think Georgiana would like a greenhouse for Christmas," he said as they walked down the path that in summer was rich with greenery and flowers. "The flowers on the table and around the house tonight came from Barbara and Win's greenhouse."

"I'm sure she'd love that. What are you going to give Brand?"

"I may order the building of the five-furlong track we've been discussing. Brand's very serious about managing this place for me," he continued as they stood beside a wood and wire fence that only a few months before had been covered by masses of red, white and pink tea roses, Ramblers, Bourbons, Noisettes, and China roses. "I'm sure that sometimes he thinks I may only be playing with this place and will just toss it all away one day."

"I think the track will convince him otherwise. But how many horses do you have?"

"A mare, a stallion, and their filly just five months old. We'll visit the stables in the morning and take two of the saddle horses out for a ride," he said as the wind grew stronger and colder and Kit leaned against him. "You want to know something else, don't you?"

"Don't be mysterious with me—it's not necessary. I know that you're getting more and more serious about making *Ballet At Midnight* into the 'quality movie' we all spent so much time discussing."

"I may just be living proof of the moth that has to hover around the flame no matter what the ultimate danger," Greg said almost lightly as he pulled Kit closer against him, more for pleasure than for mutual warmth or comfort. "I can live with danger—I just have to know which danger and from where it's coming."

Kit rested her head on his shoulder. His hands were moving gently up and down her back, and his touch through layers of velvet and taffeta was almost as tantalizing as when there was nothing between them.

"You still have to tell Sin, and he does have veto power over any project you come up with."

"He'll agree."

"How confident you are," she said as he began to kiss her throat while his hands caressed her spine, "about everything."

"There are some things that just have to be, and while we can't change them we can adjust some of the circumstances so that the power is more evenly distributed."

His mouth moved over hers, and Kit gave herself up to his kiss, to the feeling of his warm mouth over hers, and to the sweeping and savoring motions of his tongue. The increasingly cold night air was having no effect on his mounting desire, and she recognized that something primitive in him was bubbling slowly but inevitably to the surface.

There was so much about this that they had to discuss, she knew, but it was all beginning to recede to some dark corner where it would wait patiently for them. All that mattered was that in a short time they'd be back in the snug little Dutch colonial house, upstairs and in bed, interested in and hungry for each other.

She returned his kisses and moved her hands skillfully down his back to one of his most sensitive spots, and heard him utter her name and unsuccessfully try to bite back a groan.

"Wait until you're stripped down to the bare essentials and between the sheets," she promised, her heartbeat growing swifter. She knew perfectly well that he was going to take her like a Russian nobleman, like a czar, with all the passion and possession that had been bred into him. Later, much later tonight it would be her turn to show him how much she loved him. Now was only for the reminder.

"If this were summer, I'd take you right here," he promised thickly, and Kit felt a swift stab of desire that would only begin to be assuaged when he entered her. "As it is, I think I can just manage to get us back into the house."

His arm was tight around her waist, and Kit decided that it was the only thing keeping her upright as they retraced their steps back along the stone path to the kitchen door. But while her knees felt weak, the rest of her was blazing as if a thousand tiny fires had started under her skin. She felt like one of those huge, ornate fountains that was so favored by the owners of the most lavish of Europe's chateaux. She told Greg how he was making her feel.

"And you're making me feel the same way," he told her in a passion-heavy voice.

They entered through the kitchen door to find that the Kirbys had already cleaned up and left for their own house. How long *had* they been out in the garden? That could be answered by a quick look at the clock, but time had no meaning to them as they walked quickly, silently through the kitchen, the dining room, and the living room. Kit picked up the large red fox throw from the sofa and earned a pirate's grin from her husband.

"Why didn't I think of that?" he asked as they gave up all pretense at decorum and ran up the stairs to the master bedroom.

"It doesn't matter," Kit said, closing and locking the door behind them while Greg put the throw on the bed where it glowed richly against the white sheets. "Oh, Greg," she said as he switched off the softly glowing bedside lamp. "Gregory . . ."

He came to her in the darkness, and when he took her in his arms all ability for rational thought fled. Working with silent intensity, they undressed each other; hooks, snaps, buttons, knots, and bows all coming undone as one garment joined another in a growing heap around their feet.

Even with her eyes only half-adjusted to the dark, Kit had explicit proof of Greg's fully expanded and throbbing condition. She knew he wanted her as much as she wanted him, and wondered how much longer they could hold out.

There was no need to exchange a word, and with their arms around each other's shoulders they made their way to the bed. Their sensitized skin made contact with the fur throw at the same moment, and they both cried out at the slightly prickly yet very sensual softness of the guard hairs.

Instinctively, Kit rubbed her body against the lush fox, and when Greg poised his body over her, she wrapped herself around him, avid for the ultimate friction of two bodies made one.

Even before he touched them, her breasts had swelled with desire, the nipples taut, and when he placed a hand under each full globe, she stirred even more restlessly.

"You don't have to wait," she gasped out as he drew an invisible circle around each breast, teased the nipples, and made her feel like the most voluptuous woman in the world. "All I want is you."

"And all I want is to love you the way you deserve to be loved," he rasped. His skin was burning hot and he knew he couldn't hold out much longer, but tonight was like the fulfillment of a ritual, and he wasn't going to cheat her out of a moment of pleasure. "This is all for you."

It was better than the first time they'd made love together, better than their wedding night, she thought as her senses began to swirl and her nerve endings sizzled as his fingertips moved over her neck and shoulders and arms, down her breasts and along her sides to her hips and thighs. She thought she knew what the next move would be, and she waited, poised for the sweet torture of his fingers intimately exploring her.

But instead, his hands cupped her quivering hips, held them still, and raised her to the aroused center of his body. His own desire was too overpowering to extend their fore-play and he thrust deeply into her.

Kit had her first climax the moment their throbbing bodies came together, and the certainty she'd felt a short time before that tonight their love-making was going to spring from some new and deep wellspring was right—and more so.

His body was over her, inside her, and she held him tighter, aware that the next minutes were going to be unlike any she'd ever known before. For a countless moment, he held them closely together, and then with a deep groan he began to move inside her, all of his demanding, passionate Russian personality coming out of his self-imposed restraints.

At the first thrust of his hips, Kit closed her eyes to see brilliant streaks of color and began to follow his movements, matching herself to him for the ultimate pleasure. He rested his head at the side of her neck. She was aware of nothing but him, nothing but them, and she whispered her passion into his ear. She wanted him to know how much she loved him and that there was no threat from the outside that would ever come between them.

"I want you to know that it's never been like this for me

327

before. I don't think I could ever want another man to make love to me—and don't tell me that was your idea," Kit said, and laughed softly. They were curled up in the rumpled bed with all the pillows behind them and the fox throw keeping them warm instead of being the sensual aid to their love-making. "Even couples passionately in love need time to adjust, to find their depths."

"That's the best way of putting what just happened to us. And I have something to tell you," Greg went on. "Do you know how they say passion is all the same to a man and who the woman is doesn't matter? Well, it's a lie. I've never felt the way I do with you with any other woman, and after loving you, I certainly don't want anyone else."

"It's a lucky thing that we've reached this conclusion, isn't it?" she teased gently, and kissed his cheek. "Do you recall something I said to you earlier?"

"I'm tucked under a fur throw, not between the sheets, but I admit the part about the bare essentials is true enough."

"A little while ago you said you wanted to love me the way I deserved, and now I want to love you." With a single graceful movement, Kit tossed aside the throw and rose to her knees. "This is like our wedding night all over again, only all the strain and rush is over. Now we can concentrate and love each other."

Chapter 17

"My darlings, there you both are! We were getting worried about you," Vanessa exclaimed as Kit and Greg entered the library of Sin and Caro's Montecito house late on Monday afternoon, just as the rainstorm that had been threatening all day broke.

"It seems that you two just made it," Elston Harper said genially as greetings were exchanged. Thea's father was a tall, commanding man, and without the slightest bit of haste he nonetheless saw to it that no one lingered too long in the doorway of the library. Almost before the Wests knew it, they were walking down the length of the large, yet intimate and welcoming, room with its toasty colors and comforting floral prints. "I hope you're ready for tea."

"We're always hungry for tea," Kit replied, depositing her silk-lined wool jersey coat and suede hat on a small chair with a needlepoint seat. "It was too chilly to have a picnic lunch the way we did on Saturday."

"You did eat though?" Vanessa asked anxiously, sitting down in a wing chair near the fireplace, slender and elegant in a Lucile dress of rose crepe de chine finished with French-blue ribbons. "Driving on an empty stomach can be as dangerous as driving if you've had too much to drink."

"We ate our lunch in the car," Greg said, sitting down on

329

the sofa beside Kit, whose Chanel sports outfit of a pale tweed skirt and apricot charmeuse blouse contrasted pleasantly with the sofa's deep floral print.

Not to mention a few other things, Kit thought, well aware of why Greg didn't look at her while he said that. They couldn't very well tell the Harpers—or anyone else—that in the middle of lunch they had repacked the basket in favor of making love in the back seat. They hadn't bothered to undress very much, and with the large lap robe over them had made swift and passionate love. So now I—we—know what it's like to do it in the back seat, she reflected with renewed delight, still feeling the intensity of Greg's strong embrace as their bodies came together.

But this wasn't the time or place for such recollections, and she forced her attention back to her hosts. Outside, the rain was coming down in sheets, but here there was a fire glowing brightly and it was time to relax and enjoy afternoon tea.

"We'll have to try a back seat picnic," Elston said as he relaxed in his favorite chair. "We can—ah, here is our tea, and just in time, too."

In front of Vanessa, a Directoire table was covered with an ecru-colored cloth of thin Italian linen with a border of ecru lace, and an antique black tin tray holding an English bone china service of cream and gold and Spode dessert plates of deep pink. It was a traditional English tea with thin bread and butter sandwiches, hot scones ready to absorb butter and strawberry preserves, two silver cake stands holding little frosted cakes, and, for an extra touch, there was steamed orange pudding with hard sauce.

"A refill, please," Greg said a few minutes later, holding out his cup to be refilled with hot jasmine tea. "I'm usually not hungry in the afternoon, but there really must be something to all this fresh air."

"Really?" Vanessa raised her eyebrows in pointed amusement and refilled the large cup with a stream of hot amber liquid from the silver pot. "I would say that being a new bridegroom—and a very happy one—has something to do with it. Now, Greg, tell the truth, don't you remember a similar situation?"

"What do you mean, Vanessa?" Kit asked as she watched Greg blush and then laugh. "You have my husband acting like a Boy Scout getting his first lecture in the facts of life."

"Vangie has the ability to do that," Elston remarked. "And I'm frequently in awe of her."

"I'd better explain," Greg said to Kit, finally regaining his composure. "Vanessa's very astute, and her connection is quite correct. Before Sinclair married Caroline, he had a good appreciation for food and wine, but nothing compared to after he got married."

"I see," Kit said, and bit back a strong urge to giggle. "I'm glad I have such concrete proof that I'm making my husband so happy."

"I'd say it was all very mutual," Vanessa said, the look in her eyes even more knowing. "You two look very pleased with each other."

"Oh, we are," Kit said, reaching out to Greg. In a totally unselfconscious gesture, she stroked the back of his neck, and he looked at her with adoration in his eyes. For a moment they actually forgot about the older couple in the room with them.

"More tea?" Vanessa asked tactfully.

"You must think we're, we're—," Kit replied, and hesitated, not quite sure what to say, and noting that Greg looked as temporarily lost as she was.

"Very much in love," Vanessa finished.

"And very happy with each other's company," Elston added.

"A condition in marriage that does not necessarily go hand-in-hand." Vanessa added some extra hard sauce to their pudding. "Now, are you finally enjoying your new house, Greg?"

331

"Now that I have Kit I am. I never realized it was such a cozy house before."

"A woman's presence is something that should never be taken for granted," Elston pointed out gravely. "All of my expeditions over the years have certainly proved that point, and since I'm also the proud father of one of New York's best decorators, I can speak from first-hand knowledge as to how important it is to have a nice place to come home to."

"Well, I'm very happy with it, and, in a way, that's a relief. We're going to be very involved with the house we're building in Beverly Hills, and our energies have to be concentrated on that."

"That's a wise move. Are you going to live at the Alexandria until it's built?"

"It looks that way, Vanessa. Most rentals in Los Angeles are pretty awful," Greg replied, being polite about the state of available houses in the city. "It'll take about a year to get it all ready."

"And in the meantime, Greg's apartment can be our honeymoon nest."

"Which is the last way I ever expected to use it."

"If you'll take my advice, you'll begin planning your house-warming now," Vanessa advised.

"And as long as we're on the subject of parties," Kit said, swiftly changing the topic of conversation, "you *are* coming down to Los Angeles for all the parties everyone will be giving us? They wouldn't be the same without you two."

"I think we can manage a few days away from our hideaway," Vanessa said with deliberate English coolness.

"Don't take that too seriously," Elston put in. "Vangie's busy planning out her wardrobe for all the festivities."

"Oh, I admit it, I'm caught." She surveyed the tea table with a practiced eye. "My, but we've done justice to all that food."

"Mostly due to us," Greg said. "Rather typical behavior— if we were twelve years old, that is."

"Well, in that case, maybe you both should be sent to your room," Elston suggested with a slightly wicked gleam in his eyes.

"Rather, I think both Kit and Greg could probably do with a nap after their long drive," Vanessa agreed.

Kit gave Greg a sidelong glance to find his expression deliberately oblique. He was longing for this chance to depart the library with style and grace and good humor as much as she was.

"It was a very tiring drive," Kit agreed, "and we'd hate not to be at our best at dinner tonight."

"Since Elston and I plan to roll back the rug and put some new ragtime records on the Victrola, we have a vested interest in seeing that you're both lively enough to do some dancing." She consulted the slender gold watch around her wrist. "Dinner is at eight, but we'll meet for cocktails in the Chinese salon at half-past seven."

"Are you sure—," Kit hesitated.

Vanessa waved a casual hand at them. "Go, my darlings. Have a nice, cozy little nap, and when we have dinner you'll tell us all about your wonderful weekend!"

"If you think they're going to take a nap, then you must also believe in Santa Claus," Elston remarked a short time later when Kit and Greg were safely out of earshot.

"Oh, I know perfectly well that right now they're *very* passionately involved," Vanessa returned as she and her husband moved to the recently vacated sofa. "They could scarcely keep their hands off each other. It was rather sweet, actually, their concern that we might think they were acting improperly."

"It never fails to amaze me that young people always think passion is their sole province," Elston said, putting an arm around his wife. "No doubt, when we got married, my daughter and your stepdaughter thought we had a nice,

333

quiet, and unexciting relationship going."

"Probably. But then it's better to have a few secrets from one's children. Better than some secrets."

"Such as?"

"You are interested in gossip! And men always deny they are."

"We have to protect our reputations somehow. And I can tell every time you know something juicy about someone. You get a certain *knowing* look."

"Believe me, it tooks years of practice, not to give away at first glance what someone else is trying to keep secret."

"Is it Gregory or Katharine who is keeping something hidden?"

Vanessa was quiet for a long time. "Gregory," she said at last. "But that isn't the name he was born with."

"That's very California, to make that adjustment. Frank Rundstadt is an adjustment from Franz von Rundstadt," he offered informatively. "Of course, with the war on, it's better to drop any German connotation."

"Well, I didn't know that! That means he's Cosima and Raimund's son—God rest them." She eyed her husband. "How do you know this?"

"Frank told me himself. I recognized him the first time we met, and we had a nice talk about it."

"But I can't do that with Greg. Frank's obscuring his background is one thing, deliberately having to create an entirely new life is another."

"Who *is* Greg, then?"

Vanessa looked troubled. "He's come so far."

"I assume you don't mean that in reference to his once having been Sinclair's valet."

"No, I'm referring to his being Prince Ivan Vestovanova's son, Alexander."

"The one who murdered the ballerina?"

"They never found the body, and even if he did do what they say, it must have been an accident. I've known Greg for too many years to think that no matter how young and hot-blooded he was he could have done such a thing."

"How many years have you known about this?"

"Almost since it happened. When we were living in the Imperial Hotel in Tokyo during the Boxer Rebellion, waiting for the news that the siege had been lifted, we met an attaché from the Russian Embassy. How those people love to talk! He couldn't wait to tell us the latest scandal from St. Petersburg, all about the disappearance and probable murder of a dancer with the Imperial Ballet. He told us that Alexander Vestovanova had gotten out of the city, had been tracked down in Brussels, and then disappeared again. Oh, it was awful to listen to!"

"And the minute you saw Greg, you knew who he was?"

"No, not immediately. I began to suspect who he really was the day I saw he has a small scar near his hairline. It's not really visible any more. The poor boy," she finished, not quite sure what else she could say.

"I'd say the 'poor boy,' as you call him, had done rather well, and today he certainly looks and acts like a proper benedict. Do you think he told Kit?"

"Yes, and I'm also sure Sin and Caro know."

"And they never told you?"

"I'm only a mother-in-law—stepmother-in-law—if you insist on being practical. And it's not a thing I would ever discuss with Caro."

"I agree. That sort of unsolved, unresolved situation can be very dangerous."

"If I ever mention this to Caro, there's always the awful chance that the story would spread." Vanessa rested her head on her husband's shoulder. "We can never talk about this again. Greg's life is entirely his own now, and I wouldn't ever want to think that by some careless remark we revived a subject that was best left untouched and unknown."

Chapter 18

Weddings

Los Angeles

West - Allen.—On November 5th at the residence of
Mr. and Mrs. Rupert Randall, Mr. Gregory West and
Miss Katharine Allen, daughter of Mrs. Vincent
Lyman, and the late Mr. Lewis Allen.

Kit read the listing in the just-arrived advance copy of the
December 15th issue of *Vogue,* laughed with delight, and
looked up to the top of the stairs leading to the dressing
rooms where her mother sat on a chair, busily sketching.
"I'm officially married now, Mummy, *Vogue*'s printed the
announcement in their social listings! I really wasn't sure
they were going to put it in," she said, fully aware that if
things had been different and she had married Gregory as
Alexander Vestovanova, their wedding—which itself would
have been an entirely different sort of event—would have
rated at least two full pages and reams of copy about the
latest international wedding. As it was, this was going to be
their private joke, she thought.
Constance put down her sketching pencil. "They could

337

always have listed you and Greg as having gotten married in Pasadena," she called down in a wickedly funny suggestion.

"I would have cancelled my subscription if they did. Mr. Nast sent us a note saying that we were too late to make the December 1st issue, but Greg said that was probably because they had a special meeting to see if they could list Los Angeles without subscribers thinking that they were lowering their standards!"

"Greg may have something there. Now let me get back to work, darling. I want to get this sketch done before you open the door to the latest horde of holiday shoppers."

"All right. I'll go and see if Dad needs anything. I settled him in my office with the latest issue of *Vanity Fair,* but he may be getting restless by now."

In her Agnes dress, a striking creation of black satin with a pleated white chiffon trim that gave the effect of an upstanding collar and extended to a vest-like illusion, and enlivened by gold, blue, and red braid, she walked across the selling floor to her office, making sure that everything was in order, and hoping that today's cool, crisp weather, so unlike Los Angeles, even for early December, would bring in another new wave of shoppers. She caught a glimpse of herself in one of the many mirrors and had to smile. No woman could stay unchanged after one month and four days of marriage, but the last change she would have expected was the more dramatic way she was dressing: the deeper colors, the even more striking clothes, and the extra jewelry. The wide gold bracelets Greg had given her on her birthday adorned each wrist, and the ruby heart pendant rested against the white chiffon trim of her dress. It wasn't a lot of jewelry, and it was all appropriate for daytime wear, but added to her wedding and engagement rings, it was more than she'd worn at any one time before the evening hours. Still, she had found it suited her, and she enjoyed the reaction she got from people.

"Dad, are you all right?" Kit asked as she swung into her

office which was sprayed with her scent of the day. Tuesday was for Poiret's *La Tulip*. "You're not getting bored?"

"In the middle of all this loveliness?" Vincent asked, closing *Vanity Fair,* and putting it beside him on the loveseat. "Your shop is truly outstanding. Of course, after the jungles of Venezuela, I have to admit that my opinion may be a bit lopsided."

"I don't think so." Kit smiled and leaned back against her desk, observing her tall, distinguished stepfather. She valued his opinion and knew he never gave compliments simply for the sake of being polite. "If I meet the high Bostonian standards you were raised with, then I *am* doing something right."

Constance and Vincent had arrived in the port of Los Angeles aboard the *San Cristobal,* the Monday before Thanksgiving, and they were staying with Sin and Caro. After describing what it was like to sail through the newly-opened Panama Canal, they informed Kit and Greg that their stay would be of an appropriate length—long enough to catch up on all they had missed in each other's lives, but not long enough to look like interfering parents.

"It's so wonderful to have you both here. I don't think I've had a chance to tell you that before. We love showing you both off at all the parties."

"And we're having the time of our lives. Caracas is very lively in its own way, but it really doesn't know how to throw a party the way Los Angeles does. You and Greg are a very popular couple."

Before Kit could reply, there was a brief knock at the door, and Delia stood poised on the threshold.

"Excuse me for interrupting, Kit, Mr. Lyman, but I have some good news. The reorder on the scented lingerie cases and those cone-shaped satin sachets to hang in the closet just arrived."

"At last! Those two items have been practically walking out of the store on their own," Kit told her stepfather.

"Delia, put the new cases into the vitrine in the lingerie alcove and some of the sachets on the secretary. Oh, and bring a dozen of each in here. Nan asked me to hold them for her."

"That and the new Jeanne Hallee dress she wanted finally arriving should make her very pleased," Delia observed. "And Kit, Julie just told me that Mallory would like to see you when you have a moment. It's about a dining room table."

"This is a typical day," she offered informatively a minute later. "Something happening every minute."

"And from what I've just seen, you handle it all admirably."

"Most of it is just remembering details. Greg says that I'm very good at making lists, and I tell him that if I don't have lists it will all collapse."

"I'm sure Greg has made a list or two in his life. You're both so suited to each other in every other way, I can't imagine you don't mesh there as well. Is that what you wanted to hear?" Vincent inquired.

"Only if it's the truth."

"I wouldn't say that unless it was the absolute and utter truth," he told her, his patrician Boston accent strong. "You both belong together."

"I know I must have surprised the both of you tremendously when we went ahead and got married. I was worried at first that you both might just be putting on a good face because we'd already done the deed—not that I would have changed my mind in any case," she couldn't resist adding, and then brought up the matter closest to her. "What I really want to know, is do you both think as highly of Greg as I do?"

"What does your mother say?"

"Oh, you know Mummy. I asked her, and she went on for fifteen minutes about his cheekbones, nose, and hairline and a dozen other things I already know about. I think that it's a good sign that, unlike some mothers who are only pleased with their new son-in-law in relation to the size of his bank account, mine is thrilled because I provided her with an excellent artistic subject!"

Vincent laughed, but gradually he grew serious. "I don't want you to ever worry about this again, Katharine. Your mother and I both agree that Gregory is a fine man who loves you very much."

"Even at my age, it's amazing how nice it is to hear those words."

"Even from a stepfather?"

"And since when does that matter?"

"That's also nice to hear. And when we got your cable announcing that you and Greg had gone ahead and gotten married, Constance read it, looked at me and said, 'I always knew I had a smart daughter, and she's just proved it by marrying her man and saving me from the idiocy of the receiving line!'"

"Mummy never told me that!"

"She probably will while you have dinner tonight and I take part in that poker party that Sinclair is giving."

"I think that was supposed to be Greg's bachelor party, but since it doesn't quite apply any more, it will be a bit more sedate than those affairs usually suggest."

"Ah, no dancing girls then?"

"Somehow, I doubt it." Kit glanced at the clock on her desk. "I'd love to spend more time talking to you, Dad, but if I want to discuss a dining room table with Mallory, I'd better go next door and see her now."

Like Kit's shop, Mallory's had the same quiet yet expectant air of a business preparing to open for what everyone knew would be a very profitable day. She waved at Grazia and Julie, who were busy setting out fresh flower arrangements and went directly to Mallory's office. She hesitated for a moment on the threshold, looking at her friend who was sitting back in her chair, eyes closed.

341

While she was hesitating about whether or not she should say something, Mallory's lashes fluttered.

"There you are. I thought you might be too busy to come in until later."

"You said the magic words—dining room table," Kit remarked as she sat down in the chair next to Mallory's desk. "I hope it's something special."

"What do you say to a Queen Anne dining table inlaid in a sunburst pattern with Honduran mahogany and banded in African mahogany and supported on shell-carved cabriole legs?"

"The first thing I'd ask is how many chairs."

"Ah, details." Mallory crossed her legs in an elegant motion. "There are only two chairs, but side chairs shouldn't be too much of a problem—Sloane's or the Hampton Shops in New York should be able to help you out with good reproductions."

Kit agreed, and studied her friend. Mallory looked striking in a simple Lanvin day dress of french-blue flannel, and there was an invisible cloud of *Narcisse Noir* floating around her, but there was something else that was not quite identifiable.

"Mallie, are you feeling well? You look a little off."

"I am a little off, but I'm perfectly fine," she said, and smiled at her friend's puzzlement. "I'm pregnant again."

"Oh, Mallory, that's simply wonderful." Kit hugged her friend. "How is Rupert taking the news?"

"He's absolutely delighted, and even though he hasn't said anything, I know he's so delighted with Justine that he'd love it if we had another daughter."

"Well, time will tell. Speaking of which—," Kit paused and looked at Mallory's still-elegant figure.

"The end of June or the beginning of July. We haven't decided if we'll go back to New York, or if I'll have the baby here, but there's plenty of time for that."

"I'm sure. And I'm glad that you're not far enough along

to affect what you wear to all the parties being given for Greg and me."

"Oh, so am I, believe me. I'll even be able to sit on the floor for the sukiyaki dinner we're giving."

"And that will be the only sort of dinner party Greg and I will be able to give unless I can get extra chairs," Kit pointed out with good humor, and they spent a few minutes discussing the dining room table and other important pieces of furniture before Kit, with a look at the clock on Mallory's desk, stood up.

"It's almost that time again," she said lightly. "I want to take another look around the selling floor and see how my mother's sketches are coming before I open the door."

"Do you think she'll do a series of drawings of my shop if I ask? I'll pay, of course."

"Does pregnancy affect your reasoning? My mother won't take a penny in payment from you."

"I know, I just thought I'd be polite and offer. And as for the effects of pregnancy," Mallory continued with a touch of wickedness, "judging from the way you and Greg both look, you'll be finding that out firsthand soon enough!"

Kit went back to her own shop with just enough time left for a final review before it was time to open. Despite the war in Europe and the fluctuations of Wall Street, it seemed that as long as the items offered were timely, elegant, and as exclusive as possible, price wasn't much of a problem.

With a now expert eye, she surveyed the well-filled display cabinets, glad she had such swift confirmation of her taste, and that she had taken the chance and ordered in such large quantities.

The wide variety of bags were all selling well. In particular the fitted satin evening bag, the fitted black velvet-brocade bag, the black moire vanity case lined in white moire and hanging from a silver chain, and the black chiffon bag lined in white satin were all but selling themselves. The mocha leather bag with buckle fastening was the favorite daytime bag, the writing portfolio shaped like a handbag was the bestselling novelty item, and customers were buying the fitted leather vanity cases in multiples.

The only traditional present, cut glass bottles with gilt and enamel tops filled with lavender bath salts, still had a definite appeal, but so did the blue agate cigarette holder in a rose leather box and the silver cigarette case with vanity fittings. Like most of her friends, Kit rarely, if ever, smoked, but that didn't mean that she didn't want all the sophisticated accessories that went with the habit.

Kit checked the vitrine where a selection of bracelet watches with black moire straps, the faces surrounded by diamonds or enamel were displayed and made sure that there were generous supplies of Christmas menu cards showing old English scenes and address books in chased leather.

She was admiring the case where a selection of jeweled combs and hairpins were displayed when her mother joined her.

"Everything here is just a delight to sketch," Constance said, elegant in a trim Premet suit of lightweight tan corduroy with a tailored cutaway jacket and wide black silk braid girdle that gave it a very feminine look. The two women embraced. "I can't wait to do a pastel of the lingerie alcove."

"I'm going to hang all your drawings in my office and put my fashion prints in the saleswomen's room. Will you do a special drawing of my perfume vitrines?"

"Why didn't I think of that? I'll start work on them tomorrow morning. Which ones are the most popular?"

"A lot depends on who's doing the buying. A businessman bringing home a present to his wife and daughters will pick *Quelques Fleurs* or *Jicky* because they're standbys, a younger or more sophisticated man will want *Narcisse Noir* or *L'Heure Bleue,* and college girls are crazy for the heavy D'Orsay fragrances, *Cyclamen* and *Leur Coeurs."*

"And your other women customers?" Constance inquired, intrigued. "Do you have to do a lot of convincing for them to try something new?"

"Surprisingly, no. They love anything from Guerlain or Poiret. I also sell a perfume called *Ilka,* made by Piver, but so far my only customers for it are Nan and a retired Madam who lives in Pomona," Kit finished, and shared the laughter with her mother.

"And I'm sure you're very careful not to let them know about each other. Do you have many customers like that?" Constance asked, she herself having female fans who ranged from not having to pay their own rent to being involved in the upper strata of the world's oldest profession.

"The usual share, but everyone's very polite to each other." The saleswomen began to arrive, and mother and daughter temporarily suspended their conversation so that Kit could greet them and give a few last-minute instructions to the women who worked for her.

She made sure that everyone was at their posts, and after a final look around and exchanging a smile with her mother, Kit, as she did every weekday morning promptly on the stroke of ten, unlocked the door.

"Good morning," she said to the half-dozen women of varying ages who were eagerly waiting to step inside, "and welcome to my shop."

The upstairs sitting room of the Pooles' Chester Place house was the setting for the large scale, high stakes poker game that, had things worked out differently, would have been Greg's bachelor party.

The room, like all the others in Sinclair and Caroline's house, was furnished with the greatest of care and attention to detail. The focal point was the cream-colored wallpaper with a beige floral stripe Caro had found in a Pasadena paint shop where, the owner had informed her, it had been ignored and passed over for more than ten years, the woodwork was pickled pine set off by the beige velvet winter curtains, and the large, excellent pieces of furniture were upholstered in a richly flowered yellow chintz. Combined with the intricate Oriental carpet of beige, taupe, yellow, and dark green, the room had an air that was so unperturbable that not even the addition of a poker table could detract from it.

"The children are all in bed, and Caro, Vanessa, and Constance have gone over to the Alexandria, so we can now have a night of unrestrained debauchery. Just watch out for the odd stuffed animal—the children sometimes leave their toys behind when they finish playing," Sinclair said when Greg, Rupert, Vincent, Drake, Winston, Archie, Frank, Matt, and Charlie were all gathered in the room. "We'll drink to the health and happiness of the new groom and his bride a bit later."

"God, Sinclair, but there are times you have all the social charm of a prison warden," Win Lucas grumbled good-naturedly as the rest of the group laughed.

"Well, if I didn't provide direction, you'd all wander around all night, drinks in hand, and we'd never get anything accomplished."

"Take it all with a grain of salt, Win," Drake advised. "We only have to put up with Sin's bullying on those rare occasions when we gather for boys' night out. On the other hand, Greg actually has to *work* for him! How do you take it—or is that the reason you're hiding out at Hooper Studios?"

"Look how long Greg has worked for Sinclair," Rupert said before Greg could speak. "I suspect it's rather like living in an ugly house—after a while you don't really see it!"

"If there's any problem here, it's my problem. And since I'm the guest of honor here, why don't we play some poker?"

Greg suggested, taking the only stand he could before the matter got out of hand.

"I couldn't agree more," Archie said with quiet determination. True, he didn't work directly for Sinclair, but he was the man directly responsible for his paycheck and that called for a certain loyalty in return. "I feel lucky tonight, and when a Scot feels a streak of fortune coming on he tends to be generous with his bets."

"That sounds good to me," Frank said. "What about you, Vincent?"

"Every time I go out of the country to consult on an engineering project, I learn a whole new set of card tricks from the crews. I look on tonight as my first chance to try my latest collection."

"As a fellow alumnus of Harvard, I can attest to the card playing abilities of Boston," Charlie said as they began to take seats around the table. "Who else do we have represented here?"

"The University of Glasgow," Archie said. "Not a place to learn card tricks."

"The University of London," Frank offered, "and poker was something we read about in penny dreadfuls!"

"Which probably means you're the worst shark of all of us," Matt observed. "Drake and I will be responsible for upholding Stanford's good name."

"Put me down for Princeton," Win offered genially. "Of course, when I was a student there, we were going through a bridge phase and no one would admit to knowing a thing about five-card stud."

Greg hated conversations like this, and he felt some of his enjoyment of the evening ahead cloud. He had the name of a small but respected college in Western Pennsylvania, and although he sent them a substantial check every year for their scholarship fund, he didn't feel right about referring to the school as his alma mater.

I can't lie and I can't tell the truth, he thought, sitting down at the table. How many more years am I going to have to go on living this lie of where I came from? Forever, probably. My life is going to look like an old tapestry, changing and fading but never unraveling.

"Well, it's me and Rupert for Columbia, and Greg takes care of—. Well, there you are," Sin said in a welcoming voice. "I was beginning to think you'd gotten lost."

"No, it was one of those long distance calls where the person on the other end talks like it doesn't cost money to make these calls," the recipient of Sin's greeting said as he advanced into the room. He was in his mid-twenties, tall with brown hair that was almost dark enough to be black, and a pleasant face that was just short of handsome. "Thank you again for inviting me."

"Don't mention it," Sin replied, standing up. He shook hands with his latest guest and then led him to the table. "This is Mitchell Avery, who has just arrived from New York. Mitch, this is—."

"Welcome to my post-bachelor party," Greg said when all introductions were concluded. "I hope you like to play poker."

"Sure, I've been able to play since I was seven," Mitch replied, a gleam in his brown eyes. "There's nothing else to do when you're growing up on a ranch in Oklahoma."

"Do you know Brand Kirby?"

"Some. We grew up together, but when it came time for our parents to pack us off to college, we parted ways and lost touch. I heard he's a gentleman-manager on some horse ranch."

"Yes, it's my horse ranch," Greg said. So far, he liked this man, but he couldn't help but wonder why Sinclair had invited him. "Were you eager to leave New York?"

"No, I like it well enough." He hesitated for a moment. "I didn't like the man I was working for."

"Mitch was working for Curtis Chandler," Sin supplied, and the look on his face said he didn't want any questions.

348

"Curtis sent him to me. Incidentally, where did you go to college?"

"Amherst."

"Oh, well." Sin reached for the cards and expertly cut them. "We seem to be well represented here tonight, and now it's time to see how well we all learned the lessons of our misspent youths." He shuffled and fanned them with an expert motion. "It's dealer's choice, gentlemen. Are we all ready to try and win each other's shirts?"

None of the eleven men seated around the table were given to telling lewd stories about women, trading profanities, or drinking heavily, the usual accompaniments to poker nights, but they did play high stakes poker, often gambling large sums of money on a single hand. To be sure there were poker chips for those who preferred to use them, but Sin always made it very clear that there was nothing quite like a pile of large denomination bills in the center of the table, and his guests always came well prepared. Not that winning or losing mattered very much to any of them. It was only the dare of the game that mattered, and several hundred or a few thousand dollars were all part of the adventure.

They played intently for an hour, with Rupert being the big winner, but gradually the real reason why they had gathered in the Poole house on this Tuesday night reasserted itself. Mitch, Frank, Matt, and Charlie were the bachelors of the group, and when the others finished welcoming Greg to the ranks of married men, they reminded the other young men that they too were not immune from the siren song of marriage.

But it wasn't until the buffet dinner was served that it actually turned into a bachelor party. They helped themselves from chafing dishes filled with breasts of chicken tarragon in wine and lobster Newburg, did justice to both the salad and the cheese platter, and emptied several bottles of

Schramsberg champagne. By the time the Waterford punch bowl lined with slices of jelly roll and filled with rich custard trifle appeared, all of the men were in fine form.

Greg had told Sin about *Ballet At Midnight* the day after he and Kit returned to Los Angeles from Santa Barbara. He had reclined on the leather chesterfield in his best friend's antique-filled office, concentrating on the tank filled with six black fish to keep his apprehension at bay while Sin sat at his desk reading the story. Sin had been silent for a long time after he finished reading, and then he asked Greg what he intended to do about this. Now he wondered if his reply— that he was going to make a movie out of it—was earning him his somewhat acerbic treatment.

He reached for the current bottle of champagne and leaned over to refill his stepfather-in-law's glass. "I don't think that this is like any other bachelor party you've ever been to."

"Well, you are the first guest of honor at any bachelor party that I've ever been to who has already surrendered his single state. Still, it's all in good humor here, and despite my loss at the table, I won't have to wire the State Street Trust for more money!"

For a moment Greg had to fight the almost irresistible urge to ask the older man if he could speak with him privately, and then tell him who he really was and what he might have done. Vincent regarded Kit as practically his own daughter; didn't he have a right to know just whom she had married?

It was a decision that had to be made in a split second, but Greg hesitated just a fraction of a second too long and the moment was gone. But had he really wanted to say anything in the first place? Was it all brought on by a combination of champagne and camaraderie? Greg speculated as the conversation moved on to the topic of the movies, in particular to the matter of D.W. Griffith who had completed filming his epic in early November, and was now deeply involved in the editing with an eye toward a February premiere.

"I have it on a reliable source that he's editing down 150,000 feet of film and keeping three projectionists busy," Archie offered with wry distaste at the director's obvious excesses.

"That means a twelve-reel movie," Greg said wearily. "It won't be easy to compete with him. But then, as much as I hate to say it, he may be setting the trend for longer motion pictures."

"Just remember that anything concerning the Civil War is doubtful," Sin put in, and a wicked gleam appeared in his eyes. "Of course, *no one* knows what a ballet movie will do. Most Americans have no appreciation of the dance."

"Then they can learn," Greg snapped. "Going to the ballet is not like contracting a communicable disease or voting Republican."

"But you can't make a movie without actors," Charlie pointed out. "I don't think there are too many actresses here in Los Angeles who can be Tatiana."

"No, but there may be someone up in San Francisco." Greg felt ready to play a trump card. "Her name is Odette Derrenger, and she used to dance with the Paris Opera Ballet."

"Have you spoken to her about this?" Sin asked almost too quietly.

"No, but I've written her that I'm going to be in San Franciso on my honeymoon later this month, and there's a movie role I want to discuss with her."

"Well, you're not letting any grass grow under your feet." For the first time in all the years they'd known each other, Sinclair and Gregory were in complete disagreement. From his own experience, Sin knew that you didn't invite a potentially dangerous situation unless there was an obvious advantage in it for you. And right now, he thought, Greg was like a country bumpkin smoking a cigarette near a gasoline spill. If it all exploded now, even after all these years, there would be no way, not even with all the influence he could muster, to save him. "Naturally now that you have a story and at least one actress in mind, we might get down to some concrete details."

Greg looked at the other men seated around the room, listening in with great interest. "We'll have this conversation tomorrow, all right, Sin? This isn't the time and place." *As you well know,* he added silently.

There were a few awkward moments, but then the party began to flow again. There was more champagne with all the appropriate toasts, and there was still time to return to the table for a few more hands of poker.

They talked about horses, automobiles, airplanes, the Harvard-Yale game, and the Battle of the Marne and Ypres, where, despite horrendous losses for the Allies on both battlefields, the German army had been stopped in its advance and was forced to retreat.

But even while he participated in the conversation, Greg's mind was still on another subject. He had to make the movie. Not only because it was a good story and would lift Hooper Studios out of the mud of being third-rate, but quite possibly because it would provide him with some answers.

But was the cost going to be too high?

Since the summer of 1900, he and Sinclair had worked together; but now there was a rift between them that was undeniable. It could only be temporary, the sort of thing that occurs when two men with equally strong personalities clash over something important, but it was there, and as he displayed his straight flush and swept the money on the center of the table toward him, he wondered if he were now on a path where nothing would ever be the same again.

Kit opened her eyes, surprised by the darkness, and it took a minute for her to realize that she must have fallen asleep while reading in bed.

Tonight, while Greg was being entertained at Chester Place, she had had her mother, Caro, and Mallory, as well as Nan, Barbara, Grazia, Jessica, and Susan MacNeil to dinner and to see the latest arrivals in the unending stream of wedding presents.

As she had assured Greg, their sudden marriage was no impediment to people sending them presents, and like every other new bride she was now involved with the mandatory thank-you notes. But once her mother and friends left, she had undressed and gotten into bed, deciding that when he came home, Greg would rather find her reclining against the pillows, wearing a nightgown of flesh-colored chiffon trimmed with filet lace and ribbons, than at the writing table, working on yet another thank-you note.

I only closed my eyes for a minute, she thought a bit hazily. I wonder how long I've been asleep. Greg—

Turning her head, she saw him come out of the bathroom, and she held out a hand to him.

"You were sound asleep when I came in, and I turned off the light and put your book away," he said, sitting down beside her.

"And I was going to be up and waiting for you. Is it very late?"

"Just after one. What a night," he said, resting his head against her shoulder. "I think a stay in Marine boot camp has to be easier than coming up against Sin."

"Is there something wrong between the two of you?" Kit asked concerned, as Greg stretched out alongside her. He was wearing only his heavy silk dressing gown, and she put her hands at the back of his neck and began to massage the tension away.

"He's upset with me because of the movie. Oh, that feels so good. And he wasn't expecting me to have someone in mind to play Natalia—I mean Tatiana."

Kit let the slip pass. "He's only concerned for you."

"I know that, but I don't have to like his attitude. He really is my older brother—Sergei is so long ago—never mind—yes, right there—but I'm a little too old to be treated like a rambunctious seventeen-year-old."

"Aren't we all. Right now, Sin is probably cringing whenever he thinks about what he said."

"I did exact a little revenge, though," Greg said a little more cheerfully. "I won eight-hundred dollars at poker."

"So tonight wasn't a total loss?"

"Far from it." For a minute he concentrated on kissing the side of her neck. "Shall we talk about something else? I'm very curious," he went on, reaching out to touch the book he'd placed on the bedside table. "What's *The Honest House* about? It sounds rather risqué."

"It's a decorating book!" Kit laughed and rumpled Greg's hair. "The *on dit* from New York is that the author, Ruby Ross Goodnow, was Elsie de Wolfe's ghostwriter for *The House In Good Taste.*"

"I see," Greg said with a touch of male perplexity, resettling himself so he and Kit could look at each other. "But with Mallory here and Thea in New York, why do you need more decorating advice?"

"Oh, it never hurts to check out all newcomers—one never knows. And we do have quite a decorating job ahead of us, and the only thing we can be sure of is that my mother is going to paint the mural in the breakfast room. So far, we're going to have a twenty-two room, three-story American Colonial house, a tennis court, a swimming pool, and a pool house, as well as a Bohn Syphon refrigerator."

"If it's good enough for the Pullman Company, it's good enough for us. And don't forget the garage, the stable, the gravel driveway, and a Japanese tea house. Do you want a footbridge as well?"

"I think a footbridge would be a bit excessive, but we have to decide on shade trees, fruit trees, plants, and bushes," Kit reminded him, and then began to run through a rough mental count of how much all of this was going to cost. Even before a single piece of furniture was carried through the door, she knew it was going to be astronomical. "Greg—."

"I can afford it," he said, reading her thoughts. "And as Gregory West, not Alexander Vestovanova."

"I believe you," Kit said. "It just took me a moment to realize that being a Vestovanova means never having to look at a price tag."

"What's a price tag?"

"You are impossible!" Kit undid the belt of his dressing gown, parted the side, and pulled him closer to her. "But there are definite advantages."

"Whatever else is a husband for?" he asked, his fingers tangling in the ribbons of her nightgown. "A year from now, our house will be built, but right now I'm very glad we have our cozy little nest right here."

"I couldn't agree more, but if the wedding presents keep coming in the way they are, there won't be much room for us!"

"Do you know what I wanted to do tonight?" he asked a minute later, brushing her hair back from her forehead.

"Hopefully, come on back home to me."

"That goes without saying. But the truth is, I almost took Vincent aside and told him who I really am—or was. But the moment passed."

"I'm glad it did. Dad's very understanding, but he would have thought you were behaving a bit strangely."

"Why do you call your stepfather 'Dad'? I don't mean to change the subject, but I've been meaning to ask you."

"I couldn't call him Vincent, it just wouldn't be right, and one thing you *don't* call a Boston Brahmin is 'Father Vincent.'"

"I can see your point."

"You know Dad thinks very highly of you, he told me so this morning."

Greg felt himself flush. "I'm glad I kept my mouth closed. I could have destroyed his high esteem for me in five minutes."

"I think if we ever find out all the answers, we might tell my mother and stepfather. They'd be very compassionate about what you've been through, but it would be even better if we can present them with a resolution."

"You're very right, but I hope I can wait that long. Ever since that damn story arrived, I find myself getting the urge to tell someone I know all about me and what I might have done."

"Is that why you want to make *Ballet At Midnight* into a motion picture, to tell everyone what happened without really having to say a word?"

"It looks that way. It may be that I spent so many years *not* mentioning or discussing any of this that I have no safety valve left. The hardest thing in the world was telling you," he went on tenderly, "and that might have released the hold I kept on my past. I'm so tired of being a prisoner of that night, and by making this movie, I may be able to free myself of the worst of it."

"That's very possible," Kit agreed, and held him close, wanting him to know that she understood, would always be there for him.

"I want you to promise me one thing," Greg said a long minute later.

"Anything at all."

"If I ever start to get caught up in the muck of the past, I want you to tell me off in no uncertain terms. I may be a prime candidate for making a complete fool of myself, and I don't want to set myself up for a problem I can't get out of."

Chapter 19

The formal reception to celebrate the wedding of Mr. Gregory West and Miss Katharine Allen, who were married in a private ceremony on November 5th, was given by Mr. and Mrs. Sinclair Poole in their Chester Place house on Saturday evening, December 19th.

This gala, given at the height of the holiday season, was the crowning event in the series of festivities given for the newly married pair over the past few weeks, and followed by only twenty-four hours the Japanese dinner given by Mr. and Mrs. Rupert Randall at their West Adams Boulevard house on Friday night. At that party, all of the forty-two guests gathered in the drawing room that had been made to look like a Japanese tea house. With shoes left at the door, the men and women donned kimonos over their dinner clothes, and then proceeded to sit cross-legged on the floor which had been covered with thick woven matting. The suki-yaki dinner, served on eight-inch high lacquer tables by pretty young Japanese waitresses and eaten with chopsticks included *ostuimono,* a soup with mushroom and seaweed; *curi sunommo,* cucumber salad; *suki-yaki,* which is strips of beef and vegetables with cubes of soy bean curd; baby lobsters with white radish sauce; and *chawon-mushi,* egg custard. Saki was served in little bottles and poured hot into tiny cups the size of six thimbles by geisha girls Haruki, Mirdori, and Tariko, all under the direction of Madame Kato. They then played the samsen and sang old songs about the chill of autumn, the death of a bird, and lovers who are parted by fate; and at the conclusion of the evening wished the couple *omedeto*— Japanese for good luck.

But Saturday night's gala, which commenced promptly at the fashionable hour of nine o'clock, was representative of the splendid receptions we all dream about to celebrate the happiness of a new pair.

Mr. and Mrs. Poole's entry foyer, whose decor is well known to Angelinos either through invitation to one of their large and hospitable soirees or via press interview, was provided with an even higher gloss of romance by being adorned with rich arrangements of white flowers. It was in this beautiful spot that all of the guests were welcomed.

The new Mrs. West, the former Katharine Allen of New York, who is the proprietor of "Katharine's" on Spring Street where the best-dressed women in Southern California are flocking to in droves, was dressed in a special gown created especially for her by Herman Patrick Tappe. This creation of rich white satin with long, tight sleeves and a neckline of the crossed surplice style was finished with an overdress of silver appliqued lace which began with an Elizabethan collar and ended in a deep point at the knees. Even without train and headdress, this outstanding gown, set off by the double strand of pearls and diamonds that are Mrs. West's wedding present from her husband, still retained a bridal air.

All of the other women present were equally elegant-looking. In particular, Mrs. Poole, the former Caroline Worth of New York, was striking in a Jeanne Hallee creation of pink chiffon over pink satin embroidered in bugle beads; Mrs. Rupert Randall, who wore Redfern's pink chiffon gown with a lace bodice and iridescent spangles on the lace overdress, and Mrs. Vincent Lyman, the bride's mother, in Poiret's bronze lace over emerald green satin.

Other costumes of note include Mrs. Elston Harper, who is Mrs. Poole's stepmother, in Worth's blue velvet combined with blue tulle, silver lace and rhinestone motifs; and Mrs. Brand Kirby, the wife of the gentleman manager of Mr. West's horse ranch, in Cheruit's pale rose mousseline combined with Chantilly lace.

All the gentlemen present wore formal evening clothes.

Among the guests invited were Mr. and Mrs. Drake Sloane, Mr. and Mrs. Winston Lucas, Miss Grazia D'Ettiene, Mr. and Mrs. Jesse Lasky, Mr. Adolph Zukor, Mr. and Mrs. Michael Garriety, and Mr. Charles Lasky, who is the scion of the famous New York theatrical family. . . .

When the last guest had been received, everyone moved from the drawing room to the dining room, arranged to accommodate what Mrs. Poole confided to me was the largest and most gala party she and Mr. Poole have given. The table for dinner was a serpentine affair covered by ivory-colored satin as gleaming and shimmering as the bridal dress. Greenlined shells packed with gardenias paraded down the center of the table, and their progress was broken only by two crystal compotiers filled with green and white mints. The silver reflected the light and the crystal, and everyone was in fine appetite for the cold filet of sole mousse with lobster sauce, the breast of chicken on tongue with tarragon sauce accompanied by French peas and parsleyed potato balls, the raw mushroom and lettuce salad, and the strawberry and vanilla ice cream. The wedding cake was a work of art. After the style of the Renaissance, it was four tiers of frosty wedding cake appropriately crowned by a temple to Eros, and encrusted with cupids and arrows.

After a number of toasts, all made with Moet et Chandon 1909, there was dancing in the drawing room, and the wedding presents were arranged for viewing in the yellow salon.

The festivities came to a reluctant conclusion in the early hours of Sunday morning, and Mr. and Mrs. West returned to their apartment at the Alexandria for a brief respite before boarding The Coaster at Union Station at eight o'clock.

Among the presents given to the newly married couple were a magnificent pair of Imperial Oriental vases in yellow with a rubbed underglaze given by Mr. and Mrs. Poole. . . .

Thus ran Jessica Gilbert's article on Kit and Greg's reception to celebrate their recent marriage. Complete with photographs, it covered two full pages in the Sunday edition of the *Los Angeles Statesman-Democrat*. She had gone directly from Chester Place to the *Statesman-Democrat*'s office at Broadway and First, and still in her Callot Soeurs dress of ice blue satin with a long tunic of ecru lace threaded in gold, she had sat in the city room, typing out her story. Because of this, the paper had been a few hours late getting out on the streets, and when Kit and Greg boarded The Coaster at shortly before eight on Sunday morning, they weren't able to read about their own reception.

This crack Southern Pacific train offered its passengers the comfort of reclining chairs, the fine food of its dining car, and some of the prettiest scenery which began with the valley and orchards as soon as they left the city. From numerous previous trips, Greg knew to reserve their seats on the left side of the train so they wouldn't miss the thrilling sight of the Pacific's surf pounding on the beach below the cliffs as the train rushed on toward the mountains. At San Luis Obispo, The Coaster went inland, and there was the thrill of seeing the helper engine put on so that the equipment could make the grade at Cuesta, and the horseshoe-curve turn up the mountain.

But as beautiful as it was on a quiet Sunday when the train wasn't very crowded, it was nonetheless a long and tiring journey. When the train pulled into the station at Third and Townsend Street, promptly at nine-fifty that night, Greg and Kit were both feeling the after-effects of all the parties, as well as the strain of seeing to it that their businesses would run smoothly without them until after the first of the year. They felt far too tired to really absorb the reality of being in San Francisco.

Their friends each had San Francisco hotels to which they were devoted. For Caro and Sin, it was the Palace, staying there each time they were in the city, even though, since its reopening in 1909 following the earthquake and fire of 1906, it had been rebuilt further along Market Street; and Mallory and Rupert always stayed at the St. Francis, as they had on each visit since their own honeymoon in 1910. But Kit and Greg decided to stay someplace where they could make their own memories, and the Packard limousine and driver that Greg had engaged for their stay drove them from the station to the top of Nob Hill, to the Fairmont Hotel.

Like its two closest competitors in the city's luxury hotel market, the Fairmont, too, had been damaged during the earthquake, burned to the ground during the fire, and subsequently returned to all its glory; and it prided itself on the chic, cosmopolitan clientele it attracted. Even after ten o'clock at the end of a weekend, the lobby hummed with activity; and when the Wests came through the revolving door and walked across the richly carpeted floor, past the heavily veined marble pillars that went straight up to the ceiling, rich with gold-leaf trimmings, to the reception desk, every eye was upon them.

"Mr. and Mrs. Gregory West from Los Angeles," Greg announced in a quiet but thoroughly effective voice, and the reception clerk looked as if he were about to jump to attention.

"Oh, sir, madam, on behalf of the management, welcome to the Fairmont," the young man said quickly. "We have all your instructions right here, and if you'll just fill out these forms—."

"What instructions?" Kit murmured as Greg signed them in.

"The usual things—what brand of champagne we like, the newspapers we read."

"Don't forget that we have to read Jessica's story about us. It would look a little odd if we didn't want to read about the gala given in our honor."

"We'll have to send Jessica flowers," he promised, capping his pen. "We'd like a copy of the Sunday edition of the *Los Angeles Statesman-Democrat,* please," he told the clerk.

"It hasn't come in yet, sir, but it will be available tomorrow morning."

"That will be fine, we'll expect it with our breakfast order."

"I'll make a note of that right now. Everything else is in order. We have a superb suite set aside for you and Mrs. West. Since I see we have your luggage on a trolley, our chief bellman can show you upstairs."

"Now I can really see you as an officer," Kit said a short time later when the bellboys finished unloading their luggage and departed with generous tips. She took off her Tappe hat of black satin with a black crown and scarlet brim. "All you

362

had to do was look at that clerk and he was ready to do everything up to and including saluting!"

"No, I think he just gave us the standard treatment for guests who reserve suites. Speaking of which, what do you think?"

Kit looked around the sitting room, all done in pale gray silk and velvet and blue satin. The room was so cool and restrained she felt that her Tappe suit of gray and black plaid silk, its jacket open over a scarlet silk blouse, was an almost too-intense splash of color.

"It's pretty, but right now I'm a little too tired to know if it's really for us. I do think it could use a little more color."

"It is a little too neutral," Greg agreed. "It's almost Christmas, and there should be more here."

"It may look better when we get our personal belongings spread around. Do you think we can arrange for a tree?"

"We'll do that tomorrow. Look at the flowers," he said, indicating several vases of flowers. "Do they really have to be white also?"

"It's supposed to be chic. It is, but not at ten-thirty at night with a full day of train travel behind us. Ah, the prerequisite basket of fruit from the management," she said as she unwrapped the large wicker basket holding apples, oranges, several small bananas, and a pineapple.

"Do you think this is a warning about room service?"

"Oh, you think you're funny, don't you?" Kit kissed him and reluctantly turned her attention to the flowers. "From the management, from Mr. and Mrs. Kenneth Crockett, from Mr. and Mrs. Georges Bergery,—oh, I forgot Georges and Bettina were in San Francisco for the winter—and from Madame Odette Derrenger," she read from the accompanying cards, referring to the vase of white roses, the Imari dish holding several orchids, the silver bowl heaped with gardenias, and a bunch of white violets in a small Limoges vase. "Did you get an answer to your letter?"

"I have an idea we're looking at it. I'll have to get in touch with her tomorrow. I hope she has a phone."

"Is this what's known as business before the honeymoon?"

"I was thinking more along the lines of your helping me convince Odette that making a movie is in all our best interests."

"Hmm." Kit put her arms around him. "If you really mean that, I think we may be in the wrong room for an in-depth discussion. Shall we see what our bedroom looks like?"

Despite the Vuitton trunks and suitcases making a rather grand obstacle course on the heavy fitted carpet of french gray, the bedroom was generously proportioned with panels of french gray and a cornice with carved moldings. The room had a wide, restful look with simply designed furniture ornamented by very slight carvings, simple lamps, wall sconces, a few but excellent pictures, and a large double bed with a cane headboard and footboard. The maid had already been in, removing the french-blue silk bedspread and turning down the bed.

"I think we can leave all our unpacking for tomorrow," Kit said, exhaustion mingling with desire as she leaned against Greg. "I hate to be the one to throw a damper on our first night in San Francisco, but I'm so tired."

"So am I. Why don't we act like the old married couple we are, and go straight to bed?"

"So much for being an exciting Russian," Kit said lightly, slipping off her suit and blouse and stepping out of her handmade shoes.

Greg took off his suit jacket, tie, and shoes. "Right now, I'm just a tired American. I've just thought of something. Shall we take flying lessons together? It ought to take a few hours off the train trip."

"We seem to be buying everything else, why not an airplane?"

"Every couple should have one," Greg said as, free of all their clothes, they fell across the bed together. They fell asleep almost immediately. When they awoke again it was nearly dawn, a proper San Francisco dawn, heavy with fog, and their response to each other was elemental and immediate. "What were you saying a couple of hours ago about my being an unexciting Russian?" Greg asked when there was time for talk again.

"Nothing that I care to elaborate on," Kit replied with a luxurious stretch. "We have too many other interesting things to do. This bed feels wonderful and so do you. Now that's a really splendid combination to make San Francisco the best place to be!"

By Monday afternoon, they wondered why they'd ever thought that their suite was unattractive. By the time all the unpacking had been taken care of, the rooms took on a far more familiar feeling, and now, at shortly after noon on Wednesday, December 23, the day before Christmas Eve, the suite with its sweeping view of Nob Hill was as welcome to them as their apartment in the Alexandria.

A pretty little Douglas fir Christmas tree set up in one corner and decorated with hand-blown glass ornaments and bows of antique satin that Peggy Crockett had thoughtfully sent over, gave the sitting room the holiday spirit it had been lacking on Sunday night, and a silver vase filled with holly and red carnations, as well as a crystal vase holding bright red tulips were wonderfully effective in the rooms that were basically pale gray.

"We were just too tired on Sunday night to absorb how lovely this suite really is," Kit said as they dressed for the luncheon meeting that was going to be so crucial. "Also, we may have panicked at the sight of all the open space."

"That's because of all the wedding gifts we've been receiving," Greg replied as he selected a tie. "Thanks to our friends' loving generosity, our rooms at the Alexandria aren't quite as large as they used to be."

"It's still amazing how quickly we can take over a basic

hotel suite and fill it up with our belongings."

"Wait until we open our Christmas presents," he said, pausing at the open bedroom door to look at the tree with the numerous ornately wrapped boxes arranged beneath it.

"I'm glad to know that you're looking forward to Friday morning as much as I am." At the dressing table, Kit sprayed on a last mist of *Apres L'Ondee,* stood up to take off her pink satin robe, and, wearing only her lacy lingerie, went over to the closet. She considered the selection of dresses and suits for a long minute before making a decision. "Do you think Odette is going to be as prickly in person as she was on the phone?"

"I wouldn't put it past her. Frenchwomen," he said in a dismissive tone of voice.

"You sound like the voice of experience."

"I'll tell you about it another time."

"Oh, go and wait for me in the sitting room," Kit advised, recognizing Greg's restlessness. "In another minute, you'll be looking at your watch and making husband-like noises. Do us both a favor and relax and read something. I won't be long."

Greg looked like he was about to make a very husbandly comment, but instead he left the bedroom, and Kit turned back to her closet. Whenever meeting a Frenchwoman was involved, there was no such thing as being too concerned about how one looked.

Her frock was from the new house of Martial et Armand, made in the style of a "moyen age" robe de style that most of the Paris couturiers were so fond of this season. It began with an underdress of beige charmeuse with a waistcoat and bands of gold lace encircling the long semifitted waist and hem. The overdress was of paler beige silk lined in charmeuse, embroidered in tan, banded with skunk, and finished with an upstanding Elizabethan collar.

This should show Odette Derrenger that we're not some tacky, know-nothing showpeople from Los Angeles, Kit thought with satisfaction, fastening the row of five gold buttons that ran from the V neck to the end of the waistcoat. The high-handed treatment of them by the dancer rankled mightily.

As they found out from San Francisco Information, Madame Derrenger did indeed have a telephone number, and late on Monday morning, just after the Fairmont's maid and valet had completed the task of unpacking the luggage and left the suite, Greg had placed the call with Kit listening in on the extension. To say that the Frenchwoman had been cool was like saying that the weather in the North Pole tended to be breezy.

She had summarily cut off Greg's stream of perfect French, and in equally good if somewhat accented English informed him that she knew exactly who he was and what Hooper Studios did. She wasn't interested in a long conversation, and after informing him that she had another far more demanding appointment, she agreed to join the Wests for a late lunch on Wednesday.

"We're at the Fairmont," Greg began, but got no further.

"An excellent establishment, quite de luxe. I will meet you and your wife at the Magneta Clock in the St. Francis at one. Until then, Mr. West—."

"What a bitch," Kit said a moment later when they met each other halfway.

"I'm glad you said that first."

"What are you going to do?"

"Get your hat," Greg instructed. "Right now, we're going to lunch, and on Wednesday, it looks as if we'll be enjoying that meal in the splendor of the St. Francis."

Now, as she picked up her pearls which lay between a silver goblet holding a mixture of pink tea roses and baby's breath and her ornate Tiffany travelling clock, Kit noted the time. Twelve-fifteen, just enough time to get them from Nob Hill to Union Square.

Following that telephone call on Monday, they had gone

367

to lunch at the New Poodle Dog, and followed it by a long walk through Chinatown. They had stayed on in that colorful district to have dinner in a highly regarded restaurant and then went to a performance at a Chinese theatre where the actors were costumed in magnificent brocades and silks and the story was an ongoing one with a new segment played out each night.

Not once during that afternoon or evening or at any time during Tuesday which was spent with the throng of Christmas shoppers at Gumps, I. Magnin, and the City of Paris, did either of them mention the name Odette Derrenger.

Kit fastened the clasp on her short strand of pearls, put on her black velvet hat that had a wave of black ostrich feathers curling over the scrolling brim, and collected her purse and Poiret afternoon coat of fine black wool embroidered in gold. This was their honeymoon, there was a dozen things they'd rather be doing, and this churlish ballerina had better not only be worth the time and effort but also as good a dancer as Pavlova, she thought.

"If I were another sort of wife, I'd ask will I do, but since I'm not . . . will I do?"

Greg looked up from *A Preface To Politics,* and almost dropped Walter Lippmann's book. As he looked at Kit standing in the bedroom doorway he felt his throat close and his vision cloud.

Am I really going to go through with making a motion picture that's close enough to my own life to be called autobiographical? he wondered. It's utterly conceivable that I'm acting like the proverbial moth around the flame, that I'll find out absolutely nothing and destroy everything I've built up. And I'll lose Kit.

"Will you do?" he echoed, pushing aside the disturbing rush of thought. "My darling, there aren't words enough in any language to tell you how very much you will do. I'll probably have to fight off men who'll want to shove me aside, and Odette will turn green with envy."

Kit laughed and walked forward, the dress swishing expensively around her ankles. "That sounds delightful, but in either instance, it's the *last* thing we need."

Greg stood up. "You'll never be able to convince me that you haven't planned out everything you're wearing right down to your perfume, to create the ultimate effect."

"My brilliant husband." Kit took a red carnation from the silver vase, snapped the stem in half, and tucked the flower into Greg's buttonhole. "We've already conceded the first round, but we're not going into the second without all the ammunition we can muster."

"Aren't you going to kiss me?"

"Oh, the temptation, but just this once I have to think of my maquillage. Later, though . . ." She left the sentence unfinished, and laughing, Greg draped his Burberry raincoat over his arm.

"Come on, another promise like that and we won't get out of this suite."

"I've been thinking about something that I can only call *cherchez l'homme,*" she said as the elevator took them downstairs.

"I've never heard that used in connection with a man before, I'm not even sure it's correct." The operator lined the car up with the floor and slid open the doors. "What do you have in mind?"

"It's more what you do. If Odette is the right person to play Nat—Tatiana, wouldn't she want to know who'll be her leading man. Do you have someone in mind?" she asked as they crossed the ornate lobby, crowded with holiday lunchers.

"If it were possible to borrow an actor from Vitagraph, I'd want James Morrison. He was outstanding in *A Tale of Two Cities, The Seepore Rebellion,* and *The Redemption of David Darcy.* And there's Douglas Fairbanks, but I don't stand a chance of being able to hire him either." Greg stopped talking as they went through the revolving door, and waited until they were in the Packard before speaking again. "But I'm almost certain I can convince Anthony Kendall to play Nikolai."

As the driver took the car down Nob Hill, Kit regarded her husband with a mixture of surprise and delight. Anthony Kendall would be perfect, she thought. A popular Broadway actor since the moment he stepped on the boards in late 1902 at not quite twenty-one, he had swiftly managed to become that rarity, a leading man with intellect, a matinee idol with depth. He could do drama or comedy, or even a musical. He had charm, talent, drive, and the ability to inhabit any variety of characters and bring them to life.

Greg read her expression correctly, but he still asked, "What do you think?"

"That Toby would be absolutely perfect."

"Toby? Do you know Anthony Kendall?"

"Of course. Don't you?"

"Yes, but apparently not the way you do."

"There's nothing for you to be concerned about. Toby did take me dancing a few times, but he was married a year ago last June to Camillia Leslie, Alix's cousin."

"Were you upset?"

"Oh, no. But I think Richard Thorpe was. He and Camillia had been seeing quite a bit of each other until she met Toby," she related, and in the same vein, couldn't help wondering what Sebastian would think when he heard about her and Greg. "Anyway, I heard that he didn't take a show this season because of the baby coming, so he's at liberty."

"I love theatrical phrases."

"But Lesley was born in early November. Do you think they'd want to come out to Los Angeles so quickly?"

"I'll find out soon. But from the letter he wrote me, I think he may want to try making a motion picture—even though he can't talk in it."

"His fans won't care if it's silent as long as they can see him." It didn't occur to Kit to be upset that Greg hadn't discussed this with her earlier. This was his business, he had to keep certain things under wraps for as long as possible, and she certainly didn't discuss everything that went on in her shop with him—and the fact that she knew Anthony longer and better than he did had nothing whatsoever to do with the matter. "And it isn't a bad idea to keep this movie as much in the family as possible," she added. "Toby has always worked for Percy Lasky, who's Charlie's father, and since this is a first for so many people, you're right to involve as many of those we know and trust as possible."

At the moment they met Odette, the same thought occurred to the Wests: it was the greatest crime in the world of entertainment that movies were not only silent but had no color. The Frenchwoman who met them at the great Magneta masterclock in the lobby of the St. Francis was made for both.

Like most ballerinas, she wasn't terribly tall—only about five-feet-five inches—but she combined a dancer's natural grace with an estimable sense of chic. Once the maitre d' had shown them to the table that was important yet secluded, and the waiter had presented menus and recited chef Victor Hirtzler's specials of the day, their subtle testing of each other began.

Odette had removed her Premet coat of blue gabardine with a rich kolinsky collar to reveal a Premet afternoon dress of corbeau blue taffeta with a wide and elaborate girdle of blue taffeta embroidered in gold. Underneath her Talbot hat of blue velvet and taffeta ornamented with a blue ostrich feather, her rich ebony-colored hair was wrapped into a figure eight at the nape of her neck, and despite the wide brim, her incredible blue-violet eyes missed nothing.

At first they talked about San Francisco, discussing the upcoming Panama-Pacific International Exposition, how Art Hickman's ragtime band had proved so popular to the

St. Francis that the hotel renamed the White and Gold Room to the Rose Room after the musician's hit number of that name, and about the Monday night gala in the hotel's Colonial Ballroom which was planned to raise money for Belgian War Relief.

"I am choreographing and dancing in the tableau," Odette explained as they finished their lobster bisque. "There was a rehearsal last Monday afternoon—that's why I was so abrupt when we spoke. Except for me, the ladies taking part are all amateurs, and although they are all willing and well-intentioned, it is not always easy to—," she finished with an expressive shrug that said it all.

"Then we'll look forward to seeing you dance," Kit told her. Odette's cool, distinterested, and somewhat aggressive phone manner was nowhere in evidence now. Instead, she was the essence of a charming Frenchwoman, and with a silent signal between them, Kit and Greg decided to give her the benefit of the doubt—for now. "Mr. and Mrs. Crockett have insisted that we join them."

"That's Kenneth and Peggy Crockett," Greg put in, knowing that he had good reason to identify his friends from other San Franciscans with the same last name.

Her reaction was just what he hoped it would be.

"Madame Crockett is very interested in the arts, in particular the ballet," Odette observed with approval as the soup cups were replaced with plates of grilled chicken. "And unlike some patronesses, she is knowledgeable about the subject."

"I attended her reception for Pavlova and the Imperial Ballet a few years ago," Greg offered, and continued truthfully, "It was a very different evening for me."

Odette gave him a considering look. "You do not strike me as the sort of man who is either afraid of the ballet or doesn't understand it."

"I'm glad to say I'm not. You already know that Hooper Studios plans to make a ten- or twelve-reel quality motion picture. I would like to find out if you'd be interested in appearing in the film," he went on, deciding that all the social notes had been taken care of. "If you are, I'd very much like to discuss terms with you."

"Americans are so direct," Odette said, and the Wests quickly took forkfuls of vegetables to keep from laughing. "Always business first."

"I'm here on my honeymoon, Madame. My wife and I are very eager to enjoy each other's company and to see San Francisco. I believe that under such delightful circumstances, even a Frenchman would want to conclude his business as quickly and as satisfactorily as possible."

There was no mistaking the tone of his voice, and Odette had not survived her years in the highly competitive world of the Paris Opera Ballet by being anyone's fool.

"Please forgive my comments, Mr. West," she said sincerely. "I meant no slur, either upon you or your nationality. Naturally, since you're in this beautiful city for your honeymoon, business *is* something that must be rapidly concluded."

Odette spoke excellent English, and unlike some French-speaking people, she did not drop words and expressions from her native language into her sentences, Kit observed silently as she finished her chicken. Of course, in other matters she was playing the ultimate Frenchwoman, centering all of her attentions on Greg.

Not that she minded. She and Odette had already taken each other's measure, and like two elegant lionesses with only one handsome lion to share, each was giving the other a great deal of space. There was no coolness between them, but to the Frenchwoman, it was Gregory West who was the important figure.

Let her be charming and bewitching, Kit thought with a silent smile as she listened to them discuss motion pictures in general and *Ballet At Midnight* in particular. I'm the one going back to the Fairmont with him.

373

"I understand that you want to open your own ballet school," Greg said as the waiter removed the plates that had held the main course and brought out the chocolate mousse and the cafe filtre. "If you agree to make this movie, you'll have more than enough money to do just that and not have to look for a loan that would have a lot of unwanted strings attached."

"How did you—," Odette stopped. "But of course you would know of my difficulty. My husband is a very talented cellist, and although he has a very handsome contract with the San Francisco Symphony, this is an expensive city. I've had any number of offers to back me in my wish to open a school of the ballet, but then I know certain things would be expected of me. Do you both understand?" she questioned, for the first time including Kit in the conversation.

"Very much so," she told the other woman. "If you can't realize your dream on as much of your own terms as possible, then it isn't really a special dream any more."

"Exactly. I am glad, Mrs. West, that you understand my difficulty so completely. But I've seen motion pictures—sometimes far too many, I think," she went on, turning her attention back to Greg. "What assurances do I have that you won't employ a director who decides he wants to make a comedy, or has no regard for the importance of the ballet?"

"My personal word, and if you like I'll have it written into your contract that if the story you film deviates from what I've told you it would be, you can leave with full salary. But I can assure you right now that the director, Charles Lasky, is from a fine old theatrical family, and he has great respect for the integrity of the storyline."

"That is very reassuring. But it costs money to live in Los Angeles. What good is the money I earn if it all disappears into living expenses?" Odette went on, her intent clear.

Does she think I'd let her live in a hovel? Greg thought, and then recalled that with the French, you could never tell what they were going to think. He didn't like it at all that

374

Odette, despite her now-charming manner, was still playing *la belle dame sans pitie* with him. But at least she wasn't going in the other direction and making explicit overtures to him.

"Your living expenses, within reason, will be paid for by Hooper Studios," he said finally.

"And what does 'within reason' mean," Odette persisted, and Kit wondered if Greg wasn't slowly but surely being drained of all his patience.

"A small suite at the Alexandria, which is the best hotel in Los Angeles. We live there," he added.

"Then I'm sure it will be satisfactory," Odette conceded with a charming smile. "Will you want me to provide my own wardrobe?"

"Of course you won't have to do that!" Kit exclaimed, and needed a moment to regain her composure. "All the clothes you'll need for the part—with the exception of ballet costumes—will be provided for you by my shop."

"And do you dress yourself out of your own shop?"

Kit sent up a silent prayer that Tappe would understand and forgive her. "Of course I do."

"Then I don't think there will be a problem. I have to discuss this with my husband, and then I will be in touch with you again." Odette took a sip of her cafe filtre. "Mr. West, why do you want to make this movie? It is the sort of motion picture that the people who usually patronize this entertainment either won't go to see or will see and won't understand."

Kit watched Greg's face very carefully. There were any number of reasons he could give her, she knew. There was the business explanation, that a properly made quality movie, no matter what its degree of success, would attract a buyer for the studio; there was the artistic explanation, one Odette would respond to, that no matter how low the public's taste level was, one could not always play for the lowest common denominator; and then there was the explanation that came as close to the truth—Greg's truth—as possible without revealing too much. Not quite daring to breathe, she waited for her husband's reply.

"I can give you any number of business-related reasons why I know *Ballet At Midnight* is not a mistake in any sense of the word, except that they would be as boring to you as they are to me," Greg said in a compelling voice. "All I can tell you, Madame Derrenger, is that certain artistic endeavors—paintings, books, poetry, plays, musical compositions, and now movies—despite the fact they don't fit in with the accepted perception of the great mass of public taste—and no matter how impossible it seems, simply have to be done."

Chapter 20

Kit drove her brand new fire engine red Buick roadster into the newly designated parking area of Hooper Studios. She parked between Greg's Fiat and Charlie's Oldsmobile, noting with delight that the studio's quiet, almost sleepy days were definitely over. The area was full of motor cars, ranging from modest Model T's to far more expensive models, and once again Kit reflected on how residents of Southern California, regardless of income, seemed to be unable to get around unless they owned an automobile.

She walked quickly from the car to the house, still not used to the fact that Los Angeles at the end of January could be as warm as New York at the beginning of October. According to the newspapers, the rest of the country was suffering through a terrible winter, but California seemed to be immune. Even San Francisco had been warmer than usual, and once the business with Odette was successfully concluded, their honeymoon had been perfect—so much so that they had extended it for another week, and hadn't come home until January 20th, five days before.

The glow was unchanged, their closeness even more enhanced, but now they had to return to the real world where they had other responsibilities. She had to guide her shop so that following its very successful holiday season it wasn't caught in the shoals of the January Sale followed by the February doldrums when no one wanted any more winter clothes but weren't quite ready for the spring models; and Greg, at long last, was functioning as the executive producer of *Ballet At Midnight*.

Her first stop was the cubicle where the switchboard girls worked, answering the calls that now seemed unending.

"Oh, Mrs. West!" Karen did something mysterious with all the wires and plugs and pulled her headset off. "Maisie's gone to lunch with that new beau of hers, and she'll be so upset to miss you. What a beautiful outfit you have on. I simply love it!"

"Thank you very much," she told the younger woman. "Are you having a busy morning?"

"So far, it's the usual madhouse. Oh, don't go up to Mr. West's office, he's gone out to the property office. Mrs. Rigby's taking all his calls," Karen told her brightly as the switchboard began to make impatient, almost strangling noises. "Would you like me to ring Mr. Moffitt's office and let them know you're coming?"

"No, Karen, that's all right. I'll wander over unannounced, but right now you'd better get back to the board before it explodes!"

Kit was eager to see her husband, to have lunch with him so they could discuss the series of events that always greeted them on Monday mornings, but as she walked down the corridor toward the back door, the sound of a typewriter being pounded caught her attention. Suddenly, the sound of typing ceased, and Kit paused in front of an open doorway to greet Georges Bergery.

"Katharine, *tres chic, tres belle!*" the popular bestselling novelist and biographer exclaimed as he rose to his feet and came over to usher her into the small room that had been converted into his office while he went about the task of changing *Ballet At Midnight* from a good but choppy story into a filmable scenario.

"Now that I have a compliment from a Frenchman, I'm sure I made the right selection. This outfit *is* something to start a conversation with."

"Or stop it as the case may be. Do you think women's hemlines are really going to be this short?" he asked with such gentle appeal in his blue eyes that Kit had to laugh.

"Since this is only eight inches above my ankles, I hope that hemlines will get even shorter. But I don't think that's going to be for a while yet," she said, turning around so that the French-born Georges could admire her striking Premet outfit that combined a striking beige velvet dress with eight rows of shirring over the hips and a Zouave-style jacket of black velvet embroidered in red silk and finished with gold. "When I left my shop, Bettina was trying on another Premet model something like this one," she informed him, referring to his always chic San Francisco-born wife.

"By 'something like this,' I take it to mean just as short?"

"Oh, Georges, you're not going to be one of *those* husbands?"

"I think you know Bettina a little too well to even suspect I could get away with ruling on her clothes."

"I'm glad to hear that." She arched her neck in the direction of the typewriter. "How is the scenario coming? Or shouldn't I ask?"

"Ask away. Bettina says I'm the sort of writer who walks around with my latest chapter, asking my friends—or an amiable stranger—if they'd like to read it."

"That's probably one of the reasons why your books are so popular. Personally, I'd never trust a writer who hangs on to his work like he's just created a book that should be dipped in gold."

"I'm guilty of any number of faults as a writer, but not to the one of hanging on to my manuscript until it turns yellow around the edges," he said in his superb English that bore only a slight trace of French accent. "Which is probably why Greg wanted me to write this scenario."

Kit looked around for a place to sit down, but except for the typing chair, every surface was covered with books, papers and cartons. "This movie is, for all the quality involved, still something of an experiment, and it's easier to do work with people one knows and can depend on."

"Then Greg is very lucky that he has friends around him—particularly today."

"Is there something going on that I don't know about?" Kit asked, nonplussed. "Greg seemed to be a little preoccupied this morning, but—"

"He's anything but preoccupied now," Georges said, suddenly finding great interest in arranging the just-typed pages. "In fact, to use a very apt expression, he's on the warpath. I never realized he was such a perfectionist."

"Yes," Kit said, a band of fear closing around her heart. "Well, I've kept you from your work long enough. I'd better see how Greg is. Take care."

She left Georges smiling, and kept her face cheerful as she continued on toward the property office. From a quiet, almost sleepy atmosphere, Hooper Studios had seemingly overnight transformed itself into a busy, hardworking film studio, and Kit felt a strong surge of pride for Greg.

He's done all of this himself, she thought. He's saving this studio from disgrace and ruin, he's putting people to work, and every movie that comes out of here is going to be the very best possible. But is *Ballet At Midnight* too much of a strain, too much of having to relive his past?

The property office, once a collection of contents from closets and attics, had recently been moved into a one-story building that had previously been the repository for storing odd bits of lumber. It was under the direction of Montgomery Moffitt, who functioned as the studio's set decorator. Normally, it would have taken Kit only a few minutes to get from her car to the building, but thanks to all the people rushing around, her progress took quite a bit longer. Everyone she passed, it seemed, wanted to stop her to say hello, to ask about San Francisco, and to tell her how much they were enjoying all the work they had to do.

Maybe it's just my own nerves. Greg's a perfectionist, and his being on the warpath may just be Georges's writer's imagination, she told herself, opening the property office.

Inside, it was all one vast area filled with all manner and style of furniture representing just about every period known. While it wasn't a Sears, Roebuck catalog come to life, it wasn't W & J Sloane either, and Kit walked carefully down a narrow aisle toward the opposite end of the building where a small office had been partitioned off from the rest of the open space. At first, all she could hear was the low murmur of voices that grew more distinct as she came closer.

"Do I see antimacassars on the furniture in these drawings?"

It was Greg's voice: low, calm, uncolored, unemotional— a clear signal that the red flag was flying.

"Well, Mr. West, you have to remember that we're talking about private quarters here, not formal reception rooms. Behind the scenes, these people live just like the rest of us."

"No, they do not!"

"Who do you think you are, Mr. West, Nick the Dime-Bender? I'm the set decorator here."

You won't be for much longer, if you don't watch out, Mr. Moffitt, Kit thought, listening to the set decorator's rather reedy voice. She reached the doorway, but neither man noticed her, and she surveyed the scene in front of her. The best of all the furniture stored here was in this office, but it was hardly visible since it was almost completely covered by a series of sketches that represented the sets for *Ballet At Midnight*.

"And who is Nick the Dime-Bender?"

"His real name is Nick Dunaew, and he works for Albert Smith and J. Stuart Blackton at Vitagraph as their expert on Russia's aristocracy even though he's probably some sort of peasant."

"Do I look like a peasant to you?" Greg questioned in a dangerous voice.

"One never knows in Los Angeles." Montgomery sniffed disdainfully. "A good tailor and voice lessons can work wonders."

"It appears, Mr. Moffitt, that your observations are as useless as your proposed sets."

Kit watched as a red stain spread over the other man's cheeks. "Why don't you trust me in these things?" he asked in a supplicating voice.

"Because I know that what you propose to put on the screen is *wrong.*"

Montgomery was a tall, very thin young man who looked rather like a well-tailored stork. Now he believed the gossip that Gregory West had a bad temper and could take a man out when crossed. This was definitely *not* going to be the easy job he thought he'd signed on for, he went to collect his pictures and saw Kit.

"Oh, Mrs. West. I didn't see you before. You, you look very lovely."

At this point in her life, Kit was long used to receiving compliments from a variety of men, and as concerned about Greg as she was, a part of her realized that judging from the appreciative look in Montgomery Moffitt's eyes as he looked at her ankles, he probably wasn't as fey as everybody thought he was.

"Thank you, Mr. Moffitt," she responded, deciding that it would not be the best form to tell him that she thought he ought to pay more attention to the man who signed his paycheck. "Hello, darling, I didn't mean to come at a bad time," she told Greg as she came the rest of the way into the office.

"I don't think there's such a thing as a good time today," he said, kissing her cheek, "but I'm never anything but happy to see you. We were just concluding our discussion."

"So I heard."

"I've been looking forward to lunch with you all morning." He sounded as if the contretemps she had just been an inadvertent third party to was of no great matter, but she didn't like the strained look around his eyes and mouth.

"Would you like me to go on ahead to your office?"

"No, I think I've said everything I have to here." He fixed Montgomery in an unblinking dark amber gaze. "Have I made myself clear?"

"Perfectly—no antimacassars—even though you and I are just about the only ones who'll know the difference."

"And you didn't know until I informed you otherwise."

Montgomery had the grace to look embarrassed. "I'll make all the adjustments you want, Mr. West, and have them ready for your approval by five this afternoon. But you should realize that most of the people who'll go to see *Ballet At Midnight* won't have the slightest idea of what you're trying to show them. They'll come because it's supposed to be 'cultural' or because they saw Anthony Kendall on stage or read about him in a magazine. There's no interest in the finer things in life in this country. Why, if it weren't for the war in Europe, right now I'd be in—."

"Right now, you're here and working for me." Greg's clipped voice dripping ice. "I'm not particularly interested in your disrupted travel plans. What I do care about is making this motion picture the very best it can be."

"But no one will appreciate it, Mr. West."

"There's always the chance you're right, Mr. Moffitt, but I'd like to think that by the end of this coming summer, you're going to be very pleasantly surprised."

"I should have let you know I was in the property office right away," Kit said a short time later when they reached the privacy of Greg's office. "I know that no matter how angry you are with Montgomery Moffitt, you wouldn't want him

383

to know I was the audience—even though it was accidental."

"Under normal conditions, you're right, I would have considered our . . . discussion to be strictly private, but what you witnessed was not normal, and I'm glad you didn't see and hear our whole encounter."

Kit took off her Madeleine hat of black velvet with a turned up brim. "Georges said you were on the warpath today."

"He's right," Greg said shortly. "I've been making everybody's life miserable all morning—but then I don't think anyone can be more torn apart than I am. I need a drink."

Kit perched on the back of one of the chesterfields while Greg went over to the well-stocked bar. He wasn't a daytime drinker, and not that much of a drinker at any other time, but she watched while he took an old-fashioned glass, added several ice cubes from the ice bucket, and poured a healthy shot of Black & White Scotch into the glass.

"I may as well keep you company," she said. "There are times when both parties have to have a drink in hand before they can talk, and this is one of them." At the bar, however, she hesitated. Should she mix a martini, take a ladylike glass of sherry, or pour out a sophisticated measure of vermouth? What the heck, she thought, and duplicated Greg's selection.

"There's not much to toast right now, is there?" she asked as they sat down next to each other. She placed a hand on the back of his neck. "Are you feeling all right?"

"Oh, never better. I just love myself when I turn atavistic and treat my employees like serfs." He took a quick swig of his drink and closed his eyes for a moment as the liquid traced a path that burned before it warmed.

Kit took a careful sip of her drink. "I've never noticed that you were a throwback to your ancestors—in public, that is," she couldn't resist adding.

"I'm sorry you had to see me like that," he said finally. "I took one look at those sketches and almost fired Montgomery on the spot. He does nothing all day except talk about line and style and proportion, but he's a *poseur,* with no idea of what he's doing or how something has to look. Antimacassars."

"They have antimacassars on the sofas and chairs on the *France.* Believe me, it does detract from the French Line claim that it's the 'Chateau of the Atlantic.'"

Slowly, very slowly, the tension around them eased, and Greg began to laugh. "I wish I could say I'm sorry I shouted my head off, but it was a matter of principle. If this movie isn't made the right way, there'll be nothing to distinguish it from the films Hooper used to make, except that no one will take their clothes off."

This time, Kit was the one who laughed. "I can't imagine Odette in white lingerie. Incidentally, she's over at my shop having the final fittings on her clothes for the movie."

"Is she giving you or your staff any problems?"

"None at all, she's just charming. Apparently, the problems she gave us in San Francisco were all part of her act."

"That's something I should know about," Greg said, and took another sip of his drink. "I don't know if I can go through with this, Kit."

Ever since they'd returned from their honeymoon and the plans for the movie had gone into full swing, Kit had been almost painfully aware of the strain that daily seemed to grow heavier on Greg. She also had the same awareness that she could not force him to either talk about it or take some form of constructive action; but, as he freely admitted his conflict to her—far sooner than she would have expected—a wave of relief washed over her. Whatever they did or didn't do, and however long it would take to reach a solution didn't matter as long as this wasn't a hidden matter that would eventually cause a strain on their relationship and their love.

"Do you absolutely have to?" she asked, deciding to touch on the most sensitive point right away.

"No, if I wanted to I could probably close production down in less than an hour, and within forty-eight hours, using Drake as intermediary, I could sell Hooper Studios to the highest bidder. Sin's original investment would probably be quadrupled. In fact, so much money would be involved that it might smother the usual comments."

Kit had been involved in enough bad situations—her two engagements and the near-miss with Sebastian, as well as her abrupt departure from Barnard among other more minor mishaps—to know just how Greg was feeling as he described how he could set himself free. The feeling of claustrophobia would be receding, his pounding heart would be slowing down to its normal beat, and the feeling of escape, of having gotten away without being trapped, would be spreading through him. She knew all of those reactions well, and even though it might not be possible to act on it, it had to be mentioned before any more practical and difficult solutions could be discussed.

"And it's the comments that concern you the most," she stated, "because this goes beyond not caring about what anyone says."

"I have to remember that I'm a businessman, and any decision I make—artistic grounds notwithstanding—reflects back on my reputation. I can close down *Ballet At Midnight*. I can close down this entire studio, but I'll still have to deal with the repercussions. The first comments would be that I was well rid of what was a questionable investment in the first place, and lucky enough to have made an excellent profit; but eventually there would be comments about my ability to carry through on decisions, and then there would be actual doubts about dealing not only with me but with Sinclair."

"I know that you've worked for years to build up a reputation as a business leader, but keeping that trust intact doesn't have to mean that you have to stay here if seeing this movie made is going to be a physical and emotional strain on you. I'm afraid," she went on, moving even closer to him, "that I'm not going to be a noble wife, telling you that you have to push ahead no matter what the price because it will all be worth it in the end. I love you too much to stand by and watch while a problem eats away at you. You won't quit, but you can't stay on and have every day be a repeat of this morning. There has to be something in the middle."

"The only respectable thing would be to concoct some sort of story for why I can't be here full-time any more and then install an executive who'll answer directly to me. That way, I can still keep artistic control, but I don't have to watch my past being acted out on a set while the cameras roll."

A little of the strain was off his face, but Kit knew there was still something bothering him, something he had only mentioned once before and then never brought up again. Still, she had to proceed with great care in this matter.

"Could you really be happy not being here every day?" she asked. "You'd be sitting in your office in Sin's building, wondering who was doing what."

"You're right. And now it seems that I'm in a very fragile circle, and there's no way of getting out of it without shattering everything." He put an arm around Kit. "What would you say to buying a pineapple or sugar cane plantation in Hawaii? That seems remote enough for no one to care very much about what we do."

Kit rested her head against his shoulder. "That sounds like it would be wonderful—for about six weeks or so. I don't think that's the place for a pair of city dwellers like us."

For a few minutes, they sat sipping their drinks. Their discussion was too fraught with pitfalls and dangerous emotional topics to go on without a short respite; they had to prepare themselves for the next round.

"It's funny, but I keep waiting for the phone to ring or a letter to arrive with the first blackmail threat," Greg said at last. "A couple of years ago, Rupert said blackmail is when someone steals your most private past and then ransoms it back to you. I've never forgotten it."

A new fear trickled through her bloodstream. "Greg, do you still think that that's the motive behind *Ballet At Midnight?*"

"At least I don't think the Okhrana is after me any longer. If they'd found me, it would have been over by now. No, this is a part of something else. But whoever is behind this is waiting, possibly until the movie is made and ready to be released."

Kit put her glass down on the coffee table. "I'm not used to drinking scotch at this time of day, and I'm starting to feel a little fuzzy. Shall we have lunch?"

Greg held his glass up to the light. "I'm not used to drinking hard liquor at this hour either. I like your suggestion, and maybe some good food will make everything look a little more manageable."

It didn't take long to have their lunch brought upstairs and set out on the coffee table. There were steaming hot crocks of petite Marmite, a long loaf of French bread wrapped in a damask napkin to keep it warm, a salad with herb dressing, and long-stemmed dishes heaped with chocolate mousse.

They concentrated on their food, depending on it to take off the disorienting edge the liquor had given them. The door was locked, all phone calls were being held, and Greg's carefully decorated office was their private sanctuary.

"Other than the fact I'm slowly being driven out of my mind, this movie is going very well," he said, buttering the last piece of bread. "Archie and Charlie are working splendidly together, coming up with all sorts of new ideas for using lights and gauzes to get the best angles; Odette is the picture of the cooperative leading lady, and Toby is working out equally well—if the experts can ever make the movies talk, he'll have a whole new aspect to his career. Despite the fact we're all pretty much a bunch of amateurs—excluding Archie, of course—this is not working out too badly."

Kit speared a lettuce leaf with her fork. "But none of this

makes up for what you're going through or answers any of your questions."

"I know, and it all comes back to O.L. Pinchot. I wonder—"

"What?"

"I have to find something out." He put his salad aside and got up. At his desk, he picked up his phone. "Mrs. Rigby, this is Mr. West. Will you please ask Mr. Coster to come up here and bring all the information regarding O.L. Pinchot. Yes. Thank you."

"That's a perfect solution! Find the writer of *Ballet At Midnight,* and you'll find your answer."

"I hope you're right, darling. I can't think why I didn't come up with it before."

"It doesn't matter as long as you thought of it now." Kit was sure Greg must have literally pushed away any thought of finding out who the author was, and where he or she lived because he was unable to deal with the situation at that time, but that was something she could never say to him.

Before they could continue their conversation, Mr. Coster arrived, holding a leather-bound ledger and a sheaf of papers to his portly chest. Greg guessed quite correctly that the older man still resented him somewhat over the allocation of funds for Archie's new lens, and he made sure to treat him with the greatest of deference now, charming him out of his officious mood.

"Oh, I see you're having the chocolate mousse," he said, sitting down on the chesterfield. "It's really quite delicious."

"I couldn't agree more. That's why I asked the Fairmont's chef to disclose his recipe," Kit related. "He told me it's not his usual practice, but he likes to make an exception for newly married couples, particularly when they appreciate good food."

They chatted about food and wine, trading information about their favorite San Francisco restaurant and damning the prohibitionists before Mr. Coster turned his attention to the papers he had with him.

"Let's see, O.L. Pinchot," he said. "Yes, we sent a check out on November 20. But this is odd, my records show the check hasn't been cashed yet."

Of all the information they'd been expecting to hear, this was the most unexpected, and for a moment they could only regard each other with surprise.

"Of course O.L. Pinchot could be out of town or ill," Greg said in a deliberately casual voice. "Where was it sent?"

"Well, well, this is most irregular. I don't know why I didn't pay attention to this before. The check wasn't sent to an address *per se,*" he told them. "It went to Box Eighty-six at the General Post Office in New York."

"Oh well," Kit said after Mr. Coster left.

"Well, well," Greg replied in imitation of the accountant, but his quip fell flat. He held out his arms to Kit, and together they stretched out on the chesterfield. "Do you have the feeling we've just stepped into the maze at Hampton Court?"

"And every turn leads into another dead end. I would have sworn the address would have been Boston, or at least somewhere in New England." She rested her head against his shoulder. "I didn't want to say anything while Mr. Coster was here. He's your employee, and I didn't want him to think I was interfering in your business, but is it possible that the check was never picked up, and that it and the congratulatory telegram are still in the box?"

"It's a very distinct possibility, and as long as the rent is paid on the box, the post office won't take any action." He hesitated for a long minute. "But we're going to have to take action. What would you say to a trip to New York?"

"I'd never say no to that, but we can't spend our time there skulking around the General Post Office."

"Aren't you going to ask me why I want us to take this trip?"

"No, because we both know the reason why. It's difficult

enough for you to have this movie made, but it's even more impossible not to know the facts."

"And possibly one thing more," Greg added. "I want to meet this O.L. Pinchot face-to-face. I want to find out if I'm one of the few who connected with a blackmailer who lost his nerve."

"If that's the case," Kit asked as they reluctantly sat up, their arms still around each other, "would you take any sort of action—legal or otherwise?"

"No, I'd be content that even though greed was his motive, he still had enough humanity left not to be able to go through with it. But," he continued, "I want to find out *how he knew* what happened to me."

With the irrevocable stated, Greg stood up and went over to his desk, to the telephone that suddenly looked like his own personal lifeline. He lifted the receiver, and bypassing Mrs. Rigby, contacted the switchboard.

"Maisie, this is Mr. West, will you connect me with the long-distance operator, please? Yes, Operator, I want to place a coast-to-coast call to Mr. George Kelly, his number is . . ."

Still seated on the sofa, Kit listened as Greg gave the operator all the necessary information. Part of this was absolutely unbelievable. Blackmailers didn't lose their nerve; if anything, they usually got greedier. But what really mattered was why the story had been written in the first place.

"If any private detective can help you, it's George," she said when Greg returned the receiver to the cradle. If her own calls to New York were anything to go by, he would have at least an hour's wait before the complicated connection was made.

"When I first met him, he was Sin's bodyguard and bouncer." Slowly, he smiled. "He was very helpful to me then, and now it seems like a million years ago."

"I want to hear all about those days, but we both have a lot

391

of things to do right now," she said, and went over to him. "When do you want to leave?"

"If The California Limited has two connecting drawing rooms, can you be ready to leave tomorrow?"

"If that's the way it has to be, of course I can, but that means I have to go back to my shop now." She went over to him, and they spent a few minutes concentrating on each other. "And we'll work out the rest of our plans when you get home."

"After dinner we'll have to go over to Chester Place and see Sin and Caro."

"You're right, we can't tell them what we're doing over the phone," she said, holding him close, longing to comfort him for the strain he was going through, but if they were going to find out any answers, certain tasks came first. "I'll see you later, and remember that no matter how difficult any of this gets, I love you, and I'm with you all the way because I want to be."

"I owe you an apology, Greg," Sin said as both couples went into Caro's private sitting room which opened off the master suite. "I've been behaving terribly toward you over the last few weeks—in particular on the night of your party—and I want to make things right between us."

"This isn't necessary, Sin," Greg protested. "My decision was probably the last thing you expected me to do."

"That's still no excuse for my treating you like a college kid who can't be trusted." He locked the door. "Sit down, everyone. This is all nice and private, just the way you requested."

The sitting room was a rich combination of Oriental objects blended with traditional furnishings. Chinese painted wallpaper provided the backdrop for a Chippendale-style mirror, and the Regency marble mantel was graced with a pair of lusters with ormolu and Wedgwood bases, while precious personal treasures, silk-shaded lamps, and vases filled with white flowers graced lacquer tables.

"We were very surprised when you phoned and asked if you could see us," Caro said as they took their seats among the sofas and chairs covered in pale pink brocade. "You never have to ask if it's all right to come over."

"What we have to tell you is very private," Greg said, "and since we're not dressed for dinner, we had to make sure we weren't coming during a party."

"When we give a party, you're both always invited," Caro said, crossing her legs, looking thrillingly dramatic in a Jeanne Hallee dinner dress of black chiffon over crimson silk.

"In case you're wondering, we haven't had time to change clothes tonight," Kit supplied.

"That's perfectly all right," Caro responded, totally at sea as to what was going on with Kit and Greg. They both looked worn out, and their still being in daytime clothes was not a good sign. "Shall we all have coffee, or do you both want something stronger?"

"We're still trying to recover from the scotch we had before lunch," Greg admitted, reaching for Kit's hand.

"I always thought you didn't touch hard liquor during the day."

"Today was the exception, Sin, and when you hear everything, you'll see I was justified," Greg said, and then told the Pooles everything, not leaving out a single detail, not trying to make a single excuse for himself.

"And you were able to get through that whole incident and have only one drink? You have my congratulations," Sin said. For a moment he regarded his best friend, one of the few men he trusted implicitly. "I take it that you both have a plan of action?"

"When Coster told us that the check hadn't been cashed yet, I knew there was only one thing I could do, and Kit agrees with me. We're leaving for New York tomorrow."

"Good for you." Sin's voice was definite. "Of course, you may find yourself a bit red in the face if the writer you're looking for turns out to be someone eking out a living and who made the whole story up."

"Believe me, I'd rather be embarrassed than live any longer with the uncertainty."

"What arrangements have you made at Hooper Studios?"

"I'm leaving Mitch Avery in charge. We had a long talk this afternoon, and he knows what he has to do and who he has to watch out for."

"Have you done the same for your shop, Kit? I'll be glad to give you any help you need," Caro offered.

"I've put Grazia in charge, but if she has any problems, she'll go to you or Mallory. We've told everyone we have to go back to New York to replenish my stock—which is true enough."

"In Chicago, I know you'll be at the Blackstone, but where can we contact you in New York, at the Lyman apartment?"

"No, when we called Montecito, they told us that the Howards have gone up to Massachusetts to visit some relatives. We'll be at the Plaza."

Sinclair nodded, his face serious. "I want you to know how highly I think of you, Greg, for going after this. It would be easy to take off and hide somewhere."

"We did discuss Hawaii—for about five minutes," Greg said, and smiled for the first time that evening. "After California, there really aren't that many other good places left to hide."

"I see what you mean. Is there anything we can do for you?"

"No, but we'll let you know how everything works out," Greg said as they all stood up.

"We really have to go," Kit said as they all exchanged embraces. "Moss has been wonderful, helping with all the arrangements, but we still have a million things to do."

"When you're married, getting out of town isn't an easy

thing to do any longer. In my bachelor days," Greg said lightly, "I would have taken the first train out tonight."

"Now I'm happier than ever that you and Kit are married," Caro said with an arch look. "The only train out at night is The Omaha Express, and absolutely *no one* ever travels on that unless it's a deep and desperate emergency!"

Chapter 21

On Tuesday afternoon at one-ten, when The California Limited pulled out of Union Station, Los Angeles, Kit and Greg were on board.

They had finally finished packing in the early hours of the morning, snatched a few hours of sleep, and after a hastily consumed breakfast, Greg had gone to Hooper Studios while Kit had taken care of her own last-minute business at Katharine's before it was time to leave for the station. They were both assured that their respective businesses would function smoothly while they were in New York, but this trip, decided on and carried out so swiftly, had robbed them of the keen sense of anticipation that travel created.

"I don't believe that we've actually done all of this in twenty-four hours," Kit said, wearily slumping down against the familiar dark blue plush sofa, heedless of the effect on her Callot Soeurs dress of emerald-green broadcloth with an open tunic and collar and cuffs of white satin.

"I couldn't agree more," Greg said, sitting down beside Kit and putting an arm around her. "Darling, are you feeling all right?"

"No, I'm not." Kit pulled off her close-fitting Madeleine hat of dark green faille with a sharply upturned brim ornamented with two sweeping large green wings and tossed it on the table. "I shouldn't have worn this dress and hat. I think I'm about to turn the same color."

"You're not, but you do look tired and a little pale under your paint."

"So do you," Kit returned, nestling against Greg, "except that you're not wearing makeup. I have such a headache, and I'm so tired."

"This is one of the things I like about being married," Greg said as he cushioned her body against the increasing motion of the train, "we can share so much."

Kit laughed weakly and lifted her head to kiss his cheek. "It is nice when we can agree on so much."

"I take it that neither of us wants lunch."

"The only thing I'm going to eat is two aspirin and a glass of water. Do you care to join me?"

"Not only that, I have a slight addition to your excellent idea," he said, and rang for the porter who appeared at the half-open door to the drawing room almost instantly. "George, will you do us a favor and make up the connecting drawing room for us?" He handed the man a dollar. "I know it's a little early, but we're both rather worn out. Just knock on the connecting door when you're finished."

Kit had a bottle of aspirin in her dressing case, and once they'd each taken two, they began to get undressed. Having two drawing rooms gave them all the space they needed, but they were too worn out to do any unpacking or other settling in, and the only thing that mattered was the bed being made up in the next room.

"I hate to see you covered up," Kit said, watching Greg wrap himself in his silk dressing gown, "but have you thought of the possibility of a train wreck?"

"Not at all, and neither have you," he said with an appreciative look at her nightgown and negligee of pale rose charmeuse. She had washed off her makeup and her hair fell in soft dark acorn-colored waves to just above her shoulders. "When there's a bed to share with you, I don't care very much about respectability."

As tired as she was, in spite of her dully aching temples and tight neck muscles, she felt a flash of desire at his words, and moved quickly to cover the few steps between them.

"You always say the right things to me," she said, wrapping her arms around his shoulders and molding her body against his. "I think we forgot a few things last night, and even though now is not the time to make up what we lost, I don't want you to think that they're not on the agenda," she went on between kissing his forehead, each cheek, his chin, and saving his mouth for last.

"That was the best kiss of all," he murmured, and his lips came against hers while his arms tightened skillfully. With the steady vibration of the train underfoot, their kisses went from gentle exploration to full passion. Without releasing each other, they sat down on the plush sofa, and Greg pulled her across his lap.

"Is your headache very bad?" he murmured, his hands stroking her back.

"It's getting less every minute," she said, longing coursing through her, overcoming all weariness. "Aren't you tired?"

"Exhausted. I couldn't swing from a chandelier for all the money in Morgan Guaranty Trust, but as to an interlude—."

"My thoughts exactly."

"Then you're agreeable?"

"As long as it's a prelude to a long, lovely night together after we've had our nap." Shifting in his embrace so that her knees were on either side of his hips, she began to kiss the hollow at the base of his throat.

Dimly, they could hear the conductor's voice saying something indistinguishable, the voices of their fellow passengers as they moved along in the corridor outside, and the faint sound of the porter rapping on the connecting door, but none of it mattered as they wrapped themselves around each other in the most intimate embrace possible.

Their passion for each other, never very far from the

surface, had been slightly misplaced for the past twenty-four hours, but now it flowed richly between them. He slid the silken fabric of her nightgown up her slender thighs, and she undid the belt of his dressing gown and parted the heavy silk to feast on the sight of his pulsing body, and then they came together in a rush for fulfillment.

"We make love like swans," Kit murmured in his ear. She was already full to overflowing with his body inside her, and in the next moment, as his hips began to move and his arms held her in an embrace she never wanted to leave, any conversation at all seemed very unimportant.

"When we can stand up without the risk of falling down," Greg whispered heavily a long time later, "shall we go to our nest?"

"A marvelous suggestion," she agreed, caressing the back of his neck while he moved his hands down her spine. "And thanks to the past few minutes, we are going to have a wonderful nap!"

They slept through the afternoon and early evening, and when they awoke again it was dark outside and the train was hurtling along the track at full speed.

"Where do you suppose we are?" Kit asked as they cuddled together between the pristine white sheets and covered by the warm, soft blankets provided by the Santa Fe Line. "It's so quiet that it's almost as if we're alone on the train."

"That's an interesting thought. It's fifteen hours from Los Angeles to Seligman, and we can't have been asleep that long." Greg stretched out an arm to switch on the light and found his watch. "It's almost nine."

"We've missed dinner."

"Are you hungry?"

"I hate to sound unromantic, but I'm famished."

Greg laughed and turned on his side to face her.

"Normally I'd suggest that we feast on our love, except that I'm famished also. Shall we see what the dining car crew can find for us?"

Less than a half-hour later, they presented themselves at the door to the all but deserted club car. A pair of businessmen sat at the bar, and at the other end of the car, a group of white-coated waiters sat together, talking in low voices.

The ranking waiter came up to them immediately and explained that the club car was finishing up for the night, but if they didn't mind sandwiches—.

"I guess it pays to know when to tip," Kit said lightly as they settled in at their table halfway down the length of the car. She had put on a pretty Drecoll dress of blue taffeta trimmed with silver buttons and an embroidered satin collar, and now that the worst of the strain was off them, she was ready to enjoy their late dinner. "It also pays to look highly respectable," she went on, delivering a level, highly amused look at Greg, now attired in a flawlessly tailored dark suit, white shirt and foulard tie.

"If only everyone knew the truth."

"It's better that they don't."

"Our secret, and with two drawing rooms, the other passengers will probably think that we don't get along," Greg finished as their waiter returned to their table, carrying a laden tray.

In short order, the heavy white tablecloth all but disappeared under small green bottles of Canada Dry ginger ale, glasses filled with crushed ice, bowls of pretzels and peanuts in the shell, and plates of ham and cheese sandwiches.

"Thank you, John," Greg said as they surveyed the table. "This is just what we want, but I hope it wasn't any trouble to put it all together for us."

"No sir, Mr. West. It's a fairly empty trip so far. I guess people really don't want to leave California at this time of

401

the year."

"Chicago and New York do leave something to be desired in the way of weather at the end of January," Greg agreed. "By the way, where are we?"

"We passed Victorville about ten minutes ago," John replied, filling their glasses with ginger ale. "It's still quite a way until we get to Seligman and cross into Arizona."

"This is the part of the trip I hate," Greg said when they were alone again. "I never feel that I'm really travelling until the train crosses over the state line."

"I think The California Limited takes just long enough," Kit said as they began to eat. "Any longer than three days and we'd all be stir-crazy. It's the same way on the *France*. It's glorious, but five days of perfectly prepared food and deluxe surroundings are about all anyone can take."

"I'll remember that for future reference," Greg said, implying for the first time that someday, when the war was over, they might go to Europe together. "It'll be interesting to find out if first class can be stifling. All I know is steerage."

"Was it very awful for you, your crossing to New York?" she asked, reaching across the table and briefly placing one hand over his.

"I'd never want to set foot on a ship from the Red Star Line again, even if I had the best cabin," he admitted, "but in retrospect everything I went through was probably good for me. I had to learn to rely on my own strength somewhere along the line, and that was probably my last chance."

"I'm so glad you said that," Kit said. "From the day you told me all about what happened to you, I knew that as awful as it was, it came at the right moment in your life, that underneath it all you could find the inner resources to succeed. I just wondered if you knew it also."

"Let's just say that marriage has added to my perspective on life in several matters."

For a few minutes, until the deep emotion between them lessened somewhat, they concentrated on eating. Kit was all too aware that the next week could strongly affect their lives and their marriage for either better or worse, but it would never be the same again. Still, she thought, it was a little odd to know that every mile the train covered was bringing them closer not only to an answer but also to an inevitable change.

"Does George know about you, the truth, or are you strictly the erstwhile Gregori Vestovich to him?"

"I never said anything to him directly, and neither has Sin, but you know George—he probably put everything together years ago."

"I wouldn't be at all surprised. There's no private detective like George, and he's discreet."

"I'll drink to that."

"Don't even *mention* drinking. It took twenty-four hours for me to get over that scotch. I'm surprised we got any packing done last night."

"Last night—and all of yesterday—is something I'm not going to be able to consider with any sense of perspective until we've put a lot more time and miles between us and Los Angeles," Greg said as the table was cleared and they were presented with slices of chocolate layer cake and a large silver pot of coffee.

"When we're in New York, how under cover are we going to have to be? If things work out," she went on carefully, "will we be able to see some of our friends like Henry and Alix and Charles and Thea—and why are you smiling like that?"

"Because Alix did see all of me once," he said, and told her about his night at Roosevelt Hospital when Alix had been his doctor. "I almost went through the floor the night she turned up at Sin's, and ended up operating on him." His smile became bittersweet. "That was just a week or so over thirteen years ago."

"I was only fifteen then."

"Suddenly, I'm very glad that we're here together now. And I don't see any reason why we can't be social while we're in New York. The worst scenario is that we'll have to get on a boat for South America."

Kit wasn't fooled for a minute by his almost off-handed attitude, but she decided to play along. "It's summer in Brazil now, and my friend Davina Alexander's stepfather is Wilson's ambassador down there, but I don't think we'll be paying them a visit anytime soon." She took the last forkful of cake. "This was delicious."

"I couldn't agree more."

"Then are we ready to leave?"

Greg took out his billfold and put two ten-dollar bills in the center of the table. "Don't tell me you're tired," he said with an unmistakable light appearing in his dark amber eyes.

"Well, I was going to suggest that we go back to our drawing rooms, and I have lots of ideas," Kit said as she stood up in a slow and expensive rustle of taffeta. "Fortunately, none of them involve our going directly to sleep. Shall we go?"

Part Four

The Searchers

When you have eliminated the impossible, whatever remains, however *improbable,* must be the truth.
> —*Sir Arthur Conan Doyle*

I think it's a sad pity that most people go through their lives hating their work. I always tell young people they must find the kind of work they love because then they can do their best.
> —*Frances Steloff*

The things we know best are the things we haven't been taught.
> —*Marquis de Vauvenarques*

Chapter 22

To most New Yorkers, the most romantic buildings in the city are Grand Central Station and the Plaza Hotel. Both the Beaux Arts train station and the French Renaissance-inspired chateau-style hostelry are places of meetings and partings and comings and goings. In a manner of speaking, they *are* the city, representing it in its most fluid and changing form, and yet also standing for something solid and traditional; unchangeable in a world in which change is life. For Kit and Greg, both buildings were welcome sights when the Twentieth Century brought them into New York City at nine-forty on Monday morning, February 1st.

The California Limited had arrived promptly at the Dearborn Street Station at eleven-fifteen on Friday morning in a snowy Chicago bracing for yet another near-blizzard. On checking in at the Blackstone Hotel, they had wisely decided to postpone their reservation on the next day's Century to wait and see how the storm developed. The last thing they needed was to find themselves stranded on the train in case the snowfall turned dangerous.

Fortunately, the snowfall, although steady, failed to add more than five inches of white powder to the city, and at twelve-forty on Sunday afternoon, they boarded the Century. Kit was aware from their first hour in Chicago that the cold and snow affected Greg in an adverse way, threatening to bring on a very Russian mood of quiet depression, and in an attempt to keep it from getting too great a hold on him, she had seen to it that they had plenty to keep them busy.

"Are you planning to walk me through the Metropolitan Museum of Art the way you did on Saturday in the Art Institute?" Greg inquired as he put on his suit jacket.

"If the occasion requires a long walk with lots of things to look at and discuss, I will," Kit assured him, primping her newly bobbed hair. On Monday afternoon, after they'd settled into their tenth-floor suite overlooking Central Park, while Greg had gone off to meet with William Fox, a New York theatre owner, she had taken herself to Pierre's, where the hairdresser, who was a friend of the great Antoine in Paris, had cut her shoulder-length hair to a chin-length bob. Afterwards, delighted with the way she looked, she had stopped in at Thurn's on Fifty-second Street and purchased a Jenny dance dress of thin white taffeta dripping with crystals and bands of thin pink taffeta inset at the waist. Now, on Tuesday morning, she ran a comb through her hair. "How does it look?"

"If Irene Castle could see you, she'd run away and hide," Greg said, longing to run his fingers through the shining waves. "You look beautiful, and if you don't hurry up and put on your hat, I'll have the same reaction I did yesterday."

"Is that a promise?" Late Monday afternoon, when Greg had come back from his meeting, after he had looked at her hairstyle from every angle, he had taken her straight to bed. Through the dressing table mirror she could see the large and very rumpled bed that was ample proof of their passion-filled night when they had gotten out of bed only long enough to let room service in. "I'm not going to complain, but—"

She hesitated, and reality intruded.

In some ways, it looked like any typical morning, Kit

reflected as she checked her makeup. The hotel maid hadn't arrived yet, the room service waiter hadn't been summoned to take back what was left of their breakfast, and in the sitting room, the morning papers, all of them carrying stories about the latest Zeppelin raids on London, were scattered around. Books and other belongings gave the elegant cream and rose suite with its reproduction Louis XV furniture, carved plaster ceiling, and crystal chandeliers a more personal feeling. But as much as they loved the Plaza, the hotel could not protect them from the fact that in a very short time they would meet with George Kelly.

"I don't suppose it would do me any good to ask if this clock is wrong," Greg called from the sitting room, and Kit quickly put on her Camille Roger hat of slate-blue velvet with a long red plume made in the sweeping Louis XVI style and joined him.

"That depends on whether you want it to be early or late," she said, and found Greg standing in front of the marble fireplace with a mirror set into the wall behind it and a small Magneta clock resting on the center of the marble mantel. "Five minutes before ten," she went on, standing beside him.

He put an arm around her waist. "I should know by this time that the Plaza's clocks keep perfect time, but I'm torn between pushing the clock along so this meeting with George is over, and not wanting to see him at all. I feel very defenseless, and it's not a sensation I like."

"That's very understandable," she said as Greg held out her new mink coat. Designed on long, slender lines with a high, snug-fitting collar, it was a triumph of both style and workmanship from Bergdorf Goodman's new fur salon. Greg had ordered it weeks ago as a surprise, and when they'd decided to come to New York, he had cabled Edwin Goodman, instructing him to deliver the coat into the care of Fred Sterry, the Plaza's manager, who had it waiting for her in the suite when they checked in. Kit, who had never bothered ordering a fur because she considered fur cloaks cumbersome, was overwhelmed by both the perfection of the coat and with love for Greg for his perception in knowing exactly what she would like. "But it would be much worse if we had come here deciding to do this on our own or by hiring a private detective who's a stranger," Kit pointed out gently as she put her arms into the coat.

"Yes, but the first time I met George, I was on crutches with several pounds of plaster of Paris on my right foot, and I wasn't exactly tailored by Brooks Brothers."

Kit held up Greg's double-breasted topcoat of navy cashmere lined in sheared nutria and finished with a sheared beaver collar; obviously Greg was a strong believer in the theory that living in Southern California thinned the blood.

"I'm just returning the favor," she said, "and as for George, he's a wonderful man and you know he won't treat you like a—a—"

"A greenhorn just off the boat," Greg finished, and began to laugh as he let Kit help him into his topcoat. "That's what I was back then, but you're right, darling, I've got this all out of proportion. Now, where's my hat?"

Greg tilted his fedora at a dashing angle, Kit picked up her cashmere-lined leather gloves, and they were ready to leave. Together, they swept down the wide corridor to the elevators. It was inevitable that they would attract a good deal of attention, but their thoughts were centered on the meeting that would take place fourteen blocks downtown, and they paid no attention to the whispers and looks the other passengers in the richly paneled wood car gave them. It wasn't until they reached the Plaza's lofty lobby of black and white marble with ornate gold detailing, oversized vases full of flowers, and a superb, specially woven carpet underfoot that they broke the silence that had fallen over them when they left the suite.

"Now I know what the Castles or Douglas Fairbanks go through in public," Greg whispered as the operator opened the car doors and they continued their progress out of the hotel. "It's a very odd feeling."

Kit stifled her laughter. "Are you telling me that you've never noticed the covert, not to mention covetous looks given you by the ladies—all *sorts* of ladies?"

"Not until I had you on my arm."

"Of course you didn't." Kit tucked an arm through his. "Do you know the story about Caruso and the Magneta clock, or were you here when it happened?"

"I've never heard a thing about it," he said as they went through the revolving door.

It had been sixty-five degrees and sunny one week ago when they left Los Angeles, and although today was equally sunny, with the light glinting off the snow-covered trees and grounds of Central Park across the street, the temperature was hovering somewhere in the low twenties. After the steam heat of the hotel and with systems used to the balmy climate of Southern California, they both recoiled from the Arctic-like wind and hurried across the sidewalk to where Wooten was waiting beside Vincent's newly delivered, shiny black Pierce Arrow limousine.

"Do you want to hear this story?" she asked as they settled into the taupe velvet interior with the fur-lined lap robe over them.

"It'll help take my mind off the cold."

Kit laughed in agreement. "You know that all the clocks in the Plaza not only keep perfect time, but they're all connected to the main Magneta clock in the lobby."

"No annoying, ticking clocks at the Plaza."

"That's right, but they do make a very faint buzzing sound. We barely hear it, but it apparently drove Caruso wild. One day he couldn't stand it any longer, took a knife, and stabbed the clock in his suite," she related, and was relieved when the faintly distracted look that had been on and off Greg's face since they got up disappeared as he began to laugh.

"Only a tenor would stick a knife into a clock!" he said

411

when he could control his merriment.

"It's almost atypical behavior, and it's funny to everyone who knows about it except the Plaza's management—every clock in the building stopped."

"Nothing like that ever happens in Los Angeles," Greg observed as Wooten steered the car down Fifth Avenue, "and it's not only a Plaza Hotel story, it's a New York one."

When they'd spoken with George Kelly on Monday, they invited him to have breakfast or lunch or anything else he wanted with them at the Plaza, but his schedule wouldn't permit it. He was quite involved in a project with Miss Maude Adams, he explained, but he could give them more time if the Wests would meet him at ten-thirty on Tuesday morning at Gertner's, next door to the Empire Theatre.

"Tell Clara Lindy—she's the cashier—that you're meeting me, and that you want to sit at one of her husband's tables," George instructed, and now, at ten-twenty-five, the pleasant woman who took the customers' money, signalled for her waiter husband who took one look at the Wests and promptly showed them to the best table he served.

The restaurant was half-full of people all involved in conversations, but as soon as Kit took off her fur coat, all attention was momentarily on her and the dress she was wearing. It was a Chanel creation, a chemise of blue jersey richly embroidered in red and gold, the design forming around each cuff and on the front of the dress in a deep U-shaped pattern. It was remarkable in its simplicity, and Kit accepted the attention she received with the air of a woman who knew she had made a fashion find.

"No one can take their eyes off of you," Greg whispered proudly as he took off his topcoat and hat. "If this Gabrielle Chanel you've been telling me about can make dresses as beautiful as some of her hats, anyone who wears them will stop traffic."

"All of the sport clothes I wore while we were in Santa Ynez came from her Deauville shop, but all the dresses she designs in Paris are done in secret because she's licensed as a milliner and there's another dress designer in her building in the Rue Cambon, but she'll move to larger quarters eventually," Kit finished, laying the napkin over the lap of her dress. She didn't want to say anything, but she had the feeling that George wouldn't have suggested meeting in a restaurant if his news was very bad.

"I'm glad Wooten didn't go off on vacation," Greg said with a glance out of the window where car and driver waited patiently. "It makes getting around easier and— Here's George," he went on, relief apparent in his voice as he stood up to greet the private detective.

The first few minutes after George joined them was reserved for the exchange of social notes. Greg hadn't seen Sinclair's onetime bodyguard since his last trip to New York, nearly a year earlier, and on George's part, he had to congratulate the groom and kiss the bride before any business, no matter how important, could be transacted.

"From all appearances, I'd say that Gregory here has taken very well to marriage," George teased. Although well into his forties, he still retained the build of the professional boxer he'd been in his youth, and as well-barbered and tailored as he now was, he still had a hint of danger about him.

"I'm doing my best," Kit said, "and so far, it's all been wonderful. Here's our coffee."

"As the Bard of Avon said in *The Taming Of The Shrew,* 'we sit to chat as well as eat. Nothing but sit and sit, eat and eat,'" George quoted from his endless stock of Shakespearean quotations as Mr. Lindy brought them big cups of coffee topped with whipped cream and baskets filled with an assortment of cinnamon, raisin, and poppy seed rolls, and rolls with coconut frosting.

"We have a lot to discuss, George, and a lot of it very

pleasant, but I'm sure you can understand my wanting to know what you've found out," Greg said when they had their privacy again.

George nodded and broke a cinnamon roll in half. "This is really one of the oddest jobs I've handled since—well, never mind about that. It seems that the person who rented Box Eighty-six at the General Post Office is Gerald Chanfield."

"Senator Orin Chanfield's son?" Kit asked on a wave of disbelief.

"George, if anyone else but you told me this, I'd have serious doubts about his technique."

"So would I, Gregory, so would I. I couldn't believe it myself, but without a doubt the box was rented in the name of O.L. Pinchot, with instructions that all mail be forwarded to Mr. Gerald Chanfield at Adams House, Harvard, Cambridge, Massachusetts."

"How could a college senior—," Kit began, and stopped. The questions this revelation, the last one they expected to hear, were too manifold and complex to deal with at this minute.

"It's the maze again, that damn maze," Greg said in a low voice, pushing impatiently at his place setting. "No matter how hard we try, there are no explanations, only one question leading into another. It reminds me of eating my first artichoke—leaf after leaf with no end in sight."

George regarded him with obvious sympathy. "I'm sorry, Greg, but this is the only answer there is."

"Are you sure?"

"My source at the post office was quite certain. The box was rented from the middle of October to November 30th."

"That's long enough to collect the check. Thank you, George," Greg said. "I mean that with all my heart. It's not the answer I hoped you'd give me, but it's a place to start from."

They talked about more general topics, and when the Wests promised to keep George apprised of what transpired

414

with Gerald Chanfield and to come to dinner at the Kelly house in Brooklyn Heights when all of this was straightened out, the older man left.

"Gerald Chanfield," Kit said when they were alone again, and Greg waved away Mr. Lindy who was coming toward them carrying a coffee pot. "He's twenty-one, a senior at Harvard who's bound for Harvard Law, and he has his own money, *why* would he be involved in this?"

"And how—if he did indeed write this story—did he know? I'm sorry, Kit, I just can't believe this is some sort of coincidence, that the idea was just out there somewhere in the air."

"For something that changed your life so radically, you have every right to be skeptical until the last fact is in."

"Then you're still with me?"

"Try and get rid of me."

"This is a public place, so I can't kiss you the way I'd like to," Greg said, leaning closer to her. "But since we can't do anything else about this today, what would you say to taking advantage of our being in New York and spending the day out on the town?"

"Greg, look, this one is exquisite, just perfect for our house when it's built," Kit said as they paused in front of a painting of tiger lilies, one of the many superb Impressionist paintings on view in Durand-Ruel's gallery on Fifth Avenue.

"It is beautiful," Greg agreed. "And I think a painting by John Twatchman would be a fine way to start our collection."

"I couldn't agree more. Unfortunately, you'll have to find another painting. We've just purchased this one," a familiar voice said behind them, and they turned to find Henry and Alix standing behind them.

"How wonderful to see you both!" Kit exclaimed as she and Alix embraced. "Oh, Alix, you've bobbed your hair. It looks grand."

"Thank you, darling, so does yours," she said, looking as striking as ever with her sable coat open over a Poiret dress of scarlet jersey with a crisscrossed wide black sash, and a Lanvin hat of black chiffon velvet with a wide brim and a band of sable around the crown. "But what are the both of you doing in New York?"

"Business," Greg said after he shook hands with Henry and kissed Alix. "For both of us, as it happens. In case you haven't heard, Kit's shop is the last word in fashion in Los Angeles."

"Oh, we've heard," Alix assured them, "and we're all terribly proud. I can't wait until we get out to California to see it. If you two hadn't eloped, we would have come out for your wedding, but now we'll wait until June and come out for the Panama-Pacific Exposition."

"I've done some consulting work for the fine arts committee," Henry said off-handedly as if he wasn't always being asked by one committee or other to give advice on paintings and sculpture. "At any rate, since Europe is out, seeing California is a first-rate idea, and the children should love it."

"We'll give all of you a tour of Hooper Studios," Greg promised, acting as if there were no problems and their trip back East had no great consequences for him.

"We'll look forward to it, but what have you been doing today?" Alix and Henry exchanged amused looks. "You strike us as a couple who've been doing quite a bit of shopping."

"Are we that obvious?"

"Oh, we were newlyweds once too, and every shop is fair game."

"Kit decided that we should confine our shopping to Fifth Avenue."

"What a wise decision. You've been to Lord & Taylor?"

"We had lunch there, in one of the dining rooms on the

416

tenth floor, but first we went to the Grande Maison de Blanc for linens."

"How could we resist a store that advertises itself as the trousseau house of America?" Greg asked, amused. "We decided to come to Durand-Ruel's instead of looking at furniture in the Hampton Shops." He glanced at the painting and then back at Henry. "I don't suppose I can persuade you to change your mind?"

"The very first flowers I sent to Alix were tiger lilies."

"Then consider my question withdrawn."

"In that case, why don't we all see what they have on exhibit?" Henry suggested. "And while we look, you can tell us about Los Angeles."

"Camillia seems to be quite happy out there," Alix said as they made their way around the gallery. "She wrote that Toby is enjoying himself more than he thought he would on a silent movie."

"I'll consider that a compliment," Greg decided, and joined the others in laughing.

For nearly an hour, the Wests and Thorpes viewed the paintings on display, and finally Kit and Greg decided on a work by Childe Hassam. It was only slightly smaller than the thirty-by-twenty-two Twatchman, and instead of tiger lilies, a rich spring garden, all the flowers in full bloom, were rendered on the canvas.

"Are you certain?" Alix asked.

"Beyond a doubt," Greg said.

"When our house in Beverly Hills is finished, this will be the very first thing we move in," Kit added.

"I'm very glad you feel like that," Henry said as he and Alix exchanged very pleased looks with each other. "This painting is our wedding present to the both of you."

For a second, Kit and Greg were speechless.

"You don't have to," Greg said, recovering first.

"Yes, we do," Alix said in a tone of voice that meant the matter was settled. "We weren't sure what you'd like, or what would look appropriate in the house you're building, and this seemed to be the best way to solve our problem."

"I don't think we can say anything but thank-you, and that we'll always treasure this painting no matter how many others we collect because you gave it to us," Kit finished, and kissed the Thorpes.

"My darling wife has just said everything that needed to be said," Greg added. "And to show you how highly we regard your present, we'll send it to Sin and Caro's for safekeeping instead of a storage company."

"We're appropriately flattered." Henry glanced at his watch. "It's a little early, but shall we go over to the Waldorf and celebrate with a bottle of champagne?"

"We'll take a raincheck on that, if you don't mind," Greg answered. "And when we do get together, why don't we make it the Plaza or the St. Regis? The Waldorf isn't my favorite hotel."

"We'll tell you about it another time," Kit put in. "Right now, we have a lot of shopping to do."

"Then we won't delay you any longer," Henry said, fixing Greg with an inscrutable look from under his hooded lids. "And since you're shopping, I think the best advice I can give Greg right now is to remind him that Tiffany's is only two blocks away."

In Tiffany's, Greg bought Kit a pink sapphire and diamond bracelet, and she bought him a platinum evening watch, and then they turned their attention to the more domestic needs, selecting china, silver, and crystal. Deciding to choose their stationery another time, they spent the rest of the afternoon going in and out of the myriad of department and specialty stores lining Fifth Avenue, using the Pierce Arrow as a mobile if very oversized market basket to hold all the purchases they didn't have sent directly to California.

After the strain of the past week, this day of shopping was

a necessary release for them. For just a few hours they could pretend that they were the way they appeared to salespeople, other shoppers and passers-by: a wealthy, elegant, attractive couple, obviously in love, utterly carefree, and concerned with nothing more than spending a vast amount of money on a variety of luxury merchandise that ranged from tablecloths to the best foulard men's ties, from a coffee urn from Lewis & Conger to a half-dozen pairs of women's shoes at Cammeyer's deluxe branch at 381 Fifth Avenue.

And, for a while, it worked.

They were in Bonwit Teller's on Thirty-eighth Street. It was an hour away from closing when reality, the true reason why they had had to come to New York, pierced through their almost day-long fantasy. They were browsing through the wide selection of perfumes offered when the young saleswoman who was helping them turned to a closed cabinet and withdrew a box.

"I have to show you this, Mrs. West. It was one of our best sellers at Christmas, and we don't have too many bottles left," she said, and set down a pyramid-shaped box of mottled gray paper embossed with an artistic design and a gold seal thick with Russian lettering.

For a second, Kit thought that Greg had turned to stone. He was still standing beside her, he was still smiling, but his body was so still, so rigid, that it was almost as if he'd been transformed to some inflexible object.

She felt the lighthearted mood that had enveloped them only a short time before disappear, and as they watched while the saleswoman opened the chains and remove the seal with the Russian coat of arms that held the box closed, it was almost as if the past few hours had happened a long time ago.

But how much significance can I read into a bottle of perfume? she thought. Not too much—and everything.

"As you've probably guessed, it's imported from Russia," the young woman went on, not noticing any outward change in her two customers. "The extracts are blended in Moscow, and I doubt if we'll be getting any more shipments. It's a shame, *Le Minaret* is really special."

Kit had to agree. The scent was rich and sweet and heady and unlike any other perfume she knew, even her favorite *L'Heure Bleue*. It wasn't really her, but there was something about it. . . .

"Why don't you buy a bottle, darling?" Greg said, and Kit was relieved to hear him speak in his normal voice without any of the edge that was there whenever he was under a great strain. "Even if you don't use it, it'll look nice on your dressing table."

"I have to commend you," she said a short time later as they walked toward the main entrance. "You sounded just like a husband who has spent the day shopping and is just about ready to finish it off."

"I'd say that was a fairly accurate description. Are you hungry?"

"Greg!"

"My darling, if I've learned anything in the past week, it's that there's only one explanation for why that story was written, and today, after my initial shock at the information George gave us wore off, I reached the conclusion that no matter how many wrong turns and blind alleys we have to work out, we'll eventually get to the truth. And no matter what Russian fits about signs and portents still linger, I'm practical enough to know that there's no mystic meaning in a bottle of perfume, or our coming across it now." They paused at the door to fasten coats and pull on gloves. "What shall we do for dinner?"

"I don't feel like changing clothes and I don't want to order from room service. Shall we go to a restaurant in the theatre district that I know?"

"Why not—and afterwards we'll see about getting tickets to something."

"I'm glad you're in such a good mood. I hope it holds when you see the restaurant—it's not exactly Voisin."

"As long as the food is good," he said as they left Bonwit's. "I can't forget why we're really here, but this is New York, and I'm not giving up the opportunity to take my wife to dinner and the theatre for anyone, not even for the Czar of Russia and the entire Imperial Court!"

The restaurant where Kit took Greg was on Forty-fifth Street off Broadway. Up one flight of stairs, it served Chinese food—chop suey to the uninitiated and more complex and delicious dishes to those who knew better—and was a gathering place for theatre people, reporters from the *New York Times,* and those who knew where to get a good meal at a reasonable price.

As she had warned him, it wasn't much on decor. The long room was filled with tables set for two and for four and covered with heavy white tablecloths, red and gold dragon prints were hung on the walls, wood and rice paper partitions provided a little privacy, and a Victrola in one corner supplied the entertainment. But the food, for those who knew what to order, was superb.

Neither of the Wests could speak much Chinese, but their skill with chopsticks earned them the waiters' immediate respect, and their table was filled with serving dishes heaped with steaming food, all of which they did ample justice to. The cold winter day and their endless round of shopping had given them quite an appetite.

"The waiters are probably going to talk about us for the next month," Kit said, and took a sip of the hot, smokey tea in the handleless cup. "Are you still in the mood for the theatre?"

Greg broke an almond cookie in half. "More than ever. It's funny how a good meal can put new energy into everything. What shall we see?"

"Well, we've already missed *The Ziegfeld Follies, The Beauty Shop, The Passing Show of 1914,* and *The Yellow*

421

Ticket, but whatever we do see, I'd rather it were a musical or a comedy."

"That's what I'd like to see also. After we get out tickets, do you want me to ring the Plaza and have Wooten pick us up when the show is over?"

"Poor man, we've probably worn him out. Let him have his dinner, and we can be true New Yorkers and take a taxi home."

Greg laughed. "I'm afraid, that underneath it all, that's what we are."

"I don't know if you feel the same way, but I really wouldn't want to be anything else."

"I guess that it doesn't matter where I came from or where I live now," Greg mused. "For all intents and purposes, I'm as much of a New Yorker as you are." For a minute, neither spoke, and then Greg went on, "But our being New Yorkers residing in Los Angeles is going to have to take on another aspect. We're going to have to go to Harvard and see Gerald Chanfield."

"I agree." Kit had been waiting for Greg to say this since their meeting with George had concluded. "But I don't want to go to Boston and not let Pack and Daphne know we're in town. Boston's a much more closed city than New York," she explained, "and they'd know we'd been in town and not even telephoned to say hello. We don't have to tell them the real reason why we're there, but I want to see them."

"Of course we'll let your stepbrother and his wife know we're going to be in Boston. We'll call them first thing tomorrow morning, and we'll even stay with them if they want us to be house guests."

"Their Louisburg Square house is very spacious, but it's also in the process of being redecorated. We're better off at a hotel."

"I haven't been in Boston since 1908. Do we stay at the Touraine?"

"That is a long time. No, everyone stays at the Copley

Plaza now, it's *the* hotel for Boston."

"Then it's ours as well." Greg glanced at his watch. "Seven-fifty, just the right time to show up at a box office or two and see what seats haven't been sold."

"I've just remembered the name of the train we take up to Boston," Kit said as they got ready to leave. "The New Haven Line calls it The Gilt-Edge Express!"

Greg could hardly contain his laughter. "Considering the way we've spent most of the day, the train might have been named for us," he said, paying the bill and leaving a generous tip. "And right now it's time to finish off our day by going to the theatre!"

Kit and Greg walked over to the Lyric Theatre where *Watch Your Step,* starring Vernon and Irene Castle, was playing, and were rewarded with two seats in the front row of the first mezzanine. The show had no plot to speak of, but it was all color and light, Helen Dryden's lovely costumes, and syncopated dances, the combination of which made for a sold-out house.

They loved every minute of it, and when the last curtain came down, they walked over to a small Italian coffee bar for cappuccino and pastries before hailing a taximeter cab to take them back to the Plaza. At this late hour, the hotel seemed vast and oddly silent, and in the dark privacy of their suite they let their clothes fall to the floor in the urgency to make love. But not once in the entire day, from the time they left Gertner's to the moment they fell asleep in each other's arms, did either mention to the other the almost gossamer-thin idea that had formed in both their minds as soon as George gave them the information he'd collected.

The almost invisible, not-to-be-mentioned idea that despite all evidence to the contrary, Natalia Voykovich wasn't dead.

Chapter 23

"The real reason I'm so successful is that I look like an utter twit. No one on the Boston Exchange thinks I can find the front door on my own much less put together a very profitable business deal, and every time I do, they think it's a wild fluke," Packard Lyman related with glee to his wife and Kit and Greg as they gathered in the Wests' fourth-floor suite in the Copley Plaza for cocktails before dinner on Thursday evening.

"Don't believe a word of what he's saying," Daphne assured them as they relaxed in the spacious sitting room decorated with fine Sheraton furniture covered in richly colored silks. "Pack's always being consulted by this group or that. *Everyone* wants his opinion."

"We know that, but I wouldn't let my stepbrother interrupt his set piece for the sake of accuracy," Kit said, enjoying the moment, not wanting to dwell on their having to meet with Gerald. "He has too much fun with it."

"And since your wife and stepsister are on to you, Pack, I gather it's all right to tell you I wasn't fooled by your tale," Greg added as he reached for the silver cocktail shaker that room service had just delivered. "Anyone for a martini?"

"Oh, why not," Pack said with mock resignation as he helpfully removed the long-stemmed glasses from the bed of ice from which they were resting. In his late thirties, Pack was a tall, slender man with wavy brown hair, bright blue eyes, and an expression that usually did put his business adversaries off. "That should teach me not to put on that act in front of family. Dad has a fit when I do it, and Grandmama threatens to put me out of her will."

"We won't tell."

"You're a brick, Greg, and I can tell my dear Katharine that I wholeheartedly approve of her choice of you as her husband."

Greg poured out the icy martinis while they all laughed and traded stories about travelling on The Gilt-Edge Express. It took all night to get from New York to Boston; but the New Haven Line, for reasons it alone saw fit, always removed the dining car after New Haven.

"It probably has something to do with Yale," Pack remarked in his faint English accent.

"Not another Harvard man?" Greg inquired as they passed around silver dishes filled with salted pecans and almonds. "I would have said Oxford or Cambridge."

"Oh no, Dad saved me from that fate when I was fifteen and he reclaimed me from my maternal grandfather, the old Duke of Newcrompton, and deposited me under the watchful eye of my paternal grandmother, Abigail Lyman."

"Speaking of which," Daphne interjected quickly, tucking a hairpin back into her rich blonde hair, "Grandmother wants to make sure that the two of you are coming to dinner on Saturday night. I'm not supposed to let on, but she really is planning something gala. Now you won't say no, will you?"

"We'd love to come," Kit said, looking over her glass at Greg. "Our business should be finished by then, and we may be in the mood to celebrate."

Greg concentrated on his martini in order to gain some time. For a second, the usual sense of conflict rose up in him. He was in Boston to solve the mystery that had haunted his life for the past fifteen years, not to act as if he were on a business trip of no great consequence and could take every opportunity to socialize. But the Lymans were Kit's family, and if a proper Boston grande dame wanted to entertain them at dinner, he had no right to be a wet blanket.

"I've never been known as a man who refuses an invitation to a good party," he said at last, quickly winking at Kit. "And as long as we're on the topic, I'll be the first to say that there's nothing better on an icy night than a cold martini, but if we don't go downstairs for dinner, the Copley Plaza will have four pickled guests on their hands."

"And we don't want to be late for the dancing," Kit added, her Lanvin dinner dress of sky-blue chiffon with an overskirt of putty-colored chiffon embroidered in gold and banded in mink giving off an expensive whisper as she stood up.

"Kit's absolutely right," Daphne said, her Poiret dinner dress of white crepe de chine girdled in a glowing sash of cerise chiffon fringed in gold giving her blonde beauty a sharper edge. "Besides, Pack and I are looking forward to dancing with the bride and groom."

Pack obligingly put his drink aside. "Food first—there's something about Boston in winter that brings out the appetites."

"Careful, Pack. Greg and I haven't been married very long."

"Funny, Kit. But it's time to eat, and while we have dinner, Greg can tell us what business brings you to Boston."

From its opening day in August 1912, the Copley Plaza became *the* hotel for everyone in Boston who wished to both see and be seen. Designed as the sister-hotel to New York's Plaza, and built of gray stone on the St. James Avenue site that had been the original home of the Museum of Fine Arts, the seven-story structure was also marked with the famous motif of double Ps set back-to-back and placed on linens, silver, and decorations. As in almost every structure designed by Henry Hardenbergh, there were spacious rooms, rich wood panelling and high ceilings, and in the dining room with its gilded ceiling and glorious Waterford chandelier, the party of four made up by the Lymans and the Wests were shown by the approving maitre d' to the best table by one of the large windows overlooking Copley Square.

Over lobster bisque, they discussed various war relief groups and the sometimes original ways they were going about raising money. Kit was fascinated by *Vogue*'s Fashion Fete which had been held in New York's Ritz-Carlton in early November for the European war benefit. The clothes had come from the best New York shops, and she was keeping close track of the favorable reviews of the event with the hope of doing something like it in Los Angeles.

"Tappe wrote that he thinks there may be something in doing fashion shows for charity," Kit finished as the soup plates were removed.

"Did you see him in New York?" Daphne wanted to know. "I was in the shop while he was making your wedding dress a little less bridal, and I was the recipient of several choice comments about a particular bride who couldn't live up to her responsibilities and eloped."

"How long did he rant and rave?" Kit asked while Greg and Pack chuckled shamelessly.

"Eight minutes—I timed him. Then he calmed down and was as happy as a teddy bear for you."

"I'm glad to hear that. We phoned him up when we got to New York, but it seems he's gone down to Palm Beach to visit a client."

"Kit's very eager for us to meet," Greg said as the waiter brought their entree of boneless chicken breasts stuffed with spinach resting on a bed of wild rice and draped in a special champagne sauce. "I have the feeling I'm being shown off."

"It's an experience no new husband should miss, being

428

inspected by your wife's dressmaker. Hopefully, your business won't take too long—whatever it is."

With only a quick glance at Kit, Greg put down his fork. On the train ride up to Boston, they had discussed the problem and decided that the best option was to tell her family the truth—with certain adjustments, of course.

"You already know that Hooper Studios is going to make a twelve-reel movie called *Ballet At Midnight,* and that we got the story from running a contest," Greg explained.

"And your coming here has something to do with the author of that story," Pack hazarded. "Did you find out it was plagiarized?"

"Nothing as simple as that, Pack. I found out that the check we issued hadn't been cashed, and thanks to George Kelly doing some detective work, we found that Gerald Chanfield wrote the story under an assumed name."

"Senator Chanfield's son?" Pack almost dropped his fork. "What a perfect scandal!"

"For writing a story that was chosen to be made into a movie?" Kit asked in disbelief. "I don't understand Boston Brahmins."

"Neither do I, and I not only live here, but my father was a member of the Earl of Minto's staff when he was Governor-General of Canada, and I grew up in ever-so-proper Ottawa," Daphne added. "Poor Gerald, they'll make his life miserable for this."

"That may explain a lot," Greg said with an unexpected flash of sympathy. "But we're still going to see him. The question is finding the right place."

"In a restaurant, of course," Pack advised.

"Yes, that's it. And college in February is a grind," Kit added. "He'll jump at the chance to get away for a night."

"Well, since we don't want to disappoint Mrs. Lyman on Saturday, we'll take him to Locke-Ober's tomorrow evening. I suppose it's as good as ever."

"Locke-Ober and change are mutually exclusive of each

429

other," Daphne offered, amused.

"It's easier to conduct a conversation there than in Durgin-Park," Kit put in.

"Of course if you really want to win his confidence, Gerald is still young enough to appreciate Bailey's. They have the best hot fudge sundaes," Pack related as the waiter served their dessert of pots de creme chocolate.

"The best hot fudge sundaes are at C.C. Brown's in Los Angeles," Greg disagreed.

"At Bailey's, the hot fudge drips over the edge of the silver dish."

"At C.C. Brown's, you get a silver dish of vanilla ice cream and the hot chocolate fudge comes in a silver pitcher!"

"Men," Kit said, picking up her dessert spoon as she kept her laughter under control.

"Boys," Daphne corrected, having the last word on the delicious subject before they moved on to other topics.

"I can't thank you both enough for this invitation to dinner," Gerald said on Friday evening at eight as they sat in the upstairs dining room at Locke-Ober's on Winter Place. Downstairs in this, possibly Boston's best and most historic restaurant, there was carved panelling, an abundance of silver-plated service pieces, and a long, mirrored bar with a delicately toned nude painting hanging over it; but in the proper upstairs room it was all white-tablecloth service, crystal chandeliers overhead, and windows set with heraldic-patterned stained glass. "Harvard can get pretty boring at this time of year."

"The last four months before graduation are always the worst," Greg said truthfully enough, deciding that at least in this instance the finest military academy in St. Petersburg and Harvard had one thing in common. "Kit and I thought you'd enjoy a night away from your books."

"I wouldn't think a honeymoon couple would want too

much company," Gerald said brashly. At just twenty-one, with light-brown hair and deep brown eyes combined with patrician bone structure, he was well aware of how much his good looks let him get away with.

"Oh, we've advanced past the primary married stage," Kit said a little too lightly. "Besides, Boston being what it is, the rule is contact your friends and family before they contact you."

"And we decided to see you about a little matter of $250." Greg gave him a level look. "You are O.L. Pinchot?"

The blood drained out of Gerald's face, and when the waiter arrived with their lobster Savannah, he kept his eyes on the profusion of cutlery that made up his place setting. The one small hope he'd had that this had just been a normal invitation to dinner had vanished.

"What do you want?" he asked finally, looking at the elegant couple as if they were a real threat to him and to his way of life.

"Oh, for God's sake," Greg snapped, his annoyance obvious, "you just *won*—no, *earned*—$250 and you're acting like we're extorting money from you!"

"Aren't you proud of what you've written?" Kit inquired, her own temper rising. "I read *Ballet At Midnight,* and it's good. Or is this some sort of college prank?"

"No, no," Gerald said swiftly. "I wrote it myself, and no one at Harvard knows about it."

"You haven't exactly robbed the State Street Trust," Greg pointed out. "And I always thought Boston prided itself on being the Athens of America."

"Yes, but in my family, in our circle, you have a pattern set out for your life, and you live it in a way that makes you a good citizen, gives you a pleasant life, and increases your bank balance to be even more substantial."

"And that life doesn't include writing," Greg finished.

"Not fiction. When my father leaves the Senate in about ten years and my brother, Edgar, takes over, he plans to

431

write a history of justice and reform in the state of Massachusetts. Do you see what I mean?"

"All too clearly. You rock the boat at your own consequence," Greg said, finding all too many similarities between Boston's Brahmins and St. Petersburg nobility. But there were differences. He had never been taught anything about service to others; his life had been one of wealth and luxury that had obscured the danger until it almost destroyed him. Gerald, on the other hand, knew he was being stifled, but he was too tightly tied to his way of life to pull away. "Or is it do what you want, only don't get found out?"

"Being a Chanfield is different than being a Lyman—they've always been more . . . independent," Gerald offered informatively, referring to the family that, whether he liked it or not, Greg was now involved with. "We do things a certain way. I'm expected to go to Harvard Law in September, and to the Attorney General's office in Washington when I graduate. When the Republicans win again, I'll go back to the family firm. Edgar will go into government first. When Dad retires, my brother will run for the Senate, and I'll go for his seat in the House."

"It sounds like a royal succession," Kit said, suddenly feeling very chilly despite the warmth of the restaurant and her Tappe dinner dress of gold-embroidered blue velvet.

"Except that royalty doesn't have to face the electorate, who do have minds of their own and don't always fall into line," Gerald said. "In the meantime, I have my amusements."

Judging by his barely touched glass of wine, his amusements didn't include drinking to excess.

"Such as writing fiction and submitting it under another name," Greg stated quietly.

"I guess you want me to start explaining. That is why you're buying me dinner."

"That would be nice," Kit couldn't resist saying.

"I never expected my story to win," he told them. "All of my classes are snaps, and it seemed to be a good way to kill a little time. I took the box in New York because I thought the story would be sent back to me in a week. I almost passed out when the telegram and the check arrived. Are you really making a motion picture?" Gerald asked as if he couldn't quite believe this was real.

"It's being filmed right now," Greg assured him. "And your credit line reads O.L. Pinchot."

"How did you get that name?" Kit asked, her curiosity getting the better of her.

"That was easy. My father's first name is Orin, and my mother is Louisa. Her maiden name was Pinchot, so—"

"So you have O.L. Pinchot. Why couldn't I put it all together? It was probably all too familiar," Kit went on.

"But how did you get the idea?" Greg said, asking the question he thought he might never get to ask. Somehow he had assumed this moment would be heavy with anticipation, would take longer, would be more difficult, but instead it sounded like a completely normal conversation. "Was it told to you by someone?"

"As a matter of fact, it was. When Edgar and I were kids, our parents thought the shore was the best place for us, and every summer we went out to Manchester-by-the-sea. One year, the house next to ours was let to a new couple. I can't remember their name, but she used to tell us about Russia—particularly about the ballet. She told us that she'd been a ballerina in St. Petersburg, and that there were men who would bring her flowers and jewels. That was pretty heady stuff to hear, and I guess the stories must have stuck."

This was almost anticlimactic, Greg thought as he absorbed Gerald's words. There were no bells going off, no feeling of the fog lifting, no filling in of the black spaces that were his memory of that night—only one more piece that didn't quite fit.

"Do you remember what she looked like?" he asked, and

hated himself for asking the question.

"After all these years? The stories stuck, but the woman—," Gerald flashed a quick smile. "She was very pretty."

Kit put down her fork. "How long ago did you hear these stories?"

"1903 or 1904, I'm really not sure. My mother would know, she keeps excellent diaries. One thing I've never forgotten though," he went on, "when she told me that story, the one I wrote about, she cried. Not hysterically, just very quietly with the tears running down her face. Mr. West— Greg—are you all right? You look a little pale."

"A little too much lobster Savannah." Greg forced himself to respond normally. "I haven't had it in a few years, and Locke-Ober's does it so well. And your story is very affecting."

Good, Kit thought with relief, he's handling this beautifully. This must be almost too painful to contemplate and remember, but he's not going to give himself away, at least not now.

"What have you done with the check?"

"I still have it. It can't be cashed because of the assumed name."

"Come back to the Copley with us, and I'll write you another—this one with your real name."

"And you can frame the original one and keep it as a souvenir," Kit suggested. "Imagine pointing it out when you're in Congress."

"If my father doesn't kill me when he finds out about this."

"Don't say things like that!" Greg snapped. "Look, I can tell anyone who asks that the author of the original story wants to remain anonymous. I'm the last person to invade someone's privacy. But you have to tell your mother and father."

"That won't be the best news they've ever had. Chanfields are supposed to be old and settled before they sit down to write, and then it's supposed to be very high-minded."

"I have an idea that when the war is over, noblesse oblige isn't going to be what it used to be. And if you're a successful writer," Kit continued, "no one will mind very much what you did or didn't do."

"Would you like us to tell your parents?" Greg inquired before Gerald could say a word. "We'll be glad to smooth the way for you."

"I wouldn't want to put you to the trouble of a long-distance telephone call."

"It won't be long-distance, it'll be face-to-face," Greg said as Kit looked at him in surprise. "We have to go down to Washington next week, and we'll be very happy to see your mother and father and tell them that your story is going to be a twelve-reel movie."

"I'd appreciate it, but if it's any trouble—"

"Of course it isn't. We'd be proud to call on Senator and Mrs. Chanfield—we have quite a bit to discuss with them."

Chapter 24

"So Gerald wrote the story that you're going to turn into a movie," Senator Orin Chanfield said as both the waitresses were out of earshot. Both couples had enjoyed the Terrapin stew, and now, at shortly after eight on Tuesday evening, with a light snow falling in Washington, they sat in the dining room of the Chanfields' R Street house waiting for the next course to be served. "I never knew he had such a literary bent."

"Of course you did, dear," Louisa corrected gently from the opposite end of the oblong table that was draped in heavy white damask and weighed down with old family china, crystal, and silver. Unlike many Boston women of her age and class, Louisa's clothes didn't have the slightly colorless, slightly out-of-style look that far too many women in their mid-forties favored. Tonight, her Jenny dinner dress of navy blue velvet-striped chiffon over a slip of old-gold silk was quiet, correct, and eminently suitable for the wife of Massachusetts' newly elevated senior senator. "He was always sending stories in to *St. Nicholas Magazine*."

"All children send in things to that magazine. Edgar did, so did I when I was young. But it's a far cry from submitting stories to a young people's magazine when you're twelve, and being twenty-one and submitting a story to a contest where having it selected means it will be a motion picture."

"Gerald was very concerned about your reaction," Greg said. From the contact he'd had with politicians in California, he didn't particularly care for the breed, but Orin was different, and he found himself relaxing in the warmth, welcome, and good cheer offered in this house. "Since we had to come to Washington anyway," he continued with his usual adjustment of fact, "we're more than happy to tell you about it."

"Well, actually we do know," Louisa informed them. "Gerald phoned and told us how all of this came about. He didn't feel right about pushing the responsibility off on the two of you."

"I'm glad he did that," Kit said, leaning back in her chair so that her Marital et Armand dinner dress of blue satin veiled with blue tulle and girdled with blue velvet and silver embroidery rustled softly. "Gerald didn't strike me as the sort of person who let others do his work for him. But, if you don't mind my asking, why didn't you tell us when we spoke with you on Sunday afternoon?"

"That's easy, my dear. We wanted to meet the man you married. And we wanted to hear Gerald's exciting news from the source."

"Then you don't mind?" Kit and Greg asked the senator together.

"Certainly not! Why— Ah, here's the next course," Orin said, rising to his feet as one of the waitresses placed a platter holding a roast boned leg of veal beside his plate. For the next few minutes, as Orin carved with precise skill, and dishes of whipped sweet potatoes and string beans were passed, conversation centered on Boston, on the latest exhibit at the Museum of Fine Arts, and on the party Abigail Lyman gave on Saturday night.

"Everyone is saying that the gathering for the two of you could make one of Mrs. Jack's soirees look dull," Louisa said.

"I'm not surprised it's a topic of conversation. We didn't expect to find a ragtime orchestra in the ballroom. Greg was expecting a staid little Mount Vernon Street gathering with chamber music and instead—"

"And instead I had all the guests asking me about how one makes a movie," Greg finished with great amusement and the hope that this was a good way to get back to the most important topic.

"Did my son give you the family responsibility story?" Orin inquired.

"Not only that, he implied that Chanfields didn't take lightly to the writing of fiction."

"Possibly because no one could do it before him, Greg."

"Greg had to write a new check for him," Kit related. Despite the small pocket of apprehension about what Orin and Louisa might have to say about their onetime summer neighbor, she felt warm and relaxed. In spite of their Boston reserve, the Chanfields were gracious and welcoming hosts, and tonight their conversation had covered a wide variety of topics. She was tired from the train trip the day before that had encompassed travelling on both the Bay State Limited and the New York-Washington Express, and today's tourist excursions to the Washington Monument, the Capitol, and the Corcoran Gallery. But it was a pleasant sort of tired, one that encouraged listening rather than excessive talking. "He couldn't thank us enough."

"I can assure you it's not because his allowance is meager," Orin said, and they all laughed.

They began to talk about the movies, Kit and Greg finding out for the first time what would become apparent in the coming years: *everyone* wanted to talk about motion pictures. The Chanfields were curious about D.W. Griffith's epic, the newly retitled *The Birth Of A Nation,* which was premiering that very night at Clune's Auditorium in Los Angeles.

"Archie and Charlie went to the preview showing in

Riverside on New Year's Day," Greg related as the salad replaced the main course. "Their comments are very telling."

"I take it that it's not good news," Orin said. There had already been disturbing rumors coming into his office about *The Birth Of A Nation,* and he was eager to hear more from someone who was closer to the source.

"From a technical viewpoint, the movie is a marvel, a work of art; the camera angles will be admired a hundred years from now, but as to social significance—"

Orin read Greg's face instantly. "That bad?"

"Worse. Griffith is the worst and most insidious sort of prejudiced person. He wraps himself in a cloak of cloying sentiment and high moral tone. He's mixed acid and syrup and created a poison."

"And if there was any hope of dissolving the segregation laws, the movement has just been set back fifty years," Kit added.

Their conversation continued along those gloomy and discouraging lines through the orange souffle. Neither Kit nor Greg were unaware of the importance of this conversation, but it was not the reason why they were here. Still, everything had to be handled carefully, and they had to be willing to wait and bide their time for the right moment to raise the topic.

"The couple who had the house next to ours at Manchester-by-the-sea?" Louisa repeated Greg's question when they were in the drawing room, sipping cafe filtre and nibbling at chocolate-dipped Florentines. "Are they involved in this somehow?"

"Apparently Gerald got the idea for his story from the lady of the house," Greg explained. He—they—were so close to an answer again. Was it going to be yet another blank wall or would there finally be the closing link that had proved to be so evasive? "He said you would remember their names."

"We'll understand if you have to check your diaries," Kit began, but stopped when Louisa smiled and shook her head.

"That won't be necessary, Katharine. The name is Gardiner, and they live on Rittenhouse Square in Philadelphia," Louisa informed them.

"We weren't close friends, of course, and they only came that summer, but we have exchanged Christmas cards a few times," Orin added. "The boys were so fond of Natalie."

"Natalia is still alive. There's too much fact for any of this to be coincidental," Greg said some two hours later as they lay together in the center of the vast canopied bed in the guest suite of the Daltons' elegant S Street house.

Somehow they made it through the remainder of the evening at the Chanfields, managing to act as if the information they heard was simply the answer to a slightly quizzical problem, not the earth-shattering news it was. This revelation was too important to discuss during the short ride from R to S Street, and on arriving back at the Daltons, they found Bruce and Evangeline in the library, lingering over a late cognac, the admiral having just come back from another late meeting at the Navy Department. They had to be polite to their hosts and join them for a few minutes, but fortunately, the Daltons didn't insist that they keep them company for any length of time, and once the latest war news was discussed, they were able to escape to the privacy of their suite.

"I almost expected to hear bells," Kit responded, "and when Orin said Mrs. Gardiner's first name was Natalie, I wanted to throw my arms around you and just cry because so much pain was removed from you with that news."

"You could also have said something very appropriate."

"Such as?"

Greg chuckled softly and kissed her hair. "Those famous wifely words, 'I told you so.' You believed all along that I wasn't a murderer, even one by accident. And it wasn't the sort of love-me-love-my-dog belief, either. It was quiet and

441

steadfast and there wasn't the slightest hint that maybe you harbored one small doubt." As he spoke, they turned toward each other, drawing closer together. "And without even realizing it, I began to draw from your belief in me. That's how I've been able to get through the last ten days, how I was able to enjoy our extra day in Chicago and our stay in New York and the party your stepgrandmother gave for us in Boston—and how I was able to get through our dinner with Orin and Louisa."

His passion-filled recitation ended, and Kit slipped her hands under his pajama jacket to caress his strong, firmly muscled back. "Last Tuesday, in New York, I began to realize Natalia just might be alive," she told him. "You hadn't hurt her, but there was the very real possibility that someone else did. I'm not sure how, but it led me to think that if you had been able to get away, maybe she did also."

"I was thinking the same thing at the same time, but I couldn't bring myself to say anything to you. I thought that if I brought it up after everything else that has been happening, you would think that I'd finally broken down under the strain."

"And I thought if I told you, you would think I was carrying my belief that you hadn't done anything past the point of reason."

"The only unreasonable thing going on is our hauling ourselves up and down the Northeast Corridor in the worst February weather in ten years," he said, and slowly began to move the straps of her ivory charmeuse nightgown down so he could kiss her shoulders.

"I love you," Kit murmured, holding tight to him as his tongue traced the soft skin at the base of her throat. "And I don't mind the weather when I'm with you."

"Funny, neither do I. And quite possibly after tomorrow, we may be free to go back to Los Angeles where we laugh at weather reports in the paper."

"Philadelphia," she said as they shed their nightclothes

and then cuddled with nothing between them.

"Is that what we're calling it now?" he inquired with a wicked flash, his hands moving over her hips before settling at the curve of her waist.

"You're impossible! And you know what I mean!"

"Yes, and as soon as possible," he agreed, and began to kiss the side of her neck. "There's a train at nine-ten tomorrow morning from Union Station."

"Shall we stay in a hotel or house guest with friends?" Kit didn't want to ask these questions now, but in a very few minutes they would be too passionately involved, and tomorrow morning was not the time to settle the matter.

"Since I've never been to Philadelphia, they'll have to be your friends. Whom did you have in mind?"

"Elliott and Claire Bernstein are home, and I know they'd love to have us stay for a few days."

"Are you talking about the Elliott Bernstein the art dealer?" Greg asked, feeling his burgeoning passion recede under a rush of deja-vu. "The man who sells pictures to the King of Belgium, and has a little girl named Diana?"

"I think King Albert has other things on his mind these days than buying pictures, and Diana's a sophomore at Barnard. You said you didn't know anyone in Philadelphia."

"I only said I've never been there," he said, and told her about meeting Elliott and Claire in Brussels.

"We don't have to see them if you think it might be embarrassing for you."

"No, I'm past all of that," Greg said. They held each other close, and once again their bodies were sending the distinct signals that more direct action was necessary for both their pleasures. "Besides," he whispered as he cupped her breasts gently in his hands, making the first move in preparation for their night of love, "the chances are that Elliott will never remember me."

Chapter 25

"Has it really taken you fifteen years to get down to Philadelphia?" was the first thing Elliott Bernstein said as he and Claire greeted the Wests in the marble entry foyer of their five-story townhouse on Philadelphia's beautiful and historic Rittenhouse Square. "We're really not that inaccessible," he went on cheerfully. "Still, I'm glad to know that you've become such a success, even though we couldn't help you get your start."

"Then you know who I am?" Greg asked, feeling both amazed and pleased at Elliott's knowledge of his whereabouts. He handed his topcoat and hat to the waiting butler. "Last night, I told Kit you probably wouldn't remember me."

"I didn't want to say anything then," Kit said, taking off her mink coat to reveal a Premet suit of champagne-colored cloth with a curving waistline and flaring peplum jacket, "but I've known both of you long enough to know that you don't forget people that easily."

"Actually, it was Diana who identified you, Greg," Claire, tall and blonde and elegant in a blue gabardine Callot Soeurs frock with a side draped skirt, black silk belt and upstand͏ white collar, pointed out as they went into the draw͏ for sherry and cheese puffs. "We'll have h͏

445

minutes, this is just to give you both a chance to relax after your morning train trip," she said, diverging from her explanation for a moment. "A few years ago, Diana saw your picture, Gregory, in a newspaper story about business in Los Angeles. She showed it to us and said that she was certain you were the same young man who used to fix her dolls and admire the paintings her Daddy was offering."

"I won't say anything about good deeds never going away," Greg said, "only how good it is to see the both of you again."

As they talked about Brussels and paintings, Kit watched Greg carefully. He was tired from their round of travel in bad weather and one blank wall or half-truth after another, but he was also more relaxed than he had been at any time except when they were alone together. Now that they were certain Natalia had not died on that night in St. Petersburg, he was freer and more open. But even as she noted these changes with relief, she also knew that if there wasn't a swift resolution to this latest hanging thread, he would once again begin to get defensive and edgy.

They had lunch, and afterwards Elliott and Claire took them on a tour of their house, through rooms filled with fine French furniture, furniture from the best of America's post-Revolutionary War cabinet makers, soft colors with the occasional jewel-toned touch, and a fine collection of American and European pictures. Throughout the dining room and drawing room, smaller salons, and library, it was clear that this was a private home and not an art gallery. Only in the two-room suite on the second floor that Elliott used as his office was his occupation apparent. Here, among excellent furniture and neutral colors picked so they wouldn't detract from the business at hand, were a carefully edited but splendid selection of paintings.

"How can you bear to sell any of them?" Kit asked as they looked at landscapes, portraits, still lifes, and even a few somewhat controversial Modern paintings that had been exhibited in the still-discussed Armory Show of May 1913. "Wouldn't you rather just open your own museum?"

"I've thought about it, but basically I'm a businessman, not a philanthropist, and I enjoy working out a deal."

"Of course, they all don't sell immediately," Claire added. "The Picasso, for instance, may stay here a while. People may want to collect art, but they'd rather have something dreary as long as it's by a 'safe' artist."

"I think we're inclined to be a bit more adventurous," Kit said, looking at a Mary Cassatt landscape full of flowers in the first bloom of summer.

"We just acquired a summer landscape by Childe Hassam," Greg said, deciding not to tell the Bernsteins that it had been a present from the Thorpes in case they thought he was hinting.

"The one Durand-Ruel was offering? That's an excellent purchase," Elliott said. "I'd recommend the Cézanne over in the corner," he went on as they admired a painting that showed a green, rich hillside in France, painted in 1902. "I'll even throw in the frame."

"Very funny, darling," Claire said, and laughed. "Elliott always says that, and you should see some of the looks he gets from European clients—they really have no sense of humor."

"They also don't have too much of an appreciation for American Impressionists," Elliott added, leading the way into the connecting room. "Look at this," he instructed, "Carroll Beckwith's Woman in White Hat with Veil. It belongs in California, and since Kit has such an elegant shop, it should go to her."

"I'll hang it in our bedroom," Kit promised, entranced with the graceful painting. "First at the Alexandria, and then when our house is built."

"It looks like our choice is made," Greg said, putting aside the real reason why they had come to Philadelphia in ord to enjoy the paintings. "Fifteen years ago, in Brusse used every excuse I could think of to come into your suite so I could see the paintings you were offering, I never would have believed that someday I'd buy two paintings from you."

"I knew you were meant for more than trying to step back into the woodwork, but to make one small correction, you've only bought one painting," Elliott said, and he and Claire exchanged pleased looks. "You're paying for the Beckwith, but the Cézanne is our wedding present to you."

"Do you really think that we didn't know that Henry and Alix gave you the Childe Hassam?" Claire asked.

"We wouldn't have said anything," Kit replied as she tucked an arm through Greg's.

"And we're overwhelmed," Greg assured them. "We came East almost on the spur of the moment, but the kindness and the warmth we've been received with goes beyond hospitality and into the realm of something much greater."

"We're going to have to tell Claire and Elliott the entire story," Greg said a half-hour later when they were alone together in one of the lavishly appointed guest rooms on the third floor. In the bedroom, decorated with beautiful Georgian pieces created by Philadelphia cabinet makers in the early part of the last century all rubbed to a high gleam by the best polish, a rug that was a beautifully sculptured piece rose and cream wool, and Oriental vases with arrangements of winter hothouse flowers, they could talk freely. It was welcoming and private and conducive to talk on the most intimate of levels. "I realized that as soon as we walked into this house and Elliott recognized me. If I continue to use the evasions that are my usual bag of tricks, I'll be throwing every bit of kindness and concern back in their faces, and I won't do that no matter what the cost."

"I love a high-principled man because he always seems to know when it's the right time to take a certain stand," Kit said as they walked into the large bathroom with its soft lighting, black-veined white marble surfaces, and abundant mirrors. Sitting down on the broad ledge of the tub, she opened a crystal jar, tossed in several handfuls of bath salts, and turned on the faucets. "I also admire your restraint more than I can put into words. We're closer to finding Natalia than we ever supposed we could be when we left Los Angeles. Two weeks ago, all we wanted was a simple answer, now we may be about to come face-to-face with the last person either of us ever expected to see."

"I'm almost afraid to think about Natalia. I'm still coming to grips with the fact that she's been alive all these years. But I still don't know what happened that night—all the blanks that have been there for fifteen years are still there. The past week has been a revelation, but it's not an answer."

"But anything is better than thinking that you're going to be blackmailed. I don't think a new marriage could take a strain like that for too long."

"And this—what we're going through now—is easier?"

"In a way, I think it is. It's almost like unravelling a mystery."

"You've been reading too many whodunits." Greg smiled. "The mirrors are steaming up."

Kit turned off the taps. "Shall we see about keeping them that way?" she asked, slipping off her pink silk robe.

"I thought you'd never ask," Greg returned, and took off his own dressing gown.

With the door closed and only the soft light from one wall sconce providing illumination, the bathroom became a warm, secluded, perfumed refuge from both the cold, damp, snowy Philadelphia afternoon and from the knowledge that at this very moment, Natalia Voykovich might only be several hundred yards away in some other grand Rittenhouse Square townhouse. The marble bathtub was more than big enough for two, and side by side they slid down until the silken water topped by soft bubbles lapped against their shoulders.

"Will you tell me something?"

"Almost anything at all," she responded to his husky whisper.

"That . . . device you use, how effective is it?"

Kit laughed and tossed a handful of bubbles at him. "Of all the things you could ask—and all you want to know about is how well my diaphragm works!"

"So that's what it's called."

"If you want to be progressive, yes. And the doctor I saw in Amsterdam last summer assured me that this was a great improvement over the old Dutch Cap. She said it was about ninety percent effective, but are you hoping that I'll fall into that ten percent margin for error?" she inquired, amused.

"I was thinking more along the lines of a pleasant accident." His fingers brushed away the bubbles that clung to the tops of her breasts. "Nothing so glorious should be hidden when it doesn't have to be."

Greg's right arm was around her shoulders, and under the warm, richly scented water, his left hand cupped first one breast and then the other, sending a delicious shiver through her. "Oh, Greg, do you want me to forget about being careful and just see what happens?"

His fingers traced a half-circle under each full globe. "I have to admit that I wouldn't have minded if we were going to have a baby from our weekend at the horse ranch."

Kit looked at him through her lashes. "That's one way to live up to the term stud farm."

"It's the only way," he corrected, lowering his head for a kiss that sent them sliding down the tub and ended with their dissolving into laughter.

"It's the only way if we want to have a baby and not drown ourselves in the process," Kit said as they recovered. "The shower might be safer."

"All we need right now is a slight adjustment," he said, pulling her on top of him, his eyes turning to dark amber as she molded herself against his body while her hands

450

massaged the back of his neck. "Any complaints?"

"Not as long as we're like this. We may have to postpone starting a baby right away, but we're going to have a wonderful time getting into practice for when we do!"

"Aren't you going to give me a chance to—"

"Not this time—remember our adjustment," she murmured in his ear, putting her hands on his chest. "Semi-underwater activities have a very therapeutic effect—just perfect for easing the strain after a tiring train trip."

His hands curved around her hips, and he closed his eyes as he pulled her even closer against his body. Kit pressed herself down on his vibrant flesh, the demanding sensations increasing as the water, stirred by the motions of their bodies, waved around them. Both of them knew they were at a stalemate in their attempt to find Natalia and the truth behind what had happened on that long-ago night in St. Petersburg. There was no going back, and with no more information they couldn't go forward. The only certainty they could depend on at that moment was the strength of their love.

"Elliott, when we met in Brussels, did you wonder why I was so intent on melting into the woodwork and wallpaper?" Greg asked a few hours later as they sat around the elegant Georgian table in the Bernsteins' dining room. He was playing this by ear. If Elliott showed no signs of being interested, he'd revert to half-truths and evasion to get his information about the Gardiners, but if the answers went the right way, he would tell his story in exact detail. "I couldn't have been very expert at what I was doing."

"You were about the worst valet I'd ever seen," Elliott responded. They had finished the variety of hot hors d'oeuvres, and now that the squab en casserole and string beans had been served, there was enough privacy to talk undisturbed by servants offering food. "Half of the time I wasn't sure if you were going to hang away my suits or try them on. That's an exaggeration, of course, but you weren't like any servant I'd ever met."

"You also didn't have the hands of a servant," Claire added. "There was something about you that didn't quite measure up to what I can politely call servant status, and when I heard you tell Elliott you had a debt to pay, I knew you must have a very special reason for being there."

"I used to think that no one would ever believe what happened to me. Only a few other people know about me—it was hardly something I ever wanted to discuss except with those closest to me. And up until a week ago, there was a strong possibility I had committed a major crime—not that I planned it in advance—but a crime all the same."

"And now you've found out that you're innocent of that crime," Elliott stated.

"I have to say that Kit never believed for one minute that I was guilty of murdering Natalia Voykovich in St. Petersburg in 1900."

"*You're* Alexander Vestovanova?" Claire said in a voice that was clearly disbelieving.

"I'm very much afraid I am, or was, whichever the case may be."

"But—," Claire began and hesitated. "Oh, when am I going to stop being surprised by such things? You poor dear."

"Kit, you've been very quiet all of a sudden."

"Oh, Elliott, as much as I love my husband, this is *his* story, and he has to tell it his own way. And Greg isn't going to tell you anything I haven't already heard or that we haven't discussed together. But if I contribute too much to this conversation, then I'll be exactly the sort of wife I don't want to be."

"I thought you'd tell me something like that." Elliott smiled and turned to Greg. "I hope you realize how fortunate you are."

"Now more than ever. And I hate to ask this question, but did you know about—," he paused painfully, "—about the incident?"

"Not in any great detail, and then mostly from gossip and newspaper squibs. As you can imagine, we're hardly on close social terms with Russian nobility."

"I'm sure that's by your choice—and it's a very wise one."

"You couldn't have been more than a boy when it happened."

"Technically, I was a man, but you're right, Claire. I lived my life like a carefree, careless boy. A spoiled brat. I was smuggled out of Russia and sent to Brussels. It was only a stopping off place until they could get the proper papers for me to go on to America. I had every intention of taking you up on your offer, but I wanted to earn enough money first to arrive in Philadelphia in style."

"I'd say you did—just a little bit late," Elliott remarked dryly, and everyone's laughter broke the tension.

"For years, I thought that a woman had been murdered and her body put in the Moika Canal which feeds into the Neva," Greg continued a short time later. "Now I know it was only meant to look like that—with me as the culprit."

Across from Greg, Kit sat silently, listening as intently as if this were the first time she was hearing the story. She knew that people tended to get very protective of the people who were their neighbors, even when they weren't very good friends, simply because those asking the questions became outsiders.

But it's too late to back out now, she thought, her hands holding tightly to the dinner napkin in her lap while her heartbeat grew more ragged. And in a few minutes, nothing is going to be the same again.

The tension was weaving its way around them again as Greg leaned forward and said, "That woman is alive and living in Philadelphia."

"There are vaudeville comics who'd disagree with you on

453

the total veracity of that statement," Elliott said mildly. "Are we supposed to know this woman?"

"I think so," Greg said. It's almost solved, he thought. "The woman I'm looking for lives here on Rittenhouse Square, and she goes by the name of Natalie Gardiner."

"Just another quiet dinner party at the Bernsteins," Elliott said in cryptic good humor. "Are we all finished eating? Good, let's have dessert, and then we can go into the drawing room and finish this discussion in privacy."

Dessert was pears flamed in liqueurs, and when they had eaten what they could, both couples adjourned to the drawing room. The servants had already set out coffee and tiny cookies and Remy Martin, but those pleasant after-dinner activities held very little interest for them tonight.

"You do know the Gardiners?" Greg asked when the doors were closed. "Do you at least know of them."

"Relax, Greg, we know the Gardiners, but you have to realize that you have dropped something of a bombshell on us," Elliott reminded him. "The story you told us is horrific. As far as I'm concerned, you were made to suffer for a crime you not only didn't commit but which never really happened. But we've also just found out that a woman we've known for years isn't the person she's always said she is, and that her husband, a man who is greatly respected, had helped her maintain and build this fiction."

"Elliott, I don't want to ruin Natalia's life or that of her husband, and it's not going to end up in the newspapers. All I want to do is see her again."

"We can't take another blank wall," Kit added hotly. "The past few months, ever since *Ballet At Midnight* arrived, have been an experience in abnormal psychology, and it can't go on much longer without some resolution."

"What would you like us to do?" Claire offered.

"Call up Carl Gardiner and find out if we can see him and

454

his wife," Greg said, feeling like a runner at the end of a very long race. "All I want to know is the truth behind that night."

Elliott stood up. "I'll be back as soon as I can."

He left, and Claire moved from her chair to the sofa where Kit and Greg sat holding hands. "I want you to know how splendid I think the both of you are," she said. "Telling us your story, Greg, couldn't have been easy, and I wish we had known about this fifteen years ago in Brussels. I'd like to think that we would have given you the same protection and help that Sinclair did."

"I'm sure you would have," he told her, "but I was too frightened and confused to trust anyone to that extent then."

"Then Elliott's offer that you come to Philadelphia must have come as quite a surprise."

"I was dumbfounded, but it was also a ray of hope that I held on to for a long time. If it hadn't been for that offer, I might not have been able to accept the warmth and help that Sin offered me a few months later."

"As trite as this sounds, in a way everything has gone well for you. You had to live far too long with a terrible burden, but you've also made something very fine out of your life."

"And now I have Kit to share the good things with."

"But so much of what we do from now on depends on the next few minutes," Kit added. She was sure that in a short time the doorbell would ring and then Natalia would walk into the drawing room and . . . Elliott returned, and almost instantly she knew her scenario was a fantasy. "What's wrong?" she asked, an unreasonable panic rising in her throat. "Don't tell us that we've made a mistake!"

"You and Greg haven't made a mistake, Kit. You both have done one hell of a detecting job." Elliott sat down in his chair. "I spoke with Carl."

"Did he try to deny what we know?" Greg asked. He had picked up on Kit's sudden defensiveness, and he felt as if he were being smothered.

"Please relax, both of you. In case you didn't know, Carl's

a rather noted criminal attorney, and since I'm an art dealer from a family of financiers, our conversation had more than the usual number of twists and turns."

"Will I be able to see Natalia tonight? Damn it, I feel like I'm begging," Greg said, his dark-amber eyes slowly turning cloudy with suppressed anger.

"You're not begging." Elliott leaned forward, a concerned expression in his own eyes. "Natalia's in New York, she's been there for the past ten days seeing her dentist. Oh, go ahead and swear," he continued, seeing their expression. "We've heard—and have possibly said—it all."

"All the time we've been going from New York to Boston to Washington and now to Philadelphia, Natalia Voykovich —excuse me, Natalie Gardiner—has been in New York," Greg said in a low and dangerous voice.

"*Don't* tell us that she's staying at the Plaza," Kit added, an unmistakable edge to her own voice. "That would just be too much."

"No, she's at the St. Regis," Elliott said, relieved that at least they were at different hotels. "Carl was very under-standing about this. I have a good idea that the incident has been a shadow in their life also."

"Then it's time we all got a surcease in our lives from that night. Maybe it's hurt her marriage. I don't want it to hurt mine."

"We're going back home tomorrow," Kit said, and she didn't mean Los Angeles. "At some time or other, everyone finds the answer to a particular question in New York, and now it's our turn."

Chapter 26

Kit and Greg returned to a New York City caught in a February snowstorm. They hadn't been able to leave Philadelphia first thing on Thursday morning, not because of the weather, which was then only gray and threatening, but for the lack of space on any of the New York-bound trains.

The trip was only two hours, and they were willing to stick it out in the day coach for two hours, but Elliott remained unmoved, reminding them that if they'd never ridden in coach, a bad day wasn't the time to start. Finally, after speaking with his connection at the Broad Street Station, he secured two parlor car seats for them on Express 236, leaving at four in the afternoon. By the time the train was ready to leave, the snow was falling, but even worse than the weather was Greg's mood. A mood that hadn't been helped by the unexpected arrival during lunch of Carl Gardiner.

He was a thorough Philadelphia gentleman, and he apologized profusely for disturbing their meal, but he wanted to meet Gregory West.

The meal had gone on smoothly, but Greg, already under far too much strain from the past few weeks, literally seemed to withdraw into himself, to become more and more distant as each hour passed. The train covered the miles north to

New York, and they said little and read a lot. Greg had involved himself in the new whodunit, *The Return Of The Night Wind,* while Kit had gone from *The Smart Set,* to *Scribners,* to *Metropolitan,* to *Arts & Decoration,* busying herself with the glossy magazines so that she wouldn't inadvertently add to a situation that was already groaning under its own weight.

It would be better when they got to the Plaza, where they wisely decided to keep their suite, she decided as the train moved steadily along despite the ever-increasing snowfall. They could rest, eat, and talk in private. The Hampton Court maze of false leads and obscure tales was gone, but reaching the last chapter of the truth was no easier.

The train was only a few minutes late, and Wooten was waiting for them, but the city's traffic—a combination of rush hour and the snow—was a hopeless snarl, and it was nearly seven before they reached the hotel.

To their astonishment, the Plaza's lobby was jammed. Woodrow Wilson would have gotten immediate attention, so would King George, or Prime Minister Asquith, or the President of France, but everyone else—including the Wests—would simply have to get on line and wait their turn.

"I know it isn't proper, but I should have kept our key," Greg said wearily as the line inched forward with incredible slowness. "I never thought we'd have to wait this long to reclaim our suite."

Kit tried to keep her alarm under control as she saw how white and strained Greg's face was. They flagged down a harried assistant manager who politely informed them that the weather had caused havoc with the reservations, that Mr. Sterry was deeply involved in trying to untangle the conflicting reservations of two competing Colorado copper kings and couldn't help at this moment.

"So much for your once having lived at the Plaza," Greg said some twenty minutes later as the door to the suite closed behind the generously tipped bellboys. "When it comes

458

down to pulling a string or two when needed, I can see where you rank."

Anger flashed through Kit like a sudden flash of lightning, and not trusting herself to speak, she took off her fur and folded it over the nearest chair. It was those sort of words, spoken without thinking, that started quarrels neither party knew how to stop, she told herself. Greg, out of exhaustion more than anything else, was baiting her, and lashing back at him wasn't going to solve anything.

"If I remember correctly, you've always stayed here when you were in New York on business," she said finally. "The two of us together should have merited quite a bit of attention, but tonight it just didn't happen."

"When I was a boy, and travelled with my family, the managing-director of any hotel we stayed at, plus a good number of the staff, would be waiting at the door for us when we arrived, no matter what time it was," he informed her, sounding lofty and far away at the same time. "Our patronage was so valued that if my father wished it, the managing-director would have cleared the hotel for us. Two fatuous copper barons wouldn't have stood a chance."

"Then I'm glad you can't go around pulling that particular trick," she shot back without thinking, and wished she hadn't opened her mouth. Round one, she thought.

"Oh, you would have gotten used to it quickly enough," he returned. "You would have liked my taking a whole floor at the Ritz in Paris or the Savoy in London for no other reason than that I could afford it."

"You can still afford to do those things, but what does any of it matter any more? We have a whole other world."

"Do you really think I've ever been able to totally forget where I came from, who my family was, and how I lost them?" he asked, his eyes flashing at her, and then he spun on his heel and went over to one of the windows.

"I imagine that sometimes it must have been the only thing that kept you going," Kit hazarded. She looked at him, standing with his forehead pressed against the glass, watching the snow fall on Central Park. He was rumpled, needed to shave, there were dark smudges under his eyes and his nerves were nearly rubbed raw, but he was still the man she loved—even if right now she thought he was on the verge of needing a good swat. "But you told me yourself that living in the past was something you couldn't stand."

"I didn't have much choice in the beginning, and when I went to work for Sin, I was caught up in his struggle to clear his father's name and had no time to think about my own father or to wonder what happened. What did he think when he came to my room and found that I wasn't there? Did he call the Okhrana immediately, or did he wait just long enough to let me complete my escape? Has he kept looking for me all these years, or did he stop after Brussels. Kit, I don't even know if my father is still alive."

Instinctively, she'd known this was coming as soon as his tirade began, and she crossed the space between them. She put her arms around him, but he remained unresponsive, and Kit tried not to feel as if he were rejecting her. She recognized that he was finally coming to grips with the reality that he hadn't committed a hideous crime, and in a way it was as bad as if he had been guilty all these years; but now it also felt as if he were pushing her away, trying to find some fault in her that would prove to him how much better his old life had been.

"If you really want to find out, I can help."

He shook her off. "How?" he asked, swinging around to face her, the hard glint in his eyes making him look like a stranger. "With that crew of 'connections' I've suddenly found myself in league with?"

"What do you mean by that crack?"

"Your mother's an artist, your father wrote a financial column for Adolph Ochs at the *Times,* your stepfather's some sort of renegade Boston Brahmin, and your stepbrother seems to enjoy pretending that he doesn't know the difference between his left and right hands!"

For a minute, Kit stared at him. A slow stain of pain and disbelief was spreading over her heart. He doesn't mean this, she thought, but as much as she wanted to comfort him, she was too tired and cranky herself to let him denigrate her family and friends and not stand up for them.

"I don't want to believe you mean a word of what you've just said," she said finally, managing somehow to keep the worst of her temper under control. "If you did, you couldn't have been as amiable as you were in the past two weeks—*no one* is that charming."

"I've been known to be able to make the best of a bad situation. I can hold my own with an assortment of stockbrokers, politicians, and art dealers."

"Judging from what I saw of the best families both times I was in St. Petersburg, I'm pretty sure we could hold our own in that crowd."

Greg's eyes flashed bits of amber at her. "Now it's my turn to ask what you mean by that remark."

"I mean that I saw or heard about more than my share of wastrels, womanizers, perverts, and drug addicts to make me think that this whole tale of how much you had to give up when you left Russia has taken on the proportions of a fairy tale. I'm not talking about your family, just about the flawless existence you had."

"Are you calling me a liar?"

Kit was suddenly aware of on just what dangerous ground they were on. In another minute, unless one of them put the brakes on, they'd both say things that wouldn't be forgotten after the heat of the argument was over. They had to talk about a lot of things, but not now.

"I'm tired," she told him evenly, "and crumpled, and I have a headache. The only thing I'm going to do right now is take a bath. Then I'm going to rest and order dinner. What I am not going to do is stand here like an idiot and trade insults with you."

"And what am I supposed to do in the meantime?"

"Stop trying to either get me to leave you or have me say something that will give you the chance to walk," Kit said quietly, her neck muscles growing tense with nerves. "You can sit down and read or take a nap, or if you're so desperate to get rid of some of the pain you're carrying around you can get another room or even go to another hotel. You have dozens of options—that happens to be one of the great things about America," she couldn't resist adding over her shoulder as she went into the bedroom and slammed the door shut behind her.

When she opened the door again an hour later, Greg was still there.

She had been all too aware that his pride was strong enough for him to take her snappish remark literally and decamp. But instead he was sitting in a corner of the sofa, a variety of reading matter around him, and a far calmer expression on his face.

"I was so worried that you might have gone off to some all-male club," she said, relief flooding through her as she noticed the conflict-laden look in his eyes was replaced by a much more tender emotion.

"I don't belong to any clubs, all-male or otherwise, and the only one where I'm even vaguely known is the Metropolitan Club, and there's always the chance that they would want me to steam a suit or iron a shirt," he said as he stood up and held out his arms to her. "Please forgive me for everything I said."

Kit ran into his embrace and wrapped her arms around his shoulders. They had been in such close communion with each other over the past two weeks that the rift had been almost inevitable, but now the only important thing was how quickly they could mend it.

"I've missed you so much this past hour. I couldn't believe

I said such stupid things," Greg murmured, sitting down and pulling her onto his lap. Kit was wearing a Callot Soeurs at home frock of pink crepe de chine designed with a round neck and a dropped waist and sleeves edged in pink satin frills, and her freshly washed hair waved around her face. Greg held her close, and they kissed over and over, and each time was as binding and as magical as the first. "I love your family and friends," he said when they drew apart. "They've been wonderful to us, and all I can say in my own defense is that I was worn out and ready to find fault with everything."

"It's all right." Kit ran her fingers through Greg's hair. His jacket and tie were off, his shirtsleeves were rolled up, and despite the fact that he was rumpled after their long and tiring day he was still very irresistible, and the longer they stayed cuddled together on the sofa the more likely it was that they'd make love right there in the sitting room. "And considering both of our tempers, it was probably safer that I walked out on you before. If I hadn't, I don't think we'd be very cozy right now."

"I agree, my darling, but if you don't get off my lap now, we're not going to have dinner, or talk, or do anything rational for several hours."

"Is that a promise?"

"One I intend to keep—after a suitable interval," he added, laughing as they both stood up. "Why don't you order dinner while I wash off our train ride?"

"Are you as hungry as I am?"

"Famished."

"Then I'll order a feast. And don't put on your dinner jacket—pajama and robe will be fine," she said, and kissed him under one ear. "It'll save time later on."

"I think we'd better talk about Natalia now," Greg said some ninety minutes later as they finished the last of the succulent Chincoteagues that had been arrayed on a platter lined with crushed ice. "You've been very patient, and have put up with a lot today."

"But you've had to deal with much more, and you needed time to absorb and adjust to it."

"I don't know if I can ever really adjust to it," he said as they stood up and went over to the serving trolley to get the hot consommé. "Thanks to you and your belief in me, I've been able to accept that I hadn't committed murder. It's Natalia's being alive that's a shock I can't begin to describe."

Carrying the bowls of soup, they returned to the table that their waiter had set up. "You were a victim that night in what the underworld likes to call a set-up," Kit said, aware that she had to proceed very carefully. "But was Natalia also a victim, or was she part of the plot?"

Greg gave her a conflict-filled look. "I don't know. I'd like to think she was totally innocent, whatever the plot was, but you know as well as I do that things in Russia are never what they seem. I hope that enough time has passed so she can tell me the truth."

"I'm coming with you when you go to see her."

Greg dropped his spoon into his consommé. "You're going to do *what?*"

"I'm coming with you when you go to the St. Regis to see Natalia," Kit repeated. She put down her own spoon, leaned her arms on the table, and looked at Greg. "We haven't come this far together to slip up now. I'm not going to sit here while you go off on your own and wait for you to come back or telephone me."

"You'd make a terrible officer's wife," he said, and finally smiled.

"That isn't something I'm going to have to worry about, is it?"

"It's not too likely."

"How badly did Carl upset you?"

"I felt like a specimen about to be examined by a naturalist. There may have been a little husbandly jealousy on his part, and it's understandable. I'd heard about Carl Gardiner for years, I've even read some of the articles he's written about the criminal justice system—it's something I have more than a passing interest in," he added needlessly, and his smile held little amusement.

"It's odd to think that while you were reading his articles, he was involved in a part of your life."

"There's far too much of my life that's odd in one way or another," Greg said as they returned to the serving trolley for the entree of quail with wild rice. "I want to settle as much of my past as I can, and then I want to go on to the next stage of my—our—life without that night sinking its tentacles into me."

"Then why don't we make some plans for after . . . after tomorrow?"

"Business or personal?"

"Both, and I'd like to go on record right now as wanting to spend the first night we can dining and dancing—preferably downstairs in the Rose Room. I also want you to see the apartment in The Mayfair, we have friends to look up, and there are several shows we should take in."

"I'd rather see *Watch Your Step* again."

"So would I. *And* I have to place a lot of orders for clothes. I'm counting on a lot of business this spring and summer, and I don't want to be caught short on stock." Kit regarded Greg over a forkful of quail and wild rice. "I saw that you had a rather thick letter from Mitch. Is it anything you can discuss?"

"You can read it if you like. Apparently, *Ballet At Midnight* is going more smoothly than anyone could have imagined."

"I hate to say it, but maybe there's something in the theory that everything goes better when the chief executive officer isn't around," Kit teased.

Greg laughed so hard he had to stop eating. "I can think of at least one person at Hooper who's glad that I'm here in

New York."

"Poor Mr. Moffitt. I think he's going to get the shakes every time he goes near an antimacassar."

"He'd better, if he wants to keep his position. Mitch wrote that Montgomery's very cooperative. He also wrote that filming should be completed at the end of April or the beginning of May. That means if the editing goes well, *Ballet At Midnight* can be released in July or August."

"You have that look again."

"What look?" he asked as they finished their salad and took their dessert of lemon mousse and petit fours.

"The one that tells me you're thinking about something very important but you're not ready to discuss it yet."

"I am, but I should be able to discuss it with you after we see Natalia," he said, and they were back to the real reason they were in New York.

"Do you think Carl went ahead and told her?"

"No, I'm sure he's a man who keeps his word. But that's not to say that he didn't want to. If he loves Natalia—and it's impossible not to—he must be very concerned for her right now."

Kit tried to ignore the dart of jealousy she felt; considering the circumstances it wasn't at all appropriate. "It's too late to call her now. You were going to call?" she asked, pouring out coffee.

"I really wasn't sure how to handle this," Greg admitted. "I wouldn't be sure what to say over the phone, and the idea of just turning up at her door—"

"No, of course you can't do that. I do have an idea."

"I was sure you would."

"The only way I could come up with to get to Natalia is for me to call her up tomorrow morning, tell her that I'm Katharine Allen West, a friend of Claire Bernstein's, and that she suggested I call because there's a dress from my shop in Los Angeles that would be perfect for Mrs. Gardiner." She reached across the small table for Greg's hand. "What do you think?"

"That I could never come up with anything that good. Natalia has no reason to connect the name West to me. How would I be able to get through this without you?"

"Lucky for both of us, you're not going to have to," Kit said as she stood up. "This is about all we can do until tomorrow morning. Now, are you as much in favor as I am of going into the bedroom and concentrating on each other?"

"Greg, sweetheart, how old were you the first time?"

"Is this part of our concentrating on each other?" Greg was sitting up in bed with all the pillows piled up behind him, and he looked lovingly at Kit, arrayed for the night in a Lucile nightgown and negligee of the palest blue hammered satin ornamented with satin ribbon and silver lace. "That was one question I thought you'd never ask me."

"I've been waiting ages to ask you. And since you're *finally* wearing the pajamas I gave you for Christmas," she went on, regarding his long, lean body draped in the bold, blue-and-white-stripes of the Sulka pajamas she'd had made for him, "I decided that this was as good a time as any to ask all those questions that intrigue women."

"And what is so intriguing about a randy seventeen year old boy on his first assignation in Paris?" he asked with a rakish look, and pulled her down onto the bed, settling her between his legs.

"That boy is intriguing only because he turned into you," Kit responded, adjusting her body so she could look at his face while they talked. "You must have been darling."

Greg choked on his laughter. "I'm trying to remember if I was ever called that."

"Unless your ladies were so overcome by a very handsome young man with the proper combination of eagerness and inexperience, they must have told you how adorable you were."

"That's a bit much."

"Just the right combination of arrogance and innocence," she continued, tracing a line along his jaw and over his chin. "You must have been treated like royalty."

"You don't really want me to answer that one," Greg said as he began to remove her negligee.

"I was wondering when you were going to do that."

He kissed her shoulders. "What is it that you really want me to tell you?"

"Did you ever make love to Natalia?"

He lifted his face from the perfumed hollow at the base of her throat. "By making love, I assume you mean what we're about to do?"

"Yes."

"No."

Kit felt an almost indecent sense of relief wash over her. While they had both thought that Natalia was dead, the idea that Greg had once been her lover hadn't seemed that important. But now that she knew the ballet dancer was still alive, the woman had become a source of very unfamiliar jealousy to her. Men, she knew, very often retained idealized memories of a particular woman they'd made love to in their youth.

"I told you about that night in Peter Ignatov's apartment," Greg said after a long time. "Natalia was supposed to make up her mind between me, Sandor, Georgi, and Kinstantin. Before then, I bought her chocolates and sent her gifts. In the times we did manage to be alone together, there wasn't enough time for us to make love."

"*Now* I know," Kit replied as they stretched out across the bed together. "When you talked about it, you put it in such romantic terms that I wasn't sure what had gone on."

"And that mattered so much to you one way or the other?" he asked tenderly. "You're the only woman for me, you have been from the moment I saw you."

"I know, I know, and I'm not doubting either your loyalty or your fidelity, the only thing I was worried about was—"

"Was the faulty and frail male memory that every so often comes up with the idea that the woman he knew back when was the ideal—everything he'd ever want or need," Greg finished, and without giving her a chance to reply, he lowered his mouth to her lips in a kiss that held as much promise as the first one they shared in the corridor of the Blackstone Hotel.

"We're a long way from the warm weather of California," she said, stroking the back of his neck. "But do you know, I think there are times when making love absolutely demands it be a cold and snowy New York night with the wind sweeping down Fifth Avenue." Her fingers slid along his neck to his chest and began to undo the buttons on his pajama jacket. "It makes being together so much more special."

"It's never anything but special with you," he said as she stripped his pajamas off him. "I never want you to think that I have any old or overworked illusions about Natalia that can get in the way of our happiness, of our life together."

They slept through the night while outside the weather was typical for a stormy February night in New York. The snow continued to fall in thick, white flakes, the wind whipped through the leafless trees in Central Park and roared down Fifth Avenue in angry gusts, but in Gregory West's life, the dark cloud of changing size that had hung over his life for so long, tonight, after fifteen years and six weeks, finally, and at long last, disappeared.

The telephone call to Natalie Gardiner at the St. Regis Hotel was so seamless, so effortless, that Kit speculated on the possibility that Carl Gardiner had indeed called his wife;

and Greg, having heard his wife describe in great detail a dress he was sure wasn't in her wardrobe, marveled at how easy it was for her to arrange the meeting so that at least the start of this potentially difficult and awkward, and even dangerous meeting would get off to a smooth start. But there was one aspect that concerned them.

"Did it sound like Natalia?" was the first thing Kit asked after she hung up the phone and met Greg, who had been listening in on the sitting room's extension, halfway between the two rooms.

"No, but then I didn't expect it to," he replied as they sat down on the sofa. "Her English had been good back in St. Petersburg, and after years of living in Philadelphia—" There was no need to finish the sentence, and after a few difficult moments, he continued, "I can't start to tell you how skillfully you conducted that conversation. Is there really a Paquin suit of beige buckskin covert cloth?"

"Of course there is, but it's over at Thurn's. I saw it the day I bought my new dance dress, so I really wasn't making anything up."

"Just taking a bit of creative license," her husband said, and smiled faintly. "At least it's stopped snowing, but I wish we could see her now instead of at three."

"Oh, so do I. But you know what going to the dentist is like." Kit glanced at the clock. "It's half-past eleven now. Why don't we order something like waffles and bacon? We have to eat, and by the time we've finished our food and gotten dressed, it'll be time to leave."

It was amazing how much time eating and deciding on what to wear could take up. Kit was torn between two dresses, all her tension coming out in selecting the right thing to wear. But which would make the better impression: a Jenny model of blue serge tied at the waist with a blue satin sash, with buttons down the front, three fitted flounces at the hem, and a crisp white Eton collar and satin bow; or a dress of tan silk with a scarlet ribbon and white lace collar and two tiny upturned ruffles accentuating the short—nine inches from the ground—full skirt that had just been delivered to her, a present from Tappe's atelier?

She decided on the Tappe, choosing it as much as a wish for good fortune as for its pretty and distinctive lines. She topped it off with a Reboux hat of black faille with a tan satin band, and she was ready promptly at half-past two.

They made the trip down to the lobby in near silence, too nervous to say anything after exchanging the hope that deciding to take a taximeter cab instead of having Wooten drive them wouldn't make them late. Fortunately, there wasn't a long wait, and then the taxidriver was taking them east along Fifty-ninth Street to Madison Avenue where he turned into the southbound lane until he reached Fifty-fifth Street, then it was another right, and three-quarters of the way toward Fifth Avenue, they pulled up in front of the St. Regis's doorman.

Since September 1904, the St. Regis held its own special place in the hearts of New Yorkers, and although it came after the Plaza in terms of favorite hotel, it was never in any way second best. But on this Friday afternoon, the Wests were far too agitated at the meeting they were about to have to give more than perfunctory notice to the luxurious lobby.

They held hands during the trip up to the tenth floor, and they didn't let go of each other until they stopped in front of the door bearing the numbers Natalia had given Kit over the phone.

This was no place for any last minute considerations, or for stage fright, and Greg rapped quickly on the panel. The door opened almost immediately.

"Mrs. West, welcome. I didn't mention it over the phone, but I've read about your shop. It sounds delightful—more than worth a trip to Los Angeles."

"Thank you very much." Kit knew she had no hope of slowing down her rapid heartbeat or stilling the butterflies in her stomach, and she pressed ahead while she still had a slight advantage. "My husband, Gregory, is with me, and he's been waiting a long time to see you again."

The slender, lovely woman who called herself Natalie Gardiner drew back slightly. "I don't understand. . . ."

Kit moved aside to let Greg step into the room. Everything that had transpired over the past fifteen years had come down to this moment, and now time seemed to stop as they all stood together. Her breath caught in her throat as Greg took off his hat, and then her attention was riveted on Natalia, waiting for the other woman's reaction.

There was no long wait. Natalia's already large, dark, expressive eyes seemed to grow even wider, and she breathed only one word, but it was more than enough.

"Sacha."

Chapter 27

"Sacha. Oh my darling Sacha. I thought you were dead!" With a sob, Natalie Gardiner threw her arms around Greg's shoulders and drew his face down to hers. In a split second, the years fell away, and the Rittenhouse Square matron and the wealthy Los Angeles businessman once again became Natalia Voykovich and Alexander Vestovanova. It was a moment neither had dreamed would ever happen, and Kit, as deeply involved in all of this as she was, suddenly felt like an interloper. Blinking back her own tears at this reunion, she began to back her way out the door. She had nothing to worry about. They weren't going to run away with each other, but they did deserve privacy.

"Kit, where are you going?"

Greg's voice, choked with emotion, stopped her retreat, and she met his dark-amber gaze. "I don't want to intrude," she said, rapidly blinking her eyes so her mascara wouldn't run. "I'll wait for you in the Ladies' Restaurant—you both need time to talk."

"And I wouldn't be here now if you hadn't helped, hadn't believed in me all along. Last night you said we'd gone through all of this together, and you weren't going to not see it out to the end with me."

"Please, Mrs. West, come in." Despite her pale skin and

473

large, overly bright eyes, Natalia's voice was calm and clear. "Your tact is greatly appreciated, but it is also unnecessary. You are most welcome here."

"My name is Katharine, but everyone calls me Kit," she said, taking off her coat and carefully folding it over the Louis XVI-style chair. The suite, she noticed, was one of the St. Regis's prettiest, all beige and cream with touches of pale blue and gold; a sitting room so stately and discreet that Natalia's Paquin afternoon dress of peacock-blue silk seemed to be an almost too-intense splash of color. "I'm sorry I made up that story about a dress, but it seemed to be the only way to arrange a meeting without arousing your suspicions."

"I can't believe—," Natalia began, then stopped. "Does my husband know about the two of you?"

"We were in Philadelphia on Wednesday," Greg explained as they all sat down, Kit in an armchair and Greg and Natalia on one of the sofas. "He was very understanding, but he also made it quite clear that he considered this to be between us."

"Carl is like that, a strong believer in personal responsibility," she replied, almost on the verge of tears again. "And I have to tell you that in a way I'm responsible for what happened that night. In the end, I was used and became a victim, but it didn't start out that way."

What a brave woman, Kit thought, watching surprise and pain form on Greg's face. She could have insisted that she'd been used all along, but there's a lot to be said for anyone who tells the truth when the going can get rough.

"Why did you do this?" Greg asked in a raw voice. "Was it supposed to be some sort of joke?"

"Yes, a practical joke. All your friends were in on it. It was supposed to be so simple, and then it all turned so ugly."

"Was this the reason why my friends denied they were in the apartment with me—was it all part of the 'joke'?"

"No, that all came after and wasn't part of the plan.

474

Oh, Sacha—"

"Don't call me that!" Greg snapped, and Kit jumped at the tone of his voice, one she'd never heard before. "Do you know that I've thought I was a murderer all these years? I thought that because of my stupid irresponsibility I caused your death. And now you tell me it was all some sort of prank."

He stood up, and with a strangled cry, Natalia followed. "Sa—I mean, Gregory, don't, please. It was all Vladimir's fault."

Greg's stare was icy, and for a single moment he thought it was all better when he knew nothing. "I should have stopped searching when I knew you were alive," he said at last. "It was better when I thought you hadn't betrayed me."

"But I didn't!" Natalia protested, plucking at his sleeve. "Please sit down and let me tell you the whole story. I never wanted to hurt you, but we were both at the mercy of a diabolical plan. Kit, please make him listen," she implored.

Natalia's look was heartbreaking, and Kit wished she'd followed her first instinct and left them alone. A third party is never a help, she thought. If Greg were here alone, he'd walk out, calm down, and then come back.

"I won't tell my husband what to do, Natalia," she replied quietly, firmly. "In a way, I'm responsible for our coming out from Los Angeles, but there's a point where my involvement ends and the story of what really happened becomes a matter for the two of you to discuss. It's not for me to tell my husband to stay when he doesn't want to just to satisfy my own curiosity about this."

"It's all right, darling. I shouldn't have exploded like that," Greg said, coming over to where she sat. He bent over to kiss her lightly. "I don't want you to ever choose sides."

She touched his face, as if trying to erase the weary look of strain that had suddenly appeared. "You'd have to do something a lot more awful to get me off your side."

"And that's the only reason why I'll stay now," he said,

straightened up and turned around. "Why would a Grand Duke want to destroy me?" he asked Natalia. "I was no threat to him."

"You were young and handsome and unlike your friends you had a great deal of money that was readily available. Vladimir didn't have to concern himself with the 'puppies' as he called them, but you were another matter entirely."

"He loved you that much?"

Natalia's laughter was tinged with hysteria, and for the first time Kit finally saw the other woman as human. The patina that was her ballerina's training as well as the years of living her own secret life had cracked.

"You are still a romantic, Gregory, even after all these years. That is undoubtedly wonderful for your wife, but it has nothing to do with me." Natalia sat down. "I was Vladimir's possession, nothing more and nothing less, and although I was easily replaceable, he couldn't stand the thought of anyone else having me."

"And that was me. He planned the incident."

"No, your friends and I planned that. It was worked out to the last detail, even to your seeing me carried out. They wanted to frighten you, and the champagne you drank was drugged, not enough to make you truly unconscious, but enough so that everything would get very fuzzy."

"And when did the Grand Duke Vladimir add his distinctive touch to our little party?"

"I never said a word to him. He must have overheard my conversations with your friends, or else someone told him. I swear I didn't."

"I believe you, Natalia. It's all too incredible not to be true—every miserable word of it."

"After you had come around to see me being carried out wrapped in that rug, we went to the apartment next door," Natalia continued. "We were congratulating ourselves and laughing. It was our plan to wait until the drug had worn off and you were sober again to produce me, alive and well."

Suddenly, Natalia looked startled, as if remembering some long-forgotten detail. "You hurt your head when you fell. Were you injured?"

Seated beside her on the sofa, Greg tilted his head so she could see the faint scar at his hairline. The last physical remembrance of that January night and what might or might not have happened.

"A few stitches courtesy of Dr. Butz. It's a souvenir I could have lived happily without."

Natalia looked miserably unhappy as she continued her story. "We were toasting our success with champagne when Vladimir walked in and informed us that he was taking over and merging our plan with one of his own. He said no man was going to have me except him, and that all of us were going to have to pay the price."

"He threatened to kill them, didn't he?" Greg asked, already sure of the answer. "Vladimir's rages were very well known, and the threats he made were not idle ones," he explained for Kit's benefit. "No wonder my friends insisted they hadn't been in the apartment, and anything that happened was all my own doing." He regarded Natalia with the first glimmer of sympathy he could summon up for her. She was right, he thought, she was as much a victim as he was, and at this moment, if he wanted to be a true gentleman, he would let the matter rest. He had more answers than he ever thought possible, did he have to know every single gory detail? Greg searched his conscience and came up with the only answer possible.

"What happened next?"

"Vladimir was determined that one of you would pay, and since you, Sacha," she went on, instinctively using his old nickname, "were the one most attracted to me and had the wealthiest father, the one who would take the swiftest action on his son, you were going to take all the blame.

"That very night, I was taken by private train to his house in Paris, and before he placed me in the care of his guards,

477

Vladimir took great joy in telling me I was not so special. I was not a *ballerina assoluta*, I was still a year away from being ranked as a *premiere sujet*, and that after a few weeks, when no one found my body, very few in St. Petersburg would remember me, and by then your family would have banished you to the countryside and punished you for your transgression there."

"Then it was Vladimir who convinced my father to put into effect a plan to have me murdered," Greg said, not even feeling very surprised. Evil, as he'd learned both from sad experience and the passage of time, was bottomless, ruthless, and could spread itself over everything.

"He took great pleasure in telling me how he planned to tell Prince Ivan how evil you were and how you had to be taken care of so you wouldn't besmirch the Vestovanova family honor again."

For several minutes, they were all silent. Natalia was exhausted, drained of all energy, her beautiful dark eyes full of tears; Greg was also pale and drawn, now he knew why the blank spots in his memory had never been filled in, now he knew all the answers, and he couldn't help wondering if he'd be better off if he didn't have such strong confirmation of betrayal and vengeance; and Kit, for all her sophistication, felt as she had on her first visit to St. Petersburg: like Alice down the Rabbit Hole, through the looking-glass, and guest of honor at the Mad Hatter's tea party.

It wasn't fair, she thought. It wasn't fair that he should have to find out that he was a victim of another man's obsessive jealousy and ability to manipulate. But more than anything else Greg had wanted to find out the truth, and if that was the ultimate aim, she could not complain because the truth revealed was a prime example of cruelty.

"Poor Natalia," Greg said at last, and reached for one of her hands. "I'm sorry I was angry with you."

"You have every right to be. We played a stupid joke on

478

you. We meant no harm, and then it all turned into a horror tale."

"And you were right when you said that ultimately we were both victims," he told her, and finally felt some of the strain lift off him.

"I didn't see Vladimir for weeks after I arrived in Paris," Natalia continued as if she hadn't heard him. "Then one night he was there. I waited for him to tell me how you were destroyed, but instead he told me that you had escaped, gotten out of St. Petersburg somehow. I thought he'd be enraged, but he was almost uncaring. He said it was only a matter of time until his agents found you, and when they wired that you were in Brussels, he went after you."

"I only knew that someone had found out about me. I thought it was my father," Greg said, and he told Natalia everything. Even now, he would not bring Boris' name into the conversation, and only said that he'd been offered help from an unexpected quarter, but otherwise it was a recital of the life he'd begun to lead in January 1900.

As Kit listened, hearing again Greg's tale of escape, perseverance, and eventual triumph, she couldn't help but wonder how this conversation would sound if it were being held in Russian—that is if Greg and Natalia could still speak the language of their native country. She'd assumed he was speaking in English for her benefit, so that she wouldn't think he was closing her out, but now it occurred to her that he spoke English to Natalia because he could no longer speak Russian.

At least he doesn't look as pale and angry as he did a while ago, she thought with relief. I don't want him to hate Natalia any more than I want him to feel the same passion he did for her when he was twenty-one, but this isn't anyone's idea of a reunion.

He told her about *Ballet At Midnight*.

"Imagine, little Gerald remembering my stories after all

479

these years. I only told my stories to the Chanfield boys because I knew they wouldn't spread the tales around."

"It's a good enough reason, and I'm sure it's sweet for you to think about—unfortunately, I had quite another reaction."

"You must have been sick with terror."

"Let's just say sick. And before we discuss Gerald, we have to go back a few steps. Before you got to summer at Manchester-by-the-sea, you had to get out of Vladimir's house in Paris."

"When he went off to Brussels, I made my own escape. The guards had grown disinterested, and the servants were French and more interested in padding the bills than in watching my every move. One morning, I simply walked out. In Paris, everything is available for a price, particularly if one goes to Montmartre."

"I assume that when you left you remembered to take your jewelry case," Kit said, deciding just this once to forget about her decision to only listen in and not say a word. "That's very helpful in times of need."

"It can also be a lifesaver," Natalia said, oblivious to Kit's sarcasm. "A diamond bracelet can buy many things. In my case, it was false papers and first-class passage to America."

Natalia paused, waiting for Greg to say something, but he remained silent.

What does she want me to do? he thought, recalling his own hasty passage to America, the trip in steerage, his arrival at Ellis Island, his first weeks in New York. Does she want me to tell her that it's all right that she didn't suffer as much as I did—as if suffering made one a better person.

Slowly, it began to dawn on him that he wasn't the only one who had spent fifteen years with the free-floating anxiety, the dark cloud that wouldn't go away. The only difference was that while he longed for an explanation, Natalia had wanted forgiveness.

How human we are. And Natalia's only crime—and I

know that isn't the right word—was being young and very pretty and infuriating an older lover who feared losing her, he thought, and felt the surge of bitterness that had swept over him when Natalia began her story start to recede.

"It's all right, Natalia," he said at last, and moved closer to her on the sofa. He put an arm around her shoulders. "No, don't cry. Look how well we've both come through this."

Natalia touched his face. "For all these years, I thought Vladimir had succeeded."

"When—when did you tell Carl? I don't want to pry, but—"

"I owe you so much. If I'd found you again after all these years and you were lacking in anything, I would have taken care of you, but you have money, success, and love, so the only thing I can give you is answers. I told Carl everything two days after I met him. I knew something was going to happen between us, something very important, and I didn't want it built on sand." Suddenly, Natalia smiled. "Did you think we had a marriage of convenience; that I married Carl only for the safety he gave me?"

"The thought did cross my mind, but I'm glad it's an erroneous one. Did you tell people you were Russian?"

"No, French with a Russian grandparent. My French was always as good as my English, and you'd be surprised at the questions people *don't* ask. Carl was a widower when we met, and everyone had given up on his remarrying. In a very strange way, some things work out for the best."

Greg looked at Kit, and the expression in his dark-amber eyes said it all. "Yes, it does." He hesitated for a moment. "About Vladimir—"

"I never heard from him again. Or should I say he never found me. He could be dead by this time."

"I wouldn't know. I don't follow Russian society."

"Neither do I."

They were through the worst of it now, Kit realized. Together, Greg and Natalia had gone through all the pain, anger, and bitterness, and now, as suddenly as it had all begun, it was all but over.

We spent so much time running into blank walls, and now, in one afternoon, it's all over, solved, and all we have to do is get out of here with style, Kit thought.

She didn't have to worry. Greg seemed to have a new aura around him, and if it wasn't exactly one of peace, it was at least a new calm. He wouldn't forget himself as a gentleman, and with a great deal of skill—as if he were the host at a party where the guests didn't quite get on—he guided the conversation down to another level. All the important questions were answered, and when the last pleasantries were exchanged, it was time to leave.

"I know I haven't said very much, and I'm sure you know I did that deliberately," Kit told Natalia as they prepared to leave. "But now I want to tell you how brave I think you are. You could have made up any sort of story, but you told the truth, even though it must have been incredibly difficult for you."

"How perceptive you are, Kit, and I'm very happy to say that you and Gregory belong together and deserve every happiness possible." The slight European cadence that her speech had taken on was gone now. She sounded just what everyone thought she was: a very attractive Philadelphia matron showing her guests to the door. Except that proper society women usually didn't kiss their male guests. "Until we meet again, Sacha."

"Until we meet again." Greg returned her kiss. "And don't hold yourself responsible for what happened to me after Brussels. That's when I finally took control of my own life, and for both of us, despite one man's rages and plots, we won out over hate," he said as they stepped outside the suite. "And in the end, that's what really matters."

"I hated to have you sit through all of this," Greg said a

short time later as the elevator began its descent. "I know you felt my meeting should have been strictly solitude *a deux.*"

"There were so many times I wanted to say something, and I almost had to grind my teeth to keep quiet. Except for that one comment."

They spoke in low tones so the elevator operator wouldn't hear them.

"And it was the best one you could have made." Instinctively, they began to hold hands. "I didn't ever want you to think that to spare you some details I made deletions or adaptations. I wanted you to hear everything along with me." He paused for a second. "Not only because you believed in me, but because I knew when the meeting was over I might not be able to repeat a word of it or discuss it in any depth for a long time."

"I know," Kit said softly as the elevator reached the lobby. "And I promise you I won't mention a word about this afternoon until you want to talk about it. Now I think it's time we went home. We've done all that we came over to the St. Regis to do."

Chapter 28

"When you said 'home' a moment ago, were you referring to the Plaza or to Los Angeles?" Greg asked as they came through the revolving door that took them from the warm lobby to the cold weather outside. "Not that it matters—"

"Of course it matters," she replied. "We don't regret living in Los Angeles, but we've already agreed that we're New Yorkers to the core."

Slowly, he began to smile, and the look on his face made the cold more bearable. "Shall we walk home?"

She tucked an arm through his. "I was waiting for you to ask."

In New York in February, the dark comes early, and at only a few minutes past five, the streetlights were on, ready to burn throughout the long night ahead. It was definitely not a night for a leisurely stroll up Fifth Avenue, but this was a perfect time for an invigorating and head-clearing walk.

"Are you all right?" Kit asked as they crossed Fifth Avenue, the sidewalks piled high with newly shoveled snow.

"I finally can say I am—in every way. It's so odd," he said as they began to cover the short distance between the two hotels, "but one of the things I'd almost forgotten about the establishment I was born to is the tactics Vladimir used. Revenge can become a very concentrated thing. Even when I was no longer in a position to be a threat—if I ever was—I had to be removed just to prove his point. I wonder how long he kept looking for me after Brussels, or if he's stopped even now."

"He's not coming after you, Greg, deep down you know that. If he had been able to trace you here in 1900, it might have been another story, but in general, Russian nobility doesn't think much about America."

Greg chuckled quietly. "It's funny you should say that. When I first told Sin the truth about myself, I asked him if he were surprised, and he said not really; servants come to this country and pretend to be princes, why shouldn't a prince say he's a servant. It's all relative, and now that I have you and more answers than I thought I'd learn, things seem a little more equal. I—we—have to look forward to other things now."

"As long as you don't hate Natalia. I meant what I said when I told her how brave I thought she was."

"I know you did, and no, I don't hate her. I even have the grace to be embarrassed about how I acted toward her earlier."

"You know that we're probably going to see her and Carl again. We're hardly going to invite each other to dinner, but we'll all run into each other socially. Will that bother you?"

"No. I see people socially now that I'd rather push in the Pacific. Compared to them, seeing the Gardiners shouldn't be a problem at all."

"I'm so glad to hear that."

"I've been thinking about my family an awful lot lately," he said, finding it easier to speak with the darkness to shield him. "Particularly my sister, Vava. The last time I saw her, she was a child, and the week before all of this began, I took her to Boissonas and Eggler so we would have our photograph taken together."

"Oh, Greg." Kit hoped that any passers-by who looked closely at them would assume that the tears in their eyes were caused by the cold wind. "Of all the tragic things you've told me, this is the worst." She tucked her arm more firmly through his. "Have you ever tried to find out about your family? American magazines never seem to get tired of writing and photographing European nobility. We have all these bound back issues of *Vogue* and *Harper's Bazaar,* and tomorrow we can go over to the apartment, sit down in the library and just look through the old magazines and see if we can find some mention of your family."

"I know that's the best way to fill in a lot of years, but I can't do it, at least not yet."

They crossed Fifty-seventh Street in silence. Looming up ahead of them was the block-long Vanderbilt mansion. Fifth Avenue was graced, or cursed, depending on point of view and architectural taste, with seven Vanderbilt mansions; but this 137-room tribute to excess gingerbread, gables, peaks and dormer windows looked as though it had been lifted from a book of fairy tales illustrated by a third-rate artist. Kit and Greg had exchanged any number of witty, biting comments about the mansion, but now he was walking past it as if it was not there.

The blue mood again, Kit thought. It's two-hundred feet from corner to corner, and we can't go back to the Plaza like this. Anything I'd say is going to sound trite; I have to find another way to take his mind off the past. How . . .

All she could see was snow, and then she began to smile.

Greg was halfway up the block before he realized that he was walking alone. Anger at his own self-absorption swept through him. Acting like a demented character in a bad drama was going to get him nothing but trouble, he thought, and calling Kit's name, he swung around to find her a few feet from him, holding a newly made snowball in her gloved hands.

"Have you had a snowball fight lately?"

"A favorite pastime in Los Angeles," he responded, sure of what was coming and deciding to play it out as long as he could.

"You must have had some practice in St. Petersburg."

"Not fair."

"You couldn't have been *that* grand."

"You know the answer to that." He smiled, his depression gone, and held out his hands to her. "You're going to ruin your gloves."

"Oh, in that case—"

With an accuracy that Christy Matthewson of the New York Giants would have envied, the snowball whizzed past Greg's ear and splattered against the high wrought-iron fence that surrounded the mansion.

"Was that an accident or on purpose?"

"Wouldn't you like to know."

For a long second, they simply looked at each other. Then, since there was no one else on the block and traffic was light, there was only one other thing they could do.

"One thing about throwing snowballs is that you never lose 'the trick of it,' as the line in *Trelawney Of The Wells* goes."

Greg watched Kit plunge her hands into the shoulder-high drift for a handful of snow. "When he wrote that, Sir Arthur Wing Pinero was referring to acting," he said, and reached for his own handful of snow.

As snowball fights went, it would never be ranked as a great one. Neither wanted to hit the other, and they certainly didn't want to break a window, or hit a passing vehicle or pedestrian. Kit was far more adept at this amusement than Greg, but they were having far too much fun to care about who was better or that they both looked a little odd.

"Oh, let's forget about this and do something a little less icy," Kit said a few minutes later as they fell into each other's arms.

"What an impetuous woman I'm married to."

She brushed a light dusting of snow from the shoulders of his topcoat. "That's one of the joys of being married.

"Besides, we're not supposed to laugh so hard that we can't hit anything."

"There isn't much we want to hit around here."

"True . . . and since we have some plans to make, there are warmer places to discuss them in."

"Let's take the long-range ones first."

"Yes, but can we talk while we walk? I saw someone peeking at us from behind the curtains."

"Have you ever been inside?"

"More times than I care to count, but I wouldn't like to tell that to the police."

"Then it's definitely time for us to go on the lam!"

"There's something so romantic about hurrying up Fifth Avenue in February!"

"What would you say to our having an apartment here?"

Kit stopped walking. "Now?"

"No, but in about five years or so we should be able to divide our time between Los Angeles and New York. Do you think you can run your shop like that?"

"I may not only be able to do that, but I may be ready to open a shop here in New York, and if Los Angeles ever gets around to building a hotel on the scale of the St. Francis or the Fairmont, I'll have my shop incorporated into the premises," she said as they resumed their walk.

"And in New York?"

"I'll look for something in the East Fifties or Sixties, very small but very exclusive. I suppose we'll have an apartment on Park or Fifth Avenue?"

"That's the general idea. One problem of living in Los Angeles that I've seen over and over is that people get too comfortable with their lives. They have the house in town, the beach house and the ranch, and San Francisco for weekends. That's not how I'd like us to live," Greg said, and paused for a crucial half-second. "And I don't have to hide any longer, either," he continued, and Kit knew he was finally free of that night. He wasn't healed, and might not be

489

for a long time, but the worst was over.

"Oh, people are still going to point to you in restaurants—they're going to say there's Gregory West, the man who runs Hooper Studios!"

"And the man who's married to Katharine Allen, whose shop has the best clothes."

"Well, at least no one will ever say that we're a boring couple!" Kit replied. "Oh, Greg, look—"

They reached the corner of Fifty-eighth Street, and looming up at their left was the Plaza Hotel, gleaming with light from within. The Champagne Porch was closed for the winter, but the Rose Room at the Fifty-eighth Street corner, and the Edwardian Room at the Fifty-ninth Street corner were both full of light and movement as the dinner hour approached, and for twenty stories up, lights glowed from nearly all of the windows.

"A good sign?" she asked.

"A very good sign," he said. "Even if we are standing on what is probably the windiest corner in New York City."

Kit laughed and flung her arms around Greg's shoulders. "Who cares about the wind when we have each other? And why don't you think of the Plaza as your reward—we can go inside after you tell me what your more immediate plans are."

Greg put his arms around Kit's waist and pulled her close. "Well, if we don't get frostbite, we're going to spend a few hours dancing in the Rose Room."

"I mean something a little more advanced, and since propriety forbids my mentioning in public what we'll be doing after we leave the Rose Room—" Kit laughed, and then gave him a level look. Standing so near a streetlight drained the color from his face, but he was still heartbreakingly handsome, and her heart filled with love. "I have my shop, and it's as wonderful as I thought it would be when all I had was a handwritten plan on paper. I saw your face during

490

dinner at Locke-Ober's while Gerald told us how he had to live up to the requirements of others, to do what they want and think is right. I want to know if you feel the same way about Hooper Studios as I feel about Katharine's?"

"I never thought I'd say this, but I like running Hooper. I like making decisions that concern more than reports and figures. I don't want it sold. I want to run it until the movie industry has its course set straight. There's lots of room for improvement, and I don't think any of us will be happy until there's sound *and* color, but I wouldn't pull out now for anything—the next few years are going to be very exciting."

"In every way—and what excitement you don't find at the studio, I'm going to provide for you at home," Kit assured him. "We're still in this together, and don't you ever forget it!"

"I wouldn't dare."

In another minute, Kit knew, they would start to walk toward the Plaza's main entrance, eschewing the small doorway and narrow passage between the Rose Room and the Champagne Porch that was the only entrance directly on Fifth Avenue, and braving the cold wind once again in order to sweep through the grand entrance facing Central Park. On a night like tonight, they could do nothing less, but right now she had to know one more thing.

"What about *Ballet At Midnight?* Full speed ahead?"

"That's the only way. When we get back to Los Angeles, I'm going to supervise its completion for a premiere in San Francisco in August at the Panama-Pacific Exposition," he told her, all his plans falling into place. "We'll have a gala, take half of a floor at the Fairmont for all our friends, buy that Russian perfume to hand out as favors, and give all the proceeds to Belgian War Relief." He grinned like a schoolboy. "Have I left anything out?"

"Nothing that I can think of." Kit tightened her embrace. "And afterwards?"

For a long minute, they exchanged the sort of kiss seldom seen on Fifth Avenue, even under the safety of a February evening. Slowly, very slowly, they drew apart, reluctant to separate after their first real kiss without the shadow of Natalia between them.

"How are you going to like being married to a man who makes movies?"

Author's Note

Unfortunately, trying to find out exact information regarding Los Angeles in the early part of this century is rather like trying to find out the exact birthdate of an aging movie star—you can find the information but, inevitably, the dates vary. Happily, Tom Owen, Library Assistant, and Mary S. Pratt, Department Manager, History Department of the Los Angeles Public Library were a great help to me, and I want to express my thanks to them for taking time out of their busy schedules to answer my questions.

Thanks also go to Jim Boyd for sharing his expertise in the area of American railroads with me; to fellow writer Muriel Bradley for sending me maps of Southern California; and to Cynthia Cathcart of the Conde Nast Library for her usual invaluable help.

Hotels are their own special world, and my appreciation goes to Susan Larson of the Fairmont Hotel Company; Alan Tremain, Managing Director of the Copley Plaza in Boston; and Janet E. Martin, Advertising and Public Relations Coordinator, and Marilyn Curry, Sales Manager, both of the Plaza Hotel in New York; all of whom answered my letters and provided invaluable information.

Herman Patrick Tappe, the couturier who plays a featured role in my store, was an influence in New York fashion for approximately forty years. Unhappily, little information except for snippets and magazine illustrations and photographs remain about his establishment, and I had to depend on writer's instinct and imagination in recreating him. If there is a reader who remembers Tappe (either the man or his establishment), I hope they will forgive any errors I might have made.

A word to my readers about the Plaza Hotel.

There were two Plazas, the first structure, built in the 1890s, proved to be too small for the ever-growing city and was replaced by the hotel we all know, which opened its doors in October 1907. At the time my story takes place (1914–1915), the elegant entrance facing Fifth Avenue did not exist. That space was taken up by the Champagne Porch (for a description of that delightful place, see my previous book, *Keepsake*) which fell victim to Prohibition in 1920. Until then, the only way into the hotel from the Avenue was a small, not-too-impressive doorway between the Rose Room (later the fabled Persian Room, and now the location of a boutique) and the Champagne Porch. The main entrance, then and now, has always been the one facing Central Park. Bergdorf Goodman now occupies the site of the Vanderbilt Mansion, and during the time period covered in Part Four, the plans for building the Pulitzer Fountain were finalized. Finally, the story about Caruso and the clock is quite true and is described in great detail in *The Plaza,* designed by Philip Clucas, MSIAD, produced by Ted Smart and David Gibbon, and published in 1981 by Poplar Books Inc. Since an exact date was not available, I have placed it within the time period when my fictional heroine, Katharine Allen, lived at the Plaza.

Eleanora Brownleigh
New York City
August 1985

BESTSELLING HISTORICAL ROMANCE
from Zebra Books

PASSION'S GAMBLE   (1477, $3.50)
by Linda Benjamin
Jessica was shocked when she was offered as the stakes in a poker game, but soon she found herself wishing that Luke Garrett, her handsome, muscular opponent, would hold the winning hand. For only his touch could release the rapturous torment trapped within her innocence.

YANKEE'S LADY   (1784, $3.95)
by Kay McMahon
Rachel lashed at the Union officer and fought to flee the dangerous fire he ignited in her. But soon Rachel touched him with a bold fiery caress that told him—despite the war—that she yearned to be the YANKEE'S LADY

SEPTEMBER MOON   (1838, $3.95)
by Constance O'Banyon
Ever since she was a little girl Cameron had dreamed of getting even with the Kingstons. But the extremely handsome Hunter Kingston caught her off guard and all she could think of was his lips crushing hers in feverish rapture beneath the SEPTEMBER MOON.

MIDNIGHT THUNDER   (1873, $3.95)
by Casey Stuart
The last thing Gabrielle remembered before slipping into unconsciousness was a pair of the deepest blue eyes she'd ever seen. Instead of stopping her crime, Alexander wanted to imprison her in his arms and embrace her with the fury of MIDNIGHT THUNDER.

Available wherever paperbacks are sold, or order direct from the Publisher. Send cover price plus 50¢ per copy for mailing and handling to Zebra Books, Dept. 2037, 475 Park Avenue South, New York, N.Y. 10016. Residents of New York, New Jersey and Pennsylvania must include sales tax. DO NOT SEND CASH.